Peter

By Gina Marinello-Sweeney

Peter

Front cover photo by: Dieter Spears (InhausCreative); Nashville, TN
Back cover photo by: Anja Osenberg (cocoparisienne); Aachen, Germany
"My Turn to Go" (2012), Written by: Elle and Shealeen Puckett; Performed by: Poema (Elle and Shealeen Puckett)
Chapter headers by: macrovector and microone
Scene break designs by: gstudioimagen and aikstudio
Excerpt from "Sonnet 18" (1609), William Shakespeare
Excerpt from "The Lady of Shalott" (1833), Alfred Tennyson, 1st Baron Tennyson
"Danny Boy" (1913), lyrics written by Frederic Weatherly (Bath, Somerset)
Excerpt from "Stopping by Woods on a Snowy Evening" (1922), Robert Frost

Used with Permission. Thank you!

Editing and book design by Jansina of Rivershore Books

ISBN: 978-1-63522-322-4

Printed in the United States of America
10   9   8   7   6   5   4   3   2

Rivershore Books
8982 Van Buren St. NE • Minneapolis, MN 55434
763-670-8677 • info@rivershorebooks.com

The Veritas Chronicles

I Thirst
The Rose and the Sword
Peter

Dedication

For BP. You are my rock.

Part 1

He spun her world in silver-blue
Catching in the light the faintest hues
A maiden from a castle tall
Its towers spun of silk
But it could not stand against the winds
Without foundation laid more firm
And so the tide rushed forward
And took it far from view
Far, far away from view.

She bent before the boat
Laughter once in her eyes
Silenced in the morning still
And so she stepped into its web
An echo of another age
And weaving through the waters soft
Like the Lady of Shalott
Her Camelot in mind's eye
Too lost in silver-turned shadow gray
To note the one who stood afar
Beside the willowy tree behind
Eyes cast in farther distance still
Not far from where she lay.

Her heart knew only the web that spun
And onward she rowed, longer she held.

Of silk, a flimsy dash of hope
Of silk, a hope dashed in its midst
Oh, its towers spun of silk.

It could not stand
It could not stand
For, it was not a rock.

Chapter 1: Emerald

Soft white billowed about the surface, blowing gently against the windowsill in remembrance of the enigmatic swan's graceful flight. Or so it reminded me, alluringly tranquil in its flicker of light and form, but not quite translucent. Not quite here.

I leaned against the frame, hand cupped under my chin, the poetry of an earlier time momentarily capturing my heart. Before turning to the figure seated opposite me, my gaze shifted to a small sparrow, brown and neat in appearance, a comforting image that puzzled my psyche by its necessity.

It was solid and unobtrusive.

It was *here*.

And maybe I needed it less, but I would not question it.

Psyche. Oh!

I turned quickly back to my client with a half-smile, my earlier thoughts nearly fading from view. "So glad we could have this talk, Cordelia. Will that be all for today?"

I preferred keeping it casual, as if a chat between friends rather than doctor—or psychologist—to patient. After nearly a year of my own practice, I knew my youthful eagerness was blaringly transparent and, perhaps to some, foolishly naive, but I fought the all-too-easy temptation of defaulting to the standard practices of others. Their methods suited them. While my heart of a nerd often incorporated their ideas after meticulous study, mixing scraps of each into the art, the technique had to be my own—individual and true to myself. Real.

Human.

Cordelia smiled, the wished-for name of my favorite literary heroine coloring her cheek. She was a young woman in her early twenties, easy and light despite the problems that worried her. I suspected that she revealed them to few other than those present in this room. "Thanks, Rebecca," she said, "but I think that's it. It still bugs me somewhat, but I feel much better."

"In time." I returned the smile encouragingly before the words hit me, and I turned back in the direction of the windowsill as my smile slowly faded.

"How's Stacie, by the way?" I finally resumed my observation of the table, my voice suddenly light and even.

Stacie was a special client from my internship days who had profoundly impacted my life more than I could have ever foreseen. She had been a victim of many horrors, but had recovered a great deal from the time when I had first met her. The image of a client who had become a dear friend turned my thoughts to the brighter note of before. Cordelia, a much more bubbly cousin fifteen years her junior, was a less severe case, but I was always overjoyed to see her anxiety decrease in subsequent sessions.

Yes, someone to talk to.

This was why I was here. To help them heal.

I shook away the irony of that statement.

Why now? I was fine.

Cordelia stood up and groaned. "Oh, gosh, you just reminded me! I totally forgot! Stacie said you loved roses, and I meant to surprise you with the first of the summer bloom from her garden . . . since, you know, she's still on her honeymoon." She winked in a momentary shift before reverting to her earlier mood with a sigh. "Epic fail."

Rows of roses, petals circling in an iridescent maze of color and light.

Always with a . . .

"Oh, I haven't really done much with roses lately," I said.

"Even more reason for me not to forget!" She put one hand to her head in annoyance. "I can't see Stacie ever obsessing less over her rose garden. I'm sure you're the same deep down, even when you run out of time. I need to remember—"

"Don't worry about it at all, Cordelia!" I quickly interjected. "I appreciate the thought, though."

I stepped forward, and she offered a high-five. The pressure of that simple motion inexplicably seemed to bring back my focus, return me to the present moment.

"Until next time!" I called, now fully re-engaged into my surroundings.

"See ya, Rebecca!" she called back brightly as the door swung closed behind her.

I looked over my appointment schedule and instantly smiled at the next time slot. *One of my favorite clients*. Albert, or *Dancing Man*, I thought reflectively, recalling our old nicknames for each other. I always looked forward to his appointments like a Christmas gift. He had also been a client of mine from my internship days—which, incidentally, *did* largely take place during winter—and shaped them as poignantly, if not moreso, than the others. He was a Korean War veteran whose PTSD had crippled him for so long, but, much like Stacie, had begun to wake up again and step through the arduous healing process.

1 PM. I still had plenty of time to break for a leisurely lunch. *Perfect.*

As I stood up, reaching over for my lunchbag to enjoy its contents in the mild (for summer) climate of more natural surroundings, the knob of my small office door slowly turned.

I froze, baffled, my hand halfway into my purse in search of my sunglasses. I didn't expect another client for two hours, my secretary was on a week-long summer vacation, and, despite my overflowing joy at its existence, my office *was* in a rather remote section of town. Unless you sought it, there would be no reason to wander into the vicinity, and most people preferred the phone or email as a convenient means to set up an appointment.

And yet, any surprise that had filled my mind with mild curiosity in the seemingly longer-than-usual millisecond it took to enter the room quickly turned to stunned astonishment as the door opened, revealing a tall, all-too-familiar young man in his mid-twenties. At this particular moment, a midnight blue T-shirt reflected his deep hazel eyes.

"*Peter*?" I stood, motionless. "What in the world are . . . you . . . doing . . . you never mentioned . . ." I trailed off, blinking in disbelief with the certainty that it was an illusion. Surely Captain Janeway had encountered a wormhole and a temporal distortion had led to a confusion in the timeline that . . .

I shook myself out of my all-too-common tangential Trekkie thoughts.

Peter still stood there, smiling as if he knew exactly what I was thinking, Janeway and all.

Which, you know, he probably did.

I stepped forward, and then back. And blinked again. I stood, immobile, rooted to the spot, suddenly chastising myself for not rushing forward immediately to embrace the dear friend I had not seen in one and a half years.

What was wrong with me?

I stepped forward and threw my arms around him. He moved his arms around my back and pulled me closer in a way that almost made me breathless.

Don't be absurd, Rebecca. It did nothing of the sort.

"Welcome back, Peter," I whispered. My chin trembled, and I thanked the distraction of the embrace as moisture filled my eyes.

He finally drew back, his hand still on my shoulder, his signature grin—subtle yet full—illuminating his face. "Rebecca, shouldn't you know better by now than to be amazed by surprise visits? You *are* friends with Adriana Hanson."

Adriana, my best friend since third grade, was known to drive ten hours at a mere whim simply because the notion of eating frozen yogurt at a different locale entered her mind. This half-conceived plan was then enacted without a second thought and certainly no advance notice.

His hand was still on my shoulder. I smiled and took a step backwards.

Peter's brow furrowed, but he said nothing.

"As I seem to recall, she isn't the only one fond of employing such methods," I said, raising an eyebrow.

His grin returned. "I remain guilty of the aforementioned charges, I'm afraid." He stepped forward, and then stood back again, hesitating. "I'm glad to see you, Rebecca."

"You, too!" I said, smiling, too casual, as something caught in my throat. "But," I forced my voice into a more playful lilt, "you haven't told me the reason for this surprise visit.

"And what brings you to California a year and a half after the last surprise visit." My voice softened.

"A . . . somewhat different purpose." Peter shifted his feet, and I noted with considerable surprise that he appeared to be somewhat nervous. Peter was often quiet, always introspective, but to be ill at ease was seldom, and this . . . unheard of to my recollection.

I waited, and Peter finally looked up with a glimmer of a smile that betrayed the earlier mood.

"Well, I've seen your world a few times and . . . not to sound cliché—if clichés existed, that is—but I thought you might like to see mine."

I stared blankly as his words sunk in. "Alberta. You came to take me to Alberta?" My voice rose in incredulity, and something else I couldn't quite name.

"That is correct."

"And you traveled 1,654.5 miles here to bring me 1,654.5 miles back there?"

"Precisely."

I cleared my throat, knowing at the same time that overtly asking if he had lost his mind was not on the table.

And, strangely, I knew that he was not only not daft, but that it felt . . . right.

"To Alberta."

"Alberta."

"Just . . . drop everything and go?"

"Something like that, yes."

"When exactly?"

"There's a plane that leaves tomorrow." Peter waved dismissively as a grin broke out across his face.

"Peter Joseph Asturian—"

"But there is also one that leaves in a week. And another in two."

"Peter, you know I've always hoped to visit Alberta someday . . ." I paused, trying to clear my mind.

"Indeed."

"But"—I paused again—"this is a bit sudden."

"Indeed."

"Peter . . . have you considered the possibility that you have gone quite mad?"

"The thought crossed my mind, but I dismissed it."

A smile began to weave its way across my face in spite of myself.

"You know"—I ran a hand through my hair—"if you've tired of modern convention, the telephone *is* over 140 years old."

A hint of a smile played at the corner of his lips. "Too recent for my taste."

I laughed for the first time . . . barely, but *almost* truly, in a way that I had not for a very long time.

Almost lightly. Almost freely.

My gaze fixed upon him steadily despite my desire to appear nonchalant. "Why?"

His eyes met mine, only to flicker away momentarily.

"I want you to experience Alberta yourself. And . . . I want you to meet my family. They would love to see you . . . especially Little Dan." His voice was suddenly soft. "And there's something about the trip, the journey itself. It's more, I suppose . . . than just Alberta. It's going to Alberta. With you. I think I want to be a part of that, too. If you are willing, that is." His eyes were eager, almost boyish, in a way that I had not seen before, even in our adventures to the swings.

It was somehow . . . more.

And I knew that the next uncharacteristic move would not be his.

"Yes, Peter," I said.

Chapter 2: Onyx

"Are you sure you don't want me to come with you?"

"Thanks, Peter, but"—I breathed in deeply, trying to offset a prevailing trembling sensation nearly defying my resolve—"I have to do this alone."

He nodded. "I know. I just wish I *didn't* know."

Peter's eyes still followed me—I sensed this just as I sensed the instant warmth in my chest at his concern, the only balm to a coming chill—as I approached the double doors to Hempton Penitentiary, an imposing brick building of three stories.

With an old nightmare imprisoned inside.

I squared my shoulders and opened the door.

I had waited long enough.

It was a sparse room, but more normal than I had somehow expected.

The man at the desk, tall and imposing in a security uniform, looked up.

"I have an appointment to see Dr. Yin," I said.

As we walked down the halls, I realized that *this* was exactly as I had expected. Perhaps it wasn't dark like a dungeon in nightly tales of my childhood castles—and the walls were not stained or cobwebbed—but it was a blank canvas of tense solitude, endless vacuous turns of *blank* only drawn across by the murmurs of incoherent voices that were probably evidence of an overactive imagination—but made me shiver all the same.

Or was it the expectation that made me so?

The guard finally stopped at a cell and glanced at me. "Fifteen minutes, miss."

He left me to the shadows of the dimly lit room.

I had averted my eyes since our entry—and the guard's exit. But I had not come here to stare at the floor.

I had put off this meeting for almost two years. Now here, I refused to be a coward.

As I won the battle within myself, a figure crouched at the corner of the cell moved. Her head turned slowly, as she craned her neck in my direction.

"So, you have come to visit me, *Rebecca*."

I had hoped to not hear that voice again for the rest of my life.

"Yes . . . I have." I barely managed to force the words out.

I clenched my fist as my arm trembled of its own accord. I would not let her see me shake.

I met her gaze full on.

Yin was thinner than before, wrapped in an oversized orange jumpsuit. An almost sickly pallor covered her face. She looked older—older than the year and a half—and I almost pitied her, but then those hawk eyes regarding me fixedly as in the imagining of many a sleepless night caused me to stand straighter.

And then *she*—Yin—turned away, and her eyes—those eyes—almost seemed tired.

"What do you want?" she said coolly, her eyes returning with their usual scorpion-like derision, tossed forward in the trick of a dark Mad Hatter. "Come to examine your handiwork? Isn't it a bit late for a victory lap?" Her voice was ice.

"No." I forced myself to look at her. "That's not why I'm here."

Why *was* I here? I was beginning to forget.

"Not quite too late," she whispered. "Right on time."

"Why do you say that?" I tried to steady my voice. My feet sunk so forcefully into the floor that I almost winced, and lightened their hold.

She laughed, an empty, ironic laugh. "Oh, Rebecca, it's the perfect ending to your fairy tale. The word is . . . I'm dying." Emotion flickered across those eyes, for a moment human, before quickly swept away. "I'm sure you'll be pleased. You slayed the dragon." Her sardonic tone rose. "*Especially* from the delightful cause. Stage 4. Terminal." She spit out the words. "Cancer."

I froze, motionless, as the dizzying buzz of a hornet's trek wove through the pathways of my mind, cold as snow, yet somehow numb, beyond feeling.

Her head was propped up against a white pillow, pale and worn.

"I am sorry," I said softly. I had looked away.

"Sorry? You must be overjoyed!"

I turned swiftly, forcing myself to look at her as a sudden passion filled me with vigor. "*No*. I wouldn't wish cancer on my worst enemy . . ." My voice broke.

"Your worst enemy," she repeated quietly, as I realized what I had just said. "And why not?"

"Because cancer is evil," I said vehemently. "No one, *no one* deserves it." I lifted my face, and there were tears in her eyes.

No, Yin did not cry.

She turned away.

"I forgive you," I whispered.

Yin froze, unmoving. I waited, but she did not turn around. Several moments passed, and it was clear that no more would be said. I glanced at my phone, the normalcy of the action almost startling.

I only had two more minutes. I walked to the large glass window set in the door, motioning to the guard that I was ready to leave.

"Officium."

I turned at her voice as the guard neared the door.

Yin was watching me, her eyes strangely quiet yet lucid.

"I don't . . . understand."

"You're wearing an Albertan sticker." She raised a trembling, bony hand weakly to point at the bright adhesive triangle affixed below my left shoulder.

I touched it instinctively. Peter had placed it teasingly on my shirt earlier that day. If I had had any sense, I would have removed it before entering the jail. To betray any sense of a possible future location, of a potential trip, or the company I now kept from said location was dangerously foolish. Yet now I somehow knew that it did not matter.

"Take this."

The guard moved in front of me and took the small item in Yin's outstretched hand. After examining it thoroughly and putting it through a scanner, he handed it back to me.

It was a small, badge-sized fabric divided into four sections with a backdrop of orange. A creature that resembled a dragon, only with the head of a rooster, appeared in two of these sections, while a link of chains filled another square and a dark black tower the last. In the center of the badge was a circle depicting the same odd creature, surrounded by the chains.

I turned it over in my hand, the overwhelming emotion of the visit briefly interrupted by puzzlement.

"Remember what I said." Yin's voice was heard, as if a recording in the distance.

I nodded, not understanding, as the guard stood next to me, waiting.

I was at the door when she called my name again.

"Your priest. The one I told to stop coming. You can . . . ask him to come again if you'd like."

My surprise must have shown, for her next words were a return to the old Yin.

"He might amuse me."

"Of course."

"Remember what I said," she repeated.

I looked at her and nodded. Her eyes met mine, and that was the last glimpse before the door closed quietly behind me.

Six days later, on the plane to Canada, I was looking at the pages of a newspaper when I saw it.

Yin had died.

Chapter 3: Cordierite

"Hey, Rebecca!" Jeffrey glanced in my direction, as the bell on the door sounded, cheerfully announcing my arrival at the college bookstore. "I'll be just one second." He grabbed the receipt and began to stack three books into a bag for the customer in front of me. "You haven't come to visit enough since you quit last Fall, madam," he berated me from behind the stack of books. "I've missed you!"

"My apologies, noble pirate Jedi."

"You are forgiven. Argg." He put the receipt in the bag.

"I've missed you, too!"

He handed the bag to the customer, a middle-aged woman who was likely, from my best guess, buying graduate-level books. "Best of luck to you this semester!"

The woman issued her thanks, and I waited as she walked away from the register. When the door came to a close, Jeffrey turned around and smiled at me. "So, Peter's back in town! When's the wedding?"

"Jeffrey!" I protested. "We are old friends. *Friends.*" I enunciated the word.

"Uh huh." He stacked up some "extraneous" textbooks to the side of the register to put back later. For a moment, a wave of nostalgia filled me with remembrance of my bookstore days. I almost sighed. *It was so simple, for a time.*

"Well, if it helps to know, I'm Team Peter and Rebecca. Say"—he held up a golden medal, forestalling my interruption—"think the newly canonized St. Kateri Tekakwitha might make a good patron of the team?" He grinned.

I glared at him.

"Okay, okay. I'll stop." He handed me the saint medal. "Been saving it for you. My grandpa gave it to me during one of my last visits, and I knew just who to pass it on to."

"Thanks," I smiled in spite of myself, taking it. "The canonization Mass was amazing."

I still remembered it vividly, and it was five years before *on a TV screen.*

"I'll bet. I may not be Catholic, but I figure it's like the religious version of an award ceremony for Batman."

"Been talking to Adriana?"

"No, my dear." He tipped an imaginary hat. "Came up with it all on my own."

"I accept your analysis save one point. It's clearly Superman. Or, in this case, Superwoman?"

"Fair enough. Though I can see—what was that nickname you have for your favorite pope? JPII?—riding in a bat mobile."

I shook my head, smiling again. "So, how are things in the—"

My words left me as my eyes took in a small, woven fabric pinned to the front of Jeffrey's shirt.

In pattern, color, and form, it appeared to be an exact replica of the one that Yin had given me three days before.

"Jeffrey . . . where did you get that?" I asked, trying to feign nonchalance as I pointed to it.

"Oh, that." He fingered it briefly. "Pretty cool, huh? My uncle, who recently passed, as you know, had it in his things. He didn't have any kids, and his wife died five years ago, so he left most of everything to me. Didn't know him very well, but he was a funny guy—if a bit unusual—and said I was his favorite nephew." He paused. "Granted, I was his *only* nephew."

"Anyway, I thought it would look good on my daily uniform. Might make people wonder . . . Rebecca"— his light tone changed upon seeing my face—"what's wrong?"

"I've seen it before. Three days ago." I took my copy out of my purse and handed it to him shakily. "From Yin."

Jeffrey nearly dropped the square as if it were combustible material. He had been around during the Yin incident, though not participating directly in most of the related events. "Why would I—" He scratched his head. "The same . . . I've never seen the symbols before. Not in this arrangement anyway. What do you think it means?"

"I don't know. It could be a coincidence."

"You don't believe in coincidences," Jeffrey pointed out.

"Well, maybe in the . . . neighborhood of coincidence. A more acceptable cousin?"

Jeffrey raised an eyebrow.

I sighed. "I really don't know. This is kinda freaky. Okay, so, we're set to leave on Friday. Maybe I should—"

My phone buzzed.

I glanced down, but the screen was blank. "Ugh, my caller ID doesn't seem to be working again."

I picked it up. "Hello?"

In a few moments, I had hung up.

I eyed Jeffrey. "Telemarketer. No, I do not want the latest energy plan, but thanks."

Jeffrey laughed. "Yeah, those telemarketers . . . Hey, you want me to look at your phone and see if I can figure out what the problem is with the caller IDs? Tech master at your disposal." Jeffrey bowed.

"Sure!" I said with a smile, handing him the phone. "And thanks."

Jeffrey fiddled with some buttons on the screen.

"So, anyway, I was saying . . . maybe I should put off the trip for a few days and look into—"

"No, no, you go and have fun." Jeffrey drummed his fingers on the counter absentmindedly after putting the phone on its surface. "I'll look into it. It's from my uncle after all."

"Okay."

I waited for a few minutes before Jeffrey handed me back the phone.

"Hmm, I don't seem to be able to figure out the problem."

"No worries. Hey, I'd better get going. My family is expecting me for dinner."

"Have a safe trip, girlie."

I gave him a hug. "See ya, Captain."

Chapter 4: Hiddenite

I made the Sign of the Cross, dipping one finger into the holy water font at the entrance to St. Vitus Catholic Church. Its coolness remained with me as I approached the pews.

It was soon after the Thursday evening Mass, so a few parishioners lingered, bent in prayer. I genuflected, entered a pew toward the middle-back, and, kneeling, gazed up at the crucifix before me.

For the past four days following the visits to Yin and Jeffrey, my routine had become a splattering of crazed frenzy—finding a last minute ticket for a plane on Saturday and deciding not to wait for a later flight, packing, shopping, looking up weather reports, packing some more, and officially notifying my clients that my vacation, originally scheduled to last until July, would be extended until early August to allow for any discrepancies. I had not taken off much time at Christmas—only the feast day and the day before and after—so I had a lot of vacation time that I felt could justify the extended absence and quell any guilt I felt at "leaving" my clients. All the same, I managed to fit in some last-minute appointments and rescheduled sessions as needed, promising to be available for emergency phone or video conferences.

Yet there were also calm, quiet moments of slower-paced leisure spent around town with Peter. We watched the ducks at the library park, visited old haunts like the beach, strolled around the busy marketplace with a Cinnabon or ice-blended drink in hand, and enjoyed dinnertime with my family. I had realized, as Peter extended his hand for a firm handshake at the first dinner, and later that week, that he had spent very little time with my father during his past two visits—a passing hello before or after Mass occasionally when he served as an usher and at the hospital briefly after the harrowing events of a year and a half before. Yet now was a first of sorts, the beginning of a friendship different in its aspect from any other I had witnessed from previous interactions with my friends. Now they were often seen deep in conversation, Peter quietly respectful, yet full of ideas to offer, my father nodding thoughtfully from time to time and actively participating in the discourse, whether over politics or philosophy. While I did at times involve myself in the discussion, more often than not, I was content to simply watch silently from the sidelines, observing in the background, not because I did not have anything to say, but because I enjoyed witnessing the developing kinship between my father and a dear friend.

And because you're tired, Rebecca, a voice in me whispered.

I ignored it.

I looked up at the cross with the figure of our Lord nailed to it.

For us.

I sighed, and was struck once again by the Sacrifice, the Love inherent in the reality of the Crucifix. As my inner meditations and silent prayer continued, the figure of Fr. D'Angelo genuflecting and then reverently lifting a golden monstrance skirted across my line of vision.

With the perpetual adoration chapel currently undergoing renovations, Eucharistic adoration was temporarily moved to the church with a slightly modified schedule. I had decided to go to adoration today on a spontaneous yet intention-bent move, given the long journey that would begin the next day. I had considered asking Peter to join me, the profundity of the adoration chapel visit shared years before a snapshot in my mind, yet found myself drawn in this moment to solitude.

I gazed at the Sacred Host, lost thoughts suddenly tumbling forth unbidden, as if they had been long buried yet imprinted indelibly on my heart all the while. For several minutes, my gaze remained fixed, unflinching, drawn into the fathomless depths before me, the fathomless love. Several minutes passed, the quiet of the church growing as parishioners moved their after-Mass conversation to outside the church. It was in the stillness of this sanctuary that a deep peace arose in my heart, a peace that I needed with every fiber of my being in order to make the journey the next day, to embark on anything new at all. It was the source of my strength, and, as Time moved unnoticed in my discourse with Christ, I finally had to force myself from the kneeler.

I love you, Jesus, I said simply, my eyes drawn again to the Cross before I finally stood. *I trust in You. Please watch over Peter and me, and grant us safe travel as we journey to Banff.*

And please give me strength, I said in a silent plea, before exiting the pew, genuflecting. With one last glance at the crucifix, I silently headed toward the vestibule.

My hand fingered the square fabric with the strange design still in my pocket, and I took it out, examining it once again. *What is this, God?* I questioned.

Officium. The image of Yin, now more tragic than villainous, rose in my mind. *Was there something to her words and the meaning implicit as I left, or were they just the mad ramblings of a wounded soul?*

As I walked, still deeply immersed in my conversation with God, there was a flash of white and gray before my eyes, causing me to suddenly come to a halt in front of the usher closet to avoid crashing headlong into the unexpected figure before me.

Cedric stood, white and gray hair softly framing his face as his dark gray eyes took me in with a hint of veiled amusement, a glimmer of a smile forming at the corner of his lips.

"Oh! I didn't see you there, Cedric!" I moved to hug the elderly usher, and then drew back. The half-smile remained on his countenance, so faint that, if not observed carefully, would be left unseen by the viewer.

"I'm so sorry," I added with a sheepish smile. "I was lost in thought and prayer and didn't mean to crash into you."

Cedric watched me quietly. "Don't worry, Rebecca."

There was a brief silence before I continued. "Peter told you, I think, when he visited you on Wednesday that we're leaving for Banff tomorrow." I shook my head in wonder. "After all these years, I can hardly believe that I am finally going to visit his homeland. And . . . meet his family," I added with some minor trepidation.

My excitement about meeting Peter's family was unparalleled, yet there remained some nervousness as to how I would be received. After having heard about them for so long, I was fully absorbed in what impression I would give.

Cedric nodded slowly. "Yes, Peter told me about the trip. It is a journey," he said, watching me. The old sea captain and Fred, visions of the story that Peter and I had written together four years ago, flickered through his gaze, swirling until they formed the word "intermission." That single word in a mysterious note had spurred another journey beyond—or encompassed within—the story that we wrote, the one who penned the note eventually revealed to be Cedric.

A journey. As I looked back at the old, enigmatic usher, I realized with a start that he was not talking about kilometers or hours, but something fuller, deeper.

How could he know?

Could I—

No, like every other day, it would be a matter of survival.

On a sudden impulse, I instinctively grasped his hand, another emotion awake in me as my eyes met those of Cedric. He returned the gaze, the depths of his eyes fixed and unmoving. There was in that moment a sense of change, an inexplicable notion of alteration, not of the present nor of any previously conceived notion, but an awareness, a near-premonition that I could not unveil, or unravel into a concrete level of understanding. It was, simply, an essence of thought and reality, concealed beyond my grasp. And yet it stirred within me, an acute awareness tearing across my consciousness in an unyielding wave.

I blinked, my eyes suddenly filling with tears.

I released his hand, thrown from the moment as if from an overwhelming surge of power, yet it remained within me, undeciphered knowledge resting in mind and heart.

"May you have safe travels, and find whatever you seek." His dark gray eyes penetrated mine, candlelight flickering, illuminated in a reflection of soft hues and light. For a moment, his eyes lingered on the orange badge divided into fourths lying temporarily forgotten in my hand, before he nodded, and then I turned, approaching the double doors in the quickening nightfall, sensing that his gaze followed me as I moved into the cool wind and faint shadows of Thursday's dusk.

Chapter 5: Pyrite

I washed my hands at the sink, trickles of water slipping lightly across the surface of my hands, and, as I turned, a flash of white caught my eye.

I froze, my heart slammed against my chest.

Don't turn.

My breath caught, and I turned.

A soft white robe, hung quietly and unobtrusively on the door.

Just as it had for the past year.

And then suddenly I was aware of the rest of my surroundings, of the small, multi-colored floral printed towels neatly folded in a basket to the right of the sink as always, of the shower curtains I had stared aimlessly at with idle curiosity as a young girl, of the quiet smallness of the room.

I closed my eyes, willing it to all disappear, yet wishing fervently, *yearning*, for it to remain more fully present, and, turning the doorknob with precise movements, carefully avoiding a single touch of the robe, I hurried from the room.

Quickly, silently, slowly.

Slowly, with the speed of a racing Ferrari.

"Well, here we are. *DUDE*, I can't believe you are finally going to Alberta!"

A to the power of three—Adriana, Alexander, and Amelia—stood outside the airport near Peter and me. A cool breeze lifted effortlessly across our surroundings, reaching ahead to a long, structural expanse topped by a blue and white conglomeration that resembled a flying saucer.

Adriana shook her head, one hand still raised dramatically in the air.

"Dude," she repeated, a statement of epic proportions uttered with a single word and reminiscent of the DUDE-OH-MY-GOSH-NO-I-DID-NOT-KNOW-ABOUT-THIS-ONE-WHY-WOULD-I-DUDE-DUDE-ALBERTA-AT-LAST email she had sent earlier that week, followed by a similarly worded phone call upon being informed of the upcoming Canadian "adventure."

"I know." I glanced over at Peter, his quickly forming smile betraying his evident amusement at Adriana's effervescence. "It's hard to believe. But I am glad I made it to the opening night of your play before we left!"

"I'm really proud of you, Adri," I added, drawing her into a hug.

Adriana, a former theater major, had gradually received wide acclaim over the past year for her work at a theater near Los Angeles after auditioning for *The Importance of Being Earnest*. Tonight was the third night of *The Sound of Music*.

"Me, too," Peter said graciously. "I very much enjoyed your performance!"

"Definitely a top "A" performance—as in, um, *amazing*!" exclaimed Amelia, now sixteen and more shapely, her face growing thinner and her auburn hair falling more in waves and losing its self-imposed blonde streaks.

"Enlightening and enthusiastic," Alexander offered.

"Aw, thanks, guys." Adriana swept downward into a bow.

"And a musical, too!" I teased, raising an eyebrow.

Her least favorite form of theater, the musical, had grown comfortably on her after the less pleasant theatrics of nearly two years ago.

"Okay, okay, I have changed my ways," Adriana admitted with a dramatic flourish of the hand. "I may have once denounced all musicals, but I have seen the error of my ways. I now greatly enjoy the opportunity to burst into song and terrorize all by random insanity!"

"As well it should be," I said with a smile.

There was a pause, and then I followed my brother Alexander's circumvental inspection of his surroundings.

"The other letters of the alphabet couldn't make it," Alexander observed with a philosophical grin from his place beside Amelia and Adriana.

Adriana snorted.

We all looked at her, and she cleared her throat.

"At least someone finds his jokes funny." Amelia rolled her eyes, but there was a glint of a smile in them.

I turned at the sound of a quickly approaching figure.

"Oh, good! I made it!" Amelia's older sister Teresa, her long brown hair tossed over one shoulder, arrived, her cheeks flushed with exertion. "And don't be a brat, Amelia!"

"Whatever, big sis." Amelia rolled her eyes again, yet it was much different than only a year and a half before. The two sisters had grown closer during that time, a deep camaraderie and respect reforming after the traumatic events that had enveloped me personally, yet somehow encompassed others. It was now more of a put-on gesture than one holding any real meaning.

I hugged Teresa. "Thanks so much for coming!"

"Of course, girl! Wouldn't miss seeing you off!"

A voice on the loud speaker was heard in the distance, calling passengers to the next flight.

I glanced over at Peter, who nodded, heaving a backpack over one shoulder, his other hand returning to the rolling suitcase before him.

"We should probably head out," I said, one hand on my own suitcase.

In a flurry of movement and scattering of 3 As and a T, I was thrown into a group hug, encompassed by many hands. Adriana and Teresa also gave Peter a quick hug, with the rest offering waves and nods.

"Don't forget to text every day!" Adriana ordered. "Even when I'm on vacation in Colorado! Don't forget, madam!"

"Same here!" Amelia said firmly, my honorary little sister wrapping her hand around mine as we all withdrew from the hug. Her eyes suddenly filled, and she stepped forward, throwing her arms around me again. "Love you."

"I won't be gone long," I said, squeezing her tightly. "Love you, too."

"Parental unit package, submitted this morning." Alexander handed me a brown bundle as he stepped forward. "Complete with even more hand sanitizer and extra socks than were already previously supplied."

"Oh, and Dad said, before he left for the conference at school, to watch out for the Canada geese." Alexander widened his eyes dramatically, his red hair even more pronounced than usual, nearly glowing in the sunlight.

"Hug?" he squinted in that same light.

I gave my big brother another hug. He returned it, nearly choking the life out of me.

"Stay safe," he said, his brown eyes, usually comedic, almost drawn in concern.

"I will." I extended the handle of my rolling suitcase, preparing to roll it away.

And, with one final wave—and even more last-minute hugs thrown in—I followed Peter to the glass doors of the airport building as Adriana dragged a sheepish and almost subdued Alexander away.

I looked back upon reaching the doors, watching their figures retreating.

"Ready, Rebecca?" Peter's large eyes settled on me.

Was I ready? Truly ready?

Probably not, and yet . . .

I nodded, smiling, and he held the door open for me as I followed behind.

We reached the counter, a tall receptionist with dirty blonde hair standing before a display screen with flight information and continuous updates streaming through.

"Welcome to LAX. How may I help you?"

Peter held out his ticket, stating the destination, and she took it, typing on the computer.

When she was done, she looked up at me inquisitively.

"One ticket for Calgary," I said.

The great white bird lifted itself with a stuttering, and ascended into the air.

In a moment, it transformed into an airplane, the words Air Canada and the red maple leaf of the Canadian flag spilling across its surface as, with a creaking of wheels, it elevated our surroundings.

I glanced over to Peter, who was sitting on the aisle seat, having generously offered me the window view. He looked up with a smile, a smile that seemed to say *Therein begins the adventure*. I returned it, and then settled my eyes back toward the window, and there they remained fixed. It had been years since I had traveled by plane, the last occasion having been to visit Alaska with my family the summer after seventh grade. So, my first reaction, upon gazing outward, was that it was the aerial view of Google Maps—only real. I facepalmed at myself for having such a reaction before finally accepting that I had been landlocked—and not in the conventional sense of the word—for quite some time.

Buildings and landforms shrunk, suddenly becoming smaller as we gazed from above.

"Excuse me, sir and ma'am." The pleasant voice of the flight attendant, a tall brunette with red lipstick and her hair tied back in a knot, approached us, breaking me from my thoughts. She handed us a form. "Please fill out the Declaration Card for Customs at your earliest convenience. It will be requested on your arrival to YYC. Not the entire form; you only have to fill in the areas highlighted." She indicated these sections with her finger.

YYC. Calgary International Airport. The words sunk in—and, with them, the reality. In approximately three hours and nine minutes, we would arrive in Canada. *Peter's homeland.* My breath stilled in my chest, and then my heartbeat quickened, a paradoxical reality that somehow remained true as a mixture of excitement and apprehension completely obliterated my defenses.

"Thank you," Peter said, taking the form as I remained struck mute. He offered me a knowing look as she retreated down the aisle.

"Can I—fill it out?" I finally said, pointing to the form with a certain eagerness. "It's just one form for both passengers, correct?"

Yes, Rebecca, it is thrilling to fill out a form. By all means, volunteer.

Yet Peter seemed to sense, in that way of his, my exact reasoning and thought process.

Would he never fail to dissect me? I wondered silently.

Peter handed me the document. "Of course."

I filled in the personal information section, passing the paper back to Peter occasionally, such as when it came time for him to fill in his address—even though I had already, unbeknownst to him, memorized it from the Christmas cards we exchanged every year.

"Bring any birds, Peter?" I called from where I was looking at the sheet, "or other miscellaneous animals? They want to know if Noah's ark is coming with us."

Peter looked over my shoulder.

"Hmm." He rested his chin on his hand as if considering the question carefully before his signature grin, subtle yet wide, broke out. "Alas, no. Fred's parrot wasn't free at the time."

I laughed, a mild chuckle that almost got stuck in my throat like a foreign product, and then filled out the rest of the form with our arrival information and travel plans.

I handed it to Peter for his signature after I provided the same, and then returned my eyes to the window.

In a few minutes, my four hours of sleep from the previous night took over, my head nodded, and I dozed off.

And so the tide rushed forward
And took it far from view . . .

I woke up with a start.

Far, far away from view.

I groaned, taking in my surroundings. "Oh, no! I didn't want to miss a single moment!"

Peter looked down at me with a smile. "Your internal clock must be working well. You just got to the important part." He pointed ahead to my window. "Behold the Rocky Mountains."

I followed his gaze and nearly gasped.

The great Rocky Mountains, softly shaded in gray, were submerged in a sea of fluffy white clouds, feathery wisps enveloping the peaks like a kingdom of the air. I leaned on one hand—like Peter before, only in earnest—and gazed out at the new world that had emerged, marveling at all that it contained.

"It's beautiful, isn't it?" Peter said quietly from next to me.

A small boy with shocking red hair giggled from beside me. "Rebecca, what do you see in the clouds?"

"Castles and . . . remote controls!"

"*You do not! You cannot see any remote controls!!*"

"*I can, too!*"

The laughter of children faded into the distance, and the clouds looked at me, almost for a moment sentient beings, and I realized that it had been long since I had looked upon them—or the sky at all.

"Yes, yes, it is," I said, turning to Peter as our eyes met.

Shimmering blue lakes and green pastures floated by, gliding past the line of our vision. The buildings from before my unplanned nap now seemed more sparse, giving way to the natural landscape as if in a begrudging accord. As the minutes passed by, man-made structures—small in my vision like toys tossed in a child's room—rematerialized in greater numbers so quickly as if beamed from a starship traversing the universe.

And then the movement of the plane shifted, and it descended, the drop gradual but significant, as I held onto my seat.

When it came to a stop with a note of finality, there was a hush on the plane as if all had agreed to a moment of silence, and a prayer lifted from my heart.

"We're here," Peter said softly.

I looked at Peter, and our eyes once again met as the buzz of chatter and dismounting passengers filled the plane.

"Declaration Card? Excellent. Please hand me your luggage, ma'am, for inspection."

It had been about an hour since we had arrived at Calgary International Airport. Upon entering the doors to the busy airport, we had followed the signs projected above to Canada Border Services Agency-Primary Inspection. After presenting our Declaration Card, passports, and other relevant travel documents following a long wait in line—partially spent on the provided seat examining travel booklets, eating granola bars with Peter, and, with a wince, *not* using the bathroom due to the air freshener within—and answering a few security questions, we followed more signs to the luggage checkpoint. We watched as the luggage rotated on a large, circular device of gray and silver until our suitcases came into view, and Peter quickly lifted them up and handed me mine. It was a simple device that had been in existence for quite some time, and yet it fascinated me almost as much as it had when I was a child on my first plane ride.

I waited as the woman checked my luggage—clothes, a few writing notebooks, pens, and the fantasy book I had started reading shortly before embarking on this trip coming into view. Peter turned his head politely as the details of the clothing articles became more intimate.

"All clear." The woman gestured for Peter to hand her his suitcase, and he did so. In what seemed moments later—especially after the long wait in line earlier—we were standing outside, a cool, refreshing breeze brushing across our faces.

Peter glanced over at me. "It should be about two hours to Banff by the TransCanada Highway—16th Avenue North for the portion in Calgary. Do you need anything before we go?"

"No, I'm fine, Peter," I said quietly, suddenly shy.

He nodded, offering me a smile, and, in a few minutes, we were entering the rental car (thankfully with *no* air freshener—Peter had called in advance to ensure as much, causing me to appreciate anew his tendency to always be considerate) and riding down the highway.

"There's a radio, if you want to listen to anything." Peter indicated the dashboard quickly before returning his eyes to the road.

"Thanks." I browsed the stations, static and clear resonance fading in and out as I did, before exclaiming upon hearing a familiar sound.

"William Tell Overture, isn't it?" Peter asked from behind the steering wheel.

"Yes!" I settled back into my seat comfortably. "Rossini! Now we can truly begin the adventure."

Epic soundtrack to the movie of my life: beginning now.

Peter smiled, but said nothing, and I looked out the car window as we sped along Highway #1.

The first movement, Prelude: Dawn quietly lifted across in the flight of a cello.

"That's interesting," I observed when we sat at a stoplight. "The stoplights here are horizontal, not vertical like in America. Well, except that left turn signal."

"Fascinating observation."

"Why, thank you."

The car continued onward, pine trees, shops, and restaurants passing by on either side. And then, all at once, it shifted, shops disappearing and giving way to trees and land—with only the occasional billboard to disrupt the sense of another time—reaching an incline as it did so. We ascended once again—like in the plane, but a more intimate journey—and then, after several minutes passed and shortly before descending, I saw it.

A sliver of blue and white peeked out from in front of us. *The Rocky Mountains.* As its beauty struck me once again, this time from below instead of above, *The Storm*, the second movement of the William Tell, broke out, mournful violins and violas giving way to a multitude of trombones, French horns, trumpets, and a bass drum. As I gazed ahead, I was reminded of how the composition was meant to depict the Swiss Alps. And now the mountains reached before us, growing more distinct as we approached. As they drew closer, both sides of the road were lined by pines, now densely packed in a line like guards to a great palace awaiting travelers, and the palace itself was ahead, mountains standing tall, suddenly appearing as if close enough to touch and then seeming once again farther away, untouchable—and blue and white blurred to dark gray and white, as if a mirage of the desert tricking my eyes.

Movement 3: Ranz des vaches. The pastoral movement à la Cor Anglais—The French horn.

My breath quickened as signs to Banff Park came into view, and the trees themselves rose to greet us.

"We'll use the bypass lanes rather than the main entrance once we get to Banff Park," Peter finally spoke after several minutes of quiet save the music. "It's a secret passageway that only some of us Albertans know to use to avoid heavy tourist traffic."

I smiled, nodding, but found myself utterly unable to speak.

Movement 4: March of the Swiss Soldiers. A triumphant dash announced by trumpets paving the way for the full orchestra. The Finale.

And then, all at once, we were there.

I stared ahead, taking in The House that had played—tugging gently yet insistently—at my imagination for so long. It was much as Peter had described—a brown and white one-story building with a large front yard—yet so much more. The colors and shapes, ideas and conceptions, were shallow stick figures of its true form, not entirely real, not entirely *human*, an understated fortress that somehow belonged to the alps enveloped in clouds on our ascent, a castle of the air that only sank to the ground when it was able to rise. The white was not the old dusty color of a well-used home, but soft and pristine, flowing into itself rather than apart—pure and new as if just painted, while I knew from Peter that the last renovations had been years before. Yet it was not cold and hollow, an empty structure where people did not *live*, still well-used in the way that it was well-loved, the white shifting delicately into the brown like a sunset's understanding.

I caught my breath as my eye took in an unexpected sight.

A less human sight.

Long green stems, velvet of a forest cloak, spun across the white and brown, intertwined in remembrance of a sleeping young princess, as scarlet burst forth in cascading petals from its mouth.

A rose trellis.

And, in my ecstasy, I almost *forgot*.

I turned to Peter eagerly, my eyes alight. "How did you not tell me about the climbing roses?! How long has your family had them?"

Peter's eyes twinkled. "Longer than I've known you. But I wanted to keep one surprise."

"Just one?" I teased. "Much like this adventure, ahem, trip is not a surprise?"

Peter shook his head, smiling.

"I shall call it The Rose Cottage," I declared with Anne Shirley airs. "And, yes, that is most definitely an *Avonlea* reference among various fairy tale allusions. And—"

And then I remembered, and stopped.

I was almost certain that Peter observed the smile that faded, but he had the discretion to say nothing.

I cleared my throat. "Shall we—"

"Ah, yes," Peter said before pausing. He shook his head, smiling once again.

"What is it?"

"Just that . . . after four and a half years, this is where the two worlds meet. I've been in your world for so long—and wandered back to my own. But now you're crossing into mine. I'm not sure how that will be."

"Peter," I hesitated, "I—"

"—but I'm glad of it," he finished.

There was a silence, and then he opened the car door.

I realized that my heart was beating faster every step of the way. *That should be, probably is, a cliché*, I argued with myself. *But it is also exactly how it feels.*

I had only a moment to consider how his family might find me, the elusive mystery of their essence both a source of more nervousness and strangely a comfort, before Peter unlocked the door of the house, keys dangling in effervescent chatter, and somehow, at unawares, I was standing at the threshold of a large living room with pale mint green walls and mahogany brown furniture, my feet entirely unaware of recent movement.

Olivia Asturian turned, rising from the chair as if she had been waiting for us all along, and, in that first glance, I knew her to be a kindred spirit.

Her auburn hair fell in cascading waves more civilized and elegant than I was used to with Alex's rebellious locks.

I blinked once and realized that that had been my imagining, yet this contradiction existed within her, nebulous yet understood. Her hair was black like a raven's wing, shimmering in lined waves down the middle of her back as of a young maiden, The Lady of Shalott were she not fair—yet it *could* be red if it chose, her tumbling tresses, the contradiction in her spirit, closely aligned with the parallel of its paradox. A few stray locks curled elegantly in tendrils near each ear. She was, in a word, beautiful; in three, a great beauty. Her eyes were hazel, brown and green and almost blue all at once, yet never at the same time.

Her eyes were Peter's.

And, in a glance, I knew her.

She walked toward me with a smile, flowing arms of purple lightly shifting—instantly I knew it was both her favorite color and *her*.

She grasped my hands, echoing the thought as if an intimate friend of many years. "Rebecca, it is so *lovely* to finally meet you."

I nearly blinked back tears—and, with it, a remembrance of time's door—and then smiled. She returned the smile, much as I sensed Peter do the same behind me, and that was Peter's, too, only girlish, younger than she was—for surely she was well into her fifties—seeming in her essence no more than thirty-five.

Mrs. Asturian took my hand, squeezing it, as she indicated with her other hand the inner door of the garage outside. "Raphael should be in in just a minute."

Indeed, at that precise moment, as if at the words, "Close Sesame," the shuttling sound of a closing garage door reached us, and then the certain steps of a deep-rooted man drew closer with an almost-comforting strength.

Raphael Asturian stood, and I instantly saw in him the scientist—of various patented designs—the painter—of subjects unknown—and the jam shop owner—by trade— all at once. There were no glasses perched on his nose, yet the faint red marks on his nose indicated that perhaps reading glasses (I knew no member of Peter's family used glasses regularly) or lab goggles had been recently worn. His eyes were brown and warm, taking me in with a faint smile not unlike that of his son. But his hair was darker, and thicker in parts, like that of his wife, yet lightened when compared with hers into the color of the chestnut brown furniture ahead, and gray specks fell like strands of tinsel at regular intervals. Raphael Asturian was wearing a suit in odd contrast with the garage that he had just left.

But he was an Asturian.

And everything came to surface with the trueness of that recognition.

Mr. Asturian came forth and shook my hand, his smile quieter than Peter's somehow while nevertheless remaining more direct.

"You must be Rebecca," he said.

And, as he shifted his position slightly to the left, I saw behind him a young boy of about ten years of age in a silver-gray wheelchair.

The boy's gaze was on me, unwavering, and I instantly knew that it had been so the entire time I had stood in this room, as he waited silently.

I walked toward him and almost instinctively reached out my hand to touch his.

This was Little Dan. This was Peter's life.

"Yes." He nodded, as if answering an unspoken question in his mind. "You are Rebecca." And he reached out his hand.

I took it, now blinking back tears that I had previously held at bay. "You must be Little Dan. But"—I smiled through the emotion overcoming me—"I've always wanted to call you Danny."

The boy nodded again, as if thoughtfully considering, light brown curly hair falling in short locks around his face. "Yes, you may call me Danny, but just you, and especially when we're reading poetry together." His big brown eyes, strikingly more like Peter's than even those of his father which held the same shade, addressed mine. "It will be our pact, like a secret code that the pirates make. Shall we begin this afternoon?"

I loved him.

I smiled, and met his eyes. "Of course. If—" I glanced over at Peter, whose eyes, too, were moist. "If Peter does not mind."

"I am willing to postpone the previously scheduled tour for a poetry reading with my brother." Peter smiled.

Little Dan's gaze reached mine again, startling in its maturity yet childlike—once again more Peter than either of their parents, yet so different. "I understand why you are Peter's friend. You are like us, in your eyes. I think we shall be friends, too."

I squeezed his hand. "Yes, Danny, we will."

I stood on the threshold of the dining room, watching. Mrs. Asturian was busying herself with the dinner plates, the succulent smell of beef stew filling my nostrils with delight. From the kitchen, Mr. Asturian approached, carrying a bowl, before taking his seat at the head of the table.

It reminded me of . . .

I pushed those thoughts aside.

Peter helped his brother out of his wheelchair, tenderly lifting him into a seat on the right side.

I cleared my throat, entering the room.

It had been only fifteen minutes since our arrival. I had used the restroom, washing the weariness of our travels from my face, and studied the backyard garden from the sliding glass door, unable to move, until I heard Mrs. Asturian call everyone to the table.

"Do you need help setting the table?" I asked, as Mrs. Asturian turned around. "I'd be happy to—"

Olivia Asturian waved me away. "Sit with Peter and Little Dan. You are our guest."

I sat down with some protest, as Mr. Asturian stood up, returning shortly with napkins. I smiled across the table at Peter and Little Dan.

"Beef stew," Peter said. "A specialty of Alberta, in a way."

"I know." I cleared my throat. "I may or may not have done a little online research before stepping on that plane."

"Somehow I'm not surprised."

"But," Little Dan interjected with a wide grin, "the best part is Mama's dumplings."

I smiled down at the little boy, his big eyes alive. "I just may end up agreeing with you. I love dumplings, or anything involving bread, really. Though I'm sure that your mom's stew is excellent," I added quickly as Mrs. Asturian reentered the room.

Mrs. Asturian placed a platter of wild berries, carrots, and nuts on the table before sitting down.

"Peter tells me that your family is known for gourmet Italian dishes. I hope Albertan fare won't disappoint."

"Oh, no!" I said quickly. "I *love* beef stew. And dumplings," I added, stealing a smile at Little Dan, who grinned back.

We each served ourselves substantial helpings of the stew into our wide blue and white bowls—Peter giving Little Dan a generous helping and two and a half dumplings—before sitting down again to say grace.

"In the name of the Father, and of the Son, and of the Holy Spirit," Mr. Asturian began in his quiet, deep voice.

I made the Sign of the Cross and bent my head in prayer.

"Bless us, O Lord, and these Thy gifts, which we are about to receive from Thy bounty, through Christ our Lord. Amen."

"Amen," we each responded.

From the first bite, I knew that reports of the stew had not been exaggerated.

"It's delicious!" I said enthusiastically.

Mrs. Asturian smiled. "Thank you, Rebecca. Glad you like it."

"Did you try the dumplings?" Little Dan asked eagerly.

I took a bite. "Very yummy, Danny. You have excellent taste."

Little Dan beamed.

"So, how do you find Banff, Rebecca?" Mrs. Asturian asked, daintily wiping her lips.

"It's lovely," I said sincerely. "Just as I imagined—only moreso. I can't wait to see Lake Louise tomorrow."

"Can I come?" Little Dan's large eyes addressed me.

"Of course you will!"

"The terrain is a bit rough in parts—" Peter said guardedly.

"Oh, I didn't think about that." My face was flushed.

"—but I know a good entrance. Little Dan has been there many times before, even after . . ." Peter's voice trailed off.

Little Dan reached his hand to squeeze that of his brother. "I'll be fine, Peter," he said, his large, expressive eyes so eager and young moments before now suddenly wise beyond his years.

Peter smiled. "Of course you will. You'll be with me—"

"And me," I added quickly with a smile.

"Peter tells me that you have been working as a psychologist for a year now," Mrs. Asturian said after a moment, changing the subject. "That's a wonderful accomplishment!"

"Thank you! I am. It is a pleasure to be in that position—to do my best to help people with . . ."

Their sorrows.

I paused. "With whatever ails them."

The space between Peter's eyebrows creased slightly, but he said nothing.

"A true blessing for you both then."

"It is," I said, warming up to the topic. "I even have a few clients from my preservice days."

"Yes, Peter mentioned the veteran who struggled with PTSD."

"Albert. Yes, we've become rather close. He smiles so much more often now. And dances . . . all the time."

Hypocrite. The word rang through my head, but I struggled to ignore it.

"At the end of each of our sessions, we actually dance together to a song by this artist from Argentina. It's . . .

a long story, but it came to hold meaning for him, and for me."

"Sounds like a beautiful story."

"It does," Mr. Asturian said, speaking for the first time. I smiled appreciatively back at him, and he returned it with a quiet smile of his own.

I served myself an assortment of berries and nuts.

"And Stacie might never have found the courage to get married," Peter added, "if it hadn't been for you."

"It's been such a joy to see her progress," I said. "But I can't take all the credit. I'm happy if anything I did helped, but it was mostly her."

"You should take more credit than you do," Peter said, studying me, and I suddenly realized that he meant more than the state of my clients.

I looked down, and took another bite of stew.

A painting in the far corner of the room caught my eye. It was of a sailboat, gliding gracefully upon sea green waves, white billows of form dancing lightly in an unseen breeze. In the distance was an intricate scene—a building, tall and almost medieval in style, with tiny figures skating and gathered before it in conversation. If you didn't look closely, you would only see the sailboat. Yet they were all one.

"That painting is beautiful," I said, pointing. "I understand that both of you paint." I turned my eyes to Peter's parents. "Did one of you create that?"

"My husband," Olivia Asturian said with pride, smiling at the man across the table from her.

"One of my most recent paintings, but it was done some years ago," Mr. Asturian said. "Now I focus more on my experiments."

"Which, in case you're wondering, are classified." Little Dan offered me a magnifying glass of a smile.

The Little Detective.

"My son exaggerates," Mr. Asturian said with an affectionate smile at Little Dan. "But, while I know you are an intelligent young woman, it would take some time to discuss. Perhaps later in your trip."

This quiet, reserved father of Peter making such an offer touched me.

"I'd love to."

"Olivia is the one who is doing most of the painting these days."

I turned to Mrs. Asturian. "That's wonderful. I'd . . . I'd love to see your work sometime if you'd like," I added shyly.

"Of course. I'd be happy to share it with you, Rebecca." Olivia Asturian offered me a warm smile, as if she had known me her entire life.

Peter had not participated much in the conversation, yet, throughout the entire dinner, as he sat watching silently, I felt as if he had.

There was more to conversation than words.

I helped myself to one more bowl of stew—and two more dumplings—and then leaned back against the wooden chair and its flowered cushion with satisfaction. "That hit the spot."

"So glad you liked it!"

I helped Mrs. Asturian clear away the dishes, despite her initial protests, and then we headed back to the table.

"As I seem to recall, I promised someone poetry." I eyed Little Dan, who sat waiting patiently at the table.

"Would you like me to show you to your room first?" Mrs. Asturian asked. "You did just arrive."

"I can wait," Little Dan said.

"No, no, it's fine. I'd love to start reading now."

"Should I help you to The Poet's Room, or do you want to stay here?" Peter asked, suddenly standing quietly behind his chair.

"Rebecca should see The Poet's Room soon," Little Dan said thoughtfully, "but I think that a dining room reading after dumplings and stew has something about it that seems *right*."

Peter smiled, moving to the bookshelves that materialized in the far right of the room as if they had never been there before. "What shall it be?"

"Let Rebecca pick. The first reading should always be picked by the reader," Little Dan said decidedly.

I smiled, and stood up to join Peter by the bookshelves.

"The second shelf is all poetry," Peter said, indicating it with his hand.

I nodded, and he returned to his seat.

I took a few moments, scanning the spines of the books before my eyes took note of the volume that, as Little Dan might have said, seemed *right*.

"Ah," I said, taking the Robert Frost volume of poetry from the shelf, and moving back to the table. "I always did love Frost's poetry. Though I haven't delved into it as much as I might have."

"You can take the rocking chair, if you'd like," Mrs. Asturian said, taking a seat at the table. "Poet's Chair."

"Almost as good as The Poet's Room," Little Dan said.

"You know, you are making me way too curious about The Poet's Room," I said teasingly, before sitting down on the old wooden rocking chair.

I scanned the table of contents, and found the right page number.

"'The Road Not Taken'?" Peter asked with a smile.

"My favorite by Frost, as you know. So, good guess . . . but this is an *evening*, even if summer, so . . ."

I looked up once my hand settled on the correct page. The Asturians sat at the table, the father adjusting his now-present spectacles as Olivia Asturian leaned forward, her hand delicately placed under her chin with an almost faraway gaze in her eyes. Peter's eyes penetrated mine for an instant, and in them was a warmth—a warmth and reassurance. He stood for a moment, helping Little Dan back in his wheelchair so that he could sit closer to me, and then returned to his chair, still silently waiting.

In almost any other situation, I would have been all nerves at having an audience. Reciting poetry was an action that spoke to the center of who I was, yet I preferred the company of no more than one, or just myself, speaking into the recorder on my cell phone. And yet, while nervousness sprang into my heart, worry about the first impression I would give the Asturians nibbling at my mind, there was a natural comfort at the circumstances and setting. It reminded me of an old writer's club from days bygone—C.S. Lewis and his friends huddling around a table in literary discussion.

I was not among strangers.

No, not at all.

But, even so, it was a first.

I cleared my throat and began. "Stopping by Woods on a Snowy Evening. Whose woods these are I think I know . . ."

As I continued to read, I became more absorbed in the poem. My voice grew softer, more gentle—less rehearsed and more *me*—as the words sifted within me, allowing echoes of their truth to be transmitted. When I reached the last line of the second stanza, my voice trembled with the enormity of it.

"The darkest evening of the year," I said.

I paused, and looked up. Little Dan's eyes were rapt with approval, and his father offered a more subdued version, yet clear on his face, as Olivia Asturian looked again, a faint smile upon her lips. And Peter, Peter watched me, an unreadable expression on his countenance until I began again.

"The only other sound's the sweep. Of easy wind and downy flake," I said softly, the lyrical quality of the verses beckoning me with their lull to the scene before the speaker in the poem. And then, the final stanza finally came with its melodic voice beyond my own:

"The woods are lovely, dark and deep,

But I have promises to keep,

And miles to go before I sleep,

And miles to go before I sleep," I finished, looking up.

Peter's eyes took in mine, soft and real.

"Well done," Mr. Asturian said quietly.

"Very . . . beautiful and true," Mrs. Asturian said in her romantic voice.

"Yes." Little Dan nodded. "You are a poet, Rebecca Veritas. And," he said, reaching out his hand, as I moved toward him to take it, "you know how to bring the woods *here*."

"I think," he said, his curls falling over his small, thoughtful face, "that we will have many evenings by the woods, you, and them, and I."

"And here is your room." Peter opened the door before me, and waited for me to enter. He remained at the threshold as I walked forward and took in my surroundings.

It was a simple room, a bed with a soft pink blanket covering its small frame, a mahogany dresser with a little mirror framed in gold reaching upward in three rows opposite it, and a nightstand of the same light pink of the blanket to the left of my bed, complete with a floral lampshade. There was a writing desk also of mahogany, modest and unadorned yet pleasing, near the dresser, with several sheets of paper lined on top and a pen of pink floral design strikingly similar to the one that Peter had given me long ago. Next to the pen sat a copy of the Bible, the Catechism, and several paperbacks, images of dragons and elegantly dressed women of a bygone age sweeping into my vision. Alongside the wall was a glass double-doored closet with rich spirals of brown adorning the surface like statuesque figures forming out of the woodwork.

Fruit trees and a splash of many-colored flowers greeted us in the backyard. I took it all in, my eye resting on a small, off-white enclosure near the branches of one tree, as we walked through the backyard in the final stretch of the promised tour.

I turned to Peter, a question in my eyes.

"Carrier pigeons," he said, by way of explanation. "My father used to train them."

"Wow, that's amazing," I said softly, reaching my hand upward to touch the cage, now wet with dew. "For how long?"

"More than fifteen years," Peter answered. "Sometimes I think he left this around in case one decided to scurry back," he finished with a smile.

A smile graced my own lips briefly, and then I saw it.

A large swimming pool, shimmering in bright blue swirls, stood near the garden flowers.

Peter stiffened, and I turned to him. "Have you—"

"No," he said briefly, and turned to the other end of the backyard. "Here are some more roses, Rebecca, and you may be interested in the thyme here that we planted . . ."

I looked down at the floor of my room to a carpet of rich forest green, and on that carpet was a rug of deep red and pink roses swirling in their wake.

Like the garden and its pool, they were animated in auroral incandescence, donning its resplendence as if a cloak or sheath.

I gazed around the room once again, taking it all in.

It was a simple room, but much, much more.

From the pink to the roses to the fantasy novels and writing paper, it almost looked designed especially for me.

"Peter," I said, my eyebrows scrunching together. "The lamp." I pointed to it in wonder. "It's almost like the one I have at home. And the pinks and roses and . . . even the books." I stopped as something caught in my throat.

"It was nothing," Peter said simply, waving it away. "My mother had some extra feminine objects for the room, and, as the guest room can be changed at any time, I requested some of these." His gaze shifted to me, his eyes meeting mine. "I wanted you to feel at home."

A sigh lifted through my heart, almost breaking through to the outside.

"Thank you, Peter," I said sincerely, emotion in my voice. "That was . . . very kind of you. And your mother," I added.

Peter smiled. "My pleasure." He glanced back at the door, and turned to me. "I'll let you get settled in. There are extra blankets in the closet if you need them. It can occasionally get rather cold in Banff at night, even in the summer."

He turned to the door, moving to leave.

"Peter."

"Yes?" He paused at the door and looked at me.

His large, expressive eyes were deep pools, reminiscent then of the nightly walk as they remained reflected in mine.

Was everything like the garden?

"And the pen?" I pointed to the writing utensil lying in wait on the desk.

"Oh, that." Peter's signature grin finally broke across his face. "I bought a pack of them when I gave you one in the spring of 2013. I've been storing them since," he said matter-of-factly, "to dispose of from time to time when the occasion arises."

I raised an eyebrow. "May I ask how many there are?"

"50. It was a variety bulk package, on special," Peter said nonchalantly.

"Perhaps," he said, looking back at me, "I will gift one at random once a year."

50 years.

"Perhaps interspersed at random locations at random times, befitting the Queen of Random," he added.

"Like an Easter egg hunt?"

"Indeed."

"I will have to make room for a collection," I said.

Peter smiled, and then left the room.

I collapsed on the bed, the weariness of our travels finally hitting, and was left alone with my thoughts.

I sank into the pillow, my head cushioned against it like a lullaby that willed comfort.

And then, all at once, an image surfaced in my mind, and a stabbing pain attacked my chest with unrelenting vigor.

I gasped, a knife searing through my insides, leaving no inch untouched, and forced myself upward to a sitting position. It penetrated farther, farther, hopes, dreams, and all I held most dear clinging to their heart as it was cruelly ripped from my chest without conscience or thought of remorse.

My lungs emptied in an instant, the breath stolen from me in a single bound.

A word. A name. A lock of hair.

And a painting.

I willed them to go away, let me be, in the quiet nightfall.

The knife plunged deeper, and turned into a pistol.

I can't do this. I can't do this anymore. I can't be here and not breathe. I can't . . . I pleaded to them, begging leniency.

But the clock read 2:30 AM, and night for travelers held at gunpoint held no sleep.

I pushed aside the covers, a resigned weakness throwing my limbs and the rest of my body into cement too heavy to move.

Yet moving was all I could do.

I paced about the room blindly, not caring where I turned or where I was, simply walking, hoping that the farther I went, the farther the memory would be left behind.

Yet I knew in my heart that this respite, once obtained, would be short-lived, retreating images and names would return, and I would still be *here*.

But, for now, I would walk.

I threw on the pink robe hanging on the door—a kindness that my mind could not even process—and opened the door.

I hesitated, looking down the hall, as something akin to air beckoned me. *Would it wake the Asturians? What would they think if, on the first night of their hospitality, they found me walking down the hallway like some strange figure of the night instead of warm in my bed?*

Insecurity overwhelmed me, and I closed the door.

This was a box by comparison. But a box that provided sanctuary.

For minutes and hours, I paced around the small room, my eyes burning with fatigue and throbbing agony, walking and pacing until I was too tired to think, walking and pacing until I could finally breathe again.

I woke up halfway through the night, and my hand reached for a piece of paper from the stack on the desk.

My hand fumbled, and, for a moment, I could not see the words that flowed freely from the pen through my blurred vision . . .

September Days

I've been going back to September Days
Seems like it's the only thing to do
Once in a while.
I won't linger, yes, I will
Can't forget you, no, I won't
And my heart's slipping away to September Days . . .

CHORUS
September Days
Oh, September Days
Endless nights
And pale feverish parades
Do you know what it's like
Waking up feeling
There's no breath in sight?
Crying the day away like no tears are left
Only to find one more falls down
Just like the past.
September Days are haunting me
Once again . . .

"Hey, Rebecca." Peter smiled from the table. "Ready to see Lake Louise today?"

"Yeah," I said, a smile plastered on my face. "We can do that."

Peter frowned slightly, but said nothing.

"It's like . . . that movie I saw last week," I plunged forward, unthinking. "It feels like that moment when the family gets ready for a vacation at an ice hotel. The preparation is like vacation in and of itself. It was a pretty chill movie, actually. And I'm rambling, um, I . . ."

I stood, suddenly frozen timid.

Anything you say will be judged. Anything you do will not be enough.

You are just a silly girl, the words echoed through my head. *No one wants to hear you.*

No one needs you.

You were always meant to be left behind.

"Oh, I'm sorry. I'm so sorry," I blabbered, my face reddening. "I didn't mean anything by it . . . I . . ." My voice trailed off.

Don't judge it, please, Peter. I . . .

Peter stared at me. "It's nothing, Rebecca."

Confusion eddied through my mind, clouding my thoughts.

Why are you feeling so insecure? It whispered to me sadly. *Why? You never felt like this before. Before, when . . .*

And yet the time before seemed so long ago, and I was left with the fear that every word I spoke could be a mistake—unwanted, undesired, and worthy of abandonment.

"I'm sorry," I stammered again.

"Why are you apologizing," he said, his brow furrowed.

"I don't know. I"—I looked at my feet, suddenly grateful Peter was the only one in the room, and I wasn't making a fool of myself in front of his entire family—"I . . . I'm sorry for apologizing, too. That was weird. I mean, I don't mean that I'm sorry for apologizing. Ugh."

"You're fine, Rebecca."

"Really? I mean, gosh, I'm not making myself sound like a total idiot?" I laughed, attempting to lightly throw it all away like a joke.

"No," he said, looking at me. "No, you're not."

"Right. Okay, well"—I looked at the biscuits on the table, jam jars of varied colors lying in wake around them—"that looks delicious."

Peter stood and pulled back the chair across from him, allowing me to sit.

He pushed me in, then returned to his seat.

"Thanks, Peter," I said, suddenly overcome.

It was a simple gesture, a routine act of chivalry, and yet, with it, all faded away for an instant. Tears formed in my eyes for no apparent reason, and I stared fervently at my plate.

"Thank you," I said again, feeling certain I was losing my mind, yet knowing I was not.

"Eat, Rebecca. It's a special family recipe. Perfect," he added with a smile, as my face recomposed and I looked up at him, "for the starting point to an adventure in an ice hotel movie."

"Or Lake Louise," I finished.

"Or Lake Louise." He smiled.

Chapter 6: Turquoise

Deep turquoise cascaded in sonorous ripples across the surface, iridescent prisms of light and hue intertwined in soft melodies of a tongue solitary and unknown—not tumbling and bursting forth in splashes of waves of an ancient sea, time eternal encaptured in ancient scrolls, but flowing endlessly younger somehow, yet time still enveloped in its ebb and flow as if holding an ageless secret—streams of nymph ballads gathering shimmering emeralds to lightly toss within its fold, scattering luminescent flecks beyond echoing sighs and whispers to a wholeness lingering in the stillness of its breath. Branches of pine shot to the sky, surrounding the whirlpool of blue and green with brambles of deep forest green, viridescent cloaks of bow-clad men revealed, as unscrambled leaf peered out from beneath Robin Hood's Merry Men. They swept down into a great V, sentinels at watch withdrawing, gray swirls and curves of mountains reaching upwards in carefully shaded lines of chalk and silhouette that overlooked the enormity of a sun-kissed world dreamt in glass-blown shapes.

There was a deep, pervading serenity, quiet and solitary, in this sanctuary of branch and water, drifting across in far-reaching swells, and I breathed it in— breathed it in as if it could purge any poison from my heart.

I gazed at Lake Louise, my eyes a reflection of its kaleidoscope of color. Peter stood quietly by my side, one hand on the shoulder of Little Dan, who sat in his wheelchair with his face aglow.

"It's beautiful," I whispered. "Even more beautiful than the picture I looked at so many times when I only dreamed of being here."

Thin gates with the image of bears lightly sketched across appeared in my line of vision, an expansive, many-windowed structure of golden-tinged white capped in blue emerging behind it. A brown sign lifted across the backdrop of trees surrounding it with the word "Fairmount" prettily written in cursive followed by "Chateau Lake Louise" in bold capital lettering. Only a few people milled about in the background at this early hour. Peter had told me that early morning was the best time to avoid tourists and enjoy Lake Louise at its finest, and so we had left the house at the quiet hour of 6:45 and traveled hence.

A small smile crossed Peter's face. "You'll have to come back at Christmastime."

"Yeah?" My eyes retreated from the scene for a mere instant, a hesitant smile of my own inching across my countenance. "Why's that?"

"Horse-drawn carriages," Peter said. "Fit for the best of your fairy tales."

Little Dan spoke for him at the same time, the eagerness bounding across his words. "It looks like *Narnia*."

I finally smiled—a smile almost full—at the little boy before me. "A Narnian fairy tale. I could see that."

"It should be," Peter said with another smile. "Lake Louise was named after a princess. The fourth daughter of Queen Victoria, Princess Louise Caroline Alberta. She married the general governor of Canada at the time."

As I glanced back at Peter, I noticed for the first time that he had a long, olive green and black bag strapped to his back. I wondered briefly as to its purpose, before he continued.

"And the lake is frozen in the winter," Peter added. "Almost like a bigger version of those ice sculptures I told you about."

"Wow." I closed my eyes, facing the lake once again, and something within me stirred. It was an airy figure of thought, an impression—not a person, but an idea, a piece of something that filled me with a touch of warmth and quiet thrill beyond feeling. It sifted through my form and into me like something foreign, but still an ally unbaleful, forcing recognition of its reality, its presence. My gaze lifted to the mountains before me, shrouded in soft colors of grays and whites.

"It isn't the John Denver song since these are *different* Rocky Mountains, but," I said almost shyly, "it almost *is*. I can almost feel the song around me as I look at them."

Peter smiled, and said nothing, and then I brought myself back to the world before me.

We stood and watched, allowing the sound of watery lulls to greet us, surround us with their vastness. I reached farther into the silence, and it shifted before me, inviting me closer. I gazed at the blue reflection before me . . .

"Pop-pop, popcorn!" the little girl giggled, her chestnut brown ringlets bouncing around her as freely as her laughter. She twirled, her sapphire puffed sleeves and filmy dress billowing around her small form. "You can have ALL my candy! The princess just wants pop-pop, POPCORN!"

A gentle, melodious voice rose from next to her, and something in me stilled. I looked closer, but a face was silhouetted from view, bidding me farther away. Go away, *it echoed. "Popcorn for the pretty princess in blue!" I heard the sound of a bag dropping into the Trick-or-Treat orange pumpkin bag, and walked further, but an invisible field held me at bay. I glimpsed a flash of golden kernels and breathed in the scent. "Happy Halloween, my sweet Rebecca," the voice etched with affection reached out. I pulled toward it, yearning to move closer, and then, all at once, the little girl disappeared, growing taller and taller, her dark curls falling below her shoulders, and a young woman in a yellow dress emerged. Her eyes were bright as she sat in a dark gray car. Behind her was a building shrouded in darkness, words forming across its surface, the first letter "A" visible, but I could see no more. A new, deeper voice spoke, but I was pulled back, down, down into the depths below . . .*

Pinpricks of needles sharper than those of the pine branches and farther-reaching than the bowmen's arrows stabbed my heart one by one, and I pressed my feet against dirt and rock, bidding them to resist the lurching feeling in my chest that promised to envelop my entire form. I stumbled against the ground, unsteady, the world tilting around me.

"Rebecca." Peter's hand was around my waist, steadying me.

"I . . . I'm all right," I said, as shifting images righted themselves, and the calm, serene surface of a lake reappeared before my eyes.

"The ground can be a bit uneven in this area," Peter said, watching me.

I nodded, less in acknowledgement than in habit, and Lake Louise drew my eyes back to it. The shimmering turquoise rippled before me, and, all at once, the beauty *hurt*. The pinpricks of needles returned, and I pressed my feet more firmly against the ground, resisting the disquieting sensation in my chest, and, with each passing moment, it lessened in intensity, as if gliding across the surface of the lake to disappear below, if only for an instant.

For a moment, I was safe, wrapped in a blue-hued embrace.

For a moment, later did not matter.

I sighed deeply, and breathed in the air and the lake as if of a balm, dove's pristine wings fluttering against the backdrop of a painting.

But this was a painting that could be touched.

Several minutes passed without words spoken, the stillness a reassuring caress much like the lake and its silent verses.

A line dropped before my eyes, plopping lightly into the water and startling me out of my wordless reflections.

I looked back at Peter, who grinned subtly from the end of a fishing pole, and a smile of my own swept suddenly across my face.

"Thought I'd see if there are any bites today," Peter said.

I shook my head in recollection—but this recollection was spun in gold and silver—turning back to the lake. "Do you remember how we once said that we would be called The Fisherman and the Lighthouse Keeper, you and I?"

"I do."

"And you, Little Dan?" I said affectionately, looking down to the little boy eying the pole with great interest from his chair. "What will you be?"

Little Dan thought for a moment. "Gus Pike," he said. "I'll bring the fish out with my fiddle."

Peter and I laughed, the feeling stuck in my chest, nudging its way out once again as if a curious sensation. "That is perfect. That makes you both Lighthouse Keeper and Fisherman."

"The Little Fisherman," I added, as Little Dan's face lit up, his eyes suddenly somber.

"Yes." He nodded, as if agreeing to an important pact or preparing to be knighted.

We watched the lake in silence, a bird's sweet call in the distance providing a soundtrack to the scene, minute after minute passing, as I stood, content and unable to break my gaze, desiring to remain there for much longer, with the lake providing a thought, a word, as it wrapped around me with its serenity. *Wrapping, closer and closer.*

A tiny silver fish, fins tinted in yellow, swung into the air, wiggling tenaciously against the line. Peter quickly reeled it in as Little Dan whooped, raising his small fists into the air, and I joined him, my hair blowing around me in a gentle breeze that suddenly stirred the air around us.

"You caught one, Peter!" Little Dan said excitedly, as he flattened his hand and raised it for a high five.

Peter's eyebrows knitted closer together, his grin slowly fading, and I saw a flash of the lake in his eyes as I remembered the true significance of the high five. Of how Little Dan used to run to greet him at the door with his little legs, swooping up to meet the hand of his brother.

Oh, how little I knew then.

And then Peter smiled, reaching down to his brother. "High five," he said.

Little Dan grinned as my heart swelled. "Our first catch of the day."

"Our first catch," I echoed, gazing at those same still waters.

I paced, back and forth, back and forth,

Until

The night relented

And I fell
Asleep

Chapter 7: Citrine

Peter and I strolled down the sidewalk past a scattering of varied stores, from candy and wares to restaurants, the chatter of the busy street shifting to the background as we walked in companionable silence.

There was something undeniably pleasant and inexplicably fulfilling about sharing such a commonplace and ordinary action as walking down the block and through a shopping center with Peter. I breathed in the air, refreshed, as we continued onward, occasionally commenting on a passing bird or peeking in the window of a bakery or pet shop to view one specialty or another, but mostly content to simply take in the scene indirectly, yet somehow *more* directly, through such a simple exercise as this.

And, with Peter, it felt *natural*.

I was so absorbed in my thoughts that, when Peter came to a halt, I nearly ran into him.

"Here we are." Peter gazed up at the building before us, the words "The Whyte Museum of the Canadian Rockies" blinking out at us in golden text from the backdrop of lines of dark brown. "111 Bear Street."

It was a large structure, extending such that it appeared to be composed of many sections divided by geometric shapes, a conglomeration of multicolored layers of stone standing like pillars. Gray steps led up to an arrangement of horizontal brown lines once again enclosed by panels of cobblestone of varied hues with glass doors at the front of the building outlined also in brown. Kernels of pink and white sand merged together in sparkling dust to form a statue of a bear, which stood to one side near a reddish bench, bordered on the bottom and right side with the same splattering of many-colored stone.

"Shall we?" Peter pointed to the steps that led to the entrance, and I followed.

Spacious halls welcomed us with the smell of fresh paint, gray carpet spread neatly beneath our feet. As we emerged on the other side, depositing our tickets purchased in advance before venturing farther, I turned around, my eyes moving back and forth as I took in what lay before me. Paintings spaced out on white walls revealed sweeping landscapes of the Canadian Rockies and Lake Louise, uncovered bears and other animals of the region, and depicted the indigenous people and their world. Peter had told me that the museum was named after Peter and Catharine Whyte, 20th century artists who painted landscapes, collected artifacts, and interacted with the native people of the area. As we continued through the museum, treasures, evidence of their existence and early mountaineering life, were scattered throughout.

I stretched my hand to touch the muted red-orange and gold clothing once worn by a member of the Stoney Nakoda Nations people, before realizing that this was a museum and I probably shouldn't touch anything.

I cleared my throat awkwardly, and turned to Peter, who bit back a smile.

He knew how excited I could get about historical artifacts and mysteries, probably since the time I had messaged him at midnight to gush about how, *dude*, the Indus Valley civilization had writings *that still had not been decoded yet*.

I stopped for a moment to read one of the historical facts printed on an adjacent blue wall, and then continued onward.

Pottery and other artifacts were a dominant theme, and I peered for a moment to examine small figurines of instruments near the figure of a Chinese woman, white lettering in her native tongue unfolding across the top. Peter took a special interest in an Alpine helicopter available for (distant) examination.

After perusing the different rooms of the museum for an hour or so, we followed a tour group outside for an extension of the main portion of the museum.

The faint call of birdsong reached us as we took in six log homes—four cabins and two houses—made of brick and log.

"Only the Moore home and the Whyte home are open for the summer tours," our tour guide, a middle-aged woman with graying hair elaborated. "Let's start with the Whyte home."

The Whyte home was a remarkable assemblage of wood, logs, and stone. Windows and a door outlined in wood were stationed between layers of log and brick. From the roof emerged a top window, appearing almost to be a person peeking out from the heights of the building. There was something about that imagery that made me smile.

Just an ordinary day in the life of Rebecca Veritas: smiling at inanimate objects and turning them into people through her over-active imagination.

"Computers are people, too," I reasoned aloud.

"What was that?" Peter turned back at me, a wry grin forming at the corner of his lips.

Did I say that aloud?

"Nothing," I muttered with a sheepish grin and followed the tour group inside.

"*Peter* and Catharine Whyte," I commented, turning back to Peter, as I waited for others in front of me to move within. "Ready to visit your second home?"

"Very funny."

There was then more space to move forward, and I took in my surroundings.

An old-fashioned fireplace, outlined in brick, greeted us, bordered on either side by shelves filled with books, their many-colored spines splashing into view. The figure of a native child and dog standing on a wide hill as they watched a circle of teepees swept above the fireplace in a panoramic painting. On the mantel below sat two figurines of horses—one large and black, the other small and brown—each mounted on green and brown, respectively, as if standing on grass or rock. Pillows of indigenous design were tossed neatly on armchairs that were interspersed with wooden drawers, lamps, and an assortment of smaller paintings mounted on the walls. Jars of varied shapes, presumably made of clay, were scattered on shelves throughout. Red curtains framed a wide window, beneath which stood a sofa of red and white, gray and black. I stepped out onto a carpet of floral hues, many of the same colors dominant.

It was as if I had slipped into another time, and I marveled at the feeling that swept through me.

"It's like time travel," I whispered to Peter excitedly. And then, something stirred in my memory, and I suddenly searched the room for another focus.

"The home was built in 1930 as a summer home for the Whytes," the tour guide elaborated, as we began to walk around the living room, "but it later became their main house. Much of the design was influenced by their taste. The logs in the front formed the original design. The rest was added on in 1931. There is a kitchen through those doors," she pointed to accordion-style doors in the dining room, "which is not open to the public at this time. The studio upstairs is usually part of this tour, but is currently undergoing renovations."

The threshold of the room led to a dark brown table, a red tablecloth similar to the carpet laid out across it. A globe sat on one side, and more paintings, artifacts, and books were spread throughout. To the right, next to another, small bookcase, a brown staircase rose, stopping at one layer much like a platform before switching direction and leaping farther still. As I neared it, my breath caught in my throat.

At the top of the first section of stairs, beneath a blanket of blues, greens, and reds that lay across the wooden rail, was a small square object of orange divided into four distinctive sections.

The badge from Yin.

The resemblance was astounding, but I had to be sure.

I moved closer, one hand on the stairwell.

"Excuse me, ma'am." The tour guide was at my side in a single bound. "I'm very sorry, but the upstairs is off limits at this time due to the renovations I mentioned.

You can come back to see the studio as early as next month."

"I'm so sorry," I stammered, my face reddening. "I was just curious—"

"The studio is indeed a fascinating part of the tour, a deeper look into the lives of these great artists."

"Yes, I'm sure, but . . ."

"What is it, Rebecca?" Peter asked softly, stepping beside me.

"That square piece of cloth on the top of the first bit of stairs, after the first five steps. Is that part of the original design of the home?"

"Hmm." The tour guide's brow furrowed, and she walked up the steps. She returned with the badge in her hands.

"That is strange," she mused. "I have been working as a guide here for twenty years, and I have never seen this design before. It is not indigenous, nor does it conform to any other design of the time period."

"Are you certain?" My heart plummeted to my stomach.

"Quite certain." She peered at the object again in puzzlement. "Perhaps . . . it is part of what remains to be cleaned up from the . . . event two months ago."

The way she said "event" did not seem to imply any regularly scheduled event put on by the museum.

"Event?"

"Occurrence. According to the report, two men broke into the cabin and used it for some sort of meeting. They were later arrested."

Peter and I exchanged glances.

"Why did they think it was for a meeting?" I ventured.

"It had the makings of one. Food spread out, hushed voices, strange evidence left behind—though I thought they had it all cleaned up. I'm very sorry, but I'm afraid I must return to the tour. You can read more about it in the paper, however." She laid the badge on one of the shelves and moved back to the group.

I thanked her for her time, and, after a moment, Peter and I followed her to the large dining table.

Yet my mind remained with the image of gallinaceous dragons and chains, orange splattered like diluted blood across the backdrop.

The tour ended approximately twenty minutes later, and then the option was presented of continuing to the Moore home, but, after a quick glance at Peter revealing mutual accord, I politely declined and hurried outside.

"Can I see it?" Peter asked quietly, once we stopped outside the house, a small breeze blowing through the near-wilderness.

He had been waiting outside when I had left Yin in her prison cell nine days before, and I had told him all that had occurred. On the plane ride over, I had also made reference to the strange connection to Jeffrey's inheritance from his uncle.

I dug into my purse, and took out my own copy of the badge we had seen in the log home.

Peter whistled. "The very same."

"Yes." I shook my head. "What does this mean?"

"I don't know, but I have a feeling that Jeffrey isn't the only one who will be doing research now."

I nodded, the images riddling within me, as my already-persistent curiosity was suddenly joined by an inexplicable anxiety that swept through my chest.

"Well, this is just as well," Peter commented, changing the subject. "Don't get me wrong; the Moore house is also a fascinating jump in time. But now we can get to the next stop in our scheduled plans a bit earlier."

"Our plans?" I arched an eyebrow.

"Well, perhaps a bit of a surprise."

"To where now, Peter the Mysterious?"

"It's a seven-minute drive via Mountain Avenue," he said, attempting to suppress a smile.

"Peter!"

"Fine." Peter held up his hands in defeat. "To the gondolas."

I blinked. "Gondolas . . . as in Venice?"

"Canadian gondolas are of a more . . . aerial bent," Peter said evasively.

I put my hands on my hips. "Care to elaborate, Peter Joseph Asturian?"

"What's that expression—you have to see it to—" Peter's eyes danced.

I sighed in mock exasperation. "Okay. Tell me this at least about the proposed activity, Mr. Suddenly-No-Longer-Precise—"

"Yes?"

"Is it epic?"

"It is epic."

I grinned. "To the gondolas then!"

Peter laughed, and then, after a moment, he spoke again.

"I knew how much you loved Lake Louise yesterday, and I wanted to give you . . . another view of it. From above. I would have showed you yesterday, but," his voice softened, "I didn't want Little Dan to feel left out. There may be handicap access to the gondolas, but I have never felt comfortable with the idea."

My eyes widened. "A bird's eye view of Lake Louise?"

Peter's Signature Grin appeared. "Yes. It's quite beautiful."

I rushed forward, my hand outstretched, in a blinding impulse.

A twenty-year-old grabbed a young man's hand, opening the door to the backyard, and dragging him across the yard of twinkling flowers, laughing.

She was young at heart and free.

My hand fell limply to my side, my body stiffening, as the image of Peter's first visit to our family home in California faded from view.

Where was that girl now?

I froze, as Peter looked on in concern.

"Rebecca?"

"Yes, onward!" I managed. "To the gondolas!"

Wires of rope extended from blue and green poles, vehicles of gray already drifting across.

I stood from afar, watching, as Peter locked up the car with a resounding beep and moved to stand beside me.

Gondolas in Canada, as it turned out, seemed to be much like ski lifts. As I peered ahead, I noted that there appeared to be two different types. Dark gray seats with a number at the top of the vehicle in lighter gray were consistent, the red maple leaf of Canadian flag imprinted on each with the words "Banff: Sulphur Mountain." They were mostly white with blue whiskers, the "head" of each gondola looking almost like a face, with a red circle for the nose, and the word "Banff" appearing much like a mouth. Yet, while there were gondolas that were closed, protecting the riders from the outside, with glass in front for easy viewing, others were open, reminding me of a large swing gliding through the air.

And, despite the appealing connotation of a swing, the height was also quite extensive, and my choice therefore clear.

"A closed gondola?" Peter ventured with a smile.

"Indeed."

In a flurry of movement and the illusion of a few minutes, we had quickly passed through the line, paid for the ride from inside the Gondola Base—a small room complete with a welcoming fireplace, a gift shop, and a candy store with snacks that we munched on before continuing—and suddenly found ourselves watching gondolas sliding by for only an instant before promptly climbing up into #56.

I looked at Peter. "This is . . . entirely safe, isn't it?"

"As far as the gondola itself, there hasn't been a reported incident in at least twelve or so years." Peter paused. "But there is that grizzly bear habitat . . ."

The indignant words, "Peter Joseph Asturian!" were heard on the wind, followed by a low chuckle, as we were whisked into the air.

"It's just a fourteen-minute ride. Or eight by some calculations. You'll be fine. I promise," Peter reassured me as I hung on for dear life.

"Since when do you make jokes like that?" I teased.

"Gondolas affect the brain, eh?" he offered, the wind whipping through his light hair as we swept forward, brambles of forest green, peaks, and alpine meadows flashing by. "And, there *was* the water balloon fight of '96 that may contest such a fact. Now, enjoy the ride, Rebecca."

Mr. Precise once again.

I looked down and gasped. Through towering trees, Lake Louise emerged, a brilliant blue-green beckoning all who would venture there. From above, it appeared even more beautiful, like looking down into a vision of cerulean, a whirlpool of light and air more ethereal than ever before.

The scent of wildflowers was carried in the breeze, and I heard birdcalls, more pronounced than possible from the ground below, as we brushed past an assortment of trees.

I leaned back in my seat.

"Look there." Peter's hand guided mine below.

And there, as promised, was the grizzly bear habitat, dozens of the brown and black bears ambling along grass and tree below. Yet, from my position above, I did not fear — as I might have a snake — the large animals, or concern myself with the notion of a gondola-gone-wrong and accidentally tumbling into their home like dinner falling into place on a well-set table. It was as if we were viewing a dozen worlds in a single instant, partaking in the thrill of it all.

Besides, I rather liked bears à la Winnie the Pooh . . . as long as we kept our distance.

And then it all came to a halt, and I scrambled from my seat, Peter offering me his hand to help me descend, and we emerged on a large viewing dock with translucent green glass and a muted tan-gray deck below.

"6,850 feet," Peter quoted, as we moved closer to view the lake surrounded by mountains. "During winter, the ice builds against the glass and looks like green snow."

"Like the trees around it," I whispered.

I gazed ahead at the lake as if looking at the lost remnants of dreams, spilling in puzzle pieces of translucent paint to form water and brush. For a moment, I closed my eyes, and was home, but a home removed from the regular, the commonplace, as beautiful as both could be. It was a home of the Beyond, a glimpse of heavenly wisps of reality.

"Rebecca," Peter said quietly beside me, and pointed downward.

At our feet was a small brown animal standing on its hind legs and looking up at us. It reminded me of a cross between a prairie dog and a sea otter—only an otter of the land, not the sea.

"A marmot," Peter said with a smile. "You see them quite a lot around here."

I moved closer, and the marmot blinked up at me, seeming to nod in recognition, as if to say, "Welcome to my lake," and then scurried away, undoubtedly to forage for nutritional material.

My eyes followed the small creature as it retreated, and then turned back to Peter with a smile.

Peter smiled, touching my shoulder lightly, and indicated the boardwalk with one hand. "Let's see the Gondola Summit."

The Gondola Summit was a modernized castle of branch and lake. The deck was nestled among pines with a backdrop of mountains and sky. The top layer providing a rooftop view was uncovered, below which were two glass-enclosed layers where figures could be seen at tables or milling about in evident conversation. The lower viewing deck stood at the very base with wired fencing extended outward from the main structure.

"Wow," I breathed, as we stopped before the Summit.

"There is dining available on the second and third layers. But I suspect you want—"

"A fourth, completely unique and entirely epic view of the lake again," I finished, eagerly rushing forward before Peter even finished his sentence, causing him to jog to catch up.

And then we reached the final ascent, and I was instantly captured in a single glance.

Emeralds of the lake sparkled luxuriously, dancing as beckoning figures of the night sky, as the sun began to descend, turning the ripples into opals of many hues.

It was as if I were in a fantasy novel, standing on a balcony of moonlight with an epic musical score lingering in the air, to eventually transition into a soft melody of flute.

Or perhaps violin and piano. I thought. *My favorite instrumental combination ever.*

I do not know how long we stood, gazing in silence at this whirlpool of beauty, but the light began to dim when I shivered, pulling my jacket more closely around me.

I zipped up my jacket and looked up at Peter, who turned somehow just as I did.

"Shall we go inside?"

I nodded, my stomach grumbling as if on cue. "I'm famished."

And so, we descended from the deck of light and song, and reached the glass dome of a palace to dine like kings and queens of old.

The simple white plates were platters of gold, my jeans and blue T-shirt a dazzling gown made of sunlight, and the crowds around us dimmed into the background as we feasted on stout braised Alberta beef short rib and bison burgers, grilled sun gold farms lamb rack and a selection of Canadian cheeses, in the Sky Bistro—a name which, in this case, I did not have to rename or reimagine, as the world dropped beneath our feet.

Gondolas and marmots hovered in my vision, as sleep overtook me . . .

3:23 AM

Approximately a year ago . . .

"Hello."

I looked up from the register, and before me stood a tall young man with dark hair—a deep brown almost black—and somber gray eyes with speckles of light brown that addressed mine.

He reminded me of a faerie prince from a foil painting I had loved as a child. It had been sold at the farmer's market, and my mother bought it for the eager seven-year-old. I had delighted in this foil depiction of a fairy prince and princess, a belonging of mine that remained in my room ever since. Its mystical romanticism and spellbinding enchantment spoke to the heart of who I was in swirls of pinks and blues (okay, and sparkly) allure. I had always meant to have it put up on the wall, but, for some reason, it never was. It stayed on the shelf.

Perhaps it was waiting for something. Or someone.

This picture was important to me, from the instant I saw it.

"This is you," it had said to me.

"And this is him," I had said back to it.

He flashed an uncertain smile at me, drawing me back to reality—his hair not quite as dark as I had imagined, his skin hardly pale enough for that of a fairy prince, his glasses, momentarily removed, obscuring full view of his eyes—which now appeared more gray-blue than steel gray. And yet the resemblance was striking.

"Sorry, is this the wrong place for checkout?"

"I'm so sorry," I stammered, my face reddening. "I was a bit distracted." I took his books and began to scan them, trying to avoid staring at him. In a word, he was gorgeous, but in a more alluring way than mere physical looks. He seemed studious, philosophical, different.

I had always felt different, too.

Was he a kindred spirit?

That bolstered my confidence, and I began to relax, hazarding another glance at him. He looked about my age, and had the faintest hint of bags under his eyes, as if he had been studying long into the night. Yet there was a confidence in him, seemingly asymmetrical, but still woven into his posture and smile.

"Sorry, just a minute." He put his glasses back on. "Forgot my contacts. I rarely wear glasses anymore, so it's an adjustment."

"Believe me, I have been there." I looked up to smile at him before glancing back down at the last book I had scanned.

A History of Western Philosophy.

"Philosophy major?"

"English lit, actually, with a minor in history. I finished my degree last year, and began the master's program this fall. But," he offered a smile, "I have always loved philosophy and am considering an emphasis. And you?" He lifted his eyes to mine. "Are you a student?"

"Always."

He raised his eyebrows inquisitively.

"Psychology," I elaborated with a smile, as I moved the seventh and final textbook to the top of the stack. "Almost finished with the graduate program—PsyD, which is close to a PhD, only with a clinical focus—since my college offered a new accelerated program to complete my doctorate at the same time as my BA save one extra year—stressful, but worth it, since my academic scholarship only lasts four years. Taking the licensing exam in a few months." I trailed off, suddenly all too conscious of the speedy-delivery infodump.

"I should be careful then."

I laughed suddenly, a trickle of a giggle, different from how I normally laughed somehow, as if unawakening some part of me, girlish and unrestrained, free yet soft all at once.

Overdissection once again.

"Analyzing people is one thing." I looked up at him with a smile as the mechanical sound of a receipt being printed arose from behind me. "It's when I begin to dissect inanimate objects and the weather that I start to wonder if I'm the one who needs psychoanalysis. 'Shall I compare thee to a summer's day? Thou art more lovely and more temperate. Rough winds do shake the darling buds of May, and summer's lease hath all too short a date.' "

"You know the Bard," he said with evident approval, leaning forward with a captivating smile.

"Of course. Since I was 9. I've been obsessed with Shakespeare longer than most," I said with a small laugh.

Two years after I found the painting of the fairy prince.

"William Adam Laverly," he said, reaching out his hand. "Will."

"Rebecca Veritas," I said, caught in wonder.

My eyes fluttered open, morning light flooding the room.

The clock read 10 AM, and I smiled as a memory materialized in my mind, and then, a name, a dear, sweet name, came to surface. For a moment, I basked in the joy of the shifting images and thoughts.

And then I remembered, and I suddenly struggled to breathe, the air stolen from me—no hyperbole or exaggeration lifted, but simply reality searing across me—the name echoed through my mind.

A single name upon my lips, and, my knuckles whitening, I clung to the bed for support, willing it to return air and life.

My heartbeat steadied, and I threw aside the covers, reminiscent of the night before that I now too remembered, and walked to the door.

A single name, and then another.

A wave of dizziness overtook me, and I closed my eyes, leaning against the door.

Breakfast. You need to have breakfast with the Asturians. Go. Don't let them think you are a strange girl. Go. Be with them.

Yet, all at once, I was too tired to stand, and collapsed on my bed. Exhaustion overtook me, an exhaustion beyond hours of sleep or any measure of physical fatigue, but deep and pervading, too full to ignore.

I could only obey its will with utter compliance.

I fell onto the bed, my limbs melding to the covers, and remained there until a knock at the door caused me to bolt upright. With my hands shaking, I recomposed myself, a shield obscuring my essence and core, and called gaily from the room, "Coming!"

Chapter 8: Fluorite

"Okay, yeah, I will call you on Friday for sure. Thanks for the call. Love you, too."

"Sorry, Peter," I apologized after completing the call that had interrupted our conversation, putting my phone back in my purse. "The family called to see how I was doing."

"Not a problem, Rebecca. Glad you got to talk to your folks." Peter smiled, looking ahead at a bookshelf.

"Thanks. So, you were saying?"

"I'm glad we went on the gondola yesterday . . . that you were able to experience Lake Louise in that way."

I smiled. "Oh, me, too. That was . . . quite an experience."

It was the day after the aerial visit. We had spent the morning and afternoon leisurely sightseeing and quietly conversing, after which I had a video conference with one of my clients that evening.

"Of course, if you'd like, we could join my parents at the jam shop tomorrow," Peter said nonchalantly, placing a book back on the shelf.

My eyes widened. "Oh my—I completely for . . . how could I have forgotten . . . YES! Oh my goodness, a thousand times YES, YES, YES!"

Peter grinned. "Thought it might have slipped your mind."

I raised an eyebrow, still breathless with excitement. "And how might you have deduced that?"

"Well, for one, you didn't mention it once on the plane ride over—even after the mention of a certain parrot—or the entirety of the past two and a half days . . . and, knowing you, that was worth at least twelve 'freak-out' sessions—"

I opened my mouth in protest before finally resigning to shake my head, smiling.

"—per half hour."

I began to laugh in spite of myself. "You know me too well."

"An honor and a privilege, I assure you."

I smiled, and breathed in deeply. "I still can't believe it . . . after all this time and our story . . . it's just unreal."

"About as unreal as you being here," Peter said faintly with a smile.

"Yeah . . . DUDE, wait . . ." My eyes widened. "Please tell me . . . Is there—do you still sell . . . DUKU JAM?!"

"But of course. Our biggest seller, in fact."

"I . . . oh, wow. Just . . ."

I trailed off, shaking my head again. "This is, without a doubt, the best day of my life."

For a moment, I was twenty again.

And forgot I had ever been anything else.

Except, perhaps, ten.

Peter grinned.

". . . of my existence." I froze, as realization once again dawned on me. "FRED."

"Still our faithful customer. But, alas, he only comes on—"

"Wednesdays," I finished, grinning.

"Unfortunately, yes. But you may be able to see him another day . . . You do plan to be here for at least—"

"Most assuredly YES," I interrupted, giddiness still overtaking me. "YES. YES. A thousand times—"

"Yes," Peter completed the thought, a hint of a smile once again playing at the corner of his lips.

"That time I was going to say . . . ¡Sí!" I protested.

"Of course you were. Rebecca Veritas can hardly be expected to limit her excitement to one language."

"My thoughts exactly."

"Of course."

"DUKU JAM."

I spun around the room, the ecstasy of the moment overtaking me along with those two words as Peter stood there, still save the smile that had now woven across his face and reached his eyes. In the distance, I could hear his father chuckling from the kitchen, and his mother peered around the corner, a playful expression marking her countenance with its lines of amusement. But, as I leapt into the air of my mind in one victorious bound, a girl I had once known surfaced, allowing the girl of today to momentarily retreat, and I only felt briefly embarrassed at the conclusion to my introduction to the Asturian family, who, almost certainly by now, knew me to be a strange girl.

Or, perhaps, simply *odd*.

Duku jam.

Sunken yellow lurched in a mindfield of black twisted cylinders, falling like poisoned honey across my vision. It cleared, and became a series of flashing images, jagged edges of memories, each more beautiful and terrible than the last, playing across the screen of blackened cement.

I leapt up, my heart pounding. A tear trickled down my cheek.

"Not tonight," I whispered, as my moist eyes overflowed. "Please, not tonight."

And the rose petals crinkled to dust as I fell onto the bed, muffled sobs pulling me closer to its surface and shaking my limp form until it was too tired to leave me awake.

I neared the kitchen, forcing a smile as I approached the breakfast table.

Peter looked up from the newspaper. "Oh, hey." He frowned briefly, his brow creased as he took me in—really took me in. "Did you sleep well last night, Rebecca? Those Canadian flies didn't get to you, eh? Or was your room too cold? I know this isn't always California weather. I could—"

This was the closest Peter had ever gotten to rambling—which said a lot, considering that it really wasn't rambling at all—and I could instantly tell that he was concerned.

I also knew that it would not take him long to accurately dissect my true state—if he hadn't already—to discern that my mood, if it could be simplified by that term, had nothing to do with foreign insects or frozen feet.

I couldn't let him.

This wasn't how I had hoped my first day at the jam shop would go.

"Rebecca?"

I quickly drew away from my thoughts and plastered a half-smile—convincingly, I hoped—on my face. "No, of course not. The room is beautiful, Peter—and you already put *five* extra blankets in the closet, not to mention the two covers already on the bed. And the Canadian horsefly may be at large, but it hasn't entered my domain. Yet." I paused, hesitating. "It's just . . . I was distracted by . . ."

Peter, now standing, waited patiently, his large hazel eyes focused on mine, even though I attempted to avert his gaze.

I couldn't do this either.

I forced my eyes to remain unblinkingly pulled to his and managed another thin smile. "Poisoned honey."

It was the truth at least, even if *its* truth would remain unknown.

Peter's voice softened. "What do you mean, Rebecca?"

And there it was—the moment I could say it all, unburden myself to one I knew and trusted, one of my oldest and dearest friends. But my lips remained tightly pressed together until I finally allowed myself to speak again.

"An image that popped into my mind during a strange dream last night. Might be good material for this fantasy series I've been brainstorming about. Though I need to finish this other story first. Probably. Well—whatever happens first . . . could be a close call . . . but I think . . . well, you never know, really. Usually."

Sometimes rambling could almost make things better, ease my quickening heartbeat with its own flurry of madness, brush aside the tendrils of the night in an assemblage of scattered words.

Even if they were the wrong words.

I still felt Peter watching me as I followed him to the kitchen counter, where steaming cranberry orange muffins lay on a platter.

"Don't forget to wash your hands," I teased.

Peter smiled, and allowed the broken moment to pass.

"Wouldn't think of it."

I flung a paper towel into the trash as the water from the faucet trickled into silence, willing the effervescence of the movement to bring back the ecstasy of the previous evening. And—it almost did.

But somehow I knew that this had more to do with Peter than throwing away paper towels.

I smiled—a real one this time. "Shall we head off on our adventure after breakfast?"

The door creaked to a close, and, with eyes wide open, I took it all in.

A long white counter entered my line of vision, and, underneath a glass circular dome on the left and right sides, jumbled an assortment of colors—the deep mauve of blueberry or plum, the orange glow of apricot (or was it tangerine?), and many more I could not pretend to name. Dark blues and light greens were perched alongside pure whites and bright yellows, an array of winter colors drawn to spring—overflowing buckets bursting with shades of flavor, displayed samples pleasurably arranged as if in an ice cream parlor.

Brown and white tables were scattered throughout the room, and the buzz of faint conversation could be heard in the vicinity of a dark-haired couple at the table nearest the blue-shuttered window.

But I did not see any of it.

I saw color.

And, in distant melodies, I *remembered* color.

I turned to Peter, my face aglow. "*Oh.*"

Peter smiled, briefly touching my shoulder, but said nothing.

He didn't need to.

As one, we walked toward the front counter, where Mrs. Asturian was bent behind the register. Her long dark locks were swept into a neat bun at the top of her head. She straightened at the sound of our approaching footsteps and smiled at me.

Peter had told me that Little Dan was at a friend's house, so it was just his parents and us today.

"Welcome to the Asturian Jam Shop," she said.

"Or *The* Jam Shop, as she has often thought of it," interjected Peter.

I let out a breath. "It is . . . incredible to finally be here."

Olivia Asturian smiled. "Would you like a sample?" She gestured toward the loaves of bread—ciabatta, wheat bread, and pumpernickel—lying in wait at the center of The Glass Dome and the array of color that surrounded them. Their delightful scent drew me in. *Definitely freshly baked.*

"At the risk of getting teased again by Peter . . ." I glanced in his direction. "YES. Would I ever."

Peter, now a scientist examining some oddity, appeared to study his shoes very closely for the next forty-five seconds.

I shook my head, smiling.

"What jam shall it be, Rebecca?" Mrs. Asturian asked, taking out a silver spoon after cutting a slice of the ciabatta I had eagerly pointed to (After all, ciabatta *was* the king—or was it queen?—of the bread kingdom.) and laying it on a small white plate.

Peter and I exchanged looks and helplessly burst out laughing.

"Duku jam, it is," Mrs. Asturian said cheerfully.

Peter drew me aside. "Still can't believe this is your first Duku experience," he said confidentially, as if relaying a great secret. "Especially after writing *Intermission.*"

He seemed relaxed—in a new way—in his parents' shop.

"Yep, it's about as common as plum." I suppressed a smile.

"If you know where to look."

"Should I have ordered it express from Amazon?"

"Indeed."

"Peter Joseph Asturian, I AM ABOUT TO HAVE DUKU JAM!" I exclaimed, finally unable to keep it in anymore as I grinned widely from ear to ear.

Peter guided me back around to the counter. "If you just turn around, you may indeed so partake."

Mrs. Asturian handed me the plate, an off-white, yet somehow still exuberant, jelly substance now coloring the top of the slice.

"Enjoy."

Peter led me to a table, and we sat down.

And sat.

"Well, Rebecca, aren't you going to take a bite?" He raised an eyebrow.

"Of course I am. I . . . am simply preparing myself." I lifted the piece of bread, paused in midair, and then dropped it lightly back down on my plate.

Peter folded his arms, and smiled knowingly at me.

"Okay! So, this is a big moment for me—"

"—eating bread with jam."

"—*important* jam on *important* bread, Mr. Asturian!"

"And?"

"And I'll know the right moment when it arrives." I paused, scanning the room superficially before glancing at the clock with idle curiosity.

I returned to drumming my fingers rhythmically on the table.

"No time like the present to pick up a new habit," I said conversationally, nodding at my orchestral fingers. "I wonder if Antonio would approve . . . ?"

"Rebecca."

"Okay, okay."

Peter leaned forward, as if in anticipation of the climax of a movie.

"Hand sanitizer, please," I said brusquely, flicking my hands toward the place where I had deposited it with a regal flair.

Peter handed it to me ceremoniously, as if Pomp and Circumstance played in the background.

I dramatically lifted the slice of bread to my lips in the final orchestral march with seeming ease, but, in reality, my heart beat wildly with excitement.

It felt like a bookend.

And then I took a bite.

It was a sweet taste—almost like a combination of grape and grapefruit, only not.

I smiled.

"And?" Peter prompted. "What is the verdict?"

"It is exactly as I expected," I announced. "Only much moreso." A smile lifted itself across my face once again. "Much like this place." I gestured at the jam shop.

Peter smiled. "Ah. I thought as much."

"Rebecca?"

I turned at the sound of a figure approaching as I finished the slice.

"Would you like to help Peter at the register? I just need to slip in to the back to talk to Raphael for a moment; we're reviewing inventory." Olivia Asturian stood, her poised form the clear prototype of Peter, a few inches from our table.

"I'd love to!" I said eagerly.

Mrs. Asturian smiled her thanks and withdrew. I pushed in my chair and, after throwing away my napkin, followed Peter behind the register at the front with my plate still in hand.

"Would you like to handle the register or the jam?" Peter asked as we moved behind the counter.

"Hmm, the opportunity to serve Duku jam is too tempting," I said, grinning, as I put my dish on a second counter behind me.

"I'll handle the register then." Peter smiled and moved to the right.

The door lightly swung open in a faint gush of wind, as if it had received a text message notifying all recipients of the changing of the guard and maintained a tourist's curiosity that required immediate satisfaction. A short, middle-aged woman, slightly heavy-set with frizzy brown hair, emerged, her bright blue eyes amiably addressing us as she walked forward.

"Welcome to the Asturian Jam Shop!" I smiled cordially, repeating the words said to me only a matter of minutes before, as she approached the register. "How may we assist you today?"

"Hi! Just stopping by to browse. My husband and I are actually vacationing in Banff and"—the woman ran a hand through her hair—"I was intrigued by the concept of the store. I've never heard of a jam shop before!"

Apparently the random tourist metaphor that had materialized in my mind wasn't too far off.

I smiled. "That makes two of us. Until I met Peter over here"—I jabbed a finger in his direction—"I had no idea that any existed."

"Oh, are you two the couple that owns the place? I saw some mention of it in the hotel guide."

My face grew warm. "Oh, no. His parents are the owners. We're friends. I'm, um, just helping out today." I narrowly avoided looking in Peter's direction. "Would you like a sample of anything?"

"What do you recommend?"

Best way to drop awkwardness: DUKU.

I grinned. "Funny you should ask."

There was a momentary displacement of air, and Peter was next to me. He outstretched his hand.

"Peter Asturian," he said warmly as she took it. "And Rebecca"—he threw a smile in my direction before returning his eyes to the customer—"was referring to what some consider our specialty—Duku jam, made with fresh fruit imported from the island of Terengganu."

"Sounds interesting!"

"Although it's a bit exotic and may not suit everyone's palate," Peter added. "Our apricot, for example, is also quite popular. You're welcome to try more than one flavor if you'd like."

"That's quite enticing," the woman said, resting her arm on the edge of the counter. "I'd love plum if you have it—it's always been my favorite. And I'd be interested in trying this 'Duku,' as well."

"Coming right up! Just a spoonful, or would you like to try them on our bread?" I indicated the loaves in front of me, still lavishly bathing the area with their delectable scent.

"Hmm, how about one of each, if it isn't too much trouble? A spoonful of Duwew, was it?"

"Duku."

"And plum on one of your breads . . . Hmm, any advice there?"

"I love all three types," I offered, a spoon ready in my hand, "but I'm partial to the ciabatta, which I ate earlier today and was delicious. Wheat bread is always a solid healthier choice. Then again, I think plum would go very well with pumpernickel."

"Let's do the pumpernickel then."

Duku on pumpernickel also would have had a nice ring to it. Ah, well.

"Sounds good." I scooped a generous helping of Duku jam, and handed her the spoon. She took it, and I stood with "bated breath," awaiting her reaction—as Peter did my own earlier—while spreading the plum jam across a piece of the pre-sliced pumpernickel loaf with a butter knife from the inner counter.

Peter moved next to me, and we exchanged a knowing smile.

"That's something," the woman said, finishing her sample. "I rather like it. Where did you say it was from?"

"Terengganu," Peter responded.

"Very interesting."

I handed her the second sample. "One slice of pumpernickel with plum jam."

The woman took a bite, and her eyes widened. Then a second—

"Wow!" she exclaimed. "I think that's the best plum jam I've ever tasted next to my mom's."

"Glad you like it," Peter said cordially. "All of our jams are also sealed here, so you're welcome to pick up a jar if you'd like."

"Or by the bucket," I added, biting my lip to contain laughter as I recalled Fred.

"I just might do that!"

A light click of heels was heard, and Olivia Asturian emerged from the back.

"Thanks so much," Mrs. Asturian said, approaching us, and nodding pleasantly at the new arrival. "I can take it from here." She glanced at the jam display. "Looks like that was the last of the Duku and Goji. Mind filling them up? Peter can show you what to do."

"Sure!" I followed Peter to the back after grabbing a portable Duku container as he did with the Goji, the sound of Mrs. Asturian's conversation with the customer retreating in the distance.

"You're a natural," Peter said with a small smile, placing the bucket down.

"Aw, really?" I blushed. "Thanks."

"Here you are." Peter handed me a red apron with the words "Asturian Jam Shop" on a lapel pinned to the apron. "Now you are officially a part of the Jam Shop Troupe."

I looked down at the apron again as I put it on, and smiled. "I'll do my best to make Monet proud."

Peter smiled as he pulled on his own "uniform," his a vivid green, walking back to his station. "Or Antonio."

"Wouldn't pleasing one infuriate the other?"

"Undoubtedly."

Peter smiled again. "Okay, here is where we keep the extra supply of jams." He indicated behind us with one hand, and I turned.

Rows upon rows of wooden bins, painted creamy white, were visible, a golden knob on each. Peter lifted one labeled "Goji," revealing a lustrous scarlet that I recalled from fruit bars of that flavor. Inside was what resembled an ice cream scooper-gigantic spoon hybrid, which he used to begin scooping into the bucket.

"Duku is three from the right on that row," he said, pointing to the arrangement of shelves opposite his.

"Got it! Thanks."

I walked over to the designated bin, bucket in hand, and lifted the lid. The ivory luster of Duku greeted me from within.

I grabbed the scooper inside as Peter had done, and began to relocate its contents to the bucket.

Peter glanced over at my progress, bit his lip to suppress a smile, and returned to his work.

"What?" I demanded, a smile of my own beginning to sweep its way across my face.

"Just making observations," he said nonchalantly, not turning around.

"Like what?" I still held the scooper in my hand, but all progress had temporarily halted.

Peter continued to scoop from his container. "That I will finish scooping first and thereby emerge victorious."

"Were we racing?"

"The best races are the ones that you don't know have begun."

"That's . . . that's entirely unfair!" I protested, my other hand on my hip. "Furthermore, you were distracting me!"

"Strategizing."

I marched over to Peter, bucket and scooper still in hand. "Is that so?"

Peter finally turned, a wry smile alighting his countenance. "I would say so, yes."

"In *that* case," I said, "I have some strategizing in mind of my own."

And then I dug my scooper deeply within the generously filled bucket, and flung its contents liberally at Peter Joseph Asturian.

Peter blinked twice, lifting his hand to examine the sticky ivory substance gleefully affixed to his cheek.

"Unexpected, but not catastrophic."

And, with that, Peter reached into his own bucket, and, before I had time to duck, threw a large scoopful of Goji jam in my direction.

It landed squarely on the left shoulder of my shirt, only barely missing the portion left uncovered by the apron.

"Okay, that's it . . ."

And then the Goji-Duku battle truly began in earnest, oranges and reds, maroons and mint greens, flying into the air as no jam was left untouched.

But—then and forevermore—it would be referred to as the Goji-Duku Battle.

I flung a scoop of plum at Peter, hitting him squarely in the chest, bursts of laughter brimming over, uncontained and unrestrained. Peter's deep chuckle joined mine as we began to sway back and forth with the movement of the jam flinging and, mostly, the weight of our own laughter.

I could not remember the last time I had laughed that much, or that hard.

The best kind of laughing fit.

A spoonful of jam from each side glided through the air, merging momentarily in an orange-blue swirl as it sped with unsatiable determination toward its opponent when, as if from a distant realm, the sound of a female voice clearing her throat pulled us back into reality.

Olivia Asturian, mother of Peter Joseph Asturian: Duku Fighter and Daniel Asturian, Wife of Raphael Asturian, and Co-Owner of the Asturian Jam Shop, stood at the entrance to the jam supply room, as she raised her eyebrows above deep hazel eyes filled with amusement.

I looked down at my apron, and shirt, and pants, now an array of color—while, at the same time, I felt a distinctive sticky substance on my nose. A quick glance at Peter revealed that he had not fared much better, splotches and splashes of orange, white, and many more colors and shades displayed on his clothing and face in an impressive depiction of modern art.

"I am . . . so sorry," I managed between laughs, breathless. "I . . . we . . . had an . . . incident . . . of sorts."

Peter snorted, and then we both burst into laughter, on and on until we nearly enacted the popular Internet acronym "ROTFL" in its most literal form, all the while attempting unsuccessfully to explain or, alternatively, apologize, to Mrs. Asturian, who turned away from time to time, covering her mouth, her large eyes merry.

I wiped blueberry jam from my face, locking eyes with Peter amidst peals of laughter, and it was an

intermission.

DUDE, THE JAM SHOP. DUKU. MARMOTS. What is next, the albino wombat?! So wish I could be there with you! BUT all your descriptions are making me feel as if I AM there. Loving the email reports. Thanks for keeping me in the loop.

We're heading to Colorado next week, as you know, so my responses may be slow in coming. Just as a head's up.

Rock on, dude, and say "hi" to Peter for me.
Love,
Adri

I smiled at the email from home and closed my laptop, beginning a hunt for my toothbrush and shower cap as a yawn reminded me of the late hour, and midnight blue unfurled around me . . .

2 AM

I exhaled deeply, gazing at the towering white arts plaza before me, lit up with emerald green-tinted windows.

This was my first official date.

Not just with Will, but of all time.

It was also my seventh date with Will.

Over the past three days, I had agonized over the wardrobe selection process, throwing half a dozen outfits—blouses, skirts, and dresses galore—onto my bed, considering some, discounting others, only for me to open my closet once again after a consultation with weather. com. At long last, I had chosen a midnight blue blouse of a light filmy material that fluttered around as I moved my arms—a loose bow tied at its center—coupled with a flowing black skirt of silk with cascading layers of delicate ruffles on its lower half. Since my ears were unpierced (a lifelong lack of desire to bore a hole in my ears despite the alluring quality of tinkling, brightly colored earrings the ready culprit), I opted for a turquoise and silver necklace, also shimmering in cascading interludes, three layers joined together at my neck in a tiny clasp. Black heels—of a moderate height, given my clumsiness and lack of desire to begin my first date tumbling to the floor—completed the look.

The Green Dress, the dress that I had saved since I was eighteen for a special occasion, had been considered. But it wasn't time yet, I had ultimately decided.

One day.

It had been nearly a month of almost-daily exchanges at the bookstore after or before Will's classes on the college campus when he asked me out. It had seemed a natural progression, our conversations never long enough, moving from theater and music to Star Trek and nebulas, beloved literary volumes and schooling to dreams and aspirations, all in one single bound. On six previous occasions, he had invited me to sit in the college centrum and bought me lunch—dates by default, yet more informal and casual in nature than the one that awaited me today. Two Sundays in a row, we had found ourselves at the same Mass, and twice a week for one week we waved to each other from a distance on the campus, a smile forever resting on my face as I looked back at him. Yet those mathematical calculations spoke nothing next to that wordless speech.

And it seemed that today, of all days, would determine if he was the boy from the painting, The Faerie Prince (or Fairy? I could never decide which spelling I preferred—the "ie" version almost more mystical and mysterious, but the "y" so classic and wonderstruck) of whom I had long dreamt.

At least, so I hoped.

I ran a hand nervously through my hair after closing the imposing double doors, glimmering in their gray hues, behind me.

Do I look okay?

Rebecca, chill. He's not going to be that shallow. If one hair is out of place or if the bow on your blouse is off center, he probably won't even notice.

Probably.

I heard the sound of a familiar voice, a man clearing his throat, and I turned.

William Adam Laverly stood, his dark hair framing his face. Will.

He took my hand, his somber gray eyes taking me in with soft approval. "You look stunning, Rebecca."

I blushed, looking at my feet before daring to raise my eyes to address his with a smile that I knew filled my entire face. "Thank you, Will. You look ... very handsome."

And he did. I had always been partial to white dress shirts; as a young girl, I had associated them with princes, and, so, the connotation remained with those who donned them today. He wore a suit—black pants and a deep gray coat over the dress shirt coupled with a midnight blue tie. The blue of the tie seemed to add to the "prince" or "knight" effect, though I could not put a finger on the "why." Perhaps this was because it was like the ocean or sky, romantic images that always remained so. His face was chiseled into perfect form, his dark eyes and hair never more brilliantly alive.

"Shall we go in?" *He indicated the second set of double doors directly ahead, and I nodded, taking his proffered arm once again.*

As we approached the door, a female usher, dressed in a black skirt and suit jacket, handed us the program for Pygmalion.

He opened the door.

The sight that greeted my eyes caused me to catch my breath. It wasn't that I had never visited the civic arts plaza before; I had, half a dozen times. Yet today it was as if the entirety of the surroundings were cast under some wondrous Narnian spell, rows upon rows of seats raising themselves into the air, ascending in circular arcs that flowed endlessly throughout the room, nearly each filled with a figure awaiting the performance. The red curtains before us were not curtains, but petals of roses falling gracefully before the room, a pre-performance guarding the platform for a story yet to be told.

The Globe Theater could not have looked more magnificent.

I looked at Will, who smiled back at me, and we proceeded to our seats near the front of the theater. He had been saving up money to buy us both tickets for front row seats. I had told him that it did not matter, that, in fact, balcony seats had their romantic appeal, but he only smiled as if to say, "You are worth it."

We settled into our seats, comfortable leather cushions a camouflage to his coat.

We dreamt in camouflage through the night.

I opened the booklet and began to read the cast list.

"Which version do you prefer?" I asked Will, looking up. "Pygmalion *or* My Fair Lady?*"*

"Pygmalion," he said readily. "I prefer the original work."

I nodded, understanding. "I usually do, as well. But, in this case, it's hard to pick. I love both. My Fair Lady *is a classic all on its own . . . and I do think that it has the advantage of a better ending."*

He nodded, thoughtful. "I suppose it depends on what team you're on for Ms. Eliza."

"And you are on the other team?"

"Au contraire. But I believe a little was lost in the musical, and I think that, while music can certainly enhance a story,

it was amiss here. A distraction from the literary value of the work, as it were."

"Interesting. I've always found that the music complemented the art of the work with its witty and thought-provoking insertions. But it's been a while since I've read Pygmalion. *We'll learn more today, I suspect."*

The curtains began to draw aside, and our conversation halted with it.

Throughout the entire play, I was fully engaged, immersed in a long-beloved story. And this version was brilliantly acted, dialogue spoken with meaning, the set design enhancing every move and word, costumes bringing us to that time and place, as if we were no longer in the theater, but somewhere else — right there in the drama itself yet beyond. I was swept away in the narrative, and a quick glance in Will's direction revealed the same of him. His eyes were intent, carefully taking in each scene with his full attention and admiration.

And, yet, we were *there.*

More than the play, more than the players on the stage, there were the "players" in the audience — two, only two, that truly mattered.

His eyes swept to mine, and mine to his, at the most compelling moments, and, at the most random, I was drawn to him again just as he would smile down at me.

The play wasn't just those on the stage. We were ready participants in the story arc.

It was Shakespeare's quote from Act II, Scene VII of As You Like It *all over again.*

We filled the intermission with ready conversation, discussing each act with scholarly reveal, our stolen glances, gazes, and smiles confined more to the duration of the play itself than the time given to us for such perusal.

When the curtains drew together at the conclusion, bookends of a new volume emerging in their closure, I rose to my feet, hearing Will do the same, my hands together as applause rang throughout the theater for the cast bowing amidst thrown flowers and smiling faces.

Will turned to me. "Ready?"

I nodded, and rose to my feet.

It was nearly 9 PM, and a wintery lull had settled over the landscape, yet it was not an icy coldness, but a refreshing chill, wafting through the air, enhancing it, making it more alive and real.

I breathed it in.

When we stopped—Will coming to a sudden halt, and my feet quickly following suit before they would result in the tumbling mishap I had tried to avoid in my preparations—it was before a large fountain, a statue of a flowing form, seeming both woman and mystical creature, gliding into the mist. The soft trickling of water over pebbles was faintly heard.

"I really loved the play," I said shyly, looking up at him. "Thanks for taking me."

"It was beautiful, and captivating. But not as beautiful and captivating as you." He lifted his hand to lightly stroke my cheek, and I caught my breath.

He moved it back to his side and looked at me, his eyes reaching mine. "I'm falling in love with you, Rebecca."

Tears sprang to my eyes. "I . . . I am, too. Or maybe I already am completely fallen. It's hard to tell where I am in the falling process. Maybe 75% there. 80. 97.5 . . ." I rambled endlessly, my nerves overtaking me.

"May I kiss you?" he said, smiling down at me, his eyes soft.

"This is a really strange confession, but I"—my face reddened—"I've actually never been kissed. Or kissed someone. Before."

He laughed, and cupped my face in his hand.

"You'll be great," he said, smiling at me. "Trust me."

A smile burst across my face, despite its growing warmth, and it could not be contained.

My eyes reached his.

"Actually, I think I'm 99.9% in love with you," I managed.

He laughed, still smiling down at me.

"That's good," he said, "because I'm over 100%, and moreso with each passing moment."

He lifted my face to his, his hand a light caress against my chin, until our faces were only inches apart.

"In fact, I'm almost afraid to say this." He shook his head. "During the play, during every moment we looked at each other, these words were circling in my mind, allowing me rest to consider little else."

"What was it?" I whispered.

"That . . . if anything happened to you, Rebecca," he said, his eyes intently looking into mine, "I think I would wear black and remain single forever . . . forgive my selfishness, but I don't think I would ever really recover from losing you.

"Now that you're in my life," he said softly, so close I could feel his breath on my face, "there isn't anything else. Just you. You and God."

He leaned forward, and our lips met in a warm softness that pierced the cold night in a world of forests and water nymphs.

At the end of the kiss, I leaned back against his chest in a warm embrace.

"You are my Maid Marian," he said, looking down at me.

"And you are my Robin Hood," I said quietly, looking up at him in wonder.

I woke up screaming.

It took a moment before I realized where I was, and then I plunged my face into my pillow, muffling the screams, which slowly turned to sobs wracking my body with unrelenting intensity.

I exhaled deeply, trying to draw breath, but each cry filled my being, my breath washed away with waves of water streaming down my face and over my head.

I was underwater, deep in an ocean without Light.

I stared up at the ceiling to steady my breath, and, in my mind's eye, I saw a small torch casting a faint beacon of light above.

It was small, barely distinguishable in the darkness, but I grabbed onto it.

I held onto it as the world tilted upside down in a dizzying vortex of lost dreams.

Chapter 9: Golden Beryl

I stepped out of the car, gazing out at the church before me.

It reminded me much of a large cottage of a bygone age, made of gray brick and cobblestone of varied hues with an arrangement of town flowers gathered before it in a near-medieval approach. Two lanterns graced the entrance as we strode forth, "St. Mary's Catholic Church" written in small lettering against white underneath a half circle of gray brick.

Mr. and Mrs. Asturian moved through the doorway, the latter gently pushing Little Dan in his wheelchair.

Peter nodded, smart in a suit with a white dress shirt underneath, waiting as I entered, and then stepping in after me.

A carpet of red extended outward as we moved forward, wooden walls and yellow hues dominant.

Yet, at the very center of the altar, it was strikingly, purely, white—and in that capsule of white, a circle of gold emerged as the Holy Spirit image made famous in St. Peter's Basilica brilliantly shone forth. From great arches in the ceiling—great despite the seemingly smaller space—a Crucifix ascended before us. I had only a moment to look at the stained glass panels on each side of the church and glimpse the paintings to the left and right of the altar—one appearing to be of Jesus and his disciples, and the other of the Pope, perhaps St. Peter, administering to the bishops, a remarkable symbolic resonance—before, nearly tripping over my feet awestruck, I followed Peter and his family to the right set of pews, genuflecting before entering the third row.

I sat down with Peter on my right and Little Dan on my left.

While I had sat with my Confirmation group or occasionally Adriana as a teen and gone to Mass alone when I had been living in Los Angeles, I had never attended Mass with any family other than my own.

And yet, now, with the Asturians, it felt like *home*.

I felt not apart from them, but as one . . . even though I was farther from home than I had ever been before.

As I sat down next to Peter, my dear, old friend, a sense of peace came upon me, a deeper sort of comfort, of *rightness*, as I felt his presence beside me. I also realized then, with a start, that, through all the days I had known Peter, all the Masses that we had attended, he had only once before sat with me in the pews. He was always the usher, offering a smile (or, in a particular instance, covert notifications via an unauthorized note in the Offertory basket). He had otherwise never had occasion to join my side. For some reason, this time, here in his parish since childhood, it also seemed . . . different.

And, despite my initial impressions, I could not describe, or begin to fathom how to describe, how that made me feel.

I looked up and smiled at Peter, just as the priest began to process from the back of the church to begin the Mass.

"There's someone I'd like you to meet." Peter touched my shoulder and drew me to the back of the church at the end of Mass.

A tall African priest—the pastor who had been saying Mass that morning—stood in conversation with an elderly couple. His countenance was filled with a quiet peace, and I could instantly tell that he was very close to God. As they withdrew, he caught sight of Peter, and a wide smile broke across his face.

"Fr. Abioye," Peter said, reaching out his hand to shake his.

"Peter, it's a delight to see you. We missed you last week when you were in America." The jovial priest shook his hand.

"Father, this is Rebecca."

Fr. Abioye Etienam offered me a warm smile. "I've heard so much about you, Rebecca."

"Good things, I hope?" I smiled back tentatively.

Fr. Abioye laughed, a pleasant chuckle. "Of course."

At that moment, Mr. and Mrs. Asturian approached, with Little Dan in the wheelchair in front of them, and Fr. Abioye shook the hands of each, stopping to bend before Little Dan and offer him a blessing.

"Still hard to believe how fast you're growing!" Fr. Abioye shook his head with a smile at Little Dan.

"Fr. Abioye baptized Little Dan," Peter offered from next to me. "We've known him since just before then."

"So, Rebecca"—the priest's eyes returned to me—"how are you enjoying your stay in Banff?"

"Very much. In fact, the other day we went on a gondola to view Lake Louise from greater heights—"

"Always something I would approve of." Fr. Abioye nodded, and we laughed.

"It was a great trip. Although, I have to admit, Peter gave me a bit of a fright when he mentioned the bear population." I looked at Peter teasingly, but he only smiled back.

Fr. Abioye nodded, a smile spreading across his face. "Ah, yes. Canada does have its share of interesting animal specimen. Reminds me of my home of Ethiopia. There was that lion incident . . ."

"Lion incident?" Little Dan piped up.

"My friend and I were walking in the forests of Ethiopia one day," Fr. Abioye began, "when a black-maned lion came along. I leapt into a tree—you wouldn't believe how fast you can scurry until something like that happens! My friend did the same."

"Wow," Little Dan said. "And then? How did you escape?"

We all waited, drawn into the story.

"Oh, we just waited out the lion, who prowled around for several minutes, and then several more . . . until it left after about half an hour. And then we ran so fast back to town you wouldn't believe it!"

We laughed.

"A pleasure again, Rebecca and my dear Asturian friends." Fr. Abioye extended his hand. "I'm afraid I must be off to my hospital rounds so I can't talk longer, but I will see you next Sunday."

"Thank you, Father." Mrs. Asturian shook his hand. "By the way, do you think you will be able to attend our annual summer party next month?"

"Of course. I received the invitation last week, and would be delighted to attend. I very much enjoyed your last party."

"And we loved your storytelling," Little Dan added.

Fr. Abioye smiled. "Always a pleasure." He shook our hands once again before departing toward the front of the church.

"Well, as I seem to recall, we have some plans after Mass." Peter eyed Little Dan affectionately.

"Ice cream!" Little Dan's eyes lit up.

I loved how children—especially Little Dan—enjoyed so fully the simple pleasures of life.

"Yes!" Mrs. Asturian tousled his hair fondly. "Your hair is getting long . . . you're about due for a summer haircut, I think . . ."

I paced around the room, a nightly routine I wished I could leave behind.

Why? I whispered to the silence of the room.

And slowly I fell into a restless sleep . . .

3 AM

"My lady," he murmured, his eyes inching toward mine *conspiratorially.*

I took his proffered hand, stifling a giggle, as he pulled me into the Economics section of the bookstore.

We stood there for a few moments, catching our breath.

His hand remained in mine.

"What is it?" I said breathlessly.

He glanced at the aisle quickly before returning his eyes to me with a smile.

"I was wondering if I might have a lock of my fair lady's hair as a token of her affection."

Oh.

It was a page out of olden days of yore, a dream conceived by my romantic heart so many years ago, and thought of in the thrill and exhilaration of a silver-lit shore just the day before.

Only it was real.

"Oh, yes," I whispered in exaltation.

My eyes reached his.

He gazed at me, and, dropping my hand lightly, stepped forward. In one fluid movement, he softly caressed the curl nearest my right cheek.

A moment passed in silence, glass chandeliers in an unseen marble palace.

"Do you have scissors?" I finally said, breaking through the quiet ecstasy.

He examined his pockets sheepishly. "I was eager to depart."

I stifled a giggle once again as the muffled sound of customers was faintly heard in the background, reaching into my pocket. "You're lucky I work here! But we must not tarry. My next shift begins in a few minutes."

He took my scissors and gently reached for the same chestnut brown lock. In a few moments, it was in his hands.

Much like my heart.

"Might the lady have a lock to keep, as well?"

"Of course." He smiled down at me, waiting until I lifted my hand.

His hair was dark and soft, every inch a prince.

I took it in one hand, memorizing each shade and line, every nuance of texture.

"I have to go." My forehead creased.

So this was what lovesick felt like.

His hand caressed mine, and I reveled again in its warmth.
"I will see you soon."

"Soon," I said, my eyes lost in his.

I tossed and turned, my mind playing catch with the shadows of the night, until I jolted awake, instantly sitting upright.

A single name rose to my lips, and, like so many nights before, my breath was stolen from me. I choked on the air as I threw myself from my bed, blankets and sheets cast aside.

I stared blankly ahead at the night.

Moisture burned my eyes and flowed freely, as I clenched the wall before me.

I would have thought that I wouldn't have any tears left, but somehow, somehow there were always more.

There were other nights when I was too numb to cry at all.

A wave of nausea overtook me, and I bit my lip to keep the sickening taste in my mouth at bay.

I grabbed a cracker from the snacks I had put on the desk, and sat down, slowly nibbling on it.

And then, my feet stumbling over the rose-carpeted floor, I ran to the bathroom and threw up.

Chapter 10: Rainbow Moonstone

"Should be fun." I grabbed my backpack, complete with water bottles, hand sanitizer, and my cell phone, and, swinging it over one shoulder, walked toward the door.

"Just one moment, Rebecca." Peter hesitated, and then glanced around, as if looking for someone. He relaxed when it became apparent that we were still alone.

"Yeah?" I turned, and walked back to him, putting the backpack back down in front of me.

Something told me it might be a while.

"Little Dan loved boats, especially riding in them, very much before his . . . accident," Peter said softly, his eyes pained. "I don't want to take more away from him than has already been lost. But . . . I do have concerns with him being out on the water like this. It is seldom that I take him out on these types of excursions. I hope you won't mind if we cut it short. The rapids can get pretty rough the farther we go out."

My forehead creased. "Of course, Peter. I don't mind at all."

With Little Dan, there existed in Peter a vulnerability, a protectiveness and a fear, distinctive from anything else I had learned to associate with him.

I resisted the sudden urge to reach out to him—clasp his hand or throw him into a hug.

For some reason, at this moment, it didn't seem right, I told myself.

Peter offered me an appreciative smile, and he suddenly relaxed, returning to his old self. "Thanks, Rebecca."

The sound of wheels and footsteps from the direction of the hall became more pronounced, and conversation halted as a small form in a wheelchair, with a tall, smiling woman behind him, drew closer.

"Hey, Little Dan!" I smiled.

Little Dan grinned.

And, as I hazarded a glance at Peter, I realized that that grin was worth it all.

It was everything.

A sash of iridescent butterflies fluttered across in remnants of topaz, dipped in distant peacock's tears as they mingled with forget-me-nots and morning glories, bluebells and cornflowers spilling through the cerulean waters in the flight of an Eastern bluebird. It was no longer solid, but a creature now made of those same prismatic tears it had once touched, too refined and elegant to lose its path even as it faded away.

Peter lifted Little Dan carefully into the boat, sunlight trickling through the meandering turns of the Bow River. Scattered pebbles reached toward the waters like a cocoon transformed to liquid sapphires, and a forest of trees and bramble framed each curve, mountains rising in the distance. I caught my breath at the sight of a glacier, barely discernible in the distance, ivory breaths of an ice queen tumbling forth on Palomino steeds, marble and lace joined as one like moon-kissed candles dripping into the river with the richness of white chocolate and the luxury of satin, each woven in a nuptial bouquet of baby's breath.

He reached out a hand, and I took it, pulled gently into the boat. Peter followed after me, and took up one of the oars of the canoe.

"Ready?" He looked over at both of us with a calm smile—a smile that showed none of the unease I knew he felt.

"Aye, aye, Captain!" Little Dan saluted Peter, prompting me to instantly smile.

Peter's gaze flickered over to me, and I nodded.

And then, in one fluid motion, the oars were dipped into the water, and the boat tiptoed forward.

I took a deep breath, examining my surroundings with a scientist's precision, but, more importantly, a poet's soul, as the boat slowly began to glide across the river in the light steps of a ballerina turning to the last movement of a *sonata*. I was reminded for a moment of my sixth grade end-of-year field trip at a ranch—in the days that sixth grade marked the culmination of elementary school. I had reveled in the experience of the paddle boats, gliding forth not in the calamity of bumper cars that my brother and father relished, but with a *softer* purpose, a quiet journey. It was a boat for three, and, while the activity was enjoyed by all, my friends and our classmates bored of it after a while—later than perhaps those of the cell phone app and Netflix express days of today would—but I never did.

I was content to merely sit in my vessel of the dawn, like the Lady of Shalott or some nymph of the evening light, and move lightly through the waters, sure, but slow, movements in a world of dappled light, and the deep *plunk* of pebbles following into the lake like rainfall lifting a many-colored bow across the sky.

I was content to merely immerse myself in the simplicity that somehow brought to my young heart excitement, as if in the legends of yore.

I was content to merely *be*.

Yes, this was like that day, so long ago.

A day when I had had no reason to seek such an excursion, and simply accepted it as the gift that it was.

Peter continued to draw the oars into the water, orchestrating our boat gently down the river with well-practiced movements. I wondered briefly how many times over the years Peter had taken a boat across the river, but left these thoughts to the immensity before me, drawing instead the wordless serenity of wonder, the changeable flow now consistent, trickles and then ripples of water moving in a pattern of their own choosing, with the motion of Peter's oars, in and out, in and out. Zephyrs of wind, mere breezes in the morning air, touched my face as I gazed at the azure of the meandering walk more purpose filled yet still wandering, turning softly seemingly at mere whim, but too placid for such impertinence. Wispy clouds moved in a gentle flight, reflected in the river as our boat slipped onward, a faint hush weaving across its expanse.

And then the boat reached a sudden turn, and it lurched forward for a moment, a stray rock falling to the side in the wake of the new pressure.

There was no danger in the movement, nearly microscopic, but the inconsistency was noted as panic flashed through Peter's eyes, and he drew the boat to the halt.

"Little Dan!"

"I'm all right, Peter." Little Dan grasped his older brother's shoulder. "It was just a pebble. It won't hurt us."

Just a pebble.

For a moment, Peter's eyes flooded with azure seas, fragments of touch and light kin to the river that granted us refuge and anchorage today. But then, just as quickly, it was as if it never was, blinked back into nonexistence.

Peter relaxed, his hand returning to the oar. "The rest of the journey should be fine."

And so we continued, the tranquil lull of the river arising, ribboning through each curve and turn, and drifted into ourselves as the soft babbling of the water became a duet with a distant bluejay or sparrow, a steady pace moving in and out in perfect azure, a peaceful serenity unmatched.

And then I heard it.

I was so immersed that I almost did not register the click of a camera's shutter from the neighboring brush, as we rounded the final curve before Peter's appointed destination.

I turned back, craning my neck to see, but we were swept away, slow as we did tread through the Bow, and there was nothing to be seen.

Probably just a tourist, I muttered to no one in particular, as Peter glanced back for an instant, before turning a wary eye to his brother.

And then there was a rustling, and scuttling as if of an animal, a natural member of this habitat, and I wondered if I had not imagined the whole thing after all.

It was 9:30 PM.

I walked down the hall of the Asturian house, light mint green walls soft in the moonlight, Peter at my right, pushing Little Dan.

It was an extraordinarily ordinary day—fun, peaceful, and almost perfect.

And then, as the image of the boat rematerialized in my mind, words, too, appeared, as if written across the pale green walls that surrounded us:

"With a steady stony glance—
Like some bold seer in a trance,
Beholding all his own mischance,
Mute, with a glassy countenance—
She look'd down to Camelot.
It was the closing of the day:
She loos'd the chain, and down she lay;
The broad stream bore her far away,
The Lady of Shalott."

The Lady of Shalott.

We rounded the corner, and, all at once, I was scared to be alone.

"Peter," I whispered suddenly, my body jerking into the tenseness I felt inside.

Peter turned to me, one hand on his brother's wheelchair, where Little Dan was already dozing off.

It was pathetic, vulnerable, and made me feel pathetic and vulnerable, too.

I didn't used to care about being vulnerable.

"What is it, Rebecca?" he said softly, leaning his other hand against the wall as he looked at me.

"It's . . . it's just that . . ."

That I'm dying inside. That everything is a mess. That I feel so broken, and I want to tell you why.

Oh, how much I wanted to tell him.

"I—" I turned away.

Please. I need your help.

My voice faltered, and I pointed to the hall, my eyes barely taking him in. "It's late, Peter. I . . . I don't want to keep you."

Don't go.

"Rebecca, are you okay?"

His voice was filled with concern, gentle yet insistent all at once.

No.

I forced a smile. "I'll be fine."

"Are you sure?" I heard Peter's footsteps grow closer, but I couldn't look.

"Yeah. I mean, I just . . ." I bit my lip and finally turned.

Peter nodded, encouraging.

"It's just that things lately . . . they haven't been . . ." I trailed off as moisture threatened my eyes, "people . . . they've . . ." I shook my head, waving it away.

Waving it away when I didn't want to, didn't want to at all.

"I should probably head to my room and go to bed," I finally said quietly. "I'm sorry that—"

"It's okay, Rebecca. You don't have to say anything," Peter said simply. "Not now."

My hand clung so hard to the golden doorknob of my room that it hurt. "Goodnight, Peter."

"Goodnight, Rebecca."

I closed my door, but not before I saw the worry painted across his brow, his large eyes drawn in concern, a fleeting moment before I heard the sound of wheels moving away.

I sank to the floor, pressing my hands to my face, as my eyes burned with tears that soon streamed down my face, renewed by a stabbing pain in my chest and its fear of a humiliating cowardice.

I was numb, yet too awake to be numb enough.

I was scared to be alone, but more scared still to say a word.

Oh, how much I wanted to tell him.

And then the dreams came.

Chapter 11: Aquamarine

"And here it is, The Poet's Room!" Little Dan announced excitedly.

I stood at the threshold, one hand on Little Dan's wheelchair, and almost gasped.

I had imagined a room filled with books circling in delight, perhaps a comfortable chair here and there, a rocking chair like the one in the family room. But, much like Antonio when he stepped into the lighthouse, nothing could have prepared me for the sight that awaited me.

The room was a world in and of itself—and divided into two. On one side, seaside images splashed into view, scattered shells and seahorses leaping across bookshelves filled to the brim with volumes, golden and silver, ancient and new. A seaside chair with an embroidered velvet cushion stood to one side. Half the floor was painted as if undersea, waves and fish so real as to touch gliding across. On the back wall were painted the words, "For cold days." On the other side, a 3-D glacier emerged, paintings of ice filling the walls around, the floor the inside of an underground ice chamber. Bookshelves lined up within the glacier, snowflakes falling against the shelves in shimmering sparkles of white light. Each image was painted delicately, expertly, with hands that clearly loved every inch of their movement. *Every inch of those who would venture here.* On the back wall on that right side were the words, "For warm days. Love, Mom."

Paintings of varied sceneries sat on easels sporadically interspaced around the perimeter — sporadically, yet somehow in an aesthetically pleasing arrangement.

And, surrounding it all, above and beyond, gleaming flashes of distant stars scattered across a ceiling as black as the night sky.

A ceiling of stars.

I picked up Little Dan, leaving his wheelchair at the entrance, as we found ourselves ascending five small steps, each painted as the spines of books of classic literature, from *Oliver Twist* to *The Old Man and the Sea*.

"Wow," I finally managed, taking it all in.

Little Dan's face lit up. "I knew you would like it."

"How . . . did your mom paint all of this?"

"Most of it." Little Dan nodded. "Dad helped with some of it. But it was Mom's idea. It used to just be the steps — and her paintings on the easels. But . . . six years ago, when I was four, she started to add in all the rest."

Six years ago. The time of his accident.

"So that, when it was cold, I'd have a warm place to be. And when it was warm . . ."

"Somewhere cool," I said softly. "This is . . . beautiful, Little Dan."

There was a moment, and then I remembered our purpose.

I helped Little Dan into a comfortable white cushion, built in the shape of a seashell, after he admitted he was in a "sea mood" despite the weather, receiving no argument from me there. "Here you go."

"Thanks, Rebecca. Oh! I almost forgot. I drew this for you."

Little Dan handed me a sheet of computer paper.

It was a drawing of a stone cottage by the sea, a garden dancing behind a fence and a sea lion playing in the ocean, grass growing across the sandy dunes before it. It demonstrated not only artistic talent and intelligence, but a poetic insight well beyond his years.

"Wow. That's beautiful, Danny." I looked up at him with a smile. "You have your mama's talent."

Little Dan's eyes grew big, and I could tell that he was pleased. "Thanks, Rebecca."

"So." I smiled down at him, taking my place in a pebble-hued chair. "What shall we read today? I picked last. It's your turn."

Little Dan grinned. "Let me think . . ."

"Emily Dickinson? Walt Whitman? William Blake?" I offered.

"Or e.e. cummings," Little Dan said thoughtfully.

"More Robert *Frost*?" I suggested.

Little Dan raised an eyebrow. "Not on *this* side of the room."

I smiled. "Well, then . . . what shall it be?"

"I like Emily Dickinson," Little Dan said, "and she has poems about the sea, even one from before she ever visited it. But . . . today I feel like an *adventure* in the forest, don't you?" He leaned forward.

"Hmm . . . that wouldn't happen to involve a "tyger, tyger, burning bright," would it?" I teased.

Little Dan's eyes widened. "How did you know?"

"It's my dad's favorite poem. He loves all the layers of meaning in the poem," I said, knowing somehow that Little Dan would know exactly what I meant. "And he likes Emily a lot, too."

"You need to tell me all about your dad," Little Dan said decidedly. "And all about your family. I want to *see* them here, in this room with us."

I smiled at his innocent joy, until I remembered something, and turned away so that he could not see the tear in my eye.

"I want you to know them, too, Danny."

"But," I said, my voice now raised teasingly. "The poem first."

"Yes," Little Dan said, "that is the correct order of things."

He was the most adorable little boy in the world.

I smiled, and stood, scanning the volumes of the shelves on our side of the "world" (for, of course, the tiger would live on *this* end, warm despite the ocean replacing the jungle), before finding *The Complete Poems of William Blake* on the third shelf.

I returned to my seat, glancing at the table of contents, before turning to the twelfth page.

"Tyger, tyger, burning bright," I read, looking up at Little Dan with a smile.

My head fell back on my pillow as sleep approached, my thoughts drifting to images from a year before . . .

2 AM

"Robin   Hood   *is   the   greatest   of   legends."*
William Adam leaned against a shelf in the literature
section of the college bookstore. "It set up an archetype that
we still see today, but nothing ever reaches the level of the
original tale."

"No,   it   really   doesn't."   A   curl   fell   across
one eye, and I brushed it back more eagerly than
impatiently. "The romanticism, the chivalry, the sense of a
deeper, fuller time. And . . . Maid Marian." I lifted an eyebrow.

"That, too." He winked, sending my heart racing anew.

"Do you love King Arthur *just as much, Will?" I asked,*
already certain of the answer.

"Just about, my darling. The Lady of Shalott,
Lancelot, Sir Gawain—"

"The Lady of Shalott!" I took his hand, and he smiled,
pulling me effortlessly to him.

I shook my head in wonder, squeezing his hand. "I still
can't believe it. We have almost all the same interests and
favorites. We have so much in common. Maybe more than
. . . anyone I've ever met."

"Very remarkable . . . and important."

"Yes."

I reluctantly withdrew my hand before moving quickly to
a nearby shelf. "Ah! Here it is—my favorite. Sir Gawain—"

"—and the Green Knight. *One of the strongest Arthurian tales. The symbol of the—*"

Jeffrey sauntered down our row, his long hair now closely cropped to the side of his head, but his almond brown eyes still remarkably Jeffrey.

"Rebecca!" *he greeted me in his usual way as if I hadn't seen him ten minutes before.*

"Hey, man." *He shook Will's hand and, with a quick smile, continued to walk forward, evidently on his way to the register.*

"Hey, Jeffrey, aren't you still on break?" *I called out.* "You can hang here a bit with us if you want. Arvind is still on call, and you know no one has opened the door since Will got here fifteen minutes ago. If you have some special project, I can help you soon, too. My break ends when yours does."

"No worries, girlie. Just need to man the phones," *Jeffrey said cheerfully, casting us a backward glance.* "You never know when we might get a call from the Vatican. Or Peru . . . Or Canada." *He cast one last glance in my direction before continuing on his way.*

I shrugged, turning back to Will as his figure disappeared in the distance.

"Should I be worried?" *he said lightly, closing a book.* "Does he have something against me?"

"No, of course not!" *I rushed to interject, touching his shoulder.* "He's probably just distracted . . . and, okay, maybe a bit protective of me."

"I'm glad. It's reassuring to know you have someone looking out for you on Mondays and Wednesdays when I'm not here to look after you myself."

He cupped my chin in one hand, and leaned forward to lightly kiss me on the lips.

"Mmm, it's always good to have a security officer à la Tuvok around." *I paused, stifling a giggle at the thought* of Jeffrey with pointy ears—not to mention his typical Californian speech patterns inflected with Vulcan flair.

"Which reminds me," I said, suddenly eager again, "you never told me your favorite Star Trek species."

He moved back, pacing thoughtfully, before finally addressing me. "Ferengi. Believe it or not, I have the Rules of Acquisition on my shelf next to The Complete Works of Shakespeare." He flashed me a brilliant smile.

"No way! You do not!"

"I do. I'll have to show you one day. It's back at my mom's house in Ohio."

His home. He wanted to show me, have me meet . . . I broke off my thoughts, breathless with the thrill of it all.

"Which reminds me . . . I have a question for you." He leveled his eyes with mine. "Do you think time travel is possible?"

"I wish it were," I answered truthfully, running a hand aimlessly through my hair. "As a little girl, I grabbed thyme from the backyard plants, clutching and scrunching it in my hand and closing my eyes as I twirled around, as if hoping Edward Eager's story would come true." I closed my eyes for a moment, remembering. "I've always loved the Star Trek episodes that involved time travel," I added. "Or any story with it, really. Why?"

He leaned forward. "Rebecca, there is this new study out from two years ago. It involves the bending of space through quantum mechanics, but this theorist, Dr. Benshurst, believes it can be done."

"Wow." My eyes widened. "That is . . . insane, if true. In the best possible way, I mean."

"Oh, believe me, the evidence is remarkable. Very well-theorized and researched. I can bring his latest paper tonight to discuss . . . We are having dinner tonight, my Marianne?" He leaned forward and kissed my forehead.

"*Yes, Colonel Brandon.*" I smiled, lifting my eyes to his.
"*Maid Marian.*"
"*Robin Hood,*" I said to the robber of my heart as the bell rang, signaling the end of lunch.

"Peter?" I sat down at the table, overcome by weariness. My eyes were bloodshot, blinking in and out of focus, the draining night having left me fatigued.

Numbness filled me, covering my body like a white sheet of snow. I reached for feeling, but it was a plaintive, small voice too far removed from the present day, too far beyond reality to feel at all.

"Yes, Rebecca?" Peter turned his attention from a mouthful of waffles to look at me.

"What do you think about the *Robin Hood* and *King Arthur* stories?" I did not meet his gaze.

Peter paused, considering. "Well, I've always loved medieval stories. The chivalry, the downright decency of the period. So, yes, *Robin Hood* and *King Arthur* both have their appeal—probably moreso *King Arthur* than *Robin Hood* due to the knightly aspect of it. I have focused more on Chaucer and Sir Walter Scott, really. You've always been the bigger *King Arthur* and *Robin Hood* expert. But you already know that." His eyes leveled with mine before I turned away.

Yes, I did.

"And Jane Austen?" I asked in a rush, keeping my eyes on my waffles.

Peter straightened his napkin. "I'm afraid I still haven't read more than one novel by Ms. Austen and, beyond that, can only judge by the Winslet movie—which I did like, by the way. But—you know I'm more inclined toward Hemingway."

"Shakespeare?"

"Of course. *Hamlet* especially. But no one will ever be the level of Shakespeare aficionado that you are," he said with a glint of humor, and then paused. "Why?"

Why.

"I . . . guess I was just wondering." I fumbled with my utensils.

"Is it important?" I could feel Peter's gaze follow me. *Was it?*

I didn't know anymore.

"And—" I paused, hesitant yet plowing forward despite myself. "Time travel?"

Peter paused. "It's interesting. Though you have more experience with sci-fi and *Star Trek* than I do. Not that I wouldn't be interested one day in looking into more than the two movies I saw nearly a decade ago. The YouTube videos you showed me were intriguing." He looked up. "But, for one, the idea of traveling to the past appeals to me the most, moreso than the far-off future."

"Someone once . . . told me it might be possible," I said quietly before looking up at Peter, "to travel through time."

"What did you think of the idea?" Peter asked, his gaze unwavering.

He wanted to know what I thought.

"I . . . I hadn't really thought about it before. And you?"

"It's a compelling theory, and I'd be intrigued to see the research behind it, but . . . no"—Peter looked at me—"I don't think it's very likely."

"Oh." I nodded, silently playing with a piece of waffle on my plate.

"Perhaps some who delve into unreality don't have the same imaginative insight as you do to maintain more than a precarious balance."

"Sometimes it is almost enough," I said.

Peter studied me, his eyes remaining unflinchingly on my own.

And, in that gaze, I felt that he knew who that "someone" was, somehow, even though he only barely knew the name referenced in emails and messages in connection to various events—for I had never told him. But surely he knew, or had wondered, just as I had wondered about a "Savannah" who seemed to frequently join Peter for study sessions a year or two before. But none of that mattered now.

"Does it matter?" Peter said softly.

I lifted my head, and my eyes met his briefly before flickering away.

I could not answer.

Chapter 12: Yellow Sapphire

The door was open.

I paused briefly, a plate in my hands, and cleared my throat to give notice of my presence before slowly entering.

Raphael Asturian turned at the sound, a slight smile forming. Thin, wire-frame reading glasses were positioned near the base of his nose, reminding me for a moment of my father.

"Mrs. Asturian asked me to give you your sandwich," I explained, handing it to him. "She's tied up with Little Dan at the moment."

Mr. Asturian nodded, taking the plate. "Thank you, Rebecca." He glanced down at the papers before him, seemingly lost in thought. It was not an impolite gesture, but one seemingly out of habit and immersion in another world—a reality of which I was exceedingly familiar—and so I took the opportunity instead to glance around the new surroundings, the enclosure that previously had been kept unknown behind a closed door.

It was a large room for an office, and, while it was not disorderly in any grasp of the word, it was *full*. Bookshelves were filled with volumes that appeared to be more technical than literary compared to those in The Poet's Room or downstairs near the dining room; some books sat upon the top of the shelves, running out of space, but never giving the appearance of overflowing or surpassing, but, rather, *flowing*. Diagrams and paintings were scattered across the walls, and my eyes wandered downward, catching sight of models of unidentifiable objects and machines, instantly piquing my interest as to their purpose. From there, easels were neatly lined in a row—prominent as if at the very center of the room, when, in fact, closer to the back wall, leading me to lean closer to examine the long paper drawn across them.

The first easel closest to his desk held the drawing of what appeared to be a step ladder, only one that seemed almost human, with branches of limbs that reached to the top of a bookshelf and no actual steps. There were labels and words that I did not understand, and each detail and line was minute, reminding me that, while this was the workshop of the inventor, it was also the home of the painter. As I scanned my surroundings once again, my gaze fell upon the smaller sheet in front of Mr. Asturian, the drawing from the easel appearing in miniature along with a series of mathematical formulas and quickly scattered words less neat than the room in which we stood.

Mr. Asturian glanced up, and I suddenly blushed furiously, wondering if I had intruded upon his privacy. Yet, while his expression was not entirely open, it was not closed off—for an Asturian wore no true mask—and there seemed to exist no concern in it.

"It's an invention I have been working on for some time," he ventured, his quiet, pleasant voice suddenly filling the room, "to help Little Dan reach books in The Poet's Room and elsewhere more easily." He gestured to another drawing near the one he had been studying, where what appeared to be a remote control lay, once again intricately drawn with many painstakingly labeled knobs. "He would press a button on this device to request a particular book on the shelves, which would activate this stepladder-like machine." He pointed back to the original drawing. "Once that process was initiated, the 'ladder' would bring down the selected volume to Little Dan." He peered at me over his eyeglasses. "There are, of course, more complicated studies at this time, but I was seeking a simpler and less expensive option than robotics."

"Wow," I said, brushing back a strand of hair that had fallen across my eye, "that's really impressive. It reminds me of when I was a little girl and was instantly fascinated by the soda machine and how that could possibly work. But obviously this is more complicated."

Mr. Asturian nodded thoughtfully. "It is operating from the same basic theories and principles as far as the remote is concerned. The key difference would be the 'helping hand,' the ladder with 'ligaments' that can retrieve the item after being instructed by that device. I have attempted the blueprint of different models, but, thus far, they have been too clumsy to risk use by my son." He looked up, and, as he did so, I found myself reflecting.

I had not spent much time with Mr. Asturian before, only having had reason to converse with him in the company of the entire family, such as at dinner, and, even then, he was more of a quiet presence, kindly present, but not interacting as fully with me as Little Dan and Peter or even his wife. When he addressed me, his eyes did not have the same penetrating gaze as Peter—or even Little Dan, having "inherited" this trait from his brother, albeit in his own way—and, while I knew that he was a dreamer and a philosopher, he did not have the same dream-like way about them as his wife. His gaze was less like a gaze, but not simply a look; it was subtle, undemanding, beyond the introverted nature that he espoused even more fully than the quiet reserve of Peter or the effervescent thoughtfulness of Little Dan. There existed a depth that could be ascertained from their aspect, even if they did not choose to, in effect, meld with those upon which they focused.

I glanced around the room, my eyes once again finding the easel, and noted then that the words "Little Dan" were neatly written across the top. On the easel directly to the left was another elaborate drawing, labeled "Peter" at the top and appearing to be some sort of eyewear.

Mr. Asturian followed my gaze. "Those are night vision swimming goggles. Of course there are already models in use, but I am attempting to develop a blueprint for one with higher quality imaging. While there are anti-fog goggles on the market, there are often complaints as to their effectiveness. It is difficult to develop a model that will not have this problem at all, but I am hoping to reach as close to the mark as possible. Should Peter ever"—and at this he paused—"have use for them."

I noticed then that, while some of the models lying near the easels and throughout the room remained unidentifiable, there were several that conformed to the diagrams and drawings developed for Peter and Little Dan that Mr. Asturian had just explained.

"The models were created by a colleague of mine from Calgary," Mr. Asturian said, looking down at the objects I examined. "My abilities are limited to drawing up the plans for others to construct."

"It is impressive, nevertheless," I said, my eyes shifting once again to the easels. The third to the left of Peter's night goggles was labeled "Olivia" and, while it was faced at an angle difficult to see from my current position, a portion of the drawing was visible, appearing to be a depiction of the kitchen. Several pages were folded back behind it, as in a long notebook, and I realized, as I looked back on the other easels, that the same pattern emerged—whether indicating earlier attempts at the same invention or completely different ones, I did not know.

For Olivia. For Peter. For Little Dan.

I turned to Mr. Asturian, as something caught in my throat. "These inventions—they are all for your family, aren't they?" I asked softly.

He nodded.

"My family is my life," Mr. Asturian said simply.

I smiled, looking down for a moment, before regarding him again. "That is . . . all of this is lovely."

There was a pause, and then Mr. Asturian adjusted his eyeglasses and focused on me. "And you, Rebecca? If you were to invent something, a device of any sort, what would it be?"

"Hmm," I said, suddenly lost in thought, "I'm not certain. I used to think of wild ideas as a little girl, but those were also the days of Mrs. Piggle

Wiggle and lying down on the sofa, looking up at the ceiling . . . imagining what it would be like to live in a house like hers where everything was upside down, walking on the ceiling as if it were the floor. I don't know if I ever really thought of an invention that could contribute anything important to society; they were mostly just random ideas."

"Have you read Saint John Paul II's 'Letter to Artists'?" Mr. Asturian asked.

"YES! It's my favorite! I love—" I paused. "Okay, point taken." I smiled. "I suppose the imaginative construction in and of itself is a useful part of humanity from even a spiritual context. But all of my ideas still tend to be random."

Mr. Asturian shook his head. "Feel free to state any ideas you have. Whatever comes to mind. I'd be happy to hear it."

"A dancing elevator with holographic characters that spring to life for the 30-second ride," I blurted out.

I coughed. "And that was literally what just popped in my head. I told you it would be random."

"That's very interesting," Mr. Asturian said thoughtfully, as if considering my idea—and he probably was. He did not laugh, even though I was close to laughing myself and would not have begrudged any observer who would have chosen to laugh with me in that instant over the random insanity of it all—but seemed to consider it as if I were a fellow scholar, fellow inventor, an equal in this area, even though I was far from his level of expertise.

And so, instead of further excusing my recent speech patterns, I uttered two words:

"Thank you," I said.

He nodded with a faint smile.

I remembered the sandwich he had taken, but not eaten, and then, making my excuses, took leave of him, allowing—or hoping to allow—the inventor the opportunity to consume nutritional material before the afternoon faded to evening and dinner approached.

I turned off the light, pulling myself into bed, my eyes closing as night descended around me . . .

4:30 AM

I smiled in contentment from the passenger side.

I did not often wear yellow, but today I wore a simple honey-colored dress, golden like a sunbeam's last flight, the modern V-neck cut giving way to the flair and ornamental swirls of an earlier time. I never bought on impulse—and rarely bought at all—but this dress in its echoes of 21st century Belle had struck me as the perfect anniversary apparel. Most of all, The Dress was delightfully "twirlable"; I had tested it in the store dressing room, despite the limited space that had almost caused me to scrape my knee on the door.

For, there exists a simple fact, even among those who do not often talk about clothing for fear of appearing superficial:

Real dresses must be twirlable.

I had never had cause to wear a dress for such an occasion, and the thrill of it all cascaded through my chest and heart, not unlike the flowing lines of the dress, for the entire week prior.

I kissed the lock of hair my prince had given to me, and twirled over and over.

"So, my darling." His gray-blue eyes caught mine as he turned the keys clockwise, the faint murmur of the vehicle fading away into the night. "Six months."

We had begun the evening with dinner at an Italian restaurant, the flickering candles at our table casting midnight shadows over the entire scene. When the music began, Will took my hand, his hand on my back as I placed my other hand on his shoulder. And then, suddenly, he pulled away, and we both laughed as if the entire restaurant had their eyes on us.

"We'll do this one day. Just in a library, a huge library."

"Like Beauty and the Beast," I breathed.

It was a promise he had made early on in our relationship—along with his pledge to one day write me a love song, but it had to be "just right"—and I eagerly anticipated the moment in which it would finally occur. Part of me wondered if that dance would lead to a new chapter—clichés aside—in our lives.

The flashback faded in my eyes, echoes of it still in my smile.

"I can hardly believe it." I grinned like a silly schoolgirl. "But we're here."

"Yeah, we are." He leaned forward to kiss me.

The kiss started out slow, soft and sweet, and then suddenly grew more passionate, more urgent. I ran my hands through his hair, reveling in his warmth, yet, as always, guarded and in control, the proper lady I was often accused of being.

For, I had nothing to fear. He was my prince.

And then his hand was on my back, catching the zipper at the top and starting to move it down.

I drew back suddenly, pulling his arms away from me in one swift movement.

Surely I imagined . . .

"Will, what are you . . . doing?" I managed to get the words out, my face reddening.

And it was then that I saw where we were.

Strange how I did not notice before. Strange how candlelit thoughts and promises of yellow ballroom dresses could turn into a whirlpool of forgotten distance.

A tall, two-story building. Simple. White. Balconies with brushes of assorted flowers.

The words: Abrego Hotel.

"You see, my dear Belle," he said almost conspiratorially—but much more flirtatiously in a way that I had never noticed—"it's a surprise I've been planning. I wanted this to be special for both of us, so I planned it all out for our sixth month. It's a high end place"—he gestured toward the building ahead almost casually as my heart beat erratically—"and I put together a lot of things to make it perfect." His gray-blue eyes flickered toward me again, his smile radiant, yet both seemed lighter, lighter than I remembered. "It's a surprise, but I'll let you know one thing: rose petals on the mattress."

Rose petals.

I swallowed the bile rising to my throat, a wave of dizziness overtaking me as I resisted the urge to lose all the contents of dinner over the side of the car.

This was him. This was him.

"But"—his confident tone took on a more gentle note—"I know, I should have waited 'til we arrived at our room. I got a bit carried away." He caressed my cheek with one hand.

I jolted away instinctively. I had to think clearly. He did not know. I thought he was . . . but he did not know. Perhaps we could talk reasonably . . .

I took his hand. "Will, I think we need to talk this over."

"Talk what over, my Rebecca?" He cupped my chin with one hand.

I turned away. "I think we have . . . different expectations."

"You're taken by surprise," he said in that same self-assured, calm voice. "I understand. Totally, babe, I do. But it will be perfect. Don't worry. And it's okay"—he looked me over with a smile—"to be a little nervous. Just like you were with our first kiss."

"I am not going in that hotel." The words drew from me quickly, firmly, and . . . solid.

"Why not?" His smile remained, but a hint of a frown burrowed across his brow.

"That's not . . . me."

And I thought it wasn't you.

"Not yet, dear one. But it will be. Just one moment here, and it'll be you. It's okay, babe, it's okay." And he drew me to him once again, his arms adorned with words of comfort that offered none.

He did not attempt anything again, not at first. But the kiss was different. With every second, I felt his true intent.

I pulled away. "Please take me home."

"Why?"

"Why?"

I was 21 years old, the first year of my job at the campus bookstore. It was a slow day—there had been hardly any customers for three hours that completed shelf perfection—and Jeffrey and I had stolen a few moments to sit by the window before our manager would order us back to our stations.

"Don't get me wrong—it takes guts, especially to *admit* that." Jeffrey's voice softened. "But I still don't . . . understand."

I turned to the window, and a smile, quietly and unthinkingly, crossed my lips. "Those trees . . . they look a century old, but today—I cannot see it from here, but there has to be an orange-red kite—perhaps yellow—left by its owner and mistaken for a leaf."

Jeffrey smiled and leaned forward.

"It's there, and a quarter of an hour ago, it was raining—and now it is misty, silver laughter of nymphs collected in a word that clings—no, *circulates*—with life to that leaf and that air and those trees. And there's a glimmer of color in the sky touching the blue in a different way—yet so much the same, every day at 6 or 7. You can see it, peeking around the corner even now. And—"

"Rebecca, I'm sorry. I didn't mean to pry. It's okay to talk about other stuff . . . I just thought I should say that, in case you—"

"And *that* is why," I said suddenly, passionately, fervently, pointing to the window. "That is why."

Jeffrey's eyes shifted, and then there was a depth and, when he looked at me, a warmth.

I looked at him, and there was no warmth in his eyes.

"Please turn around and take me home," I said shakily.

And so the two

A modern-day

Willoughby

and

Marianne

never

to

dance.

Chapter 13: Diamond

"And so, in silver fragments of the past, wisps of crowned yesterday fell lightly in the morning dew," I quoted softly, one hand on the page of the poetry book.

We were sitting on the "warm days" side of the room today at Little Dan's insistence, less so because of the weather and more because Little Dan declared, "It is a glacier-y kind of day, don't you think?"

"I like the way you read," Little Dan said thoughtfully. "It's different than the way it's said at school or in today's world. It sounds . . . *silvery*, just like the poem."

I squeezed his hand, moving The Poet's Chair closer to his wheelchair. "I'm glad you liked it, Little Dan—Danny."

"Rebecca," he said, looking up at me with those intelligent eyes of his, his small hand still warm in mine, "do you think a lot about your guardian angel?"

I smiled. "As a matter of fact, I do. Though sometimes more than others, which makes me feel more fickle than I should be. But, generally, yes . . . I've always been especially interested in angels."

"I think a lot about mine, too. My religious education teacher in grade one told us we shouldn't try to name our guardian angels because they already have a name, but we could ask our guardian angel what that name was. So, before I went to bed that night, I asked."

I nodded, lost for a moment in the past. "I did the same thing when I was about that age."

"And did you find out the name?"

I shook my head with another smile. "My guardian angel must have decided to be coy. I didn't learn it. But that fits. God knows my affinity for the mysterious. Did you find out?"

Little Dan stared ahead, his eyes thoughtful. "I woke up, and the name that came to mind was Ivanhoe."

I smiled. "That's quite a name. Do you think your guardian angel's name is Ivanhoe?"

He shook his head. "No, it's not Ivanhoe. Not that name anyway. But it felt like a clue."

"Like that fish in the corner of your mama's painting?"

It was a seaside image, and a small blue fish emerged from the right corner like Waldo.

Little Dan's face lit up. "Like Mama's painting. She always puts those in there for me, you know."

"That's . . ." I searched for the words as my heart filled in the blanks, "a mom."

"It is. Rebecca, can I tell you something?"

"Of course." I squeezed his hand.

"It's about guardian angels—mine."

I nodded, encouraging him.

"When Peter left for the states after my accident, he was really sad. And worried. About me. But he shouldn't have been because I was really fine. But I was worried about him."

I nodded, still holding his hand as I remembered the time Peter first told me his story years before.

"He was really the one to be worried about. So, when he left, I asked my guardian angel to look after him, too. I thought he might need extra-double help."

He turned to me. "Do you think my guardian angel can do that? I always ask Peter theology questions, but I didn't want to ask him this."

"I don't know . . . it's a good question. But I do know two things: that God saw in that request that your love for your brother was so big. And—" My eyes grew moist.

"And?"

"And you're a very brave boy," I said.

I drifted deeper into sleep, and the forcefields fell away,

> leaving me
> to face
> the firing
> of a dozen phaser blasts . . .

4:45 AM

"Rebecca . . ." Her voice was labored, as if every syllable were an effort.

I climbed onto the bed like a small child and took her hand.

"Oh, sweetie, I love you."

A finger lifted and softly stroked the top of my hand, and I knew that I would never forget that moment, that touch.

Tears threatened to blind me.

"I love you, too." So very much.

We sat in silence for a few moments, and then began to pray the Divine Mercy chaplet together, my voice gaining strength as I continued, as she silently prayed with me.

I didn't know that this would be the last time.

But I knew that it could be.

Silence passed again as we lived in this moment of shadow and light.

Light, pain, and veiled melancholy.

"How's your Peter?" she managed, her voice slower, deliberate, but lucidly aware.

He wasn't my Peter, but I didn't have the heart to correct her.

"He's good," I said. "He's now a second grade teacher and really loves it." I paused. "He's praying for you every day. I talk about you a lot, and he thinks you're a very special person."

"Aw. That's . . . sweet."

I heard a shuffling sound, and there he was, moving slowly with his walker. It was hard to believe that, only two years before, he had walked freely.

I looked at him, and quietly got up, giving her one last kiss.

I bit my lip so hard as to draw blood.

I could not cry. She needed me to be strong.

I touched his shoulder, and withdrew, walking to the doorway as he took his place, sitting on the bed beside her.

I turned back for an instant, my hand on the door.

His eyes were whirlpools of time's cacophony, lost in sidewalk cracks and carob walks.

His face was drawn into an agony and pain of the deepest and most abiding love.

As soon as I was far enough away as to not be heard, I ran.

I ran without direction or purpose, save the action of running.

I ran without knowing.

I just ran.

I ran through the backyard and the thyme and the patio of my youth, and fell to the ground, sobbing.

This was the last time.

"Carefree were the days when I grew up
Cherry picking and feeding grateful ducks
Seasons come and seasons go
Before you know it, we're all grown
Time can be a greedy thing

I hope you know I'll miss you so
There'll never be an easy way to let you go . . ."

"My Turn to Go"
(Poema)

Chapter 14: Rose Quartz

"Well, I guess you were right," I called to Peter from The Pink Bicycle as I rode beside him.

Peter had, this morning, suggested going out for an afternoon ride. With some trepidation, I agreed to it. For the past half hour, we had been riding along Banff Avenue, the wind whistling through the trees.

Peter grinned from his seat. "I am happy to accept that estimable statement, but what exactly are you referring to now?"

I finally came to a stop, dismounting, and Peter followed suit.

"Riding a bike," I explained, walking with Peter alongside our two-wheel vehicles previously located in the Asturian garage, one green and the other, much to my delight, a lovely shade of hot pink—perhaps belonging to Mrs. Asturian—I could imagine her riding well into her 80s. "I haven't ridden a bike since I was twelve. It's the first time in twelve years, but it feels like yesterday."

"You don't ever really lose it."

"Yeah, it comes back to you." I stopped my bike for a moment, catching my breath. "Which reminds me . . . for no apparent reason because this is completely random . . . but I really liked the honey we had on the pancakes this morning for breakfast. It took my family forever to find an acceptable one since the beekeeper who used to bring us honey—"

"—a beekeeper brought your honey?" Peter's eyes filled with amusement.

"Yeah, isn't that how everyone else does it? Anyway, he moved on to different beehives in another state, so we had to resort to store-bought honey, and you have *no idea* how many inferior varieties there are. They might as well be called *fake* honey." I paused. "They probably *are* fake honey. Anyway, it's pretty messed up." I broke off as Peter took a small notebook and pen from his knapsack and began writing something within.

Curiosity killed the cat.

Thankfully, I had always identified more with the effervescent penguin and therefore was clear to leave the exchange without casualties.

"What are you writing?" I marched over à la penguin movie, leaning to read over his shoulder just as I realized I would never have intruded on Peter's private ponderings in almost any other circumstance.

I blinked twice, looked again, and raised a half-indignant, half-incredulous eyebrow. "The *Rebecca* List?"

Below was written the following:

- Bread
- Grammar
- Italian restaurants
- REAL books vs. Kindle
- Soft water (bad)
- Paradoxes
- Symbolism
- Barbies (character Barbies ONLY for any civilized young girl!)
- Movie adaptations of books
- Pizza
- Fast food (*No.*)
- TS
- Fairy tales
- French toast (homemade only)
- Pancakes
- Aebleskiver
- Vegetables
- White chocolate
- Font (Monotype Corsiva best)
- Capitalization (poetic license)
- Jane Austen
- Star Trek
- Rain (Light vs. Heavy)

"Yes, well"—Peter's grin had now reached full circle—"you have . . . a, shall we say, tendency to require certain standards for items and subjects of interest. Naturally I found it useful to keep a record."

"And you just keep it with you at all times?" I bit my lip to contain the grin that threatened to explode.

"Only when I'm with you." Peter leaned against his bike with one hand. "Generally, I keep it by the computer . . . for when the Messenger app is opened to you."

"Peter Joseph Asturian," I protested, "you are absolutely insane." I looked down again at the list as Peter continued to grin, and paused. "You're missing oatmeal soap."

"And the Oxford comma. I need to update the list. Alas, it is of yet incomplete."

"And parkas."

"75 degrees: the perfect—and possibly only acceptable—temperature."

"Blueberry muffins."

"Possibly mailboxes?"

"Only when it's raining. Not to mention the correct shades of *pink*."

We both burst out laughing uncontrollably. It lasted for three cycles of several minutes each as I held onto my bike to keep me steady.

I finally wiped my eyes, one brief laugh momentarily ending the cycle, and shook my head. "I haven't laughed this much in a long time. Other than the first trip to the jam shop, I mean. I . . . I haven't felt as relaxed as I have these past few weeks in . . ." I trailed off, the amusement gone. "It's . . . nice."

"Yes," Peter said, watching me, "it is nice."

My eyes met his for a moment and then wavered.

"Come, Rebecca," he said, leading the way with his bicycle, "let's take the bikes back home. It's nearly dusk."

The stars swirled in beams and echoes of light, distant thoughts carefully contained in the immensity of time's tapestry.

I pulled a blanket around Little Dan's sleeping form with an affectionate smile. His mouth hung open slightly as he sat in his wheelchair, a mug of hot chocolate still in his hand. I took the mug, and laid it on the ground before casting my eyes upward.

I twirled for a moment, moonlight kissing my shoulders.

It felt like not simply the sky, but the air, was composed of starlight.

I turned my head in the final flourish of the dance, and there Peter sat, watching me with a faint smile upon his lips.

I walked back to sit next to him, readjusting the blanket under me as I did, as the smile of his eyes shifted to Little Dan.

We had decided to watch the stars tonight. Stargazing had always fascinated me, although I rarely had occasion to experience it— and briefly recalled how one notable year I did more than most. And, so, I had readily agreed to Little Dan's suggestion. Danny had been eager to find Canis Major, which he had been studying in his constellation book, but had fallen asleep after Orion's Belt and Ursa Minor, and two heaping cups of hot chocolate with marshmallows.

I sipped from my own mug, topped with whipped cream, before putting it aside with a satisfied sigh. "The night sky is beautiful tonight."

"Yes," Peter said, "it is."

We sat for a few moments in companionable silence, the night's melody stirring effortlessly within me. A luminous formation captured my attention, and I rose again.

"Canis Major?" I asked in a whisper, pointing up ahead to a glittering of stars in the shape of a cross.

"Cygnus, actually—also known as the Northern Cross. It's the Latinized Greek for 'swan.' Canis Major is over there to the right by the Big Dipper."

"Where?"

Peter moved behind me and took my hand, repositioning me so that I could better ascertain its location. "Right over there."

His hand, somehow still warm in the cold night air, filled me as deeply as the starlight.

I drew away after a moment and smiled slightly. "I remember you said you used to often watch the stars. Now I understand. You know them well."

Peter shrugged, unwilling to take credit as always. "I know some. Little Dan knows more."

After one last glance at Cygnus and the Big Dipper, we sat down.

I smiled again, playing with the blue fringe on the edge of my blanket. "Little Dan is such a delightful and incredible boy." I glanced at Peter sideways. "I can see why you love him so much . . . why you would, even if you were not brothers. I . . . think I love him, too."

"I knew you would."

Silence filled us again, and, in that silence, a solemnity surfaced that had not been there before. Like that moment by my room door the day of our canoe ride across Bow River, suddenly I wanted—needed—to tell him everything.

Because he was Peter.

Because I was me.

Because it . . . *was.*

But I couldn't.

I couldn't, but something needed to be said. *Something.* Just a little something.

"I think . . . I almost watch stars like I might have once—as I would have as a child. I mean, I do, obviously . . ." I cleared my throat, reddening. "I'm not making any sense."

"Usually, when one is making the least sense, he is actually making the most sense." Peter paused and then said gently, encouraging, "For Rebeccas anyway."

I hesitated once more before continuing, and then finally plowed through. "If I were a painter, I'd paint this night . . . the stories told in every curve and stroke, the romantic words within each starry light. But, since I'm not, I would write or burst out excitedly in conversation, wanting to talk about it, wanting to talk about something true, something real." I paused. "But sometimes I think people would see that as *too much.* View me as too much. I . . . never used to care, even when I was much shyer as a teen. But I can't help thinking that they . . . that I am too much for them . . . or not . . . not enough." My voice trembled, and then steadied. When I finished, I looked away, not wanting to see Peter's face or for him to see mine. "But maybe I used to be more that way . . . before."

Peter was quiet for a few moments before finally speaking. "Oh, I suppose we are all a bit crazier as kids. But I hope you never lose your sense of randomness. I hope you never lose the way you dance in the moonlight, your eyes filled with wonder. I hope you always care as much as you do today. 'Blasé' never looked good on anyone. And, if the world decides to be one big snob, ignore it."

I turned toward him.

Peter gazed at me, words contained in a single glance.

I closed my eyes, leaning back on the warm blanket, the lullaby of starlight still with me.

Words did not escape my mouth, yet, as Peter lay back on his own blanket, gazing above with a contemplative tranquility, I knew that he had heard it.

And so, in distant melodies and shades of quiet serenity, we remained.

Slowly, softly, I tossed and turned in the 2 AM nightfall . . .

2 AM

"Have you changed your mind?"

"No," I said. We were standing at the threshold, the buzz of airport traffic surrounding us, but remaining in the distance. "I haven't."

He shook his head, the incredulous look on his face inching into his voice. "I can't believe it. It's like you're stuck in the Dark Ages or something. It's the 21st century for crying out loud!"

"Some things transcend time," I said evenly, my heart caught in my throat. "I thought . . . you would understand that."

"Oh, c'mon! I'm Catholic, but I move with the times. I may like *medieval history,* but I don't buy those archaic rules."

Oh, how I thought he would be my forever.

I heard his voice again through the echoes of my lost thoughts. "It's just the normal progression in a relationship!" *he exclaimed.*

"You're right. It is," *I said softly.* "But not like this."

"What are you talking about?" *His voice became more and more agitated.* "Can you stop being the poet freak and be normal for half a second? Oh, wait,* normal. *Too much to ask for, right?!*"

My head was spinning, overtaking me with a wave of dizziness. Oh, how I had cared for you.

"When I"—*my voice shook, but I forced myself to continue*—"when I give myself completely to a man, it will be when forever is in the picture. When there is a complete 'yes.' Not half a yes or even three-quarters of a 'yes.' A complete yes. A promise. Because . . . that's what all of this is. A promise."

I looked up at him, tears threatening to blind me. No, please, not yet. Don't come yet.

He shook his head again, sarcasm accosting his eyes as he spit out the words. "Good luck with that. And, by the way, in case you haven't figured it out, you lost your boyfriend."

"Who are you, William Adam?" *I whispered.* "Did none of this—did it mean anything to you at all?* My Fair Lady, *the lock of hair*—"

"Of course it did. But the relationship wasn't progressing," *he said, his voice too matter-of-fact, his anger now cold detachment.*

Like a lawyer building a case.

Only this wasn't a court of law. It was a love story.

It was supposed to be.

"She is sick," I said helplessly. *"I need . . . I need you. You can't . . . not now."* I broke off, unmoving. Tears inched forward, but I forced them away.

"I am sorry about her condition." He heaved the backpack on his shoulders. *"But that's not my responsibility anymore. I'm sorry. But it isn't."* His eyes didn't meet mine.

"Responsibility?" I shook my head. *"You talk like . . . like caring for me is a . . . a business transaction."* I bit my lip, still trying to hold back the emotion that promised to envelop me.

"I'm ending this conversation."

". . . okay."

"Goodbye, Rebecca."

He turned on his heel and walked away.

Slow motion, like a movie, he sped away. Out of focus, out of control, away.

And, with his back turned, at the last moment that he was within hearing distance, something broke through the silent chaos.

"I really did love you," I whispered.

One movement. *I knew he heard it.*

He walked on.

My eyes lingered, until they lost their focus.

And then the tears came.

And then it all turned to dust
All the faded pomp and
circumstance

Until he was just
the boy who didn't
stay.

Chapter 15: Lapis Lazuli

"So, it's a dead end so far. But I'll keep researching." There was a pause.

"Rebecca?"

"Yeah, Jeffrey?"

"How were you able to visit Yin in jail? Like, how could you bring yourself to do it?"

"JPII," I hesitated, absentmindedly twisting the telephone cord around my finger. "But it took me almost two years. That's a long time."

"Still. You went."

"I went. But I don't think I could have gone again. I'm not . . . I'm not a saint."

"You're a saint to me."

"That's sweet."

"JPII, huh? Sounds like a smart guy. Maybe I'll look him up."

I smiled. "Yeah, he was the best."

"Listen, Rebecca, I want you to have a vacation that would *blow my mind*. You feel?"

"I'll try, silly."

"That's what I like to hear. Okay, girlie, gonna bounce. Time for dinner over here in the U.S."

"Okay! I'll send you a sneezing panda video later."

"That's the spirit. See ya."

"Ciao."

White, rectangular picnic tables arranged themselves in a large square, admitting striped chairs to their meeting, as the sound of humanoid lifeforms piqued their interest.

The Asturian backyard had begun to fill with the voices of ten or twelve friends from church and the neighborhood, past and present, mingling together in the summer party of the year. Men and women alike stood around and chatted, or reclined comfortably in chairs. There were a few children and a couple that seemed to be in their late-thirties, but most appeared to be around the age of Peter's parents. The hearty chuckle of Fr. Abioye could be heard from a far corner of the table, where he sat deep in conversation with another pair. Folk music played lightly in the background as white-gold Christmas lights glittered amidst the shrubbery, inching toward the thorns of roses on the balustrade.

It was 5 PM.

I took a deep breath, feeling the enormity of this simple occasion. *Time to meet the Asturians' friends.* The ruffles of my floral pink blouse blew slightly in the breeze. To keep the chatter of mosquitoes at bay and thereby avoid being devoured, I had chosen to wear gray jeans with sparkles instead of a skirt or dress. After all, it was an informal backyard party.

Even if the Asturians always struck me as the formal types.

I grabbed a plate from a small refreshments table set up at the entrance to the house, a delectable aroma filling my nostrils. I placed a piece of pizza sans pepperoni on my dish, adding two different types of cookies—one appearing to be chocolate chip and the other oatmeal raisin—and walked outside to meet the view that I had spent the past several moments studying.

"Hey." Peter was by my side in an instant, glancing at my apparel with a smile. "Reminds me of—"

"The pen you gave me." I smiled, more at ease. "Me, too."

"Shall we?" Peter motioned ahead, taking my arm, and we approached the right side of the long table.

A tall man with gray hair and wide-rimmed spectacles beneath a black bowler hat stood up, extending his hand. "Professor Darrell Blackburn, at your service. Rebecca Veritas, I presume?"

Peter had mentioned an old family friend by that name, but I had not known much about him, let alone had a face to put to a name. But the name suited the man.

I shook his hand with a smile. "Yes, that's me. Nice to meet you."

"The pleasure is mine."

The Professor (as I began to call him in my mind from the instant he shook my hand) had a deep, pleasant voice, reminding me of the "listening tapes" from my childhood, audio recordings on the cassette tapes now forgotten in today's generation of mp3 downloads and the occasional CD (*always* the CD for me), in which a distinctive voice recounted the fairy and folk tales of many a civilization and varied culture.

His voice was, in itself, a *presence*.

Professor Darrell Blackburn indicated two seats to the right of him, and we sat down.

I placed my plate on the table, glancing over at Peter, who had evidently already located his seat before I had arrived in the backyard, a half-finished pizza slice on his dish.

Mrs. Asturian emerged from inside the house, pushing Little Dan in his wheelchair. Little Dan's cheeks were flushed with excitement, and he waved eagerly when he saw me.

"Let's go sit next to Rebecca," he told his mother.

She switched direction, and moved him closer to us. When his wheelchair halted, she kissed him on the head and then moved to join her husband on the other side of the table.

"Hey, Little Dan," I said, smiling down at him.

"Little Dan?"

"Danny." I grinned, tousling his hair. "Just tricking ya."

Professor Blackburn reached down to shake Little Dan's hand, his eyes somber. "An honor, young man."

Peter murmured in my ear. "The Professor is Little Dan's godfather. He's like an uncle to him. To all of us, really."

Formality indicating intimacy.

I could see how the Asturians were friends with him.

"You call him that, too?" I whispered back.

Peter offered a grin and raised his eyebrow as if to say, "But of course."

"How long have you been friends with the Asturians?" I asked Professor Blackburn.

"Oh, over thirty years. I first met Peter's father when he was a student his first year at the university — and my last. We were both members of the Medieval Society."

"You had a medieval club at your college?!" I burst out with excitement. "I wish I had."

"Me, too," Little Dan said in a serious tone, as we all laughed.

"Well, at this rate, Danny, you'll be in college before you turn sixteen." I smiled. "You are far beyond most kids your age."

Little Dan beamed in thanks.

"He is an impressive student, that young man," Professor Blackburn said affectionately. "Will go far."

As I glanced over at Peter, I saw in his eyes a brief flash of pain, but, just as quickly, it cleared, causing me to wonder if I had imagined it.

"So, what do you teach?" I asked, brought back to the present moment.

"I'm a professor of medieval history in Calgary. But I grew up in Banff, so it is a delight to venture here for such occasions as these. At the moment, I'm staying in the neighboring town of Canmore to conduct research with a colleague of mine until school is back in session."

The music swelled, the sound of flutes and drums taking over the piano and guitar interludes of before.

"This song recounts The Battle of Bosworth Field," Professor Blackburn said, as if enumerating upon the events of the previous day. "1485. War of the Roses. The turning point in the war."

I perked up my ears, listening carefully to the song, as I heard a young man lamenting the departure of his "Tudor rose."

"Huh. I just thought it was a love song," I offered. The song sounded like a recent pop hit I had heard on the radio recently, despite its more classical instrumental choices.

"Was King Henry VII's marriage to Elizabeth of York a love story?" Professor Blackburn leaned forward.

It sounded like the rhetorical question of a modern scholar, but I knew it was not.

And Professor Blackburn was not like any modern scholar that I had encountered.

"Actually, yes," I said with a smile. "Despite the fact that it was a political alliance, they grew to love each other. He mourned her death deeply," I concluded softly. "Not that I'm for arranged marriages," I added quickly with another smile.

Professor Darrell Blackburn turned swiftly to Peter, clapping him on the back. "She is one of us."

Peter smiled. "I agree, although I also thought it was 'just a love song.'"

"So it is. Historical blasphemy at that."

"Hey," I protested playfully, delighting in my ability to do so with a newcomer, yet not fully surprised given his connection to the Asturians, "what's wrong with using medieval metaphors in today's world? We could use more of them, actually."

"In pop songs?"

"*Especially* in pop songs."

Professor Blackburn studied me, his eyes intent. "You are right. Thank you for the goblet of humility that you allowed to liberally splash in my face like the conquest of William the Conquerer under the Normans."

I bit my lip to contain a smile. "No worries."

"Peter"—Professor Blackburn suddenly burst forth, arising from his seat with the formal grace that shielded what appeared to be an impulsive move—"shall we sing along with this song as the lovely Rebecca," he said, nodding in my direction, "has pointed out its merits? It's about time for our annual sing-along!"

"You sing?" I turned incredulously to Peter.

"No," Peter said with a smile, "but I do sing with The Professor."

"And you, Rebecca?" Professor Blackburn's eyes turned to me as the sound of conversation hushed, the crowd expectant.

"No, I, for one, *do not* sing," I said, remaining in my seat with a grin.

Except in the car or shower.

Peter raised an eyebrow, evidently recalling my newly discovered affinity for songwriting— even though, I realized, a pang in my heart as I dismissed such thoughts, I had had reason to show none of it to him.

I raised my eyebrow back, casting aside the shadows. *Songwriting, not singing, Peter.*

He nodded, a wry smile forming at the corner of his lips, as if he had heard the unspoken words aloud.

"Well, my dear Rebecca, that is a shame. But we must continue onward!"

"One, two, three!" Little Dan called out enthusiastically. "Go!"

"Oh, baby, you're my Tudor roseeeee," Professor Darrell Blackburn began in his deep, solemn voice, the modern intonations escaping his version. "I can't live without the stack of cards you piled in my hearrtttt," Peter's baritone joining his in a pleasant, almost calming, lull.

I bit my lip, trying to contain the laughter that threatened to explode at the chosen presentation.

"You're the Aegean Sea, and I'm crossing, crossing over for you in the footsteps of my thoughts." Peter surveyed his audience, his eyes resting on me and then turning to his parents and brother, as Darrell Blackburn extended his hands with dramatic flair in a way that somehow encompassed the song, in his own way, without mocking it or showing disrespect for the artist.

"In the echoes of my melancholy recollection!" Professor Blackburn intonated, his voice rising, as Peter's singing transitioned into backing vocals.

"In the light of the Aegean Sea!" Professor Blackburn grasped Peter's hand and raised it, as if a too-soon curtain call, or perhaps two warriors lifting their arms victoriously in battle.

"Oh, baby, you're my—" Professor Blackburn nodded to Peter, his arms conducting through the air, to indicate that he finish the last line.

"Tudor rose," Peter said, meeting my gaze as the last words of the song rang out, the music fading into silence.

I smiled back, but I was no longer laughing.

"Thank you, thank you." Professor Blackburn bowed gallantly, Peter doing the same beside him. "We'll see you again at the next War of the Roses!"

"I still like the song," I protested when they sat down next to me.

"As do I, now," The Professor admitted in his deep voice. "There is something about singing it out that brings new dimensions into view."

"Yes, the Professor has given up all pretense at snobbish attitudes." Peter grinned, clapping him on the back. "He's what you Americans might term a 'softie.'"

I raised an eyebrow, grinning. "Don't worry, I won't ruin your cover."

"Thank you, my lady." Professor Darrell Blackburn kissed my outstretched hand as I laughed. Peter smiled from beside me, but said nothing.

I picked up the piece of pizza that was now only barely warm—yet somehow, despite my affinity for hot food, I did not mind—and began to eat again. There was a companionable silence.

I leaned over to wipe some ice cream from Little Dan's chin.

Unlike those distracted such as myself, he had proceeded happily to the dessert phase of nutritional conquest.

I glanced up with some puzzlement, as I observed Professor Blackburn pointing what appeared to be a cell phone at the sky, as if to take a picture—yet I knew immediately that it was not for such conventional use.

"Corona Australis," he mumbled. "Lyra the Harp . . . no, Andromeda the Stag . . ."

I glanced at Peter, who looked back at me with a smile, but said nothing.

He knew what The Professor was doing, but wasn't about to tell me.

How utterly vexing.

"Um, sir?" I ventured.

"Mapping the stars," he mumbled without turning. "This 'app' detects their configurations, and they appear as a field on the screen."

Little Dan looked at me eagerly, and I stood up, moving to roll his wheelchair closer to his godfather. I looked over his shoulder, a map of lines and dots filling the screen emitting into the distance.

"These devices have some purpose," he said, by way of explanation, finally turning to us for only an instant before returning to his study, his food but half-eaten in his plate.

My eyes met those of Peter, and we both turned away as laughter began to tiptoe forth, teasing us with its inevitability.

This is my home, his eyes seemed to say to me when they finally turned, almost swiftly, back to mine.

Yes, yes, it is. I smiled back, taking the last bite of my pizza, now cold, and preparing for a bite of chocolate chip as distant music and the lull of quiet conversation swelled together, soft laughter occasionally rising to meet the quickening nightfall in crinkles of summer nights, traces of nostalgia, a song of homecoming, yesterday and today, alive in its wake.

It had been a perfect evening.

I leaned back against my pillow with a sigh of contentment.

While Peter and I had spent most of the time chatting with the Professor on topics varying from philosophy to his favorite jam at the shop—which was decidedly boysenberry—there were also pleasant dialogues with other guests. I had particularly enjoyed speaking with a middle-aged couple; the husband worked at EWTN, and the wife was the owner of the parish bookshop at St. Mary's. Book recommendations came forth effervescently from both sides, and religious discussions were pursued in a delightful series of discourse. There was also a fascinating gentleman who worked as an archaeologist, and we bonded over the mutual interest in a way that led me to relax into some semblance of an excitement I used to feel.

I yawned, closing my eyes, yet, as sleep beckoned, so did a series of *words* yet to be unscrambled—begging me for attention as they insistently pursued my thoughts, allowing no respite.

My hand reached for a pen, and the words came tumbling forth before the night swallowed me in slumber, as I held on to apple blossoms . . .

Shine On

It's a dark night, one for skeletons
And pirates with a patch over their eye
I walk around in circles, dreaming 'bout something
And I remember, I remember when you were mine

With you, everything was lovely
The beauty of our theme song
But then you started to remember
To put all your black flags up

My love, please don't cry, please don't cry
I don't want you hurting
My love, please don't cry, please don't cry
You'll make it out all right

I don't want you hurting
Even though you broke my heart
Even though you left me
I want your beauty to shine on

Your coldness cuts across me like a blade
And I can't remember how to breathe
I stumble and my head is spinning

Don't understand how you could be so cruel

But I know that you put up your shields
Got this need to protect yourself
I know that they hurt you pretty badly
That doesn't mean you have to break my heart

My love, please don't cry, please don't cry
I don't want you hurting
My love, please don't cry, please don't cry
You'll make it out all right

I don't want you hurting
Even though you broke my heart
Even though you left me
I want your beauty to shine on

I remember when you kissed a lock of my hair
Said you couldn't imagine being more in love
I remember how we used to laugh together
In a way that I had never laughed before.

But then you tucked your heart under your arm
And took mine with you, too.

My love, please don't cry, please don't cry
I don't want you hurting
My love, please don't cry, please don't cry
You'll make it out all right

I don't want you hurting
Even though you broke my heart
Even though you left me
I want your beauty to shine on

I'm sitting in church and crying

Can't help myself; tears keep tumbling through
My mom puts her arm around me, and, praying,
I ask, "Dear God, please help me."

Oh, I could have loved you
For all of my life
I would have died for you.
But you killed me first.

My love, please don't cry, please don't cry
I don't want you hurting
My love, please don't cry, please don't cry
You'll make it out all right

I don't want you hurting
Even though you broke my heart
Even though you left me
I want your beauty to shine on

2:30 AM

The soft melody weaved through my bedroom, acoustic guitar and piano sympathetically playing as remnants of a cello could be heard in the distance. A young, earnest voice, introspective and broken, sang with them, partners in the music held in her heart and theirs. They were one.

"Hey." Adriana entered my room and sat down on my bed next to me. I dabbed my eyes quickly to wipe away the tears underneath, and leaned down to press "pause" on the stereo system playing "White Horse."

"What were you listening to?" Adriana asked. "It sounded familiar . . ."

"Vintage Swift."

"Tay Tay Era 2?"

"Yes."

Adriana knew that **Fearless** had become my go-to album in recent days of shattered hearts, with **Speak Now** close behind.

"He didn't deserve you, you know."

I shrugged, biting my lip to avoid talking.

If I said too much, the tears would come flooding back again.

"He didn't."

"I . . . I know. I just . . ." My chin began to shake, moisture anew in my eyes threatening to overfill, "wish he did."

There was a pause, and Adriana sat with me, staring quietly ahead.

"You know, I listened to Taylor Swift a lot back when everything happened with Robby."

Robert Donahue had been Adriana's neighbor and close friend when her family briefly lived in Colorado. They had never dated, but she had fallen madly in love with him. When her family moved back to California, their letters dwindled, and eventually halted altogether. She saw him only once since then when she was visiting extended family still in Colorado . . . but I knew, from the way she had spoken about it, that things were now different.

I turned to her in surprise. "You listened to Taylor Swift?"

"Yep"—Adriana played with the fringed corner of my blanket—"your unromantic best friend listened to Tay Tay. I wore her third CD out with the number of times I played it."

"And it helped you, too?"

"Yes . . . it helped."

" 'White Horse' is my go-to song."

"I thought *that's what it was,*" Adriana said, pointing to the CD player. "That's a good one."

"It is." I paused. "And . . . it's inspired me to write some songs of my own."

"And that has helped, too?"

"Yes, a lot. But I still . . ."

"I know, Rebecca. But writing is you. I think it helps to get it out—whether by writing your own songs or listening to songs from others that resonate with you."

I had never heard Adriana this quiet, this serious, before.

"I've been listening to 'Forever and Always' a lot lately, too."

"Okay, good. That reassures me a bit."

"Why?"

"Because it shows me that you're angry, too, and not just sad." Adriana sighed. "Sometimes I worry about you. I would be so angry in your place after what he did. For you, I am angry."

"I just . . . I still miss him so much. With all my heart." My voice broke.

"I know." Adriana put a hand on my shoulder. "But I also have a couple of choice words for that man that I won't say since I just went to Confession."

"He . . . has some good qualities."

Adriana shook her head. "I worry about you sometimes, you and your forgiving heart. Dude, he broke up with you at the worst possible moment in your life because you wouldn't sleep with him. Is that not correct?"

"Yes. Yes, he did. And I won't make any excuses for him—nor would I get back together with him if he changed his mind. But, Adri, I'm not . . . I'm not even capable of hating him. I just can't. I couldn't, even if I tried . . . and I suppose that's a good thing, but it makes it hurt even more. I still miss him so, so much. I still care for him. I still need him . . . love him. I still—"

Adriana rushed forward, hugging me tightly as I sobbed into her shoulder.

And guitar, piano, and cello raised themselves upward, soared in the lament of a lost love. In echoes of a heart that used to laugh freely, smile without shadow, speak without the broken mask of sorrow.

I had told Adriana, long ago, that one day the broken pieces would become a beautiful mosaic.

One day.

But not today.

Chapter 16: Rhodolite Garnet

"Once again, I would like to repeat, I haven't ridden a bike since I was *twelve*." I laughed, walking with Peter alongside our two-wheel vehicles. "And now I feel like I'm twelve again. It's a *refreshing* sort of feeling."

Peter smiled. "I used to always as a boy. And now—I still do from time to time. Especially when I need to think. I ride to Lake Louise. Though sometimes I walk . . ."

"Peter," I said, pausing, reaching to hold the handlebar with one hand. "Why didn't you tell me about The Professor?"

Peter remained silent, his face unreadable.

"I mean, you mentioned him, of course, as a family friend, but almost in passing. And it's clear that he's your best friend—like Adriana is to me, I mean," I quickly added, remembering who else he had named as such a few years before, "—much moreso than those school friends you mentioned, the guys your age. So . . . I don't understand. Not completely. You know about Adriana and—and the swing set that Dad built in our backyard, and the way—even before you met him—the way Alexander's laugh sounded. I guess it just seems like . . . you kept the most important details—well, not all, but some of them—to yourself. It's not—not a criticism," I rushed on, flushed. "I enjoy a buried treasure, a puzzle. But I"—I looked up—"don't understand."

"You are a writer," he began, by way of explanation.

"As are you," I interjected, as if saying so were important, but Peter only smiled.

"You thrive on description, on imagining. It's a journey of its own. Perhaps . . . perhaps I felt that, if I described it well enough, you wouldn't have wanted, have needed, to come . . . as much."

"Perhaps, if you had described it half as well as it is, I would have wanted to come even more," I whispered.

Peter glanced down, smiling almost awkwardly—awkward for him. "I feel odd, almost villainous, saying this, like I lured you here under false pretenses."

"I'm glad I'm here," I blurted out.

Peter looked up, and a trace of eagerness, almost boyish, crossed his face before quietly retreating.

"You are, Rebecca?"

"More than anything," I said.

3:34 AM

I laid flowers on . . .

"Hey." *Adriana walked up from behind and sat next to me. "How are you?"*

It was the quietest I had ever heard Adriana, even moreso than the day of "White Horse."

"People keep asking me that"—I paused—"and I don't know how to answer. Not just because my emotions fluctuate—from bad to okay to worse to somehow able to laugh—but because I don't know exactly how I am.

"But I'm better than before."

"Two weeks ago, you said that you hadn't accepted her death yet," Adriana said softly.

It was a question more than a comment.

"Part of me has now. But part of me—and I think a deeper part of me—still hasn't. It's not like those movies where the person can't cry until they've accepted the reality of a person's death. Maybe I didn't cry right when I heard the news, but I cried plenty soon after, even sobbed. Even when I hadn't accepted it. I've screamed deep inside my heart even though no one could hear. And you saw me at the rosary and funeral . . . and the burial."

Adriana nodded, her eyes filled.

"And that's why it's so hard to answer that question I keep being asked. I'm better now. But I have a feeling that, to completely heal, I'm going to have to go from better, from okay, to worse. There's a moment—or maybe a series of moments—that I haven't reached yet. The real acceptance. The passage of time that shows me that, after having her be a part of her life for all of mine, she is no longer here on Earth the way she was before. Not on the other line of a phone or in the kitchen at the house to greet me. And I don't know when that moment—or series of moments—is going to come,

but I'm scared. I don't know if I'll scream or fall to the ground and sob—sob so long I will lose the capacity for further tears, yet find it again. All I know is that I'm not there yet, and it's terrifying."

"I laid flowers on her tomb," I said, my voice breaking, "and this should be a movie, not my life."

1 AM

Oh, sing the song of the maiden of the sea.

Her song embraces past and present.

As her feet step lightly in the dance of wave and sand, clothed in flowing garments of dosinia and conch, marginella white, but brighter still, her heart a treasure of abalone hue.

There is a song of yesterday contained in the wisps of ocean breeze.

I walked by the sea.

"What's the most romantic thing I've ever told you?" I walked into the dining room, my eyes just barely registering the basket of cranberry orange scones with the delight of childhood vacation nostalgia when I realized the implications of what I had just said.

Peter, a tray of freshly baked scones in one hand, was walking toward the table when he came to an abrupt halt, one foot catching on a fallen dishcloth, causing him to nearly tumble to the floor.

I quickly helped him with the scones, a hint of a smile playing at the corner of my lips despite myself.

"You know, for someone who claims to be a klutz, this is the first time I've seen any evidence of it in all the years I've known you."

"Evidently you have not had occasion enough to see it."

I cleared my throat. "I . . . that did not come out as I intended. The, um, earlier comment, I mean."

"Yes, that was a . . . curious remark." He didn't quite meet my eyes.

"I didn't mean 'romantic' as in love stories. I meant it in a broader sense." I paused. "As in, a poetic outlook. Notions of . . . yearning for an earlier time, and reveling in that world. Looking at our own world—and everyday circumstances—with that sort of starry-eyed wonder."

"Ah, I see." Peter seemed to visibly relax, casually taking a scone and beginning to eat it as he guided me to the table. "That is a difficult question, as you have said many things that would fit that description. Let me think . . ."

I bit into my own scone, delighting in the perfect combination of flavors.

"I would have to say"—a grin of his own slipped across his face—"the time you messaged me at 3 AM just to say . . . let me see if I can recall the exact words: Moon-kissed balconies and seaside bridges are life itself."

I laughed. "I remember that."

"I believe it was followed"—Peter's eyes met mine with affectionate humor—"by the assertion that your ultimate life goal was to one day recite Sonnet 116 on a balcony."

I grinned, dabbing at my mouth with a napkin. "Obviously."

Peter shook his head, still smiling.

"You know—" I paused, trying to decide whether I would reveal what I was about to say. "This is going to sound crazy, but . . . want to hear what I dreamed of doing as a teen? And . . . maybe still do?"

"Living in a lighthouse, of course."

"Besides that!"

"Living in a castle."

"Besides THAT."

We both laughed.

"Tell me then," Peter said.

"Promise you won't laugh?"

"Of course not."

"It may appear very silly."

"Rebecca."

"Okay, fine." I cleared my throat. "I had this grand plan to walk dramatically by the sea in white, flowing garments."

I glanced at Peter sideways. "I don't think I've ever told anyone that before for some reason, except maybe Adri."

"Is there more to that, or is that it?"

"That's it. But it sounded like fun anyway."

"Just arbitrarily walking around like that?"

"Being dramatic and romantic. Yes."

I paused. "Are you laughing at me, Peter Joseph Asturian?! You promised—"

"No! I am not!"

"Okay, good." I finally looked up at Peter.

Peter shook his head, smiling. "You really are something."

The distant stars played battleship
With the light behind her eyes

A glimpse of another world
It never left her countenance
But the mirror never reflected
All this that could be seen
She was just her to herself,
Just that, and nothing more.

She loved them so, each one of them
Until—no, still, but that's hardly fair
Friend or lost hero
Just the same
She could not leave
This history.

And she took every compliment
Kept it deep within her heart
It meant more to her than
They would ever know
If she half-believed them, she never felt
Equal to the words spun of glass.

She was a doll
Of porcelain and not real at all
For why else would they
Throw her away?
Like a plaything of yesterday
One by one
They tossed her afar
"We don't need you, silly girl
I've grown up now, don't you see?
The ground where you lay
Shattered on the ground
Was too far for my eyes to roam
So I bid you good day.
The ground where you lay

Shattered on the ground
Was too far
For my eyes to roam
And I can't see a doll
A porcelain doll
No, I can't see the tears
From a shattered make-believe
On the ground below,
Below my new world."

CHORUS – add in later – *Rebecca Notes*

She had no reason
To believe that anyone would stay
But she refused to let her memories
Rule the path ahead
And so she chose to believe
The word of a trusted friend
The touch of his loving heart
And then she knew
In spite of all
She knew:

CHORUS- modified

She chose to love
And that was it
All along.

I put down my pen, filing away the song for the protagonist of a future story. For a moment, I attempted to begin writing her tale, but, as I sat there, nothing came to me, much as it had not for the past several months.

And, so, I simply contented myself with the song. *For now.*

Chapter 17: Tiger's Eye (or Pietersite)

"So, do you have news?" I leaned forward in front of the laptop in the room designated as Peter's office.

Jeffrey had requested a video conference in his latest email, and we had scheduled it for today. I wondered if he had found any new information in his research of the images on the badge Yin had given me. I had, of course, initially planned to join him in his research, but had found myself otherwise occupied.

"Well"—Jeffrey's face, framed in long waves of hair, appeared in full from the screen—"nothing new in the online research department, but I called this conference because I have something of vital importance to show you."

"Oh?" I leaned forward.

"Yes. Just one moment."

Jeffrey's face disappeared, and, in its place, appeared a YouTube video screen, the "play" button freezing the video in place for only an instant until unseen hands from the American side of the Internet sprung it into action.

A large, brown grizzly bear climbed down the stairs to a swimming pool, and, with a great big splash, jumped into the pool. He shook the water off of him, and I laughed as he latched onto a kickboard.

The bear climbed out of the swimming pool, shook himself off again, and then went back in for some more fun, this time landing right near the kickboard, his paws grasping it like the hands of any human swimmer. He swam around in the pool, still attached to his new favorite board, as the video came to an end.

Jeffrey's face reemerged like The Man Behind the Screen in *The Wizard of Oz*.

"Wow," I managed, a grin once again forming at the corner of my lips. "Truly of vital importance."

"Pretty chill, am I right?" Jeffrey leaned on one hand casually. "After your email about the grizzlies you saw on the gondola, I thought you should keep your eyes open for bears in swimming pools."

I laughed. "Thanks, Jeffrey. I'll have to keep that in mind. In fact, the Asturians have their own swimming pool. This could legit be a thing."

"That's cool. You guys go for a swim in it yet? Or is the weather too chilly out there in Banff?"

"It's pretty moderate, actually, in the summers. Usually just a little cooler than California with some intermittent chilly moments due to the proximity of the mountains. But," I hesitated, "I haven't seen anyone use the pool."

I paused, considering whether to tell Jeffrey the reason I suspected, then decided against it. *It wasn't my story to tell, and I felt fiercely defensive about keeping Peter's secret.*

"Well, hey, maybe later on, you can go in for a swim."

"Yeah, maybe." I suddenly became absorbed in my own thoughts.

"Good, good."

"Hey, your hair is getting long again," I finally supplied with a smile.

"Yep, thought I'd let it grow out again. Full-on caveman look. You dig?"

I smiled. "It reminds me of the old bookstore days." I turned away briefly as my smile faded, but he didn't appear to notice.

"Speaking of which . . . listen, girlie, I have work in a few, so I have to go. But I'll let you know if I uncover anything else in my research."

"Thanks, Jeffrey. I really appreciate it."

"See ya, Rebecca."

"Later, Jeffrey."

I closed the laptop just as Peter emerged in the doorway.

I waved him in, and he approached with a small smile. "I was just talking with Jeffrey." I stood up from my chair and walked toward him, meeting at the halfway point. "He was showing me a video of a grizzly bear in a swimming pool." I arched my eyebrow with a grin. "Pretty funny stuff."

"Sounds like it."

I hesitated, and then finally plunged on. "Peter, have you used your swimming pool at all this summer?"

"No, I have not." Peter's voice remained calm, but he seemed to visibly stiffen.

I should have taken that as a sign to discontinue that line of questioning.

"Don't you think you might like to?" I asked softly.

Peter opened his mouth, as if to say something, and then shut it just as quickly as his mother's voice called out from the kitchen.

"I have to go, Rebecca." His voice was distant as he turned on his heel and left.

I had heard "distant" before, heard it in the few conversations that had followed the day I wore the yellow dress.

"Distant" scared me.

I knew that Peter's distance was different, far removed and completely disconnected from the type of dehumanization that I had experienced in that instance.

But, in the subconscious portion of my brain, "distant" still made my heart beat faster, still stole my breath for at least ten seconds, still *scared* me in spite of the logical reasoning that I could throw back at it.

I returned to the office room, and sank into the chair, gazing ahead.

Then I grabbed a yellow sticky note from the small notepad lying in wait by the nearest computer, and began to write. When I finished, I folded it in half, wrote "Peter" on the outside, and left the room as I heard the sound of conversation fading from a distance to finally disappear in the direction of Peter's room.

Olivia Asturian's figure could be seen retreating to the kitchen as I peered from the doorway.

I walked down the hall, my heart still beating furiously, and stopped when I reached Peter's door.

I hesitated, wondering whether to knock, and then decided against it, kneeling beside the door, the note in one hand.

I slipped it under his door.

> Peter,
>> I'm so sorry. It wasn't my place. I know how difficult everything has been with Little Dan. And . . . everything. I had no right to push you.
>> Please, don't be angry with me?
>> Rebecca

I waited, holding my breath for what felt like several minutes. Then . . .

> Rebecca,
>> I'm not angry with you, and never was.
>> You were right.
>> Meet me at the backyard swimming pool tomorrow morning at 11:30?
>> Peter

Chapter 18: Larimar

Murmurs of a sifting breeze tiptoed across the backyard as I walked toward the swimming pool. I was wearing a modest, black one-piece bathing suit, but still remained keenly aware of the fact that it showed more of me than on any other occasion I had spent with Peter.

This did not, of course, matter, I reasoned. After all, I had participated in the swimming unit in high school P.E. freshman year, and, generally speaking, the recommended attire was not a T-shirt and jeans. For Peter especially, this would be routine; he was, after all, the swim team captain back in *his* high school days and thereby accustomed to the apparel of his teammates. There was nothing extraordinary or unusual about the circumstances of today.

I cleared my throat, and approached the pool, leaving the last few feet behind.

Peter's eyes were closed, seemingly undisturbed by the existence of his surroundings, lightly treading water close to the side of the pool, as if he were leaning slightly against it. A dark blue T-shirt was neatly (for boy-folding) folded (or thrown, if Peter-thrown) across the nearest lawn chair (which, again, didn't matter because of #HighSchoolP.E.). I wondered briefly how long he had been there, whether he had arrived on time, or gotten there early for reasons not difficult to discern. As I reached the side of the pool, he opened his eyes.

"Hey," I said.

"Hey." Peter looked up at me.

I sat down on the side of the pool, using the pressure of its solidity to pull myself into the pool. I entered with a small splash.

"This is the first time I have been in a pool since Little Dan's injury," Peter said, narrowly avoiding my gaze as he looked ahead. His eyes flickered toward me. "Swimming reminded me of my selfishness. Of the reason why Dan—"

"No, Peter," I said.

Peter gestured ahead, half a smile playing at the corner of his lips. "When I was treading water a few moments ago, it felt . . . natural again. I hoped . . ." His voice trailed off, and I was startled at the near-quake in his voice. In my calm, collected friend.

"So, let it be so."

Peter turned back to me with a wry grin. "I thought I should wait until you arrived before swimming for the . . . first time again. Since it was your note that brought us here, it seemed fitting."

Note. Brought us here. For an instant, I was lost in the Intermission of another time.

"I am honored."

Peter looked ahead, carefully averting my gaze again. "I half expected it to be pink and sparkly. But it . . . suits you."

I knew that Peter would never clarify that he was talking about my bathing suit, just as I knew I would never ask.

"Well, my fairy godmother was out of town," I joked lamely.

There was a pause, and, all at once, we knew—both Peter and I—that it was time.

Peter nodded at me once. "Well."

"You can do this, Peter," I said softly.

And, in one fluid movement, he was off.

I had watched the swimming section of the Olympics before, the grace and elegance of form and movement. But this was . . . more. *Effortless.* Real. I watched Peter, marveling as he spun in the water, hand over hand, barely making a splash. On and on, a falcon of the water with wings spread. Gliding, falling—but never fallen— fuller, deeper, his body below the surface, yet reaching out, ahead, and within.

This was Peter. And I suddenly realized how *wrong* it had been for him to stop.

After a few more laps, he swam back to me. He treaded water, his face flushed with the best kind of exertion, his eyes alight.

"Peter," I said breathlessly, as if I had been the one swimming. "That was . . . you were incredible."

We both laughed all at once—but not out of amusement—and suddenly clasped hands.

His hand was warm and firm, and I could not, for the life of me, ascertain who had moved first.

"Thank you, Rebecca," Peter said fervently, his eyes nearly filling—much like my own. "Thank you."

"You did it," I said in hushed tones. I squeezed his hand, suddenly shy, and withdrew mine (after all, it was unusual to clasp hands over the surface of water). "I'm so proud of you, Peter."

"Thank you, Rebecca."

Silence ensued, wrapping around us in quiet reflection, and then the solemn mood was broken by Peter's Grin.

"Now, let's see you make a go at it, eh?" He flashed that characteristic grin of his at me.

I groaned dramatically. "I haven't been swimming since early college . . . and, unlike you, Oh Expert Swimmer, I was always at a beginning level. Even if it was my favorite sport for twelve or so years."

"You'll be fine, Rebecca. It'll come back to you . . . like riding a bike." Peter raised an eyebrow in recollection.

I laughed. "Fine. As long as you swim at the same time instead of dissecting my flawed technique from afar. Deal?"

"Hmm." Peter paused, considering, as if deep in thought.

"Well? Do we have an accord?"

"Yes, madam, most assuredly."

I took a deep breath. "Okay, here goes . . ."

I plunged into the water, hand over hand in the traditional forward stroke, kicking in effervescent sweeps that sent ricocheting spurts of water upward and in the direction of the tranquil and composed whirlpool of Peter's expert swimming figure to the right.

I laughed, pulling up against the side of the pool as we both finished the lap round trip (Peter going more slowly than he was accustomed, I surmised, out of kindness). "I told you. Even when I was swimming all the time, the splashing from my kicks was, shall we say, *legendary*." I paused, giving up all pretense. "Or, um, just insane?"

Peter smiled, one hand also stretched out toward the side of the pool, as he leaned back next to me.

". . . like a duck," I concluded my awkward rant.

"More like a swan," Peter said.

"I've always liked swans," I said quietly.

There was a moment's silence.

I smiled, looking down. "It's probably getting close to noon. Should we . . . go eat lunch?"

Peter nodded, and we both lifted ourselves from the pool.

I grabbed a beach towel with a picture of Thor's hammer that lay across the nearest chair, draping it around me.

"I'll be just a minute. Need to grab the hose to water the plants." Peter paused. "If you don't mind waiting?"

"No, of course not. Go ahead."

Peter nodded, and moved toward the shed behind us.

I wrapped the beach towel more tightly around me, feeling the cool breeze in my wet bathing suit. I *always* got cold too easily, even for a California girl. As I did so, the right side of the towel fell down. I pulled it up, and it gleefully ran away again. Third time's the charm? *Or not.*

And then, suddenly, I felt a gentle hand on my shoulder, wrapping the towel closely around me.

I turned.

It was Peter.

"Thank you," I said softly. "That was . . . I thought you were already in the shed."

"I was at the door, but . . . you seemed to be struggling with it. So, I," Peter said, "so, I came back."

Came back.

I did not know why that simple action mattered. Peter had made a logical choice based on empirical data.

But it did. It did. And somehow I knew that I would remember that moment all my days.

I was about to break the silence with a comment on the depiction of Thor's hammer on the towel in use when Mrs. Asturian appeared, sliding the backyard door closed behind her. Her deep hazel eyes, now a shade of dark gray, took in the scene, and her hand flew to her mouth. Peter left my side and walked quickly to her, embracing her. When they moved apart, there were tears streaming down her face. Peter spoke quietly with her for a few moments before she nodded. With a quick glance in my direction, Peter went in the house.

As Olivia Asturian approached me, my heart hammered in my chest.

"You did this," she said, her elegant, feminine voice nearly shaking.

"I . . . I'm sorry, Mrs. Asturian. I didn't mean to offend you or your husband. Or Danny. I shouldn't have interfered. It was an insensitive—"

"No, Rebecca," she said gently, her voice now composed like a summer flower never tousled by the wind. "I want to thank you." She gestured to the pool chairs.

And, in an instant, we sat down.

"Before you, he wouldn't touch a pool," Olivia Asturian began, gazing ahead. "The closest he ever got was shortly after he returned from his first visit to America. I watched him from the kitchen window." She paused in recollection. "But he only dipped in his toes before recoiling and moving away as if something had burned him. My husband and I . . . we tried. We knew this . . . gave him life. But he was a prisoner of his guilt. Until today." Her eyes studied mine. "I never thought I would see Peter swim again, unless by some blessed miracle. And he did it today because of you."

Because of me.

I shook my head. "I . . . I didn't really do anything. I mean, I encouraged him, but he . . . I can't take credit."

"You can take credit for many things, Rebecca," Mrs. Asturian said.

I smiled shyly and looked down.

"Look around you, Rebecca. This is just a simple yard for simple people."

"Not simple people," I quickly interjected.

Mrs. Asturian smiled and said nothing. "Simple people take many forms. Scholars. Aristocrats. Housekeepers." She took a deep breath, closing her eyes briefly with a smile, and, more than ever before in my life, I was reminded of Anne Shirley and Emily Byrd Starr in a person other than myself. "You see this, too." She studied me. "You're a poet, Rebecca."

"Yes." My eyes swept through the backyard, roaming across every inch. "Yes, I do see it."

"Maybe that's why I've always loved this backyard," she said, sighing in a girlish way, as if younger than yesterday. "It doesn't change, and yet it grows beyond measure."

"Perhaps simplicity is just the ability to . . . to take pleasure in the eternity of the commonplace.

Even if . . . things change." I sighed. "Even if they change beyond measure." My voice faltered.

We waited in companionable silence, through the distant chatter of squirrels and small sparrows, in the light laughter of a breeze, in the quiet still that drew them all together and yet apart.

"I'm glad you're here, Rebecca." She squeezed my hand.

"Oh, so am I," I said, my voice finally breaking. "So am I."

4:27 AM

I placed a bowl and spoon on the table, and then moved to the other end on the far right side. And then bent to set the last place.

The sixth place.

The sixth seat.

It was when I laid down the last utensil that an image, a sound, flashed unbidden — and unwanted — before my eyes, and, dizziness overtaking me, I held onto the table for support.

No, there were only five places to set.

My hand shook as I moved, almost mechanically, to retrieve the last bowl and silverware. But my hand froze, suspended like a marionette in midair, before dropping to my side like the same limp toy fallen into a broken limb, as if that very action immobilized my body.

It was a routine, a skill learned as a child.

Setting a table, of all the actions in the world, held the least meaning.

The least emotion.

But the air around me had become solid, particles of wood and cement, and I could not find a word or thought transparent enough to breathe. Lungs shattered in glass particles too fragmented to find their fellow as I choked in great gasps, and then, in an instant, the wooden air burst into flames, heat suffocating the room—and what remained in me whole.

I stood, my arm still shaking, my vision a window of porcelain and silver spoons, and, in an instant, I wanted to run, seek and find the air that remnants of my mind recognized, air that surely still existed, existed somewhere.

But I instead folded a napkin, neatly moving the whole part into two halves.

A neat gesture. Ordered.

"Rebecca? Everything okay? Almost ready?"

"Yes," I said to the approaching voice, quickly picking up the next napkin from the pile. "Just miscounted."

Two names.

Screams jolted me awake again, as I tumbled to consciousness. It took me a moment to realize that the screams were my own.

A moment too late.

I heard footsteps outside my door.

"Rebecca?" Peter's voice, etched with concern, came from the other side of the door.

I threw on my robe, and cast my eyes around the room, darting desperately.

My heart beat wildly, and then, as I turned to call him away, to tell him that everything was all right, a large black shape scurried across the floor near me, and I screamed anew.

"Spider!" I yelled, my eyes widening. "I hate spiders!"

A scapegoat. Albeit through an authentic form of terror.

"May I—"

"Yes, come in!"

I grabbed a slipper and prepared for attack.

When faced with a spider, I instantly turn into a fearsome warrior, ready to take on my foe as the female version of Zorro. I enter the combat zone with all the careful observance and skill of the new movies' Sherlock Holmes. *I am ready. I am fearless. And I will be victorious.* Once, in a moment of true courage, I took a vacuum cleaner, pulled it to a position above my head, and fired. I was a champion that night. A valiant heroine whose bravery would be sung for many a moon . . . until wondering, hours later . . . IS THAT THING REALLY DEAD?!

My mind returned to the present.

The spider looked at me, and I looked back at IT, and then I leapt onto the bed with a terrified girl-scream just as Peter slipped into the room.

Arachnophobia is real, people. Make that a hashtag.

Peter's gaze flickered between my stance on the bed to the spider on the floor and then back again before he cleared his throat, took my proffered slipper, and smashed the ugly culprit with a loud clamor.

"Thanks, Peter," I said sheepishly, as he approached me, cleaning off my slipper. "Um, sorry about that."

There was another knock on the door even though it was already open, and I cringed.

"Rebecca?" Mrs. Asturian stood in the doorway in a light purple nightgown.

"Spider," Peter clarified.

"Oh." Mrs. Asturian nodded as if my ear-splitting scream had been the most natural reaction in the world. "Of course. I'll be heading back to bed then."

Clearly she hated spiders, too.

"Mrs. Asturian, I'm so—"

Olivia Asturian waved my half-expressed apology away. "Not a problem, Rebecca. Sweet dreams."

Dreams. No. I did not want any more dreams.

"You, too," I said.

When her steps retreated down the hallway, fading into the distance, Peter looked at me.

"It wasn't just the spider, was it, Rebecca?" he said softly.

I shivered. "It's cold tonight . . ."

"Not particularly." Peter's eyes searched mine, but I looked away.

"Thanks for taking care of the spider tonight, Peter," I said.

And more. More than the spider.

"It was nothing," Peter said, and, with one last glance in my direction, he made his way to the door.

"Goodnight, Rebecca," he said, turning back for an instant.

"Goodnight, Peter," I said.

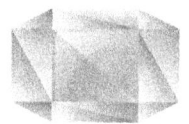

Chapter 19: Mother of Pearl

I made the Sign of the Cross, the coolness of Holy Water upon my forehead, as I entered the church with the Asturian family.

It was a cathedral of a church—not in word, but in essence—great arches reaching toward the immense heights above, as if grasping for a glimpse of the heavens before it. Stained glass windows—an assortment of colors splashed across its surface, melding together to form a heavenly work of art—filled our surroundings, reflecting the center, the heart, of where we were. The church stood in a neighboring town, and was one that Peter had said he wished to share with me.

I could see why.

I sighed at the beauty before me, glancing over at Peter, who looked back at me with understanding. Mr. and Mrs. Asturian walked forward, their posture and formal stride a flashback to the demeanor of a young usher on that fateful Ash Wednesday four and a half years before, basket in hand as he weaved in and out of the rows, capturing my attention because of the *oneness* that he held.

We followed his parents, Peter gently pushing Little Dan in his wheelchair, as we approached the middle left of the church, to the section marked "handicapped."

And yet the thought occurred to me that Little Dan was perhaps the least handicapped of all.

The bells rang from the outside of the church, and Mass began.

I gazed ahead, immersed in the Mass, and the face of a child caught my eye.

It was a newborn baby, big brown eyes blinking in the light and then finding my eyes. I smiled at her, and her entire face lit up, innocent joy spilling across her face, the very definition of "adorable." *And sweet. And perfect.*

And then I looked beside me, at Peter, who was tilting his head here and there, a smile on his face as he played "hide and seek" with a second baby from the family seated next to the newborn. The little boy's large, trusting eyes were drawn to Peter, a smile likewise bursting across his face before slipping into an insatiable giggle.

I leaned down, and squeezed Little Dan's hand.

He grasped my hand, and didn't let go.

As my eyes flickered ahead, from one child to another, and then to the right of me, falling on Peter, there was in his countenance an unreadable expression as he gazed back at Little Dan's hand in mine.

3 AM

I tossed and turned, my heart heavy in the pale glow of the night.

And then, once again, I was asleep.

"Babies are just perfect," I gushed after showing Will the famous video of quadruplets laughing in their mother's arms on the home computer. "Don't you just adore them?"

"They are cute," Will affirmed off-hand, his dark locks falling across his forehead. He paused. "I don't really have much of an opinion. I held a baby once . . . but I can't really say how I felt about it. To be honest, I can't say I felt much of anything toward the baby at the time."

"Oh! Well, it's not like—"

"But I would feel differently about my own children," he said quickly, winking.

"Oh, of course! And it's not like you've had much exposure to children, so it's natural that . . ."

I woke up, rubbing my hands against my eyes, thoughts circulating through my mind.

Strange how you don't see it until it is over.

"I'm glad you are feeling better today, honey," I said, concern etched in my voice. "Last conversation you were a little subdued. My poor, tired baby."

"Yes, our last conversation was a bit lackluster."

I froze, my brow furrowed. That wasn't quite what I had meant.

"Well, I . . . I was a bit sick, and you . . . you were tired," I babbled on lamely, fumbling through the words.

"That is true. But it wasn't like previous conversations. Conversations should always be artful, like a carefully sculpted letter," he pronounced, severely yet somehow gently, like a professor delivering instruction. "Not give way to random ramblings."

"I'll . . . try to do better next time," I said.

Until

          it

    is

      over.

Chapter 20: Obsidian

Serpents with dragon wings swooped down, leering at me with their rooster heads. I ran, screaming, as one lunged for my face, the entire world around me turning a sick hue of orange . . .

I bolted upright in my bed, my heart pounding.

Images drifted through my memory, and I collected them, their familiarity suddenly striking.

That twisted form of a dragon. I had seen it before in a fairy tale I had read as a child.

The clock read 9 AM.

I switched my laptop on and did a preliminary search.

A cockatrice.

I quickly changed from my pajamas and headed downstairs.

Peter was sitting at the table with a mug of coffee, and looked up.

"Peter," I said breathlessly, "is Professor Blackburn still in town?"

I closed the door of the car, and squinted in the afternoon sunlight.

We had taken a picture of the badge with my cell phone that morning, uploading it to Google Images to search for anything similar, and even tried an assortment of keyword searches to no avail . . . before resorting to Plan B.

It had been a twenty-one minute drive to Canmore, where Professor Blackburn was conducting research while school was not in session. Before us was a three-story building with many-eyed windows peering down at us against a gray backdrop, much like a hotel for tourists. It was, however, in actuality, a series of offices.

"The Professor's office is on the first floor," Peter said, as we entered the lobby.

The woman at the front desk, neat and trim in appearance with sparse lines of gray among her black hair, typed lightly at the keyboard before her. Small, emerald green earrings dangling from either ear were the only anomalous element in her appearance, and I found myself strangely reminded of the dichotomy of Professor Blackburn's personality.

She looked up as we approached her desk. "How may I help you?"

"We are here to see Professor Blackburn," I said, as Peter stepped next to me.

"Do you have an appointment?"

"Yes. Rebecca Veritas and Peter Asturian."

"Right this way."

We followed the secretary down a long hall, office doors on either side. A whiff of air freshener from the third door on the left wafted unbidden, funneling through my nostrils without invitation as I began to cough. But I somehow could not picture The Professor using it.

The woman knocked on a door labeled #7, and a familiar deep voice arose from the other side.

"Your 4 o'clock is here, Professor Blackburn."

"Tell them they may come in."

The woman nodded, and opened the door for us, before disappearing down the hall.

Professor Blackburn looked up from the desk, his spectacles precariously balanced on his nose before he took them off, rubbed his eyes, and returned them to their former position with a smile. "Rebecca, Peter, have a seat. It's a delight to see you. I just had a dream the other night wherein the two of you were spies, dressed to the nines, assisting me in the restoration of the monarchy under King Louis XX."

I blinked. "Wow, I'm honored that you—" My voice trailed off.

"Yes, it was fascinating. Peter kept repeating, 'Failure is not an option, failure is not an option.' Now I must say," Professor Blackburn continued without pause, "I am very curious as to your 'research.' Peter did not go into detail on the phone earlier today. I hope that I may be of service."

"Yes, that would be amazing, Professor."

"Deluxe fountain pens," he added, pointing idly to the specimen on his desk. "Collectible variety. I highly recommend."

The office, the Blackburn residence of only a few months during the summer session, already had the clear markings of a home—and, to be precise, *his* home. Piles of paper and books were scattered throughout—on the floor, on the two tables, on his desk—a deep walnut with two drawers—all in a scrambled semblance of disorganization that I suspected had some unknown order to it that only The Professor could unscramble.

It was, in effect, a kindred spirit to my own room at home.

Okay, so, maybe it just made me feel better about the messiness of my room.

Professor Blackburn followed my gaze. "I'm afraid that my ideas leap forth without much time for collecting them all in one place. Just don't trip over any artifacts."

I glanced down at a collection of paintings, mugs, and scrolls, colors both bright and subdued blinking out at me, Medieval Gothic-style drawings, illuminated manuscripts, and Romanesque Art throughout.

"I won't." I held up a hand with a smile. "And I rather like it. Neat rooms are much like one-dimensional characters—they remain static, unchanging. They lack depth. Now *this* reminds me of a dynamic character— much more personality!"

A deep chuckle came from the other side of the table, and I saw the lines of Peter's lips curve up into a smile in my peripheral vision, just as a loud commotion from above caused the Professor to leap upward.

A large box had fallen from an overhead shelf above his desk, gleefully landing with a thump on said desk, narrowly missing the head of its owner.

Professor Blackburn offered us a studied expression, his eyeglasses now balanced philosophically. "Perhaps I should attempt a more boring character. At least, for those personalities taking residence above."

Peter and I burst out laughing, and then the three of us were suddenly in hysterics.

I wiped my eyes, then looked up.

Professor Blackburn leaned forward, surveying us. "So, what is the business of the day?"

My heart began to pound as the seriousness of the topic again weighed on me. I unzipped my purse, and retrieved the badge from Yin.

I handed it to Professor Blackburn. "Are these symbols medieval?"

Professor Blackburn took the object in his hand, and his eyes suddenly clouded over as he appeared fully immersed in its study.

"Yes, yes, they are," he said finally, placing the badge in front of him on his desk. "It has been quite some time since I have seen this. I had begun to wonder if it were mere legend."

"What do you mean, Darrell?" Peter finally spoke from next to me.

"The group called themselves the Denticulatus," Professor Blackburn said gravely, "an organization that fought against the knights who followed the chivalric code under the support of the Catholic Church in the seventh century. They have often been considered a 'ghost' group, only appearing in scant records, such as a few ancient Church records and epic ballads—only a handful of short stories—from the time, though I have also traced what I believe to be evidence of them in some visual art based on descriptions of their heraldry."

"Denticulatus. That's Latin, isn't it?"

"Yes." He nodded. "It means 'indented.' In this case, the name was taken as to form the meaning 'inverse of'—the inverse of chivalric values. In effect, they were an organization that, at first, followed a system of codes and formula much like the knights, only their purpose was the opposite. They despised everything the knights stood for, from the code of chivalry to the Church itself. Their initiation ceremony was too grotesque to repeat in present company, and they even developed a system in which . . . women of the night were required to accompany a member to the meetings, not because they held any status or rights, but to prove that the members honored *their* code."

I shuddered. "That is . . . awful."

"Yes," Professor Blackburn said absentmindedly. "But indeed such is the culture that has developed today." He looked up. "If a group is adopting the traditions of this ancient medieval sect, this would be the time, if any, to do so."

"But, as you said, records on this group are hard to come by—which is probably why we haven't found anything about them by Googling their coat-of-arms," I prompted. "How would a modern group—perhaps a network of criminals, as Peter and I suspect—come across it?"

"To put it quite simply, heritage. Blood relations." Professor Blackburn's eyes focused once again on the badge, and he pointed to the background. "Orange, meaning 'worthy ambition,' an apt symbol for the Denticulatus if it weren't for the word 'worthy.' In medieval society, a family's colors would be passed down over time, displayed on their coat-of-arms and even their steeds and clothing. I have seen reference to the family of Segora in nearly all of the sources that mention or allude to the Denticulatus. In art, there is always a man depicted with a crown who wears orange and holds up the images you see on the badge here. Indeed, it would not be too far to imagine that the Denticulatus would be filled with such illusions as to consider themselves as powerful as kings."

"What do the symbols mean?" Peter asked, peering ahead at the badge at the same time that I blurted out, "Is that a cockatrice?"

Professor Blackburn smiled briefly, and then the somber expression returned. "Yes, a cockatrice, said to be hatched from a cock's egg by a toad or a snake. The latter in particular would seem to have the most significance. As you can see, it is a serpent-like beast that also appears to be a cross between a rooster and a dragon with only two legs. It is said in legend that, if a cockatrice simply *looked* at you, your life would be forfeit. It could only be killed if it were somehow tricked into looking at its own reflection."

"I remember that," I said, suddenly reflective, "in a story I read as a child. The heroine of the story was saved by such a trick."

"Indeed, cockatrices are in many of the older stories, even if less commonly known than dragons."

"And the lines here?" I asked, pointing again.

"The zigzag lines that divide the picture into four different sections signify 'fire.' Interestingly enough, the heraldic name for these lines is 'indented,' once again referring back to the group's namesake.

"The badge appears in much the same format as a medieval shield, which was divided into different sections," Professor Blackburn added. "As you can see, the cockatrice appears here and here—both on the right side of the shield, known as the 'dexter' on the top or 'chief,' as well as the bottom or 'base' on the left side or 'sinister,' and in the small circle surrounded by chains at the center or 'fesse.' On the bottom right, you can see a dark tower. A tower symbolizes society or wealth, once again pointing to the high status the Denticulatus claimed to maintain."

"And the chains on the top left and surrounding the circle in the middle?" I asked, pointing.

"A chain represents 'obligation,'" Professor Blackburn said at last. "In this case, I'm afraid such 'obligation' could only be considered servitude to a dark purpose. The Denticulatus were a group without scruples that enacted their hatred for the knights in a concrete way. They often murdered entire families of knights—or coaxed their children into taking 'colorful' potions that were more or less equivalent to the mind-altering drugs of today—and attempted to burn down churches for no reason other than hatred."

"And evil," I said.

Professor Blackburn nodded gravely, and then silence ensued as we were each left with our own thoughts.

"Yin was trying to tell me something," I said softly, finally turning to Peter as something caught in my throat. "The man from last summer, the one you . . . defended me from, The Man with the Cool Blue Eyes—"

"—the man I killed," Peter said quietly.

"He wasn't alone, was he?" I finished, my breath quickening.

Peter's eyes met mine.

"Could they be connected?" I whispered.

I turned to Professor Blackburn, who sat stoically behind his desk, his face unaltered despite the conversation that had been taking place from the other side, involving words such as "the man I killed." The thought crossed my mind that he trusted Peter unreservedly, and me by default, and required no explanation unless it was offered. And then my mind hovered above other words and thoughts, just as quickly tossing aside the one that had left it. The word that Yin had told me when I left the prison stirred once again in my consciousness, a word I had planned to look up long ago, but had been too distracted to focus on, causing it to nearly slip from my mind altogether.

"Officium," I said softly.

"Latin for 'obligation,'" Professor Blackburn said, watching me.

I fingered the badge, the chains touching my hand until I retracted it, as if from a stove that had burned me.

He should know *something*. After all this, we owed him that much.

"A woman that I . . . knew said that to me shortly before she died when she handed me this badge." I looked up at Professor Blackburn.

"Interesting choice of words. If it is connected in any way to the badge—and, by default, the Denticulatus—I would hazard a guess that this was no accident. There is more than one word in Latin that translates to 'obligation.' The legal term is 'debitum,' but 'officium' suggests a greater moral purpose, a philosophical motivation and mission. Ultimately, that would move one to an end more effectively than anything else." Professor Blackburn's eyes met mine.

"This is a lot to take in," I said finally. "But thank you for your help, Professor."

"Darrell, please." He shook my hand, and then I pulled him into a quick hug, much to his surprise. Peter followed suit.

"Wait." We were at the door when the Professor's voice carried back to us.

I turned.

"Godspeed," Professor Blackburn said.

I tossed and turned, wrapping myself more closely in my blanket and sheets . . .

4:30 AM

Tendrils of jarring orange tainted the heavens, warped into tattered remnants of distorted nebulas, the antithetical sunset thrown into macabre shadows of disarray until it became whole, but always broken, a growing mass that rushed sickeningly nearer, as I stared in horrified disbelief through the screen glass door in our living room.

Bright orange flames quickening.

Bright orange flames visible from our backyard.

Breathe.

"Dad."

He was beside me in an instant.

I looked from the view at the door—the flames of the fire like the villain from the TV screen, Beowolf's monster, imaginary now real. Like an explosive compound unexpectedly discovered by the crew of Star Trek Voyager *with the abrupt opening of the latch at* the end of the Jefferies tube, it simmered like some twisted joke of a birthday gift, a broken Christmas ribbon bleeding into a chaos that forgot its name. In short, a nightmare come to life.

The imagery that presented itself was dramatic, wild, but it was real.

Oh, it was real.

I looked at my father, his face drawn into tense lines of anguish. He glanced back at me, his face nearly unreadable now, yet I knew him and saw.

"I think we should prepare for the . . . pack things up in case. I'll tell them," he said, touching my shoulder briefly before leaving the room.

I stood, motionless yet throbbing with every bit of who I was. And then—

I grabbed my phone.

It was 11:17, and Peter had already sat with me from a distance since the report of twin fires in our community had reached him. Without being asked, he had found the fire map online, seemingly refreshing it every few minutes, even though he knew I was doing the same. It was a mixture of phone calls and Facebook messages that had lasted hours since the moment I had barely made it home before the road was closed due to evacuations stemming from the first fire. Wind had whipped around me as I closed my office door in a desert storm I had never known in Southern California, once again a movie, unreal, yet here.

"Based on what I'm seeing now, the Cedar Heights Fire is moving farther inland, and the larger fire that came later would have to jump the freeway and burn through significant shrubbery to get to you. I think you're okay."

I had breathed a sigh of relief. "Thanks, Peter. Let's call it a night."

My hands now shook as I took a photo of the backyard and typed:

Peter, I can see flames from the backyard door. Need to prepare for evac. Scared. Pray.

I clicked "Send," staring again at the translucent door, my breath quickening.
Breath 1, 2 . . .
The beep of my phone alerted me.
Peter hadn't gone to bed.

What?? That's . . . horrible. Okay, I see it now on the map. Praying right now.

I threw down the phone, blindly dashing across the house. I picked up an old paper grocery bag and ran, throwing in my old photo album, a few notebooks of my latest writing, birthday and graduation cards that couldn't be replaced . . .

I looked about wildly, dizziness overtaking me as my eyelids pulsed from the sleepless night before and the current hell that now enveloped us.

I stood, breathing heavily, my body thrown into frozen panic.

I didn't know what to bring.

I didn't know what to leave behind.

I had rehearsed the list in my mind half a dozen times before of what to bring should a disaster or emergency arise.

But that had been done from the safe comfort that it did not exist. There was nothing like living it.

My mind was a blank canvas accosted by jumbled thoughts.

And I knew nothing.

As I stared ahead, a small object on the piano caught my eye—a photograph of two.

Last year's Christmas card.

I jerked forward, gingerly grasping it, my vision blurring.

I held the photo tightly to my chest, shaking.

I had lost half of that photograph again and again in circling, relentless nightmares since it happened four months ago.

This place was my childhood, my youth, my present, my now.

My home.

If I lost it today, it would be like losing her all over again.

I stood, unable to move, hostage to everything I knew.

But a frozen figurine of ice—even a woman transformed to hail—had to run to stay alive.

I sprang into action, throwing more items into the bag, a favorite shirt, a book she *had given me on my last birthday, only dimly aware of my actions, dimly aware as I grabbed my phone at intervals of ten, then fifteen, more messages blinking into view, advice, words I tried to heed and understand, typing back in one quick, spastic movement as if life depended on speed—and did it not?—glancing at the fire map, at the flames, and—*

Adriana.

Oh, dear God. Please.

I threw the phone to my ear, then remembering I had to dial, pulled it back.

The fire was even closer to her than to me.

She picked up.

I breathed a sigh of relief.

"Rebecca! We got the evacuation call! I'm by the car—"

"Are you okay?" we both spoke at the same time, our voices a jumble of emotion and half-conceived words.

I glanced down as the phone beeped, and a text message appeared on the screen.

"A warning text. No orders yet."

"Okay, stay safe, dude. I'll . . . call you later. Have to go."

"Stay safe! Love you."

"You, too!"

I ended the call, a movement too ordinary, mechanical.

Dear God. Keep the Hanson family safe. Please protect their house . . . and ours.

I said the prayer silently, but my voice choked anyway—and then, once again, I ran.

I whirled around each room in panicked madness, looking ahead and about, my bag growing heavy.

Too heavy.

I returned to the living room, the flames burning my vision, the night sky that I knew.

The faint sound of footsteps.

I turned.

A figure with dark brown hair mixed with white stood in the hall, approaching the dining room table with a labeled file folder in hand. She wore a maroon sweater, and her eyes flitted back and forth, seemingly in search. As she drew closer, I could make out the words "Important Documents." Important. *Alex could be heard across the house, his easily recognizable footsteps a near mirror image of those of Dad in the Fourth Bedroom, also known as the Library.*

Oh!

"Your wedding dress!"

She was already in the hall and turned back.

She shook her head. "Oh, honey. The box is too big. We . . . can't bring it."

Her words sunk in as I stood, motionless, while she walked away.

I looked back at her retreating figure, tears spilling from my eyes, and ran to help Dad, who called me from a distance.

Oh, how much we could lose.

I swayed back and forth, nearly losing my balance, before jolting to awareness.

The flames loomed ahead, demanding my watch.

I covered my face.

This is my home.

"I know," Dad said from behind me. "I don't want to look anymore either."

I pulled two more filled boxes and bags to the front door.

Peter.

I took my phone, eyes drawn to the flames again like some perverse beacon that forced my attention, and wrote:

Stay.

I stared with a mixture of unexpressed sorrow and horror at the sight before me and then looked down as the phone buzzed to see Peter's response.

One word.

I held it close.

It was 6:21 AM.

I pulled myself to the living room door, my eyes having fought sleep for the past seven hours as Peter and I wrote throughout the long night.

Gray colored the blue in great clouds of smoke.

No orange.

No flames.

And I fell to the ground, choking on smoke as my eyes caressed this beautiful sight.

11:45 PM Rebecca Veritas
             Stay.

11:47 PM Peter Asturian is writing.

12:03 AM Peter Asturian
             Always.

Chapter 21: Amethyst

The soft voice of a piccolo glided through the airy expanse of a small, brightly furnished room. A tall painter, dark locks falling across her face, moved her brush fervently in a wave of inspiration—and yet her ardor seemed simultaneously as calm as the ripples of the lake that she depicted.

Olivia Asturian stood in The Poet's Room, a long white paper balanced against an easel. She looked fixedly at the canvas before her, a pensive smile coloring her cheeks.

I cleared my throat, suddenly feeling as if I were intruding on a conversation—or perhaps a sacred moment.

For, true inspiration always came from a source beyond our own reality.

Olivia turned, and smiled at me. "Come in, Rebecca."

I hesitated, and then stepped into the room. "Little Dan asked me to give you this. He was hoping to keep it here." I handed her the piece of computer paper.

Olivia looked down at the picture Little Dan had drawn, four expertly shaded figures of the family depicted against the backdrop of a blue sky and flowered garden, complete with a fish in each corner of the page, and smiled affectionately before placing it gently on top of the bookshelf. I noticed with a start that barely discernible in the background of the painting was a swimming pool. "Thank you for delivering it, Rebecca. I love seeing my son's drawings. He is still so very much . . . alive after all that happened. Too much for one his age."

"Yes," I said.

"And yet he is stronger than many think." Her gaze swept up to me. "Even my husband and I, protective as we are, are not as much as some."

Peter.

"It's . . . hard for him in a different way, I think," I said softly.

"Yes. It is. And yet I wish that somehow both of them could find a way to be whole again." She sighed, suddenly a girl again, and then looked up at me with a smile as ancient as the images in the painting she had begun. "But there has been a beginning." She returned to her previous station before the easel.

"Lake Louise," I noted, gazing at her half-finished painting. "It's beautiful."

And indeed it was, the light of the sun reflecting off of the shimmering waters seeming so real as if to touch.

"I have painted this lake so many times," Olivia said almost dreamily, absentmindedly adding a streak of green to a tree. "And yet there is always more to uncover." She turned to me. "Your visits to the lake with Peter and Little Dan brought it back to my mind."

I craned my neck to look closer at her painting, a true marvel of artistic depth. "Has it been a while since you visited Lake Louise?"

"It seems so. Of course we go from time to time since it is so close, but it seems that, with the work at the shop and other commitments, the image of this place is more vivid in distant memory." Olivia Asturian looked at me thoughtfully for a moment. "Do you paint, Rebecca?"

"Not really," I admitted, settling into one of the chairs nearby. "I painted a little in various art classes spanning throughout my academic career, but that's about it. Though . . . I did enjoy doing water colors with my mother when I was young," I said, suddenly lost in memory. "But that's a bit different."

"And drawing?"

"Sometimes I've occasionally felt drawn to sketch, but not very often and not in years."

"Why don't you take up a piece of paper and paint with me?" Olivia indicated a stack of white parchment piled on a set of drawers to her right.

"Oh, no, I am not very good at all," I stammered, "especially next to your masterpieces." I cast a wide scope around the room with one hand. "Writing really is my art form, not drawing."

"My ears look like bananas," I added.

Olivia smiled. "It does not matter what you think of your art. It just matters that you create it."

"It . . . can be therapeutic," I added almost shyly, "at least according to some psychological journals I've studied."

"It can be, and it is." Olivia moved one of the easels on the opposite side of the room and stood it next to her own. Her eyes flickered over to me, and she smiled again. "Just paint, Rebecca."

And, so, I picked up the thick paintbrush lying in wait by the paints and parchment, discounting, for some reason, the thinner brush next to it, and, after closing my eyes for a moment, began to paint.

We stood there, the strokes of the brush the only sound against the ticking of the large grandfather clock before us.

I dipped my paintbrush in pinks and purples, cleaning the bristles from time to time in a glass filled with water. I painted without thinking, simply slipping the brush across the parchment, allowing colors to spring across the painting, sometimes with distinct impressions, but, more often than not, with formless expanses, waves or thoughts, of color.

With each stroke of the brush, I felt tension released, replaced by a sense of peace.

I stepped back, minutes or hours later, and viewed my painting, a calm serenity sweeping more fully through my entire body as I was left with finality.

Olivia Asturian paused in her work to glance over at mine. She walked to stand beside me, looking up at my painting with an expression that was half studious and half poetic.

A sunset of purples, pinks, and blues swirled about the landscape, reaching the light strokes of grass—painted briefly with the thinner brush—in a way that seemed almost to envelop them. It was a simple painting, and one defined more by hue than any particularly distinct picture. Yet it was *mine*.

"It's beautiful, Rebecca," Olivia Asturian said softly, and, for a moment, she reminded me of her son.

He handed me back the notebook.

"That was . . . beautiful," he said simply.

His eyes penetrated mine, and I knew that his words were sincere. Yet I couldn't help blurting out, my face reddening with a ridiculous grin,

"Really?"

"Yes. It expresses the complicated . . . simply. And," he said softly, looking searchingly into my eyes, "I can tell that it's . . . you."

And I realized suddenly that, while it was different— very much so—the connection existed because a kindred spirit stood next to me.

"I can tell that you painted from your heart," she said. "To me, that is what makes a painting truly great. Not expertise of form, but, simply, a great thought that rises from the heart."

"Thank you," I said quietly, looking up at my painting as unspoken peace settled over me once again. "And thank you for suggesting that I paint."

"It was my pleasure," she said in the now dim light of the room, the sea of a garden behind us.

My eyes flitted open, and I reached for a pen . . .

And then, a page in my notebook caught my eye, and I laid down my pen to read what it would tell . . .

September Days

I've been going back to September Days
Seems like it's the only thing to do
Once in a while.
I won't linger, yes, I will
Can't forget you, no, I won't
And my heart's slipping away to September Days . . .

CHORUS
September Days
Oh, September Days
Endless nights
And pale feverish parades
Do you know what it's like
Waking up feeling
There's no breath in sight?
Crying the day away like no tears are left
Only to find one more falls down
Just like the past.
September Days are haunting me
Once again . . .

Strange
How in an instant
An entire future
Can disappear
Before your very eyes
It's more important
That you're happy
I let go of a dream
When it seemed the right thing to do
Yet I don't see anything
But memories piling up
My heart can protect me
But it can only block so much . . .

CHORUS
September Days
Oh, September Days
Endless nights
And pale feverish parades
Do you know what it's like
Waking up feeling
There's no breath in sight?
Crying the day away like no tears are left
Only to find one more falls down
Just like the past.
September Days are haunting me
Once again . . .

Wish I could return to summer
Winter's had its charm
Anything but September
And I might feel like I'm here again.
Every time you absentmindedly break off
A piece of glass already shattered
The fragments scatter farther
Don't you see that the distance
Couldn't piece together the seasons? [*painfully
passionate*]
I'm half a memory, faded.

[*slower, more quiet*]
I know you'd probably notice
If I died
But lately it's hard to tell.

CHORUS
September Days
Oh, September Days
Endless nights

And pale feverish parades
Do you know what it's like
Waking up feeling
There's no breath in sight?
Crying the day away like no tears are left
Only to find one more falls down
Just like the past.
September Days are haunting me
Once again . . .

I can't hate you
And being angry at you
Doesn't fit right in my world
It's an autumn leaf that glides slowly
To the ground.
But, when you're careless with my heartbreak,
My frustration is colliding
I'm drifting between time and space
I'm caught in the worst embrace
Perspiring in the blind dream
A lost page I can't erase
A fatal disease I can't cure
I'm half a memory alive.

[*light, but firm, touch of piano keys*]
But I've healed
So they say.

Maybe this song
Will help take away some of the pain . . .

[*Passionate instrumental interlude*]

I keep you tucked away in a pocket
Still wondering why I do

You're a distant melody that I can't get out of my head
But yours is the most beautiful melody
I have ever known.
[*pause*]

So, please forgive me
Oh, please forgive me
Forgive me
If September Days haunt me
Once again.

[*fading out of piano melody*]

I gazed out of the window, my eyes cast into the distance of the night. In my mind's eye, a turquoise lake filled my vision, and, for a moment, September Days lay forgotten miles away.

Until I fell asleep.

Chapter 22: Agate

"It's so very nice to find ourselves on a picnic," Little Dan observed. We were sitting by an old oak tree in the fields of a community park not too far from Banff Park. "There's something *otherworldly* about it." He turned to me, his large eyes set in that small face thoughtful. "Wouldn't you say, Rebecca?"

"I think you have it right, Danny," I said with an affectionate smile. "Perhaps it feels *otherworldly* because it reminds you of another time when people took the time for simple, joyful activities such as this. So, even if it's commonplace—"

"—it's special," Peter finished, leaning back against the red and white checkered tablecloth on which we sat, a wicker basket lying to one side. His smile turned to his younger brother. "Rebecca would call it an 'intermission.'"

I smiled, looking down, but said nothing.

"I remember," Little Dan said. "Peter told me all about your story. He read a little of it to me, too."

"Oh? And who was your favorite character?" I leaned forward to tousle his hair fondly.

"Well, I very much liked both Monet and Antonio—Morena, too—but my favorite is probably Elise. She can be silly, but in a very *good* way. I wish I knew more about The Owner, though. He never appears in the play, does he?"

Peter and I exchanged glances—and a smile.

"Oh, he's one of those mysterious background characters lurking in the shadows." I took the opportunity to tickle Little Dan gently in the ribs, and he laughed hysterically.

"Is he really that bad?" Little Dan mused, his eyes brighter from the exertion yet thoughtful at my conclusion.

"Oh, no, he is a very noble sort." I sat back on the cloth. "We just will have to have an *Intermission: Part 2* to reveal anything more about *him.*"

Little Dan smiled, and I heard a chuckle from Peter on my right.

Silence then reigned as we sat together, gazing around at our surroundings. A small blue jay perched on the branch of the tree behind us before fluttering away. Little Dan followed my eyes to the tree.

"That tree reminds me of an old man," he said, "with gnarly arms, but not a tree that is quite *human*. I think perhaps he records time moreso than many other trees. Perhaps he has a story to tell that only some may listen to."

I smiled. "Perhaps you are right. In fact, maybe I will tell you a story about this tree, but first, we

must eat more than the tangerines in this basket."
I moved forward, taking out the sandwiches that
Mrs. Asturian had packed.

"Which sandwich did your mom pack,
Danny?"

"The marmalade," Little Dan was quick to interject.
"My favorite."

"Like a little Paddington Bear." I tousled his hair
affectionately again.

"I always quite liked that bear, even more
than Winnie the Pooh. But they were both very
good sorts of bears. Not like the kind you find around
here."

"And that," Peter said with a smile once
again directed at his brother, "says more than you
may think. I rather miss the days when Paddington and
Pooh bears walked about."

"And picnics were to be had," Little Dan added.

I tossed Peter a peanut butter and jelly sandwich
and found my ham and cheese. "Now, let us feast
with our resident Paddington."

I bit into my sandwich, the flavor somehow
improved upon even more by our surroundings.
A refreshing breeze stirred the air and washed over
us without any presumption of great force. It
simply became part of the fabric of the scene
as three companions cast their eyes around them
from a great field of green.

I handed the boys some blackberries, as
well as chocolate chip cookies made by Mrs.
Asturian, when they had finished their sandwiches.

"This is the most perfect day," Little Dan sighed,
closing his eyes in contentment.

"That it is," Peter squeezed his hand, and I
reached up to take his other hand.

At that moment, from the distance, Mrs. Asturian appeared, a flowing floral skirt blowing softly in the wind as she approached us.

She bent next to Little Dan, whose eyes opened.

"I'm sorry, honey, but it's time for your doctor's appointment."

"It's all right, Mama. It's been a most splendid day, though I wish I could stay longer."

"I know, sweetie." Mrs. Asturian nodded at each of us, touching my shoulder briefly with a smile before departing. I watched as the two figures retreated, the mother pushing her son in a wheelchair, until they reached the street and were out of sight.

"Just a checkup," Peter said, and I turned to look at him. "He really dreads them, so I thought an excursion beforehand might be nice."

"You'd never know from the way he acted."

"Yeah, he's a real trooper."

"Is there any chance—"

Peter shook his head, and looked ahead. "There was too much damage. If anything, it is expected to progress further. That is what we are hoping to prevent."

Little Dan was crippled. How could it progress further than that? I did not want to consider what that might mean.

I returned my focus to the scene, my eyes lost in the distance.

After a few moments of sitting in contemplative silence, Peter rose, offering me his hand. "Shall we walk?" he asked.

"Sure." I took his hand.

At first we were simply walking across a grassy field, side by side, and then the topography of the land changed to an incline, leading in to rolling hills. Peter stepped forth first, reaching his hand down to help me should I need it, but I managed the ascent. It had been a long time since I had hiked, and so, by the time we reached the second set of hills, I was a bit out of breath.

"Rest?" I said with a small laugh.

"Of course." Peter came to a stop and moved to the side. He took a water bottle from the knapsack he had been carrying across his back. "Water?"

"Thanks!" I took the plastic water bottle from him and sipped the refreshing liquid.

"There's a lake not too far from here," Peter gestured ahead. "Rather small, but it's an interesting spot."

"I should be happy to see it," I said with a cough, and then refastened the cap of the water. "We can go now if you want."

Peter nodded and began the ascent, once again in front of me.

As I climbed higher this time, gazing from time to time at the clouds forming above, scattered across a blue sky, the stillness of the peaceful scene settled in my chest in a way not like the previous climbs of the hills as an inexplicable feeling, unnamed, rose. I shook my head as if to clear it, and yet it continued like the steady rhythm of a song.

"Almost there," Peter called back, glancing to make sure I was safely behind him, and then the connection was momentarily severed, and I focused merely on the climb. In seemingly an instant, the land dropped forward and down, revealing a small clearing. I carefully made the downward slope, heeding Peter's advice in front of me to watch my step since it could be a bit steep, and then we descended into the clearing.

It was a field of long stems of grass, a multitude of flowers throughout—mostly yellow, though a few purple and orange were scattered about them. A small lake lay toward its center, light glistening across its surface like the reflection in a mirror.

And then, just like that, *it* happened.

I saw the sun, the same sun that I saw every day, and, in an unfathomable way that can never be understood without knowing true loss, it hit me—images reeling in a haphazard, dizzying display flashing in bright colors that never seemed clear, yet were so real, a kaleidoscope dodging my resolve and refusing to retreat in the scorching summer rays ahead, tearing away at the protective lens of sanity that I had devised, as everything I had tried to keep safely contained over the past five weeks burst forth in agonizing reality.

The sun reflected it, passing through the eyes of a smiling child.

And I ran.

Like before, long ago, but so, so different.

I heard Peter's voice calling me, but the calm ripples of the dark blue lake were overhung by branches clung to by snow, and summer, all at once, was over.

There was a small cabin—a shack, really—and I ran faster until I reached it, out of air and breathing heavily, my arms wrapped around my knees as I sank to the dirt-laden floor.

A few moments, or perhaps several minutes, passed—but I had no sense of time.

"Rebecca." Peter knelt beside me, his voice filled with concern.

"The lake will turn to ice. The snow . . ." I choked out the words.

"There is no snow, Rebecca."

"You don't know." My hands were shaking.

"Then tell me."

"I can't," I whispered.

"I'm here." His voice was soft, undemanding, but ever present. "Try, Rebecca. That's all I ask."

"I can't . . . do this." My voice shook. "I don't know how. I've forgotten how to *be*."

"Be Rebecca," he said simply. "That has always been enough."

"How can I? People I thought would never leave are *gone*, Peter. They left. *By choice.* They tossed me aside like a child's plaything, and I don't know how to *be* anymore. The world is so tumbled upside down that sometimes I feel as if I don't know how to be."

"And then—after them—"

"Your grandma," Peter said gently.

"I was never prepared," I whispered. "I knew, and I was never prepared."

I felt a hand softly wrap around mine.

"When the cancer—we knew . . . only a week before they said it was Stage 4. And then it was only a month, and she . . . But, before, she was there, always. In my life. It isn't just how much I miss her and how much losing her just *hurt*; it was the reality that my world had been shaken. She had been a constant in that world for my entire life, and I had grown to expect her to stay in that world. When she passed away, part of that world was confused, scrambled, out of alignment . . . and I knew that I had to learn what a new world would become when reassembled. But the thing is, I didn't know what a world looked without her, and I . . . I still don't." A sob released, and the hand held firmer, squeezing, gently stroking mine.

I looked up at Peter, tears glistening unbeautifully in my eyes. "I'm scared. The world is so shattered that I'm scared, Peter. I know true joy and freedom and beauty, and yet it's as if I've forgotten. I'm scared I'll never be able to see it with the lightness of before." Sobs, barely treading forward a moment before, now wracked my chest uncontrollably. "I don't want to lose that, Peter. I don't."

My eyes closed, and it was then that my body, holding back that one last thread, relented, and, shaking with unexpressed grief, left me in utter surrender, as if no tear was untouched or forgotten.

And then—

It was him.

I opened my eyes, and it was him.

Peter, his eyes full, pulled me to my feet, lifting me up into his arms until I was gently cradled against his chest. I closed my eyes—but this time it was different, knowing inexplicably and unreservedly that I was safe. And yet none of these thoughts were consciously mine, only hidden at the back of my mind, for, numb from the pain, I could think of nothing. I simply allowed my limp body, broken and nearly lost, to fall against his.

He carried me to the entrance softly as if carrying something breakable, precious, and into the still lull of the quiet night, the door opened.

He carried me farther and farther, but my eyes remained shut, my head relaxed more firmly against his chest.

When I opened my eyes again, he had stopped.

The park was barely lit by the moon overhead. I had not realized so much time had passed in our conversation, not realized that so much time had passed in my tears. It had seemed so short, and yet it must have been hours. The tree was still there, its silhouette stark against the sky, its breath held in a mere whisper of night air drawn forth, its form strong and sure, and somehow, somehow, waiting.

And beside the slides and the monkey bars of youth, the eternity of the swing lay like a forgotten child.

Then I understood that the dark evergreen tree was not waiting for me, but only for *it*.

And there he lifted me into the swing of yesterday and tomorrow, drawing it back and forth, back and forth, cradling my limp body as he gently rocked the swing, tears now streaming forth fully and free as the cool night air caressed me, sobs untethered and no longer restrained wracking, overtaking, my body as he held the swing and me for what seemed—and may have been—hours, and somewhere, in that moment, I found the healing balm of swaying trees softly stirring.

And it was the beginning.

Part 2

Chapter 23: Opal

"I will have to learn what a new world will become when reassembled. When I discover it—"

"You won't be alone," Peter said.

It was 2 PM the next day, and we were sitting outside on the patio, sipping lemonade as if the shadows had all but retreated.

And maybe they hadn't completely, but I had never, in the past year, felt so free.

It was the first time in an eternity that I felt alive.

A world confused, scrambled, out of alignment.

Pain enlarges the heart, increasing its capacity to understand and care. Joy enters the heart, bathing it anew.

And yet an image passed through my mind once again, of two hands clasped, a young woman and one older sitting on a sofa.

"I . . . the last time I saw her when she . . . could still . . . when she wasn't completely bedridden. When she wasn't so weak." I closed my eyes. "It was such a simple visit, a simple moment . . ."

Peter nodded encouragingly.

"—and we were sitting there, just the two of us. Grandma had one of her shows on, one of those British ones she liked to watch, and she was explaining this or that to me since I hadn't watched it before . . . and also just *sitting* there with me. At this point, we . . . we knew how things could go, we knew how sick she was, but it wasn't . . . I mean, it's never a sure thing, but . . ."

"It's okay, Rebecca," Peter said softly. "You don't have to. I understand."

I nodded. "At some point, I took her hand, and we just held hands there for a while. Grandpa was sitting there then, and he *saw* it. Not just saw it with his eyes, but really *saw* it, I think, the significance of it all. And the love we both . . ." I broke off, taking a deep breath. "I'll treasure that day with all my heart, just as I will never forget the last day I held her hand—as much as it kills me—for the rest of my life. But mostly, mostly, I wish I could . . . hold her hand again." I cast my eyes downward, as Peter waited in silence.

I finally looked up, managing a small smile. "I suppose . . . there will be more crying fits, and sobbing fits. And you were there for the first . . . real one."

"I want to be there for all your crying, or sobbing, fits," Peter said, as the blossoms of tree branches softly danced, mingling reassuringly in the wind.

She looked out into the yard, and her emptiness was filled with recollection. Girlish laughs of yesterday sifted through her gaze, as if the yard kept it for her, held it in worn pages of trunk and leaf through soft gales of wind gently commanding the landscape. She called the names of each, companions of her childhood, in her mind, tears flowing freely as she yearned for all of them together again as one. They had a name for themselves, once, when all was free and unburdened, effortless, but very real. She cried for all they had been, for the end of childhood and youth, for a loved one in heaven, and others who still traversed the earth, dear to her heart, but never to be the same again in reality.

Her eye took in a small bird—was it a sparrow?—and another, of not much greater height or width. And then, with a start, it was as if all were alive again, the birds a time capsule bringing in their vitality what once was—five girls, distinctive yet one in their friendship, their love for one another, dandelions—blow and make a wish—scattering fragments of billowy white through tracks of smiling children, running without constraint, Christmas and Santa gifts, hot chocolate dollar bills and pirate voices singing, meaningful conversation and random fun, a child's party with friends transitioning to a smiling woman with spectacles and soft gray-white hair passing out muffins and bagels.

It was a silent sob, the purest and most full pain as the trueness of the scene unfolded. But soon it was as if she closed her eyes and rocked back and forth, a smile filling her heart as the tears continued *to flow in that landscape of memory. And then she walked to view the yard in another room, and the clouds parted, revealing a large sliver of golden light breaking the clouds in such splendor and glory as only the Greatest Painter could create. And in it she found a stillness and peace, a beauty that gently wrapped up the unraveled ends and lost questions and unresolved threads of life's journey.*

In it, she found the entirety, the end, the beginning, and the moments in between, the essence of all she was and had ever been, and all the world was and had ever been.

And so, she picked up a pen and wrote it all down to the boy that she loved, who understood and loved what she understood and loved.

I put down my pen, and gazed silently out the window, as the soft staccato of footsteps drew near.

I turned.

Peter stood behind my chair, a ghost of a smile upon his face.

Peter. Naturally.

"May I read it?"

He stood close, but at a slight distance. I knew that it was out of respect.

His eyes became soft as they approached mine, taking in my hesitation.

"If you're not ready, it's okay," he added gently.

If you're *not ready. Not "if* it's *not ready." For some reason, his choice of words made a difference.*

No, I was not ready.

I handed him my notebook.

"It's really not that good," I said quickly. "I mean, I'm not the best writer anyway, but it's not the best . . . of my worst. Well, I mean . . . it's not exactly the worst of my best either, but . . ."

I let my words trail off. Once again, I was rambling.

He had not yet opened the notebook and was simply smiling into its cover.

"Which is why it's attached to the front cover . . . almost" —*his smile broke into a grin*—*"as if for inspiration." His hand moved to open the notebook.*

He had caught me red-handed.

"Well, I do like to look at it sometimes before writing," I mumbled.

A small smile played at the corner of his lips. But it was soon replaced by a more serious expression as his eyes concentrated on the notebook before him.

"Poetry," he commented.

"You don't seem surprised."

"It was obvious," he said simply. And then I saw that he was absorbed in another world, and I knew to say no more.

I blinked, as the images of another time faded away into the present, a smile of my own dawning.

"Hey, Peter."

He didn't ask this time if he could read it. I think somehow he knew it wasn't time.

"A story or a poem?" he asked simply.

I arched an eyebrow, recalling the previous occasion. "Don't you already know?"

"Of course. A story." As I began to open my mouth in protest at his dissection, he continued with a wry grin. "The space between your eyebrows scrunches up when you are writing a story, and your eyes scurry madly to and fro. When you're writing a poem, your eyes glaze over like you're in a dreamlike trance, and then the lines under your *eyes* crease, your ears twitch, and you breathe to a metronome of eight."

"I do not! They . . . do not!"

Peter merely smiled and said nothing.

"Peter!"

"Fine. Everything except the ears and the metronome; that part was a joke."

I laughed in spite of myself. "Do you know that you can be utterly vexing at times, Mr. Precise?"

"Thank you."

"Anyway . . ." I cleared my throat, and then the sense of silly fun dissipated as I grew thoughtful.

"Okay, you're right. A story . . . I think," I said softly. "It's a reflection of sorts that . . . I think is combining with other reflections to form a story. It's about a girl who has dealt with loss—different kinds of losses than I have been experiencing lately, and others the same. For some reason, ever since yesterday, it's been like the dam has broken. I just keep writing and writing. I had been writing songs lately, but barely any stories. But now . . . I am again."

Peter smiled, briefly touching my shoulder before retreating. "Then I will leave you to it."

I stared at the ceiling above me, lost in the blankness of its creases and lines, as an image swept into my mind like so many sleepless nights before. A tall boy with glasses and dark hair drifted with it into my mind's eye, and my throat caught.

Yesterday had been the beginning. *But it was not the end.*

The stab of pain had lessened in my chest and heart, and, as I gazed aimlessly at the ceiling, as if willing for its assistance, I realized that even the ache was less pronounced than it had been a year, six months, or five days ago.

Yet there remained in the distance a melody, hauntingly beautiful—soft yet clear—that lingered like lost archives of the past.

And what scared me the most—even though I knew it was for the best—was that one day I would have to let go of that melody.

With a pang in my heart, I realized that the melody had already begun to fade, and I clung desperately to it, holding it close, willing it to not escape me.

Please. Don't go, sweet melody. You are so beautiful. You were . . . you were my life. For a time, you were my life.

Tears surfaced in my eyes, and, like so many nights before, spilled down my cheeks.

The boy turned to me in my dreams of awakening, and his eyes were vulnerable, like a child who had been broken too many times. In that moment, I thought of Yin and the jail, and the words I had offered. And, in that moment, three words appeared in my mind and in my heart, softly stirring throughout my entire being, penetrating my defenses engraved in the past to capture the essence of all that I was and might be. I knew their truth, even as I heard them fade into the quiet, even though I knew that this too was a start, and not the end, that the words would have to be reinitiated like the renewal of a contract again and again before they were finally complete.

But the words, the words existed.

"I forgive you," I whispered to the ceiling, and the boy far beyond who had captured my heart, then betrayed it. "Oh, I forgive you."

Thorn

Lyrics and Music by Rebecca Veritas

[*lower keys on piano*]

When you walked away
Did you stop to see
If I was still alive?
When you walked away
Were the words from the past week
In the back of your mind?
I remember you said
That you'd sooner wear black forever
Than lose me in your life
But a rain of cold words
Left that moment in the dark.

You haven't been a dream wanderer
For quite some time
I forgave you
Moved on
To the entrances
Of new light.
But that's not the point . . .

CHORUS
This isn't a love song
This isn't about you
It's about the moment
When I began
To feel small inside.
You're a ghost
From the past
Whose love doesn't haunt me anymore

But there's still a thorn in my heart . . . [*hold onto last note*]

As the seasons changed
There reentered another
The dearest of friends
He honored the code of chivalry
And so, with idle curiosity
As I looked through the tear-stained glass
I wondered, "Would you have thought he cared too much?"

CHORUS
This isn't a love song
This isn't about you
It's about the moment
When I began
To feel small inside.
You're a ghost
From the past
Whose love doesn't haunt me anymore
But there's still a thorn in my heart.

[*instrumental; faster pace*]
I pulled the thorn from my heart
It's almost all the way out
I'm not small at all
I'm not small, no, no . . .
I'm a little flower
That will shine so bright
Over every empty and callous word
I'm a little flower [*hold onto last note; intense*]
[*quieter*] And a thorn won't hold anymore.

[*pick-up of instrumental speed*]

This isn't a love song
This isn't about you
It's about the moment
When I began
To feel small inside.
This isn't a love song
This isn't about you
It's about the moment
When I began
To feel small inside.
When a thorn was placed
In my heart
But it won't hold anymore.

Long ago, before the thorn
Someone said, "I love you."
I wonder when I will hear it again . . .

I forgive you
I forgive you
Oh, I forgive you
Tonight.

    I put down my pen, only to take it up again. A partial chorus remained:

CHORUS 2
This is a love song
But it isn't about you
It's about the time
I began to feel alive again . . .

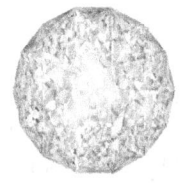

Chapter 24: Jade

I walked beside Peter, pushing Little Dan's wheelchair as the sound of drums on Banff Avenue reached my ears, filling me with excitement.

It was July 1.

Canada Day.

"Did you enjoy the pancakes?" I bent down to Little Dan with a smile once we were stationary.

Each year on Canada Day, the Lake Louise Fire Department hosted a pancake breakfast. We had therefore started the day at Lake Louise in Banff National Park before heading back to the town of Banff itself for the parade at 11:30 AM. It had been the perfect start to the day, especially for any pancake aficionado.

"Yes!" Little Dan grinned back. "Not quite as good as Mama's, but . . ."

"They hit the spot?"

"Oh, yes."

Olivia Asturian looked back from next to her husband. "They were very good. No comparison necessary."

"I have to agree with Danny, having tasted yours, but I did love that stack of blueberry pancakes drenched in honey," I sighed in satisfaction.

Peter smiled from next to me, and then I took in the sight before me.

Men clad in the red and black uniform of a Mountie rode upon dark steeds. They wore light brown cowboy hats, and some proudly held up the Canadian flag, a flag divided into three sections—red, white and then red again, with a red maple leaf depicted across the middle white section. Other Mounties marched before them, ebony-dipped caps with a golden crown displayed on the right side replacing the Western-themed hats much like the plaid skirts substituted for dark pants. They held drums, black as night before reaching a bottom of shining silver. Capital white letters, unreadable from my position, were imprinted across the top of one side of each drum, leading down to the badge of the Royal Canadian Mounted Police. I had previously viewed the badge in television series and websites from that country, and so, its markings were vaguely familiar to me. Green-yellow maple leaves surrounded the image of a bison—which was itself further enclosed by the words *Maintiens le droit* in a circular insert filled in with blue. A crown marked the very top of the badge—red, gold, and white, with tiny jewels of sapphire, emerald, and ruby at the base of the royal symbol.

"St. Edward's Crown," Peter said, following my gaze. "The bison causes us to recall our earlier connection to the buffalo, and the Mounties' connection throughout time to the grasslands of the western prairies. Though, it is interesting to note that it is thought to have once been the depiction of a bull."

I nodded, immersed in history and time, place and culture, as I marveled at the scene.

Young women, their hair tied back in a bun, followed, wearing similar colors—a red vestment outlined in gold, with white sleeves reaching to their elbows, and a plaid skirt. More trailed behind, light brown horses mounted by older men in green with dark cowboy hats followed by a firetruck, also decked out in the national colors. Automobiles, both vintage and modern, continued to join the procession, red and white balloons streaming from above. Canadian cowgirls dressed in white with tinges of red maple leaves saluted from above snowy hats as they merrily held up poles of Canadian flags from a standing position on their horses.

I stood in a crowd lined in rows of green pine, a red brick, two-story building behind me, as the gray peaks of the Canadian Rockies extended farther still. Yet my eyes were glued to the procession.

"What is your favorite part, Rebecca?" I heard a young, excited voice from beside me.

"That's a difficult question, Danny," I considered thoughtfully. "I love it all."

"You'd better watch it," Peter teased. "You may become an honorary Canadian before you know it."

"Well, you were already knighted an honorary Californian during your last visit." I grinned back at him. "Might as well continue with that theme."

Mr. and Mrs. Asturian smiled from beside us, and I felt, in that moment, as if I were one of them, almost a part of this beautiful family.

I gazed ahead to the other side of the street, where others crowded together to watch. A clocktower stood from the top of a white structure, the Canadian flag joined by three others, including the American flag. The tall buildings, washed in a smattering of subdued colors, reminded me in their structure of another time, the feeling of a town of yesterday filling the streets and stirring my heart.

And then, as if an afterthought, my feet suddenly began to march with the beat of the drums, barely distinguishable by any save myself, and an exuberance, a *lightness*, fell across me in breathless elation that could not be repressed.

I curtsied before Little Dan, glancing over at Peter, who stood at attention from the other side, knowledge slowly filling his eyes.

"Shall we dance, Danny?"

I took his right hand, and Peter his left, and we swayed back and forth to the sound of the music, stepping from side to side yet remaining close to the base as Little Dan's hands moved with us. I glided behind his wheelchair, spinning around as Little Dan laughed gaily, and then stepped forward again, catching Peter's hand for an instant before returning it to the little boy that we both loved.

Again and again, spinning close, but without reserve, we danced with the boy in the wheelchair, and he with us, unmasked emotion filling the eyes of his parents as they watched. For a moment, I thought that Mrs. Asturian meant to join us, but instead she stood back, content to look on at the three who circled before her.

I finally came to a stop—and Peter soon beside me—my cheeks flushed with merry exertion—still holding Little Dan's hand.

Little Dan looked up at me, his eyes never more bright, and a smile like Christmas morning swept across his face. At that moment, he did not speak, nor did any of us, as the march, the procession, continued before us, ourselves participants immersed yet apart from it in our own corner of the street. For, the words that we needed were already expressed without a single utterance.

And so the dance continued without a single step.

We sat in the field of Banff Secondary High School—Peter's old school—awaiting the pyrotechnic show. Food and game booths surrounded us, and I opened the foil enclosing the BBQ sandwich I had bought at one of the concession stands.

"Rebecca?"

Little Dan looked up, a beckoning gesture, and I moved closer, allowing him to rest his small head against my shoulder. He closed his eyes and smiled in contentment. Mrs. Asturian rose to kiss his head and then sat down next to her husband. Peter remained on my right, silent, at a slight distance, yet closer than I recalled sitting next to him before.

I bit into my sandwich, and, once Little Dan opened his eyes, I handed him his, helping him with the covering so I could throw it out in a nearby trash bin. I returned, hands empty, and sat down on the grass.

"I can't wait for the fireworks," Little Dan said, staring dreamily ahead, "and the way the sky lights up." He turned to me. "Do you watch fireworks in America?"

"In fact," I said, "only a few days from now, my family will be watching the fireworks from our porch for the Fourth of July."

"Your Independence Day from the British," Little Dan recalled.

"Good memory." I touched his shoulder with a smile.

"Do you miss them?"

My smile slowly faded. "Miss who?"

Peter watched from next to me, studying me as if reading my mind and the thoughts that had automatically hurried forth. For, there were those I missed who no longer awaited me in California.

"Your family. Your parents and brother in California."

I relaxed, yet a bittersweet note filled my voice as I spoke. "I do. I love it here in Banff, but I have never been this far from home for so long. It's funny, I was just thinking about them. How crazy it is that Alexander—my brother—happened to text me the same crazy video this morning as Jeffrey did—one of hiccupping koalas. I don't know why that matters, but somehow it does. I miss . . . Alexander's craziness, my dad's smile over his spectacles—his glasses look a lot like your father's, actually—and my mom's knowing way about her whenever I need to talk." I finally allowed myself to sigh, and then composed myself with a smile before looking back at Little Dan.

Little Dan's eyes grew thoughtful, and then they lit up—in a soft, more reserved way than usual, but still illuminated as if from some bright light of an idea.

"Maybe we can celebrate both today. Your holiday and ours. So that . . . you can imagine your family here around us, too. So that we can all be together." He turned to me and then to Peter in a question.

"I think that is a fine idea," Peter said quietly.

"As do I," I murmured, sitting closer to Little Dan again, noticing as I did that Peter also grew closer, the red and white blanket soft beneath our feet.

As if on cue, the first spark flashed across the heavens, golden and silver all at once. It grew, like the flame of a candle softly rising into focus, until it shot upward in great streaks across the night sky, the sound filling the field and the crowds around us, hushed in silence. Red and white gleamed across in shimmering banners of the nation in which we sat, giving forth then to the entire spectrum of colors, blues of a multitude of shades mixing with purples and pinks, each color stepping out, together or separate, as if awarded its own performance, its own moment to shine.

The fireworks illuminated the summer night sky, bursting forth with triumphant hues, ribbons and streams of sparkling light, outward and farther still from its center, that first spark that started it all.

That first spark ignited a celebration begun long ago in a parade, but, really, many, many years before.

I sat, gazing at the fireworks before me, a vibrant yet quiet serenity filling my heart, four kindred spirits, travelers of the same road, beside me, until the last sparkling ray left the sky.

I walked down the hall, a smile of contentment from the day's events still weaving its way across my face, and, out of the corner of my eye, saw a room with a door slightly ajar.

Peter's room.

I hesitated.

Rebecca Veritas, don't let your curiosity get the better—

My hand reached for the knob, and it slowly turned.

If my room at home were to be described as a dynamic yet disordered disarray, Peter's was the opposite. Lined notebook paper was arranged neatly on a blotter, with a file system situated to the left and a symmetric stack of books organized on the right side of a wooden desk. An already-made bed with a cerulean blue coverlet was reflected in the mirror of the double-doored closet opposite it, and a simple black alarm clock with green numbering stood on a nightstand to the left of the bed.

Across the room were a dresser and five shelves. Books—textbooks and small paperbacks, as well as assorted notebooks, lined most of the shelves. Swimming trophies—half a dozen—lay haphazardly on the bottom shelf in a scattered heap, as if wished to be left unnoticed, the only disorganized part of the room. And then my eyes took in the dresser more fully.

There was a framed portrait of the Asturian family, which appeared, as I drew closer, to be about six or seven years old; Peter looked slightly younger than when I had first met him, and Little Dan considerably so in his face. Yet my eyes did not linger long on the portrait.

A leather book stood on a glass stand, as if a precious artifact on display at a museum. I knew before I leaned forward to have a better look that affixed to its surface was the print-out of "Mi concha del mar"—my favorite font Monotype Corsiva standing out clearly in its elegant swirls— that I had given to Peter so long ago after writing the poem in his honor.

In the center of the dresser, to the right of the book and its stand, was another framed photograph. My breath caught as I recognized it. It was the photo Peter had taken of me at the beach during his trip to California a year and a half before. I stood on a rocky formation that jutted into the water, offering the camera a regal stare, with one hand posed on my hip. Yet, behind the steely look, there was a smile in my eyes as I looked back at the cameraman. At Peter.

"Do you remember . . . the poem I wrote for you?"

"Aye, I should say so. I read it every Saturday."

I touched it lightly with one hand.

"So"—I moved to a more natural position—"what are you going to do with the photo?"

He put the camera back in its case before looking up, his eyes once again resting on me.

"I'll put it with the poem," he said.

And to the right of the photo sat "la concha del mar," the seashell I had found on the beach that day and given to Peter, its peach-white, creamy underside shimmering in the light.

My heart swelled.

The sound of distant, but approaching, voices snapped me out of my reverie to alertness, and I hurried from the room, the door swinging quietly to a near-close behind me.

"Rebecca?" Peter said, looking up from his dinner plate filled with roast beef.

He had spoken, or perhaps asked a question, but I had not heard.

"Some more peas?" he repeated.

I looked up.

"Yes, please," I said softly, emerging from my thoughts.

Will.

I leaned against the pillow, my chin propped up with one hand, as I stared ahead, my mind and heart lost in the silence, as that single name echoed through my thoughts like so many nights before. *That name I had loved.*

It would be simple to say that I had been in love with who I thought he was. But it wasn't that simple.

No, it was that I had loved the good I saw in him, the truest parts of him.

The man he could have been.

The man he could still be. One day.

For someone else.

My jaw shook, and I burst into tears, unrelenting and full, choking my breath yet this time a deluge that was healing like rain after a long dry spell, the pain of the year before afresh in my eyes and heart, as I sobbed—not for that boy, but for the girl who had believed in him.

And I forgave him.

Again.

And, in a way, forever.

It was a different kind of forever than I thought we would have.

But it was the most beautiful kind we could ever have.

Chapter 25: Kyanite

"Wednesday again, Wednesday again!"

I looked up from the counter at the Asturian jam shop to observe a bright green parrot, having just squawked out two words, perched on the shoulder of an elderly man. The old man was slightly stooped, and wore the white shirt of a sailor and dark pants, a conical-shaped hat balanced on his head.

Fred.

Or, to be more precise, Captain Zachariah Bainbridge.

He was like the Fred of our story, I mused, and yet Cedric seemed somehow more like that fictional creation—Fred, Cedric, and the Lighthouse Keeper all at once—and this man more one than all three.

As I stared at him unabashedly, my heart beating rapidly in excitement at this encounter that was truly four and a half years late, Captain Bainbridge stared back at me unblinkingly, eyeing me as if I were a strange sea creature who had been landlogged for too long.

"I'm . . . sorry," I managed, still wide-eyed. "I've just heard so much about you. You're . . . Captain Bainbridge, aren't you?"

The captain nodded, his eyes still unwavering. "That I am, missie. And you?"

"That I am," the parrot echoed his words back at him.

"I am Rebecca Veritas." I extended my hand and shook his, gnarly and weatherworn, but somehow still with a softness to it despite its many callouses.

"A seaworthy name," he acknowledged, tipping his hat. "And this here be Battersby. He goes where I go, rain or shine."

"Rain or shine," squawked the parrot known as Battersby.

"Nice to meet you, Battersby." I nodded cordially at the parrot.

The parrot blinked at me, for a moment taken aback at being so directly addressed.

I returned my glance to the captain, and opened my mouth to deliver a line that I had been dying to say since my first visit to the jam shop, eight jam shop visits before.

"Duku jam, I presume?"

As if on cue, Peter emerged from the back of the shop as those words left my lips. He nodded with a smile at one of his oldest—and most epically eccentric—customers just as Battersby squawked, "Duku jam, I presume."

"Captain! Battersby. Nice to see you."

"This young lady was about to get old Battersby and me some Duku."

Peter nodded solemnly. "Eight buckets of Duku coming right up."

When I had read in an email from Peter back when he was visiting California for the first time that the Captain ordered *buckets* of Duku jam—on Wednesdays—for reasons that continued to evade all, I would never have been able to anticipate the reality of it until Peter left from the back, Mr. Asturian at his side, each rolling a cart that carried four large, wine barrel-sized buckets.

"Already packed up," Peter confirmed, stopping his cart upon reaching the counter.

"Thank you." The elderly captain nodded. "This shall suit us just fine."

I finally couldn't take it anymore, the mystery of the past several years pestering me, demanding an answer.

"May I ask what the Duku jam is for?" I burst out, as Peter coughed from beside me, evidently covering a laugh. I glared at him before turning back to Captain Bainbridge.

"Having a party, we are, Battersby and me," the sea captain with the conical hat said evasively.

"I'll help you bring them out," Mr. Asturian offered, and Peter nodded as if to confirm that he would do the same. It seemed to be a weekly routine.

"Thank ye. I'm much obliged. Reckon the great spring of the great cavern of Banff itself couldn't contain these here buckets, even with the help of those man-made tunnels."

A Banff cave with a mysterious spring?

My interest was instantly piqued as my imagination excitedly overtook me.

"Banff has a *cave* with an *epic spring* and *tunnels*?!" I exclaimed.

Peter grinned from beside me, clearly pleased with my outburst. I wondered then if it was mere amusement, or if I also detected a sense of relief that I was able to give forth to enthusiastic outbursts like the Old Rebecca.

And, in that moment, I realized that I felt more *free*— that I had since that moment in the cabin and on the swings—even if pain still lingered within me, as if now a part of me.

But it was also different.

At least for today, I was myself again—the old me, and yet more different than ever before.

"The Cave & Basin National Historic Site," the parrot squawked, somehow beating his master to it this time, as we all burst into laughter—even the old seaman, a deep chuckle rising to meet ours.

I turned to Peter, my eyes alight. "*DUDE.* We. are. going. to. a. cave."

I stood in front of the entrance, the word "Cave" flashing across a glittering sign of purple that led to a dimly lit passageway. To the left, a more basic sign written on a long octagonal shape held similar words, "The Cave" written in white against a periwinkle blue background and divided by a line, beneath which was also printed "Grotte Cave." Mystery and adventure beckoned me beyond, "Ali Baba and the Forty Thieves" and every other girlish dream of fantastic lands circling in my head.

"Well," I said quietly to myself, looking ahead at the opening, " 'Open Sesame' would seem to be redundant in this case."

And then I took a step forward.

Peter had already been promised to a day with Little Dan at a local family fun center for children, and, much to his regret and Little Dan's protests, it was an event with tickets already sold out, and I could not participate. I had lamented the situation, but told them that we would have to plan a group outing soon and that this would give me the opportunity to visit the Cave & Basin National Historic Site, which had been tugging at me insistently since yesterday when "Fred" mentioned it. I had planned to visit it with Peter, but he waved away my concern and said to simply "have fun" and tell him all about it when I returned for dinner. And, so, I borrowed one of the Asturians' cars—as well as their parking pass for free parking to travel about a mile west of Banff Town before finally leaping across the great steps leading to the small museum and Banff's first national park at approximately 4:15 PM. I had chosen a later time to avoid crowds since it closed at 5 PM and was a hot tourist spot. Despite some lingering hesitation given the glorious notion of sharing this journey with another adventurer—especially Peter—part of me also wanted to embark on said journey alone.

The Lone Explorer.

And, once again, you are over-dramatizing the "adventure" of this self-guided tour through part of a museum, I reprimanded myself.

When I entered the cave, my eyes widened as I took in my surroundings.

No, Rebecca, this is an adventure, no hyperbole needed.

I walked down a narrow brick tunnel, occasionally touching the railing to ensure secure footing, lights glimmering briefly from above before dimming further as the mouth of the cave itself stood before me, awaiting my entrance. As I stepped forward, the brick sides gave way to the natural elements of the cave. Crumbly yellow and brown surrounded me from above and to the sides, until lights shone once again through near-pitch darkness.

And then—I came upon a great pool.

The whirlpool splashed into view, swirls of blue and green simmering against an outcropping of grayish-brown rock in the glow of half-light. I stared out at it in fascination and wonder, feeling as if I had entered the setting of a fairy tale and this was a magical pool, perhaps the looking glass of a unicorn or the home of an enchanted prince, ancient as time itself. A small set of steps led on the left to a closer view of the pool. I climbed upward, reaching a few reclining chairs at the top in seeming contrast with the raw nature around me, one in use by a young woman, her silhouette strangely less anachronistic than their modern convenience. And yet both faded from view as I approached.

I walked closer to the pool, gazing down into it. Soft ripples broke across the surface in a quiet melody yet more rapid than that of a lake, and I was reminded when a distinctive scent wafted upward that this was a basin-sulphur spring. Now that I was closer, I could see that the surroundings were not rocks, but simply a continuation of the yellow-brown structure of the cavern itself. And yet around the front of the spring a gray border extended that appeared to be man-made. As my eyes flickered across its surface in continued study, somehow unable to move away, I recalled my brief online research from the night before, curiosity having overtaken me, that this mysterious spring had been discovered deep within the cave in 1883 by some railroad workers and was believed to have healing powers. Unlike the Banff Upper Hot Springs, which I had not yet visited, it was not open to swimmers. The small forms of a handful of the endangered Banff snail—no more than five—were barely discernible in the light across the undulating surface.

Minutes scurried by before I moved on, still drawn to the strange, almost mystical pool, bits of stories mingling in my mind and set aside for a future writing date the longer I contemplated it.

I looked back for a mere instant, suddenly aware of a light from above. At the roof of the cave above the springs was a skylight, a blinding beacon of golden hues shining through the surface, reminiscent of a picture I had used as an Easter morning cover photo on Facebook. As I peered upward, I wondered if this hole was the one that, according to my research, Native Americans had used for a rope. The historical significance of such a simple break in the pattern of the cavern sobered me for a moment, but it was the poetic casting of light that remained with me long after I stepped away.

I continued down the tunnel, now more filled with light than the previous section, for I no longer had to squint as I walked. I was led then to a brightly lit room so distinct from my recent venture in the cave that I paused, feeling as if I had moved on to another, much more modern world. A group of three apparent tourists left as I entered a typical, yet intriguing, museum room that instantly made it difficult to believe I was still in the cave with its spring and series of tunnels. The light dimmed as the lanterns inlaid in the walls became more sparse, but it was sufficient by which to see the path ahead. I began blinking momentarily. I was greeted by a Canada 150 banner with the traditional maple leaf of the flag in white against red-orange fabric. There was a wall display with a splattering of different shapes forming animals of "Canada's National Parks" and ships with historical figures drawn in miniature against a bronze backdrop. Displays of railroads, accompanied by a statue of what I surmised was a railroad man, were visible at the front of the room near large display screens showing the treasures of the Cave and Basin. Below the screens on lower displays, historical data was written in French alongside old photographs of the time period. I examined them quietly despite the fact that I did not know the language, glancing between that and the screens above me for some time.

When I finally moved on, strolling past interactive displays of park history and local wildlife, the model of an old white automobile flashed into view. I realized then that, while I had happened on some tourists as I continued through the cave, it had been some time since I had encountered any. I stopped for a moment, and glanced at my watch.

5:25 PM.

The museum closed at 5 PM.

Great.

I hurried back down the way I had come, my heart pounding rapidly as I wished suddenly for transporter technology from *Star Trek* to expedite my exit despite the clash of time it would further impose on this series of tunnels and cave.

As I moved forward, speed-walking, my foot caught on an area of uneven ground. I fell, sprawling to the ground, with a yelp.

My knee burned, an abrasion greeting me from within the beginnings of a bruise. I quickly dismissed it with a grunt, wiping off my clothes in frustration before continuing on my way, now paying closer attention to my footing and overall surroundings.

It was several minutes before I reached the entrance, breathing heavily from the exertion, and stepped out of the tunnels.

I sighed deeply, half in frustration, half in fear, as my worst suspicions were confirmed.

The museum was closed.

"Hello?" I called out, taking in the counter from behind which a receptionist had sat earlier, the chair now vacant, as my hopes quickly sank.

I walked around aimlessly, scanning for any sign of human life, chastising myself all the while for losing track of time.

"I am still in the museum!" I finally yelled out to no one in particular.

There was no reply.

I hesitated, and then moved behind the desk to pick up the phone to call Peter and have him contact whoever was in charge of the facility, and then a small sign in front of the phone gave me pause.

Out of service.

On this day of all days, when I was *trapped in the museum*, the phone had to be unusable.

I groaned, resting my face in my hands, and then realization dawned upon me.

I *do* have a cell phone, don't I?

I reached into my purse, fumbling around for the correct shape before finally retrieving it, clicking more times than necessary as the blank screen sleepily transitioned to icons against an ocean background photo. I quickly dialed Peter's home number, impatiently waiting until a loud beep blared through my ears, stating in a distant, computerized voice, "This call cannot be completed as dialed. Please try again."

Are you kidding me?

I grimaced, and tried three more times before giving up, the words "no signal" appearing in miniature on the top of my screen before I attempted the fourth.

I ran to the front doors, glass bordered in black, and pounded on them with my fist.

I peered out, but it was too dark to see if anyone was there. After several minutes flashed by, I finally withdrew from the doors, thoughts circulating wildly in my mind before they formed a conclusion.

There had to be another way out.

I would return to the tunnels and see where they led.

I dashed through the entrance, the purple-lit sign no longer holding the same appeal for me. When I reached the tunnel, I finally slowed, remembering my minor mishap earlier when showing less awareness for my surroundings.

The second trek through the tunnels seemed much longer, even though I skipped past the exhibits and barely noticed the hot springs cavern, hurrying along as a hint of fear played at the corner of my consciousness, stumbling and then careening forward, before rushing with full force through my chest.

When I finally stopped for breath, I discovered that I had moved beyond my previous venture into the museum, whether deeper into the cave or closer to the surface, I did not know. As my eyes adjusted to the changing light, I began to step forward when an image on the wall caught my eye in a splash of orange and curved lines, causing me to freeze where I stood.

It was a replication of the badge that Yin had given me, the exact same symbols that formed the coat-of-arms of the Denticulatus painted across the surface. As my eyes scanned ahead, I found that it continued, the same set of images no larger than the span of my hand repeating in a line that led down the corridor.

My concern over my current predicament momentarily wavered as I was drawn forward by the strange set of symbols, curiosity filling me.

Why were they painted on the tunnel walls? I wondered, ignoring any side displays or deviations in the path as I simply followed the wall of repeated images.

And where does it lead?

A slight breeze wafted into the tunnels as I drew close to an exit.

I stepped out onto a boardwalk leading to a gravel and dirt trail, glancing about before quickly dismissing another boardwalk that I knew led to the cave vent.

The Marsh Loop loomed ahead, coiling and bending around the river marsh.

I remembered then that the cave was located close to the Bow River, across which Peter, Little Dan, and I had taken a boat several weeks before.

I took a deep breath, checking for cell phone service one last time to no avail before moving ahead in the approaching darkness.

Wildflowers, their distinctive colors barely visible in the waning light, surrounded me, their lightness of the day appearing in my mind suddenly sinister as I continued.

I trekked onward, an outcropping of pine trees rising around me as I ventured through the meandering trail until I reached a forest. I squinted at the sign in the dark, and could barely make out the words "Middle Springs Wildlife Corridor" and "Area Closed" in red.

Great.

I turned away from the sign and began to move in a different direction when the trees retreated slightly, giving way to a large field, and it was then that I halted.

A scattering of tents appeared ahead, at least ten or fifteen in number, if not more, a large, white banner with the words "Renaissance Faire" sweeping across. A wood cabin stood behind them, simple and much in the same design as the one I had viewed at the Whyte Museum. As I took a step closer, I heard the sound of murmuring voices, and drew backward against a series of brush and trees along the path to listen from a more secure position. The voices drifted toward me as I remained concealed, and, while I could not make out every word, nausea coiled inside of me with every passing moment as my heart beat so rapidly that I was sure it could be heard.

"The cave was a much better headquarters," a man's voice was heard. "I don't like being out in the open as much."

"Swarming with tourists now." Another voice, dry and not as deep, answered.

"It was ours by rights—"

"—and we will rise up and take it again. Our basilisk has promised us this. But we are safe here. No one expects anyone to be down here, especially at night, and no one will be using these tents until the Renaissance Faire in the spring."

There was a pause, and then some muttering that I could not make out. Then—

"Did you hear about the Asturian boy?"

I froze, my breath caught in my chest.

"The nerve of him parading down the river so close to the cave—did you see the photos?"

"Yeah, I did. I think that it's time for . . ." The sound of retreating footsteps was heard as their voices faded away in the distance.

I pressed the sidebar button of my phone, my heart pounding furiously.

Still no signal.

I said a Hail Mary silently.

Maybe, if I headed back quickly enough, they wouldn't notice. And, if I could get to a phone *somewhere* . . .

I cautiously stepped backwards, away from my present surroundings, once again paying more attention to what I was leaving than what I was going toward. When I turned my head, I collided face-on with a hooded figure.

"Nice to see you, too, though that's not the kind of welcome I was hoping for."

Jeffrey.

His eyes peered from underneath the hood, the feigned lightness betrayed by worry creases underneath.

"Jeffrey, what in the world are you doing here?!" I hissed. "You . . . we need to get out of here . . . those men . . ."

"Yeah, I know," Jeffrey sighed, plunging his hands in his pockets as a lock of his long, disheveled hair fell across one eye. "Turns out my dearly departed uncle was one of their leaders."

"*Leader* of this?!" My eyes widened, and, with increased trepidation, I glanced nervously at the small clearing from which still emanated the low rumbling of voices.

Jeffrey took my hand and drew me farther away. We stopped several feet from our previous position.

I breathed a little more easily.

Just a little.

"Yep." He finally nodded. "A criminal network known as the Denticulatus. Hence the weird, borderline-creepy-rooster-snake-dragon-thing-and-chains." He pointed to his badge. "Pretty wild stuff—lots of drug trafficking with no scruples when it comes to, um, offing people. One of the basilisks—that's what they call their leaders, the same thing as a cockatrice or those weird, borderline-creepy-rooster-snake-dragon-things—killed a new member who arrived two minutes late to a meeting, saying he could have taken those two minutes to betray him and call the police. It was pretty gruesome. They already brand members, so he took a—never mind." Jeffrey glanced at the horror rising on my face. "Anyway, when I was researching, my grandma caught on and finally told me everything. Apparently Uncle Tod was more merciful than some . . . if that says much of anything, I don't know. Anyway"—he glanced nervously about—I had never seen Jeffrey this nervous—"you know that creep Yin hired?"

I shuddered. *The Man with the Cool Blue Eyes.* I wouldn't soon forget.

"Turns out only half of his duty was to harass you via Ms. Yin. He was also sent to shadow me."

"What?!"

"He worked for the Denticulatus. Apparently I was supposed to take over for Uncle Tod when he died—it's one of the rules. Only Grandma didn't much care for the idea. That man had come over and intimidated her." Jeffrey shook his fists. "She bribed him or something, and he agreed to only *watch* me for now—but gave it a couple of months. Guess that's how he showed up in my um . . . circles.

"Anyway, they've been playing it safe since their minion croaked, probably so as to not draw any unnecessary attention to their organization. But I suspect they'll make contact again soon enough. Which is why I have decided to beat them to it and make contact first."

"Are you *insane*?!"

"Yes," Jeffrey said cheerfully. "But it's the only way to get them off your back . . . and Peter's. Peter, by default—"

"—would be held responsible for the death of The Man with the Cool Blue Eyes," I finished. "One of their valued members."

"Okay, good, Spoiler Queen. So. If I return as the long-lost nephew of their beloved former leader meant to rule them all—"

"This is serious, Jeffrey!"

"I know, I know. If I do, I may have the leverage to get them to back off."

I paused. "Wait, Jeffrey. How the heck did you find me?"

"Oh, I installed a tracking device on your phone," Jeffrey said nonchalantly. "Back in the bookstore when you were having cell phone problems."

"You did *what*?"

"Did I ever mention that I was a computer science major before I dropped out of college?"

I glared at him.

"Okay, I'm sorry. I should have asked you first. But there was always something fishy about my uncle, and I didn't trust the sitch. I thought I should have a way to keep an eye on things if needed. As it turns out, I found in my uncle's notes and map that this series of tunnels and cave lead directly to their secret headquarters. When I saw that you were probably nearing that location, I headed over."

"What, just jumped on a plane?"

Jeffrey leaned casually against a tree. "Girlie, I've been here in Alberta for the past three days. Ever since I found the map. I've been monitoring your progress from a hotel room in Banff."

"You—you are incredibly frustrating, do you know that?"

"Yep, guilty as charged. I wonder if it runs in the family." Jeffrey winced. "Actually, I'm kinda over hearing about my family just about now. Anyway, my idea—"

"—is insane and incredibly dangerous! We need to go back and call the authorities—"

"No reception last I checked."

"We could wait it out in the cave until morning. Someone would come . . ."

"Armed guards posted there." Jeffrey pointed in the direction I had planned to head. "The guard switched about five minutes ago, so that's probably why you made it this far without being seen."

"We could sneak past. Come up with a distraction. There has to be a way—"

Jeffrey held me by the shoulders. "Rebecca, I know this is scary. I'd be lying if I said I wasn't a bit freaked out myself. But you have to understand that these are *trained assassins*. They will not hesitate to shoot—"

"And they won't shoot if we approach their camp?!"

"If I approach them as friends, as allies, we may have a better shot."

"The police—"

"Look, I'm really sorry. I shouldn't have taken the chance. I wasn't too worried when the tracking device picked up your signal from the front entrance to the museum since it seemed too popular an area for much to be amiss. But, when your signal continued after closing time and you were far enough into the tunnels that I could no longer track your precise location, I decided to head over just in case to take you home. It wasn't a sure thing, so I didn't think to call the cops until later. By that time, I was on my way with only my cell on me, and no signal."

"I understand." I looked at the ground. "I'm sorry. Thank you for coming."

"No problem, girlie."

I forced a smile.

"This small space is literally the only obstructed view from the clearing. The only one. We can't even count on it for long; based on the notes my uncle left, their nightly routine is very precise, almost mechanical. They *will* monitor the entire area, including here. And there's no way out, except . . . well, you know." He sighed. "You got dragged into this, and I don't want you to get hurt if things go south." He raised a hand as I opened my mouth to protest. "Which it won't. You can wait here."

"Unlikely."

"This isn't the time to be a hero, Rebecca. You need to wait here."

"I have information you don't."

"Then tell me."

"No, I won't. I'm not staying behind. Believe me, it's tempting. I'm not as brave as you think, and I'm not some ultra-feminist who won't let a guy protect her. And it's more than the fact that I hate letting you go off by yourself—call that a contradiction if you want, but it's true—because you're my friend. It's that . . . if I figured out things correctly, you need a female companion."

"Please tell me that doesn't mean what I think it means—"

"It probably does. But it doesn't matter. I trust you."

He pulled up my hood. "Then let's make Adriana proud. Your acting debut begins now."

Jeffrey paused. "I always liked that girl." And then he drew his own hood, and took a step forward.

There are walks of pain—the pacing-around-your-house-lonesome-heartbreak kind. There are walks of joy—leaping and bold, ecstatic with good news. There are walks of new beginnings—the first steps of a child or a young woman learning to become like a child again.

And there are hornets' nests of walks that sting you with living terror.

We approached a guard in the fading light, a hooded figure tall and dark in the night, a horror movie of reality that was somehow becoming more real with every step.

Jeffrey and I held up our badges.

"Password," the man said cooly.

"Officium," I said.

"So, this is the nephew of Todrick Everett." A tall man who appeared to be in his early forties emerged from behind two guards.

I pulled my hood further down, covering half of my face, as my heart beat wildly.

An earring dangled precariously from one ear while two more erratically pierced his nose at asymmetric intervals. His eyes regarded Jeffrey with mocking shrewdness that somehow remained respectful. *For him*, I surmised.

"Yep." Jeffrey nonchalantly grabbed a piece of gum from his pocket—I had finally convinced him to stop smoking about a year ago—and promptly began to chew. I noticed that the guards—also multi-earring-infested—instantly put a hand to their holsters when Jeffrey's ventured to his pocket.

They didn't trust him yet.

I swallowed.

As if able to hear the nearly inaudible sound, Leader (?) turned, seeming to see me for the first time—which I knew could not be true. Jeffrey's confident voice drew him back.

"You know who I am. You?" Jeffrey jutted his chin in the other man's direction as if the answer hardly concerned him. "Didn't catch your name."

But I saw that his hands were shaking.

"Basilisk Ibex is my title. My given name is irrelevant," the man's deep voice was strangely more ice than velvet. "Your second-in-command, you might say. The one who's been keeping things together while you've been bumming around at the beach."

"Thanks for that, pal. Really appreciate the help. But remember also what you said." Jeffrey's eyes narrowed. "Second. You'd be wise to remember that, and who I am."

My heart beat rapidly. I wasn't sure if that was the smartest or the stupidest thing that Jeffrey had ever done.

The man laughed. "Got some backbone to you after all. Good. That should serve you well in our . . . society. And who is this?" Ibex's eyes—I could have sworn they were yellow—turned to me again as if reading my thoughts. He nodded at one of the guards, who immediately came toward me.

My heart beat more erratically.

"Oh . . ." Jeffrey's feigned "cool" was beginning to wear thin as I noted the panic sweeping across his eyes for an instant, desperately hoping I was the only one to notice.

"That's just a 'friend.' If you get my meaning." Jeffrey winked.

"Let's see for ourselves," The-Man-With-the-Yellow-But-Non-Warm-Light-Brown-Eyes (Note to self—I really needed to come up with new nicknames when panicking in dire circumstances) known as Ibex said softly. "Why not enjoy her ourselves?"

The men behind him, numbering about ten, not including the two guards, let out a harrowing laugh.

I shivered.

Gray. His name was Gray.

Hail Mary . . .

A guard stepped forward and roughly pulled down my hood.

His eyes widened in recognition, and suddenly the eerie silence broke into chaotic commotion, as I desperately wished for the disturbing quiet to return.

"That's her!" one exclaimed.

"I saw her with that Asturian brat!" the guard who had uncovered my head spat on the ground.

"That's the girl we were following!" another guard said in the most callous tone I had ever heard in my life.

Gray raised an eyebrow. "How interesting."

I swallowed hard as knives and guns appeared, as if emerging from a dark mist that, until now, had concealed reality.

Gray raised a hand. "No need. Let's talk this over reasonably." He smiled widely, revealing two empty spaces amidst a plethora of yellowed molars.

Jeffrey's face was white. As Gray turned to him, I saw his face recompose.

But what would Gray not see?

"My apologies. I did not know the connection of this—"

"Liar!" one man growled. "She's a Papist. They don't sleep around."

"If you had allowed me to finish," Jeffrey glared at the man, his old confidence returning, "I would have said that I didn't know that she was in bad standing with this association. Certainly I know how she pines after the Asturian boy. And I know all about her saccharine piety." He laughed ironically in a way that almost convinced even me. "But she trusts me. So, I brought her here to have my way with her after reclaiming my position. But, thanks to you, I probably lost my chance. Way to roll, dude."

Gray watched him carefully throughout the speech. "What a shame. I hope she reconsiders."

I overheard one of the guards whisper to the other, "What does saccharine mean?"

"I don't know, man. What's piety?"

In other circumstances, I might have smiled. But this was no movie.

And Gray was their leader. *A group of mindless wolves led by a man with the intelligence of a sci-fi villain.*

"So, where are we now?" Jeffrey's nonchalance was in full force.

"Well, it's late." Gray waved a hand dismissively. "We can discuss arrangements tomorrow. For now, you can both stay here for the night."

I wasn't sure if I was relieved or terrified.

"Sounds good, man."

Gray pointed ahead to a series of tents several feet from where we stood. "There it is. I'll send a guard with you."

During this painfully long, yet ultimately brief, exchange, nightfall had grown, casting more darkness around us. Jeffrey quickly threw me a look of reassurance through its concealing mask.

Jeffrey turned, and I followed behind him, trying fervently to stop shaking, although my pulse was racing.

We had walked only about two feet when I heard a single word uttered in Gray's calm, disconnected voice.

In a quick blur of movement, Jeffrey threw himself in front of me.

And that was when a knife was plunged through his back.

Chapter 26: Tourmaline

No. No. No.

A single word.

Jeffrey fell haphazardly to the ground, his form twisted sickly as I sank beside him, eyes burning.

I grabbed his hand. "Oh, Jeffrey."

He looked up and smiled at me weakly, a thin, painful smile—but a real one. *Oh, a real one.* "I didn't save you when I should have." For a moment, a snapshot of a movie theater emerged through the fog in my mind. "I knew those two guys were dirty, but I was desperate to belong, to be accepted." Jeffrey winced in pain. "By their crowd." A glimmer of a smile, more peaceful and lucid, surfaced. "But now . . . now I can save you."

His fingers moved slightly against the surface of my hand as his breath became more labored. "You know, Rebecca, you . . . you are my only real friend."

A sob burst forth, and suddenly I was weeping.

"There, there. It's okay, Rebecca," he said softly. "You are worth it."

And then he began to sing.

At first, I could not make out the words—they were so faint—but then a single, distinctive note arose, each subsequent note wracking my body over and over, growing more than the last with the agony of recollection.

He was singing "That's Amore."

We were in the college bookstore, laughing without restraint, living without knowing pain. Jeffrey pulled me into a dance, twirling me around and around to a symphony of lightness and air heard through the words of an old Italian song.

"When the sun hits your eyes like a bowl of lasagna."

The two times became one, shifting beyond recognition, as the teasing modification of a song lyric became the plaintive chant of a dying man.

Jeffrey smiled once more, and then his eyes closed, his hand suddenly limp.

I was still screaming as they dragged me away.

Chapter 27: Hematite

The door slammed shut in tones of brass, as one of Gray's men, tall with a cocky smile and dark blond hair, threw him roughly in and then left.

Peter.

I reached for him, nearly falling over the decayed apple cores and cigarette butts littering the floor as I stood, throwing my arms around him so tightly it hurt my wrists. He pulled me gently to the floor, my iron grip still firm as I fell against his chest, sobbing, my streaming tears staining his bright red shirt.

Tears of sweat and blood.

"Peter," I choked out. "It's Jeffrey . . . he . . ."

"I know. I saw his body as they dragged him out. I'm so, *so* sorry, Rebecca."

And then there were no more words to be said. My body shook, the sobs unrelenting, broken only by a cry more like a scream, yet silently burying my heart as we rocked back and forth on the floor, Peter reaching up to lightly stroke my hair from time to time. In each tear was Jeffrey.

In each tear was Grandma.

And in each tear was Peter.

I pulled back, my eyes searching those of Peter. "You shouldn't have come for me. You . . . how did you find me?"

"I was concerned when you were still not home so late after the closing time. So, I went to look for you. I am familiar with the trails around here, and knew how to access them from behind the museum. I assumed that you had ventured there. But it was also because of Jeffrey. When he arrived in Banff three days ago, he gave me a call. He told me to promise not to tell you since he knew you had enough on your mind, but shared with me his concerns about a local drug ring connected to his uncle." Peter paused. "That was all he said, but it was enough to quicken my pace tonight. He was worried about you, Rebecca."

The truth of his words struck my heart again in silent stabs of pain.

I closed my eyes, my jaw shaking, as I choked back more tears.

"Oh, Peter."

"I know, Rebecca. I know," he said quietly, touching my hand.

"And now what?" I said, jaw still clenched as my hands shook. "We're . . . we're . . ." My words trailed off, too horrible to utter.

We're stuck here. We're prisoners. We could die here.

"Well," Peter said with a thin smile, his voice measured, "as I see it, we have two options: The Divine Mercy Chaplet or the Rosary."

A smile settled weakly at the corner of my lips, as my back ached with renewed vigor. "You pick." I closed my eyes and leaned against his shoulder, too exhausted to care at the moment how my actions seemed.

"Well, my first thought was Divine Mercy . . . but today is Friday," Peter said, looking ahead with seeming calm. "The Sorrowful Mysteries." He glanced over at me—don't ask how I knew—and my eyelids fluttered open, as I bit down hard on my lip, forcing myself to stay awake.

"That is fitting," I said. I made the Sign of the Cross and watched him do the same. It was a prayer in and of itself, giving strength where I had none.

And he reminded me of it—of that strength.

I grabbed his hand, my frozen fingers, nails tinged with blue, enveloped in a soft blanket of warmth—like before, only more in its urgency, an echo, a reminder of comfort where little existed.

"I believe in God, the Father Almighty, Creator of Heaven and Earth."

My trembling voice joined his, steadying with each word.

"In Jesus Christ, His Son our Lord, who was conceived by the Holy Spirit, born of the Virgin Mary . . ."

The Creed swept through me, through our surroundings, warming the cold, dark room of disarray.

"Our Father who art in Heaven . . ."

"Holy Mary, Mother of God, pray for us sinners now and at the hour . . . of our death."

The words spun faster, yet remained ever still, calm as a serene blue lake.

"As it was in the beginning is now and ever shall . . ."

"The Agony in the Garden," Peter said, naming the first decade
as the night brightened
  softly
        into
    Light.

The jostling of the wooden door against its hinges startled me awake, my head snapping to attention, as I whirled quickly from my position against Peter's shoulder.

I stood, my heart beating wildly in my chest, as a man in the dark gray clothing of the Denticulatus emerged in the shadows of the room. Peter stirred beside me, but appeared to remain asleep.

I stared back at the man, my breath quickening with every heartbeat.

He has come to attack me.

I moved back against the nearest wall in helpless desperation, grabbing the sharp end of a broken coat hanger that had been lying haphazardly on the floor.

"Get out," I said shakily, yet with as much firmness as I could muster.

In a moment, Peter was in front of me, shielding my body with his own.

I breathed heavily, grasping at the back of his shirt.

"Stand back," Peter said, his voice calm but commanding.

"You misunderstand." The man held up his hands to show that he did not have a weapon. "I come in peace."

"Then why are you here?" I said, moving to stand beside Peter, still clutching the broken hanger.

"The boy. They had no right to kill him. His uncle . . . he was a good man . . . a good leader. As good as we can be anyway." The man slouched, his hands in his pockets. I considered the fact that he could have a weapon stored there, and that this was some sort of sick game to play with our minds, yet I somehow sensed that he was telling the truth, that I had no cause for concern.

"What is your name?" Peter asked, his voice now more gentle.

"Dmitri."

"And why have you come, Dmitri?"

"I want to help."

I paced back and forth, the four hours of sleep following Dmitri's visit providing a brief respite for my incessantly twitching eyes. "It could be a trap. An excuse for another bloodbath, only sooner this time than they had planned."

I did not verbalize what we both undoubtedly thought—that Gray probably planned to kill us off at one point or another anyway.

After all, he had already tried to kill me once. The image of Jeffrey's crumpled body came again to my mind's eye, and I bid it leave before I lost control. *Why had he spared my life then?*

And then the sick realization dawned upon me, that he was toying with me like a broken doll.

Peter nodded, sitting thoughtfully on the other end of the room, leaning against the wall. "It's possible. But I looked into that man's eyes . . . and saw *something*."

"He could be a good actor."

"Yes," Peter admitted.

"Why didn't he just save us then? Why the wait? It was dark after all."

"Dmitri said that they had been partying last night, celebrating our capture. It checks out; we heard quite a lot of it. He would never have been able to get us out with so many outside. We're lucky he was able to slip in to give us some food. And we'll have the advantage of them sleeping off their drink. Gray doesn't start operations and begin relocation until 8 AM—three hours before the Cave and Basin Museum opens—and he is the one most likely to question Dmitri's 'orders.' "

I turned, looking back at him. "I wish I could be as calm as you are."

I walked to sit beside him, staring ahead.

"I'm not calm, Rebecca. You know that."

I sighed heavily. "I know. That was stupid of me to say. I just . . . thought that, if I pretended there was nothing beneath that calm exterior, I could *survive*." My eyes met his. "I'm sorry."

Peter nodded, his face unreadable. "No need to apologize. Besides, I won the Contest of Tranquility back in '96."

I laughed, the feeling of it in my throat startling, foreign.

His words were so *him* that they provided some comfort.

"Rebecca," Peter said softly, "is there anything you want to talk about?"

I knew he meant something deeper, older, fuller. And yet:

"So, if we do this . . . there will be the exchange of the guard, so to speak . . . he will chat with one of them, a good friend of his, get ahold of the keys while asking him to look over one of the maintenance reports . . . slip the keys to us . . . stand guard, pretend that he is under orders to escort the prisoners if we're intercepted." I froze, caught in realization. "He's risking his life for us, Peter. I . . . I don't want another person to die for me . . . or die at all."

"Nor do I. And I hope that it does not come to that. But," Peter said, his large hazel eyes penetrating mine, "he gives his life freely."

As did Jeffrey. He left the words unspoken, but I heard them.

Silence wrapped around us, lifting a faint hush across the small room. A memory stirred within me.

"Do you remember . . . what I said outside the church a year and a half ago?" I said suddenly. "After the miracle . . . Anyway, it doesn't matter if you remember—"

"I remember," Peter said quietly.

You are dear to me. Very dear.

"I thought I'd . . . finish my book. And you," I glanced over at him, my eyes glazed. "You have so many more to teach. But still, here we are, in this moment. This moment exists, exists and somehow . . . matters."

"Hold on to it," Peter said.

And I held on tightly as my eyes closed, the room fading to the quiet of the night.

Tapestry of a Life
Lyrics and Music by Rebecca Veritas

[*Instrumental: Piano with chimes in background. Brief violin solo with piano then returning. Piano consistent for the rest of the song.*]

Fireworks dart across the sky
Colors of an American dream that two once shared
It's the first time I've felt alive
Since you were gone.

I stare at the photograph on the piano
Half the frame is empty
And it makes me want to
Scream inside.

I remember the moment that
I sat by your side
On the bed, so frail
The last time I held your hand
We were praying and
I turned away so you wouldn't see
The tears in my eyes . . .

CHORUS
Oh, I'm going to miss you
'Til the day that I die

There'll never be another one of you
My grandma, darling, oh, no.
I could cry a thousand times
And it would never measure up
I don't know how this world could be
Without you here
And yet I know that somewhere up above
You love me even more than before
[*pause*]
And that is your tapestry.

He stood by the door
You know he's so lost without you
With no hint of wind
It blew open wide
With a touch from Heaven
An embrace he needed so much.

A neighbor walks by
That ol' mango tree
Oh, it lined the years of my youth
He stood there, and said aloud
"What's going to happen to
The mango tree without her now?"
As soon as the words left his mouth
A bright mango came tumbling down
And hit him in the head
That Sicilian pluck
Oh, you haven't left us at all
You'll never be gone . . .

CHORUS
Oh, I'm going to miss you
'Til the day that I die
There'll never be another one of you

My grandma, darling, oh, no.
I could cry a thousand times
And it would never measure up
I don't know how this world could be
Without you here
And yet I know that somewhere up above
You love me even more than before
[*pause*]
And that is your tapestry.

Distractions come and go
I need it, and then suddenly
I have to get away
Close the browser
On a television smile.
My friends ask how I am
And I don't know what to say
You know, it really depends on the day
[*rushed*] Or the hour or the minute or the second
It's hard to tell
When it will hit me.

I remember countless times
You and I
We were making gnocchi
Rolling into strips
Cutting into cubes
And then, with laughter in my eyes,
Sending them flying on the tablecloth
I felt so light and free . . .

CHORUS 2
Oh, I'm going to miss you
'Til the day that I die
There'll never be another one of you

My grandma, darling, oh, no.
I could cry a thousand times
And it would never measure up
I don't know how a world could be
Where you are not
And yet I know that somewhere up above
You love me even more than before
And that is your tapestry.
Oh, oh.

[*increased speed of music; guitar riff with piano*]
I walk into the kitchen
And past your room
In the bathroom
Those little towels
You always put out for company
Are still there.
Strange how the simplest thing
Can break your heart.
Is that your robe hanging
On the door?
I call on the phone
And you're not there
[*backing vocals*] Only a voicemail remains
Laughing at the table with you
And now there's just an empty chair
The coffin is carried out of the car
And I don't want to see
But I'm frozen there
I squeeze the hand of a boy of mine
But he's not really here
And tomorrow is.
I put the flowers on your tomb
The priest's final words ring out.

[*slower*]
One day I'll walk down the aisle
I always thought you'd be there . . .

CHORUS – EXTENDED
Oh, I'm going to miss you
'Til the day that I die
There'll never be another one of you
My grandma, darling, oh, no.
I could cry a thousand times
And it would never measure up
I don't know how a world could be
Where you are not
And yet I know that somewhere up above
You love me even more than before
[*pause*]
And that is your tapestry.
Oh, it's your tapestry.
Your tapestry, oh, oh.

[*Instrumental; Backing vocals*]
Oh, I love you.
I love you.
I love you, Grandma.
I love you.
Oh, you know I won't forget
Your face, your voice
Indelibly imprinted in my heart.

I'll miss you for the rest of my life.

[*Ending of piano ballad*]

Chapter 28: Zircon

The click of the key against the lock of the door sounded against the erratic beat of my heart.

I hazarded a glance at the clock. *5 AM.* The time Dmitri had designated for our escape. I hoped against hope that it would be him. I turned to Peter, who looked at me reassuringly, as the door quietly skidded open.

Dmitri slipped in, casting furtive glances outside and then within, to ensure that we were not alone.

"Any problems?" I whispered.

"No." The tall, lanky man shook his head. "I got the keys with no problem, but we have to be quick. It won't be long before they notice."

"Okay." I took a deep breath.

"But I will have to tie your hands," the man said apologetically, "in case we are discovered."

"We understand," Peter said, waving it away.

Dmitri quickly bound our hands behind our backs with the efficiency and precision of one who had done this many times.

Could we trust him? I wondered.

You don't have a choice, my mind reminded me.

"Here." Dmitri slipped a knife into Peter's jean pocket. "When you are safe, you can use the knife to free yourselves. And . . . in case you need the knife for anything else."

I swallowed. *In case there is a fight.*

At least the knife was reassurance that Dmitri was on our side.

And so, with that, he exited in front of us, moving stealthily ahead, his footsteps muffled against the pavement as he remained close to the shadows of the buildings, Peter and me closely behind, struggling to move as quickly yet quietly as we could with our hands bound.

With each step, my breath came in short wisps. All it would take would be one false step.

The first sound of human activity reached me after about two minutes. I took a deep breath again, reminding myself that this was to be expected.

"Hey, Dmitri!" One of the guards called out to our "captor." He made a signal in the shape of the insignia from the badge Yin had given me, which I had recently realized was also a greeting. Dmitri returned it with a casual smile.

Okay, he was good. Almost as good as . . .

There was a pang in my heart as an image of Jeffrey's face flitted before my mind's eye, but I cast it aside.

For him, we had to get out of here. So that his sacrifice had not been in vain.

"Hey, man!"

"Escorting the prisoners out so early?" The guard blinked in the morning light.

Another reason why I had dearly wished we had escaped under the cover of nightfall.

With the rising sun, I felt so exposed.

"Yeah, a bit early for my taste," Dmitri said lazily. He kicked Peter hard in the leg with a grin. Instinct compelled me to rush forward, but I knew it was all part of the act.

Peter groaned, and I had a feeling that part wasn't an act.

". . . but their execution is at 9, right after breakfast. The boss has other plans for them before."

"I'm sure he does." The guard winked back in understanding, as my stomach turned over.

The execution. Was Dmitri's answer true, or a fabrication? Surely he would not risk the fact of such a small detail. The reality of it settled in me. I had known the risk, but we were scheduled to die, actually scheduled to die, this morning.

God, please get us out of here, I prayed an urgent prayer.

"The usual place?"

"Yep, yep."

"Should be fun." The other guard waved as Dmitri moved onward.

I exhaled, and almost smiled in relief, but continued looking down, the role of the downcast prisoner about to lose her life.

We were only about five feet away from our destination, the forest stretching ahead with its promise of safety, when the sound of a softly dangerous, familiar voice was heard.

"Where do you think you're going?"

We froze, and then turned.

Gray stood, his earrings still dangling in ironic symmetry, his green eyes hard, yet almost translucent, as they surveyed us coldly.

The man who killed Jeffrey.

I breathed heavily, anger and fear intermixing, as I attempted to quell both.

"Got orders to escort the prisoners." The man nearly faltered in his words, as my breath failed me.

We wouldn't be able to complete the plan.

"From me?" Gray loomed closer. "Strange, isn't it? I don't remember giving any orders."

From behind me, I could feel a barely discernible movement.

Peter. Our binds.

"I," the man fumbled in earnest now, "I am very sorry. I must have been misinformed . . ."

"No." Gray's voice was calm, too quiet. *Dangerously quiet.* "I think," he said, staring at Dmitri with cold precision, "that you thought I would be a fool. That I would party last night with the rest, and be too drunk to go out early. I think that you know my pattern of staying in my tent until late morning."

Peter's hands were behind my back, loosening my binds.

"I am not a fool," he whispered, a hiss barely heard above the wind around us, but discernible, somehow I knew, in any storm.

"You're right," Dmitri said, all pretense leaving him as his voice suddenly rose in confidence, the voice of a desperate man who believed he had nothing left to lose. "I no longer serve you. Not after what you did to that boy."

"Now," Peter said in a low voice.

In an instant, there was a flash of silver, and a knife in Dmitri's hand. "Go now!" he yelled, as he lunged for Gray.

Peter grabbed my hand, and we ran, blindly falling ahead as if our lives depended on it. *Oh, how real that now was.* Gunshots pierced the air, sickeningly real, one so close that I feared for a moment that Peter had been shot, but heard his presence beside me, his footsteps reassurance of his safety.

For now.

I did not dare to look behind us, but, based on the sounds that I heard, we would not be alone soon.

Minutes passed by in gasps of breath and lost footsteps, always plunging ahead, but never really seeing, only visualizing the destination, our purpose all that mattered.

We stopped when we reached the safe distance of the glen, an entrance to the forest beyond, as I choked on my breath.

And, at that moment, somehow I knew, knew before he even spoke, that the escape would soon mean little to me.

Little at all.

I heard his voice, as if a sound in the distance, but it was close, oh, so close.

"Rebecca," Peter said softly, turning to me. "I have to go back."

"What?!" I fervently shook my head. "We just escaped. What are you even talking about . . . thinking about . . . we have to hurry . . . before they catch up to us . . . it won't take long . . ."

"For Dmitri. It was . . . always my plan to help him if it came to that. I just needed to get you to safety first."

"No, Peter." I looked about wildly, and then my eyes settled on his face.

Not him. God, please, I can't lose him.

Not him.

I tried to steady my feet, swaying back and forth in exhaustion and an incoherent confusion.

"Peter, *no*, you can't go. I . . . I can't lose you. I can't lose you, too."

Peter's eyes shifted quickly from the approaching figures in the distance to me, concern and conflict briefly wavering across them.

"Rebecca, you have to go. I have to help him. Go, and *live*, Rebecca."

"But I . . ."

I swayed back and forth, image and form blurred, my eyes pleading with him. In the distance, a bluejay called, blissfully unaware, blissfully whole.

"You are my rock," I choked out.

Peter's eyes were filled.

"I know. And that makes this that much harder. But you . . . have to go. Now."

I grasped his hand, and he held it, meeting my gaze. For a moment, nothing else existed. We were on some plane of unreality, and it was just him and me, Peter and Rebecca, laughing over Duku jam and some silly scene with Antonio and Monet forever quarrelling, flying high on the swings, living, breathing, *being* more than existing, in the world that I knew.

But he was that world.

"Peter, I . . ."

The words swirled around me, begging entrance, but I wouldn't let them be free.

Because these words, these words could kill me.

"Go, Rebecca," he urged, his eyes penetrating mine.

I need you.

Shapes shifting out of focus. The soft hue of a pink-colored pen. Waves echoing in candle shades of blue, over and over, insistently, pure and real.

I love you.

The words startled me in their clarity, breaking through the shifting images of my mind, blurred shapes of my surroundings, and I instantly knew their truth.

I loved him. I loved Peter.

Why now? Why did I have to know now? After all the years, the intermissions, the misadventures.

The last few years I had lived with so many scars, abandoned, lost, holding desperately to my desire to *trust* despite it all. And through the haze of it all, so many people I found I couldn't count on anymore, it was like a camera lens out of focus, blurry . . . but, with him, it came into focus. It was clearer with Peter.

I knew.

Now. When he could die.

I had to tell him. He had to know.

Yet, when I opened my mouth, emotion lining my face, all I could manage was one word:

"Stay," I said.

"Always." His eyes met mine for one last instant, a flicker of pain crossing them before he pulled me into the forest, and, in the faint lull of distant footsteps, disappeared from view.

Chapter 29: Intermission

"I love you," I whispered, the sanctuary of the forest green fading to black.

I love you.

I love you.

I love you.

Chapter 30: Ruby

I had dreamt of fairy tales where the heroine was lost deep in a forest, mystery and danger intertwined in the carpet of green.

I still loved those tales.

But roleplaying a story is more convenient than active participation in real life.

Branches tore at my shirt and arms, and I resisted the urge to cry out as they cut deep red against my wrist. I pushed through them, moving ahead, caught between the caution needed to execute my departure without further injury and the desire to move quickly to avoid any wild animals that might live within my newfound abode.

Dorothy's lament from *The Wizard of Oz* was brushed aside in my mind, as my thoughts added "giant spiders" and "slithering creatures" to the obligatory list, reminding me why I had not gone hiking in seven years until this summer.

Just move. One step at a time. One step . . .

Peter.

I halted for a moment, catching my breath, tears rushing down my mud-speckled cheeks. *For him, you need to run.*

I had collapsed on the forest floor when Peter had left me within its then-safe confines, trees momentarily consoling me with their solid, overarching forms, surrounding me in a solemn meeting that even called the attention of a small butterfly, a painted lady with yellows and curious patterns of purple and blue. I had fallen asleep, exhaustion overwhelming me, and then saw her when I came to, blinking as the sunlight suddenly accosted my eyes with its brightness.

She had scurried away, her flight all at once a mere dot on the horizon, and I had stood up, resolve suppressing my sobs for as long as I could walk.

I walked, and walked, and walked.

After what seemed like hours, but could have been minutes or half an hour, a glimmer of light, an illuminating glow of sunkissed daffodils and scurrying rabbits, reflected off the trees before me. And then the trees, tall and ancient, wise yet dangerous as a famished eagle, grew wider apart, no longer a dense mass of bramble and limb.

I strode forward, and found myself in a glen of dappled light, wildflowers as purple and yellow as the butterfly I had encountered streaming forth beneath my feet and carpeting the ground.

I lifted my gaze up to the heavens above, uttering a silent thank you. My limbs were fatigued, but now separate from the limbs, the trunks and branches, of the trees, they flew, descending through the valley and fields until they reached a sidewalk, cement and gray and white, and saw civilization, a civilization I had never been happier to see.

Thank God.

It was a small town street, one of the older sections of town that Peter had shown me briefly on the way to Mass. I scanned my surroundings quickly, my tired eyes aching with the effort, and moved forward, ignoring all but the nearest grocery store.

In that moment, it was all that existed.

I walked in, took several steps, and almost fell in front of the counter.

"I need to call the police," I managed, coughing, as my allergies and asthma caught up with me.

The girl at the counter, around my age with long brown hair and dark eyes—reminding me for a moment of Teresa—looked at me with concern and alarm. "Of course. We have a phone right here . . ."

She dialed the number, and I reached for the phone, grasping at it as if at a last morsel of food, when she made the introduction and passed it on.

"Officer, I'd like to file a report . . ."

I poured out the entire story, leaving out details unimportant given the urgency of time yet providing enough detail so that the pertinent facts would be understood, rambling incoherently at times, fearing that it would not be enough. I paused, considering, and then quickly plunged forth again at another thought to include the story about the man who had helped us, providing a brief physical description of both Peter and Dmitri, in the chance that more than one life might be saved today.

There had already been enough loss.

There was a pause on the other line, and he said, "Bow River and the Trans-Canada Highway, you say? A few miles from the forest?"

"Yes, sir, that's it. And please don't think I'm crazy . . . I . . ."

"I'll check the deets about the convicts with the officers in charge of their alleged case later. We'll be on our way."

"Thank you." I handed the girl the phone, and leaned in near-defeat against the counter. I did not know that my eyes had closed of their own accord until a voice drew me back to awareness just as my head nearly sank against the granite surface.

"Ma'am?" The girl, who had likely been listening to the whole story—but I didn't have energy or time to think of whether she could be an accomplice (*Man, I was getting paranoid*)—looked at me, her forehead creased in concern. "There's a place to sit over there." She pointed to an arrangement of neat tables and chairs (*neat* stood out to me at the moment) near a coffee shop within the store. "I'll let you know if we receive any further calls. Or you can come back here if you need to use the phone again."

Should I call the Asturians?

The image of a young boy, beloved yet small, sitting in a wheelchair flickered through my mind. And a dark-haired women, strong yet so filled with heart. And a man with wire-rimmed spectacles who spoke little, but said much.

No, I could not worry them. Not yet.

I thanked her, then collapsed gratefully onto the nearest chair, my legs still shaking.

I closed my eyes. *Our Father, who art in Heaven . . .*

Please protect Peter.
Please protect the love of my life.

I woke to the sensation of my shoulder being shaken, and immediately bolted upright.

The young cashier's brown eyes addressed mine with sympathy.

I looked at her, a question in my own.

"They found signs of what you described. The men there have been arrested—not sure if it was all of them, but that's what the officer said. The man you said helped you—he had serious injuries, but he was taken to the hospital. They think he'll be all right. I . . . should have let you talk on the phone, but you had fallen asleep, and I felt bad waking you." The girl shifted her feet awkwardly as if expecting a rebuke.

"Thank you. It's okay," I dismissed her concerns quickly, my own propelling me ahead. "But . . . Peter. My friend. They found him, too, right?" My heart beat fast, rising in hope, quelling in the worst kind of fear.

The girl shook her head. "I'm sorry. They searched the entire area, the perimeter . . . they didn't find him."

Oh, dear God, no.

"They had another emergency a mile away involving a shoot-out at a drugstore. They're short on officers given a recent incident, and, well . . . they said they'd try again later."

I quickly pulled myself to my feet, nearly jumping from the chair.

"Where are you going?" she asked.

"Back to the forest," I said.

Sometimes there are moments colored in shades
that glimmer like soft silver light
　　　Like a poem, they bid us on.
　　　　　　Their direction unknown, but clear
Sometimes the color is only dirty gray, ugly,
coarse, unrefined
　　　　But it propels us forward,
Because, without it, the silver will not stand.

The trek back into the forest this time was easier.

Primarily because I didn't care a whit about the scratches biting my face and body, and only hazarded a glance at my ankle, swollen with possible infection, but meaning nothing to me.

A single name was all I had.

I ran through the glen, trampling through the grass so urgently that I nearly tripped on a tree root once the forest began to take shape.

I brushed through it, protecting my eyes and moving forward.

Our Father, who art in Heaven . . .

The girl at the register, at the last moment, had called me back, throwing a glittery pink cell phone in my hand.

"Just in case you need it."

I opened my mouth to speak, but she brushed it away with a wave of the hand. "You can bring it back. I'm pretty good at spotting trustworthy people." She paused and looked up at me with what appeared to be admiration.

"You really love him, don't you?" she said in wonder. "Like in the movies?"

I didn't answer—half out of the newness and half out of the strangeness of first confessing my recent understanding to a stranger—but I almost nodded.

"I hope you find him," she had said softly.

I nodded my thanks, promising to return her phone, and dashed out of the store.

I arrived at the clearing, towering trees that had once been a sanctuary surrounding me, as I looked furtively, madly, around.

There was no sign of him, and I was nearing the other side of the forest.

The end.

I spun around, turning and shifting, dizziness overtaking me. In a last swoop, I tripped over a mislaid tree branch, falling to the ground. My knee stung, as my head began to throb painfully.

I caught my breath and scrambled upward, resisting the urge to sink to the ground as my entire body—and heart—wished to do.

If I left the clearing, this could be the end. No more wistful thinking, or leftover hopes.

But I had to do it.

I took a deep breath, my eyes filling, and turned in the direction where everything—or nothing—awaited.

And then I heard it. Faint, almost a whisper of thought. A sound barely discernible among the call of birds and the trampling of moss under my feet.

As I grabbed a broken branch, lying idly on the ground as if in wait, now with the potential to use as a weapon—for I did not know who or what approached—a tall figure with golden brown hair and deep hazel eyes that I loved with all my heart and life within me emerged.

Bruises covered him, and his T-shirt was a sad scramble of cotton, twigs, and dirt. There was a jagged cut on his leg, whether by intentional injury from an enemy party or accident, I did not know.

Peter's eyes met mine, and I ran.

My arms fell around his neck, pulling him closer in a crushing hug, squeezing so hard that I did not know if I would ever be able to move away. He rocked me back and forth, his strong arms reaching securely across my back, around and around, the light falling in the clearing around us as we clung to each other, minute after minute speeding by, laughing, and sobbing, and almost screaming, dirty, and sweaty, and broken—

And alive.

Peter pulled back, grasping my hands, and looked into my eyes. That penetrating gaze of his, the one I had always loved, but had never known why.

I was looking into the eyes of a friend, a best friend, but much, much more.

The words of my grandma circled in my head, filtered awake in my consciousness as they came back to me. *How is your Peter?*

My Peter.

I looked at him, vulnerability evident in a single glance. *He had the power to break me more than anyone in the world.*

But I chose it.

I chose him.

We both spoke at once, our words overlapping . . .

"I was so scared for you, Peter. I called the police, but they couldn't find you and—"

"I was looking for you, too, and I—"

"Headed back to the forest," we both rushed out, and then stopped, the image of the other reflected in our eyes as we stood once again in silence.

He looked at my arms, concern creasing his brow as he reached for one with his hand. I winced at the pain where he touched it, but didn't push his hand away. I just looked at him. And looked. And looked.

And would never tire of looking.

"Let's get you home." Peter broke the silence, his hand still firmly wrapped around mine, as he eyed a cut above my right brow. "And you may need to have a doctor take a look at that ankle . . ."

How had he noticed the injury on my ankle so quickly?

"No, I'm fine—"

"Rebecca Veritas—"

"Peter Joseph Asturian." I pointed to his form in one sweeping gesture, raising an eyebrow (which *did* hurt) as if nothing had transpired and we were just silly kids joking again. And then my finger's projectory landed on his leg, and, while it didn't look near fatal, it made me wince again.

"Okay." Peter brushed a few leaves from his head. "Fine. We'll both take a closer look when we get home to see if you—we—need further care. Just in case. But, really, Rebecca, I'm fine—"

"I am, too. Now that . . . I've found you," I said breathlessly.

"And I you, Rebecca." His words were soft, but warm, almost shy.

And, in the midst of this solemn moment, my stomach growled.

Peter raised an eyebrow. "Perhaps we should eat after we finish with the bandages . . ."

Peter had offered to carry me as far as possible—which made me blush furiously now that I knew how I felt.

Speaking of which, when are you going to tell him, Rebecca?

Um, eventually.

Like Duku jam on pumpernickel bread, it just had to come at the right time.

Or so I convinced myself. I was glad at least to have these random thoughts, which kept me from having a complete meltdown over all that had just occurred.

I was due for a very long nap.

While I was examining my feet, as if expecting my *shoes* to have some sort of injury, I waved away the idea, reminding him that he had already carried me during the last misadventure, and we could call a cab this time.

And then, when he opened his mouth again, as if to argue the point a second time—almost as if he didn't want to lose the opportunity to carry me—which made me blush furiously *again*—I raised my eyebrow, offered him The Teacher Look that he had taught *me*, pointed again to his leg, and vowed to sit on the forest floor making friends with all the rabbits and birds at the risk of encountering a *creature*—and you know, Peter, how I hate *those*—if he did not immediately, irrevocably, and fully agree to my terms.

Peter closed his mouth in reluctant submission, and I handed him the phone that the girl at the register had given me.

Approximately fifteen minutes later, we were in a taxi heading to the Asturian home. Our request for aid had been answered by a park ranger who also happened to know the Asturians (*Did everyone know the Asturians?* I thought in wonder. For a quiet family, they sure were well-known. But it was a small town . . .). He had transported us by golf cart to a waiting taxi near the museum where it had all begun.

I leaned back, reveling in the comfort of the cushioned seats. The aches and pains all over my body, ignored earlier, reemerged in the safety of the vehicle. I closed my eyes, but forced myself to stay awake.

Peter had had the advantage of a surprise attack. When he arrived back at the clearing, he had watched from behind the surrounding shrubbery as Dmitri's knife fell to the ground. As Gray rushed toward Dmitri with the knife now in his possession and a second flash of silver arising from his belt, Peter had jumped on him from behind, throwing the full weight of his body onto his back. There was a brief struggle, but, with Dmitri's help, the two were able to overpower Gray and ultimately prevail.

By the time some of his lackeys returned from their scouting on the forest outskirts, moving forward to attack, and others emerged half-inebriated from their tents at the commotion, Peter already had a knife placed warningly against their leader's throat. Since there were enough men loyal to him, they backed off. Gray, staring down his captors coldly all the way, was tied to a pole outside one of the tents, and Peter and Dmitri took turns at watch. In a short period of time, a few members of the Denticulatus had defected—evidently of a similar persuasion as Dmitri—and Peter reassured them that the law would be more accommodating with their cooperation. However, they refused to answer when he asked about my whereabouts. When the sound of the police sirens was heard several hours later, Peter had felt confident that the situation was now under control, and, leaving Dmitri in charge of the camp, headed toward the forest in search of me.

I glanced at Peter, who looked back at me with those warm, expressive eyes.

I returned my focus ahead, closing my eyes again.

When the taxi pulled to a halt in front of the Asturian home, I jolted to near-consciousness, having slept in spite of myself. A gentle hand was on my shoulder, my eyes fluttering open as it pulled me awake.

"We're home, Rebecca," Peter said softly.

He paid the driver, and helped me out of the car, an arm protectively around my back as I emerged. As we approached the door, I stopped for a moment, turning back to Peter.

"Your mom is going to freak out when she sees us." I pointed to both of us, tatters and injuries galore, in one wide, all-encompassing sweep.

"I know."

He opened the door.

Olivia Asturian was standing in the middle of the living room, speaking to Little Dan. As the door opened, she turned, her relief at seeing us quickly replaced by horror, as she rushed forward. "Peter, what happen—"

"Peter?" Little Dan's eyes widened.

"Dan, Mom, I'm fine," Peter said reassuringly. "And Rebecca, too, though I think someone should see to her ankle."

"And your leg," I interjected firmly.

"Sit now." Mrs. Asturian ushered us to the nearest sofa with a no-nonsense look.

After a detailed examination from Mrs. Asturian, who seemed to be an expert at diagnosing bruises, sprains, and the like—no doubt due to the fact that she had raised two boys—she ascertained that we had gotten off a lot easier than we might have. There were some jagged scrapes—in particular, she was concerned about Peter's risk of infection and applied Neosporin with a mother's speed—but my ankle was declared to be a minor sprain, if that, which would heal quickly.

I had leaned back against the sofa with a sigh of relief. *I really didn't feel like going out to see a doctor.*

Then we were hustled to the other side of the house for quick showers and a change of clothes. When we returned, hot chocolate and ham and cheese sandwiches were waiting by the fire. Once we were found to be in "less of a sorry state," as Mrs. Asturian put it, the questions came flying in— from three sources, as Mr. Asturian had emerged from his lab soon after we arrived—and we told the story, leaving out the detail of Jeffrey's fate for Little Dan's sake. We would tell Peter's parents the full account later.

After the story concluded, there was a brief silence.

Mrs. Asturian breathed out deeply. "Thank God you are okay."

"I had hoped that we were rid of those men." Mr. Asturian shook his head. "But thank God you are okay, my son. And Rebecca."

Peter kissed his mom's head, and quietly embraced his father. My eyes were suddenly moist.

Little Dan remained silent and simply grabbed my hand and one of Peter's, his eyes addressing ours without a single word.

"I'm okay, bud," Peter said quietly, brushing the curls back from Dan's forehead. "Nothing's going to happen to me."

I had never heard Peter use the word "bud" before, and, for some reason, that made me almost break out into a fresh round of tears.

Mrs. Asturian eyed me thoughtfully. "I think that perhaps a nap is in order. Dinner won't be for a few hours."

I hadn't even realized that evening neared. The day had seemed to pass in minutes, yet, at the same time, a millennium.

"Yes, thank you," I said eagerly, rising from the couch.

"And you will do the same," Mrs. Asturian said, raising an eyebrow at her son. Her usually soft eyes and easy demeanor were firm now.

"Yes, mother."

"I'll—"

"It's okay." Peter waved her away as she offered to help him reach his room at the top of the stairs. "I can manage."

I smiled for the first time since the embrace with Peter in the woods, and left for my room, the possibility of slumber filling my heart with a gladness that I could not contain.

We were alive.
I loved Peter.
And I was going to take a nap.

Chapter 31: Scolecite

I woke up to a mid-afternoon sun reflected in long strands against the wall opposite my bed.

As I stirred, opening my eyes tentatively, remembrance of the past forty-eight hours darted through my brain—and heart. I leaned back against the pillow, gazing upward before closing my eyes again with satisfied contentment.

Peter. A silken mist enveloped me, a deep peace that relaxed my body as never before—and I remembered the love I now finally realized. But, all at once, aches in my body from the strenuous past events became more pronounced—and then there was a pang in my heart as I recalled what I had lost.

I pulled the sheets aside and quickly dressed, barely conscious of what clothes I had donned.

After a moment's pause, I returned to sit on the bed and stared meditatively at the wall.

There was a knock on the door.

"Come in!" I called.

Peter stood in the doorway, his appearance considerably less disheveled than the previous day, yet with more wave or curl to his hair than usual. He wore a dark green T-shirt and was so very much *Peter* that I felt certain my cheeks reddened—even if imperceptibly.

"Good morning," I said, even though it was the afternoon.

"Good morning." Peter remained in the doorway, whether simply out of propriety or more, I did not know. There was a flicker of concern that crossed his eyes. "How's your ankle, Rebecca?"

"Much better." I smiled back at him—and it was, even if still sore.

"That is good to hear," Peter said, as relief washed over his face. "Little Dan wanted you to meet him in The Poet's Room, but it can wait. I told him you needed rest. I know he will understand."

I shook my head with a smile. "The Poet's Room is never a source of fatigue—nor is Little Dan an imposition. Of course I will go."

A faint smile reached his eyes. "I think he means to spoil you. Something about him 'treating' this time, and reading to you."

"Sounds perfectly delightful."

"We . . . heard from the Cave and Basin museum," Peter said. "The security system was down that night, as you might have suspected."

I nodded, my body tensing unexpectedly as I suddenly wished for the topic at hand to disappear. *To leave. To be forgotten.*

For, what came with it could never be forgotten. *Never leave.*

". . . but the error was such that it appeared to be operational. The screens showed what they thought to be a live feed of the museum, but it was actually old footage stored in the backup system. They apologized profusely for what happened near their premises and offer monetary compensation for any . . . losses."

"Oh. That is kind of them."

Peter moved, as if to go, and then paused, turning back to face me. "Rebecca, I thought you would want to know . . . when the police called earlier today to get my statement, they mentioned that Jeffrey's grandma had been phoned. They plan to ship the body back to the U.S. He will have a proper burial."

I looked down. "I'm glad of it." I lifted my head after a moment, and Peter's large eyes, filled with understanding, were reflected in mine.

"Is there anything I can get you, Rebecca?"

I shook my head with a smile.

Peter moved toward the door.

"Peter?"

"Yes, Rebecca?" He turned even more swiftly this time.

"Thank you . . . for going back to the forest for me," I said softly.

"And you, Rebecca." Peter nodded at me—more like a bow—his face unreadable, and then retreated, closing the door quietly behind him.

Throughout dinner with the Asturians that night, I studied every contour and line of Peter's face—as if to commit it to memory. It took the clearing of a throat to the right for me to be jolted from my thoughts.

"Are you moving on to portraits?" Little Dan proposed, lifting an impish eyebrow.

"Portraits?" I smiled back at him.

"Mama says you've been painting landscapes and abstractions."

Olivia nodded with a smile from across the table.

"But, to paint the best portrait, you have to carefully study the subject."

"Well, I know exactly who the subject of my first portrait will be," I said teasingly.

Little Dan grinned. "Who?"

"You!" I leaned forward, tickling Little Dan's left arm. He exploded into giggles.

There was a brief displacement of air, and Peter was now standing on Little Dan's other side, a playful expression alight on his countenance. For a moment, our eyes met over Little Dan's shoulder, and I drew in my breath quickly as I realized how close Peter's face was to mine. Yet, just as suddenly, the moment passed, and Peter was tickling Little Dan's right arm, and I his belly—carefully, but not so that the little boy would know—as Little Dan shrieked with laughter, until Olivia Asturian's amused voice called us back with a, "Now, now, you two, that's enough. Let's let Little Dan finish his dumplings."

Chapter 32: Jasper

It had been three weeks, and I still had not told him. *Three weeks.*

Three weeks since I had been captured and almost died.

Three weeks since I had tried to forget that an old friend *had* died, swallowing it up in a box in my heart that refused to be opened.

Three weeks since I finally discovered I was madly, head over heels, in love with Peter Joseph Asturian.

Three weeks had passed without telling him how I felt.

I looked up at the boy across the table—the boy, it would seem, of my dreams—and, in that way of his, he sensed my observation, lifting his eyes from perusal of the menu to return my gaze unblinkingly.

"So, what do you recommend?" I managed, my voice taking on a conversational tone. "I know this is one of your favorite restaurants, so you must be the expert."

"Apple strudel," Peter said without hesitation.

I raised an eyebrow, suddenly more relaxed. "Apple strudel? For the main course *and* dessert?"

"It wouldn't be amiss." Peter rested his arm on the table briefly before returning to his usual statuesque posture. "Best apple strudel in the province. Or the country."

"Or the world?" I grinned.

"That would not surprise me."

"Most excellent." I glanced over as a waitress approached us, her white apron decorated with the maple leaf of the Canadian flag.

"Are you ready to order?"

"Just a second." I looked quickly through the pages of the menu, which had been lying idly on the table while I had been lost in my own thoughts. "Ummm—let him order first."

Peter nodded cordially at the waitress. "Hi, Barbara. I'll have a hamburger, a glass of water, and then one of your large apple strudel desserts—" He glanced over at me. "If you want to share, Rebecca?"

"They're pretty big," the waitress offered.

"Sure! And umm—I'll take the classic cheeseburger and an um mug of hot chocolate."

"As long as you don't have any ten-dollar bills nearby," Peter whispered, leaning toward me as he called to mind a previous occasion when he had not been present, but of which I had told him—one involving a ten-dollar bill somehow leaping ungracefully into my hot chocolate on the first day of an internship that proved to be likewise tumultuous—and then having to give said bill to my new mentor.

"Hey!" I protested in mock indignation. "Even ten-dollar bills needed a bath."

I coughed, realizing that my voice had reached a volume louder than a whisper, and then looked up at the waitress, who stood waiting in bemusement.

"And that will be all," I managed, as I heard Peter cough beside me, evidently to cover up a laugh.

It was, I noticed, starting to become a habit of his.

"Hey, at least I didn't order the Bleu Cheese Salad without bleu cheese," I protested, as she left. "I do that at Mimi's with friends all the time."

"Indeed. That would have been . . . fascinating."

I resisted the urge to swat Peter with my menu, which I then realized I had kept hostage from the waitress in my lap.

"She can get it later," Peter said, following my gaze.

For the next twenty minutes, Peter and I were engaged in an intense discussion of stories that reminded me of the year that we met. *Of the old days.*

"We really should write *Intermission 2*," Peter said, after we both finished laughing over a recent development in a story of mine, wherein a character had simply refused to do what he had been told, no matter what I tried, instead maintaining a plan unknown to The Author.

"At the very least, for Little Dan," I hurried to say, my face reddening.

Why did this make me nervous? We had written a story together before.

And yet that time spent together, now that I *knew*, would be . . . very *different*.

But that was no reason to be rude.

"And because I would also greatly enjoy the chance to embark on that adventure together again," I said softly, "and become reacquainted with all our old friends."

"As would I."

At that moment, a server approached with two plates, interrupting our conversation.

"Cheeseburger and hot chocolate?"

"That's me." I moved the menu aside, which the bus boy took once he had laid down my plate. He then put down Peter's ordered meal, and, with a bow, withdrew.

I squirted hand sanitizer on my hand, and then looked up at Peter, who was smiling.

"What?!"

"Nice new hand sanitizer bottle."

"Oh." I looked down at the pink, sparkly design, suddenly reminded of a day in the Asturian backyard involving a swimming pool. "Well, they weren't out of that variety . . . when it came to this."

I cleared my throat, raising an eyebrow. "Would you like some?"

"Well . . ."

"Peter!"

"Fine. I fully support cleansing one's hands."

"Good." I squirted Peter's hand with exuberant abandon, allowing far more to exit the bottle than necessary. "*There.*"

"Interesting choice of amount."

"Oh, hush," I said playfully, and then realized that I had never said that to Peter before, and in this teasing way.

I blushed again, and began my first bite of the sandwich.

"Oh, wow, this is good," I said, wiping my lips with a napkin. "And I'm not even a cheeseburger fanatic."

"Banff has the best of . . . almost everything."

I shook my head, as if to protest, but a smile wove across my face, and I found myself unable to contradict that statement when that particular boy was sitting across from me. I resisted a sigh of satisfaction and watched as Peter bit into his sandwich.

"Observing for reactions?" Peter asked, now the one raising an eyebrow.

"Nothing less than a full review," I teased, and then returned the measured study to my own food as my stomach began to growl.

I had taken another bite from the cheeseburger when I felt a distinct pressure, cold and metallic, against my back.

I turned around to face two men with dangling earrings and light blue eyes.

"Get up slowly, and don't say a word."

Chapter 33: Spectrolite

Dark gray duct tape wound itself tightly around my mouth, unyielding and cruel as I tried to scream.

But I knew it was futile. I had struggled uselessly for several minutes with the rope biting into my dry hands and sealing them behind my back as I furtively scanned the back seat of the dirty white truck for anything that could set us free.

I had found nothing.

I looked at Peter, gagged and bound beside me, pleading at him with my eyes for any suggestion. He looked back at me, his large hazel eyes drawn into greater depths, and shook his head.

No escape.

Once, long ago, Adriana and I had escaped from a similar predicament with no means to untie ourselves save a technique learned from a YouTube video. But today it had all happened so quickly, somehow more quickly than before—my reflexes had then been more sure—and I chastised myself for not managing to move my wrists slightly apart or taking a deep breath to expand my chest as I had been tied up.

And, even if I had, the rope today had been fastened more tightly, enough that it had produced welts when one of the men first roughly pressed the rope around my wrists.

And, even if I had, that same man put a knife against my throat the instant he perceived any rustling, presuming that I, as hostage, would discourage Peter sufficiently from any attempt to escape.

I could not speak to Peter in that moment because my lips were sealed shut.

I could not touch him—grasp his hand or rest my head on his shoulder for one of the first—and perhaps the last time.

In that moment, as tears welled in my throat, I realized that the gazes, the penetrating looks, so much a part of our friendship, of *us*—to speak without uttering a single word—now were fortuitous.

Now they were all that we had.

Peter's eyes held mine, soft yet firm, as the car looped and then shot through a winding country road, a rock in a stormy sea as we ascended with the incline of faded pavement until the truck, an hour later, came to a halt, and every recollection, every laugh, every breath was contained in that

instant as I allowed myself to meet his gaze, resting and falling
> into
>> him.

We stood in a field, daisies lying beneath our feet, long blades of grass lingering restlessly against us, but the field held no growth.

Peter stood opposite me, a knife flashing against his neck.

His eyes flickered in recognition as they met those of the two men. And, as he mouthed two words, almost instinctively, my heart plummeted.

I struggled against my captor, who, just as quickly, pulled a blade against me. "You are the men—"

"That Asturian put in prison," the man finished, a dangerous edge to his voice. A look of utter hatred, beyond a glare, was raised to Peter. "He stuck his neck where it didn't belong. Or, should I say, legs?" he sneered coldly, and I winced as the image of a young boy falling to the sound of gunshots passed before my eyes.

Little Dan.

"But now we're out on good behavior." A mad grin flitted across the second man's face. "We did our time. And *maybe*," he said the words lightly, "maybe we could have let that go."

"And then you killed our brother, the one who held the fort when we were in prison, thanks to you Asturian scum." The second man swore under his breath.

"Your brother?"

And then it came to me in a flash.

"Our own flesh and blood. He was under Yin, but he always served himself, and us, first. After all," he said with a flash of pride, "we are the true descendants of the Segora family. The Denticulatus belong to us by rights, far more than the false leader that we had."

The Man with the Cool Blue Eyes.

My eyes shifted to Peter, understanding also on his face, as the blade of the knife at my throat scratched lightly in warning, drawing a small trickle of blood.

"Let her go," Peter's voice rang out, strong but laced with deep emotion, and I knew the seeming calm was a facade. "This doesn't involve her."

The two men exchanged looks with hollow, jagged laughs.

"Let her go," he repeated again, a hoarse whisper.

"It's too late for that, Asturian," The taller man—the older brother—spit out the words. "She's involved. She has always been involved."

My brow creased in puzzlement for a moment, and then, all at once, it dawned on me—the sense of being followed that day on the boat, the moments before and in between—it all made sense now.

But *always*?

Before I had time to consider his words further, I was roughly thrown to Peter's side, tossed as a discarded remnant of lint, garbage laid to waste in the eyes of those who would wish it.

The second man lowered his hand to his belt, and, from it, emerged a pistol.

He raised it, an eyebrow cocked. "This will give me great pleasure. I've been waiting six years for this moment."

His brother laughed, reaching for his own gun now, just as quickly, trained on me. "And don't worry. When we're done here, you can be sure that we'll find the invalid, too." He grinned sardonically.

Peter's jaw tensed, and his voice was low with warning, despite the weapon pointed at him. "Don't touch him."

"Oh, Peter," the first man said mockingly, as if speaking to a friend. "It's time to wipe every last Asturian from existence."

"And all those who care about them," he hissed.

He lifted his weapon, preparing to aim.

"Goodbye, Peter Asturian."

I looked at Peter, and his eyes reached mine, an intermingling of pain and deep regret, anguish written across his face before drawn to an expressionless sadness.

"It's not your fault," I whispered, as I heard the flick of a trigger. "I will never believe that, as I long as I—" I couldn't finish the words.

As long as I live.

It would have to be longer.

I closed my eyes. *Oh, my God, I am sorry for my sins . . .*

"It's finally time." The mocking voice reached my ears, assaulting my meditations, and I opened my eyes to look at Peter one last time. His eyes were closed, a prayer evident on his face, before softly flickering open.

Our hands closed the distance, grappling across the darkness, and, clutching his against mine, we looked ahead at the barrel forced into our vision, black and shining like a twisted beetle, an overwhelming darkness swallowing the scene.

And then, in that moment, in a stuttering of shapes and movement, the world shifted.

A whirlpool of Light spilled across the field in luminous echoes—echoes, yet clear—golden like an unfolding dawn flower bursting to full breath, an aureate star's final trek flickering across the night sky in flashing pinpoints, leaves of silver shimmering softly throughout in untrodden paths of yesterday, aglow with incandescent streams of consciousness as deep as the refulgent yellow, and then, unforgotten and pure, a light also of white, a soft moonbeam glimmering and flowing in distant melodies of a wave's foamy lace, the underside of a shell shifting and turning, dove's flight echoing in the distance.

It was golden, and silver, and white, all at once, blinding my vision, yet illuminating it.

And, through it all, a great wind stirred—but it was not a wind of this earth, nor was it heard apart from the light, as, for a single instant, there was no separation between sound and touch and sight—all one in a breeze that lifted through echoes of light.

There was a piercing cry as the two men, frozen by terror and then hastily scurrying away, were enveloped in the essence of light and wind—not like a storm tossing travelers aside, but as if they faded into a mirror of yesterday, and then were no longer there.

I blinked, my hand still in Peter's, as the Light and Wind remained so that I could see in the distance a figure, bent slightly with age, yet somehow raised to a greater height. He walked closer and came clearly into view, and I moved with a start.

"Cedric." I stood, frozen as if in a daze, my hand still in that of Peter before it flew all at once to my mouth.

I looked at Peter, whose perplexed face reflected the same awe, as Cedric approached us.

His deep gray eyes addressed ours, speaking with a single glance—a near-glow—that was not quite here, not quite human.

"Are they—" My eyes scattered to where our captors had once stood.

"Lost to time, yes, Rebecca," Cedric said softly, his gaze unmoving, holding at once both Peter and me. "They will never trouble you again. Or Peter." His great eyes shifted to the young man who had once been his fellow usher in a day that now seemed a century before.

We stood in silence, the light still echoing in the distance.

"Who are you?" I whispered. "What . . . what are you?"

Was he an angelic being? The apparition of a saint? Or a saint of today, gifted with an understanding beyond our own?

Cedric watched me, his deep eyes steady, silver hair framing his face, as the gray retreated, as if to another realm of thought. "Rebecca," he said quietly, almost gently, "what I am does not matter. I was called for a time to be in this place, and in this time. And that is what I have done."

Peter stood silently by my side, and yet he looked ahead at his old friend—and Cedric back at him—a conversation shared that did not need words. The old man smiled at him, a faint turning of the lips.

It was at that moment that I noticed that the man I—we—had come to love, a man always in the background, but forever in the forefront, the man of Intermission, was stooped and weary, his eyes still penetrating, but his ashen face etched with fatigue, wrinkles more pronounced, his frame at once grand yet frail and thin, nearly fading into the light around us. And then realization dawned upon me in stabbing strokes.

"This is goodbye, isn't it?" My voice broke, my words soft and hushed. "Cedric, you're . . . you're leaving us, aren't you?" I looked at him, my eyes raised to his like those of a child as they grew moist. "You're . . ." The words stumbled out jarringly, as if through a choke. "Are you . . . dying?"

"Not dying as you would call it," he said quietly. "But, in this form, yes . . . you could call it dying."

A sob shook my body, and Peter stirred beside me, pulling me closer.

"Don't cry, little one," Cedric said gently, as the sobs burst forth anew. "I am leaving because my time is up here, in this way and in this form. But I will always be with you and Peter as I always have been." His eyes penetrated mine.

"Oh, Cedric," I choked out. "I'll . . . I'll miss you." And then I rushed forward, throwing my arms around the old man who was somehow more, but always, always was more to me, my tears intermingling with the fabric of his shirt, as I remained so for moments, or minutes, an embrace that I wished could last forever.

"Yet tears can have in themselves beauty," he said, watching me, as if he heard my unspoken words as I finally drew back, "and the depths of them last forever."

And then Peter rushed forward himself, embracing the man who had been both mentor and friend, a choking, suffocating hug that gave nothing but life.

"Peter," he said, and, in that single word, he said every nuance and meaning and echo of more.

Peter grasped his hand, and then withdrew to stand by my side.

"Goodbye," I whispered, as the figure turned, retreating back into the Light glimmering still in the distance.

Cedric turned.

His deep gray eyes filled us once more, and then a small smile graced the corner of his lips—and in that smile was a gift, a gift I would somehow never forget—and then he walked forward.

I stood, my head cradled in Peter's shoulder, as we gazed ahead, tears streaming down our faces as we held each other, weeping in joy and grief and wonder, as the figure faded softly from view, and remained so long after the Light dimmed.

Chapter 34: Chalcedony

I sat beside Peter, gazing out at Lake Louise, my heart in my throat, and then, as slowly and yet suddenly, it began to clear in the dim silence.

We had arrived at the house deep into nightfall—approaching 1:30 AM, but feeling much, much later—and had fallen exhausted onto our beds. I had not even taken a shower, an event that had never previously occurred in my life, and slept a dreamless night. When I awoke, the clock read 5:30 AM, and I had wrestled with the notion of trying to get back to sleep. But, as memories from the night before tossed through my mind, startling me into further awakening, I knew that sleep would be an impossibility, so I threw on my robe and headed downstairs.

It was Sunday, the day the jam shop was closed, and I had expected to find no one when I arrived. Yet Peter looked up from the table where he had been staring ahead thoughtfully, an empty plate before him that appeared as if it had not been touched at all.

"Can't get back to sleep," I had said, settling down next to him with a sigh.

"Me either." Peter's eyes met mine, and he rose from his chair. "Should we—"

"Take a walk to the lake?" I finished.

Peter had nodded, and then grabbed a piece of paper. "One moment. Just let me write a note to my parents so they don't wonder where we are, especially since they did not see us last night."

And then we were here, blinking through half-lidded eyes in the sunlight, the deep azure of the water swirling in shades of mossy forest canopies, at times transforming into emeralds of the royal court, while, as now, taking a simpler form that, in that moment, we needed more.

We were sitting, perched on a slight elevation near the bank, and our eyes reflected in the lake as we sat there in companionable silence.

It was as if the lake sensed our exhaustion and demanded no great exertion. We simply gazed ahead, lost in the watery depths and forest outskirts, weaving in and out of ebb and flow, as a light breeze drifted like a comforting caress across our faces. A slight rustling—perhaps of another marmot or a rabbit—could be heard alongside the trill of bird song, but none of these sounds disturbed our sanctuary.

I sighed, my forehead creased with beauty bittersweet, and the lake took my sigh to its depths, allowing only the melody of softly treaded ripples to emerge from that heavy sigh.

Peter turned, squeezing my hand briefly before allowing it to drop lightly to my side, and our gaze returned to the lake.

The lake understood, as if the heartbeat of a great creature resonated through the ripples of the water's serene flow, returned the gaze as if it had waited for us, and we sat in quiet contemplation, without thought or understanding or attempt to understand, and simply were, simply *being*.

No words were exchanged—or required—between Peter and me, as minutes, and then hours, ticked by. Wordless prayers rose also across the expanse of space, and perhaps time, lifting our hearts and souls in the stillness of its contented repose.

I stared ahead, and, enraptured by its thoughts, allowed the pure serenity of Lake Louise to flow over me in silent elation, the wind blowing and Peter sitting quietly beside me a part of its essence. For a moment, it was all that I, that we, needed.

Adoro te devote. My eyes flickered above to the heavens reflecting the same majestic, tranquil azure for a moment, before returning to the lake.

I reached for the door.

When we emerged on the other side, my eyes took in four figures—three familiar and one unknown. But it was not simply the presence of a newcomer, a man in a white coat with words on an unreadable nametag, that gave me pause. It wasn't that Mr. Asturian was frozen, seemingly unaware of our presence, his body unaccountably still, his chin balanced against one hand. It wasn't the emotion filling Mrs. Asturian's eyes, unshed tears awake in every expression, as her face was drawn into a depth I could not name. No, it was not simply what filled my eyes with scientific precision, or even through psychological or literary analysis. It was a sense, sense that something had shifted, something greater, deeper, and more poignantly real than my imagination could conjure, or even venture to ascertain. Out of the corner of my eye, I perceived a small figure in a wheelchair, but, before I could take it in completely, there was a flurry of movement and dark hair, and Mrs. Asturian flew to Peter.

I looked at Peter. In his eyes existed unfiltered panic, wild and filled with a tragic understanding of the scope of years.

He knew the man.

"Peter." Mrs. Asturian clasped his hands, tears filling her eyes.

"Mother"—Peter's voice shook with emotion, despite his attempt to steady it—"why is Dr. Anderson here?"

"It's all right, Peter." Mr. Asturian had spoken, his form no longer immobile as he addressed Peter, his dark eyes solemn but traced with a soft glimmer of peace. "Or perhaps . . . more than all right."

Dr. Anderson spoke for the first time, his voice deep and quiet. "Your parents called me this morning after . . ." He shook his head, his brow drawn in confusion with the studied look of one who spent much time bent over papers in dim light. "I cannot find any medical explanation for it. I saw your brother on Monday for his regular appointment. There was no sign of this . . ." The doctor shook his head again as if to clear his thoughts.

It was then that my eyes—and I could sense the same of Peter beside me—shifted to Little Dan, seated in his gray wheelchair. He was smiling, a smile that reached his eyes.

I turned to Peter, but his eyes never left Little Dan.

"This morning, Little Dan reached for a book on the lowest shelf." Mrs. Asturian's soft voice was heard beside him. "His foot caught on the rest plate of his wheelchair, and he lost his balance and fell . . . I was in the kitchen, and hurried over when I heard the noise. I reached to help him up from the floor, but he . . . knew. He . . ." Her voice quaked unabashedly with emotion, and she could not continue.

"It's okay, Mama."

All eyes turned to Little Dan. His voice was quiet, but eager. Mrs. Asturian moved toward him, but Little Dan shook his head.

"I'll show him," he said.

And then, in an instant, he was standing. And, his feet shaking only for a moment, he straightened his back, moved forward . . .

And walked.

For the entire walk, short yet imbued with a pervading length, his eyes never left those of Peter, studying them and *filling* them all at once. And Peter's eyes flickered back, meeting his in a gaze measured throughout, two brothers united then in the pervading silence unbroken.

Little Dan was only about two feet away when Peter rushed forward, throwing his arms around his brother. He sank to the floor, clinging tightly to Little Dan, as his body shook, loud sobs—audible, real—wracking his body in the faint hush of the room. My eyes filled as I stood there, unable to move, much like Mr. Asturian a few moments before.

Little Dan looked over Peter's shoulder, a tiptoeing glance, smiling at me as a smile of my own briefly lifted across my face through the tears spilling down my cheeks. Peter still held him in a tight grip, seemingly powerless to draw away.

"Rebecca, will you read to me in a little while?"

"Yeah . . . Yeah, I will, Danny." I smiled back at him as tears once again pooled in my eyes. "What book?"

"The one I dropped. It's on the table over there."

I moved to retrieve the book, approaching the table and then stopping before it.

It was a worn volume of green with silver-tinged pages. I picked it up, and read the title.

"Chapter 12," Little Dan said. "Cedric of Ivanhoe."

I stood, watching, by the patio balustrade, an afternoon wind filtering through stray locks falling across my face, scattering an assemblage of curls in airy breaths that did not disturb or annoy, but simply *were*.

Peter. Peter and Little Dan.

I stood. I watched. I watched as Peter gently held him in the swimming pool, supporting his small form with his larger one as he kicked his feet—*Oh, those beautiful, tiny feet*—and moved his arms in the front stroke, turning every so often to tousle his hair or smile down at him. And then again, in shifts and turns—and sprays—of dolphin Light, forward together, arms and legs and movement, Peter and Little Dan, together.

Oh.

I turned the corner, and it was dusk, velvet darkness cascading across the surface above with stars appearing interspersed throughout in glimmering pinpoints of golden light.

"Oh, Danny boy, the pipes, the pipes are calling," Professor Blackburn began to sing in his deep voice.

We were sitting in the Asturian backyard, picnic tables set up with pizza from their favorite local pizzeria and fresh strawberries that the professor had brought from his garden.

Little Dan reached for a strawberry, Peter behind him, forever guarding his brother with every breath.

"From glen to glen, and down the mountain side."

I cast my eyes above, gazing at the flashes of golden light.

Peter and Little Dan laughed in the pool through splashes of water and afternoon light, glancing momentarily over at me, Danny with the great big smile of a little boy again, Peter's smile caught more in his eyes as he looked at me.

"The summer's gone, and *all the roses falling*."

I closed my eyes.

A lake, frozen by winter ice, waiting in the distance.

But it was still there. Oh, it was still there.

"It's you, it's you must go, and I must bide."

A tall boy with long, dark hair, much like a caveman in appearance, but genuine, real, beloved.

Oh, my old friend.

"But come ye back when summer's in the meadow . . ."

Jeffrey sent me a teasing glance as we shelved books, and I grabbed a mop, throwing it at him, laughing in his direction as he grinned back, one hand on my hip as I ordered him with a regal glare.

"Or when the valley's hushed and white with snow."

Dancing in circles without end, the mop forgotten in a rendition of "That's Amore," as snow suddenly fell in the bookstore, filling the room with pure white.

"I'll be here in sunshine or in shadow."

Tears gently fell down my cheeks, a balming touch through my closed eyes.

I clung to the image of his face, his dark eyes smiling at me through the snow that covered the screen of the photograph, a lullaby lightly erasing him from view.

Yet it could never be erased.

"But when ye come, and all the flowers are dying."

I felt a hand on my shoulder, and it was Peter.

"Oh, Danny boy, oh, Danny boy, I love you so!"

Little Dan fell into my arms, and I put my hand on the small boy's back, squeezing him close as the image of the tall, lanky man overlapped with his in the night sky.

The healed and the hero, drawn together by a single name that marked one and defined the other.

Danny boy. Who was the Danny boy?

Rose petals cascading around and around, lotus flowers bidding them welcome in daffodil laughter, as I turned with them.

I looked ahead, and it was again the day before.

Little Dan and Peter spun in the water across the expanse of darkness.

A recovered hope.

"If I am dead, as dead I well may be."

I squeezed my eyes shut more tightly . . .

"You'll come and find the place where I am lying."

. . . my face shaking with the sobs that soon drew across my body, but a pain not in the same shade as before.

It was a pain that honored him in this moment . . .

Jeffrey looked up at me from the snowy winterworld, and smiled.

. . . a Light, the joy of remembrance mixed with the melancholy of loss.

Through my closed eyes, a smile lifted at the corner of my cheeks, remnants of what once was, what I knew, lifting, too, with it.

"And kneel and say an Ave there for me."

I opened my eyes, and walked over to sit near Professor Blackburn, family friends of the Asturians chatting lightly in the backyard while others sat and listened quietly.

I prayed a wordless prayer, his face imprinted in my mind.

And heart.

"And I shall hear, though soft you tread above me . . ."

Turning, hand over hand, Peter and Little Dan. I smiled and drew closer, leaving my post, but never quite approaching the pool.

This was for them.

The scene turned to black again, and the stars blinking in my half-open eyes stirred to awakening, as I handed Mrs. Asturian a piece of pizza.

She squeezed my arm, and retreated.

Jeffrey's voice.

"See ya, girlie."

I heaved a great sigh, looking at the sky above and then at Peter, who stood silently beside me.

"And all my grave will warmer, sweeter be,

For you will bend and tell me that you love me."

I took his hand, as images of Jeffrey and Little Dan intersected with one more, a face framed with gray-white hair.

"And I shall sleep in peace until you come to me."

Professor Blackburn finished the song, and lifted his dark, somber eyes to me.

I met them, and the snow and summer existed together then, the laughter of Peter and Dan in the distance, pool and nighttime gathering all at once, Mrs. Asturian and Mr. Asturian, friends and loved ones, as one, sun and starlight the same, water and moonlight alike.

Oh, I would remember.

I closed my eyes with a smile, as I let the images of today and yesterday filter through me in a new dawn.

Chapter 35: Moonstone

"Angel of God, my guardian dear, through whom God's love . . ."

I slipped into Little Dan's room, superhero posters lining the walls of his sanctuary alongside colorful images that I now knew to be painted by Olivia Asturian, and silently sat next to him.

Little Dan glanced over at me and reached for my hand.

I took it, memorizing the soft smallness of this little boy that I loved.

"Through whom God's love," I prompted gently.

"Through whom God's love commits me here." We continued together, our words the only sound in the room save a slight bubbling from a tiny aquarium holding one little, orange-blue fish.

"Ever this day be at my side."

Light flickered through my mind in great waves of color that went beyond color.

"To light and guard, to rule and guide."

Amen.

I made the Sign of the Cross, Little Dan following suit.

And then I stood, managing a tiny smile for him.

Little Dan turned and threw his arms around me. I wrapped my own arms around him and held him close, tears springing to my eyes. When we finally let go, one large tear fell from those beautiful brown eyes across his small cheek.

"Today, isn't it?" he said, his eyes lifted to mine, childlike and unveiled.

"Today," I said softly, a bittersweet melancholy weighing down my mind and heart.

I stood at the entrance to the Asturian home, rose trellises bidding their farewell from the white gates.

"So, this is it," I managed, forcing a smile. "I . . . thank you so much for your hospitality."

Thank you for your hospitality. It seemed so formal, so limited, given the extent of their hospitality.

"Thank you for everything," I said more sincerely, my eyes filling. "Thank you *so* much."

Olivia Asturian moved closer, and squeezed my hand. "It was a gift to have you here. We were so, *so* happy to have this time with you. Please promise you will come back one day."

I nodded, suddenly overcome by her kindness, as I held back tears that threatened to overflow. "I will."

Olivia smiled, and then embraced me, standing back.

Mr. Asturian came forward from behind me and extended his hand. I shook my head, and pulled him into a hug. At first, there seemed to register surprise, but he soon awkwardly patted my back. "It was a pleasure to have you with us, Rebecca. Don't forget to keep composing, inventing, in your own way."

"And painting." Olivia smiled again.

"I will," I repeated softly.

I braced myself for the next goodbye, knowing it would be one of the hardest, as I walked to the second-to-last figure in the line.

I knelt beside Little Dan and looked up at him. "Hey, Danny."

Little Dan stood—*stood*, the word sprang to my mind and heart with immeasurable joy—looking up at me. "You meant what you said to Mom, right?" he said in a small voice that nearly shattered my heart. "You'll be back?"

I bit my lip and met his gaze. "I promise."

Little Dan nodded. "Rebeccas keep their promises."

My forehead creased, and I simply nodded, unable to speak.

"And," he said, still looking at me, "you won't forget The Poet's Room? This is for you, just in case." He reached out his hand.

It was a drawing he had made of the Room that I had come to love, the initials D.A. written in small, neat writing at the bottom right-hand corner—every detail and shade outlined to the best of his ability, only with added warmth that was definitively him. *Little Dan.*

In his other outstretched hand was held a small pebble from the warm side of the room, a remnant of the time spent in this world.

"Of course I won't, my Danny!" I choked down a sob, and threw my arms around the small boy.

"I love you, Rebecca," Little Dan said, his large eyes addressing mine. "I think you're part of our family now."

I covered my mouth.

"Oh, I love *you*, Danny."

I pulled him into another hug, my vision blurred as my hands clutched the back of his shoulders.

I withdrew, managing a small, but real, smile, squeezed his hand once more, and turned to the last figure standing at the gate.

Peter.

"Hi, Peter," I said quietly.

"Hi, Rebecca." Peter's eyes penetrated mine as he looked back at me.

"I . . . it's going to be hard not going to the jam shop and . . . Lake Louise. And"—I fumbled for words, my eyes finally meeting his again—"I will miss you, Peter," I said softly.

When would I see him again? And when would I tell him what was in my heart?

It almost seemed as if the opportunity had passed. Would it be another two years before I saw him again? Could I survive that separation time and time again, and especially now, now that I knew?

The sob lodged precariously in my chest flowed closer, and I bit back tears with everything that I had.

Peter smiled. "I would miss you, too, but"—he arched an eyebrow—"as it turns out, I will be taking a leave of absence from Alberta again." His eyes finally rested on me. "I have a ticket to leave on a plane for California, and, if you don't mind the company, I would like to come with you."

Peter was coming with me.

I wasn't leaving him behind.

"I . . ." I choked out the words. "That would be . . . great, Peter."

Peter's gaze lifted across to me, and I stared back, willing my eyes to remain affixed.

But the sound of traffic and a sudden blaring horn across the street reminded me of the place and time.

I bent down for my luggage, swinging a carry-on bag over my shoulder before lifting the handle of my rolling suitcase.

"Goodbye," I said softly, and they looked back at me, a smile in their eyes.

I rushed forward to hug them each once again, and then looked up at Peter, whose suitcase had magically emerged from its previous area of concealment (or perhaps it was simply my emotions that had not taken it in before).

"Ready, Rebecca?" Peter asked.

I cast one last look around me, at the house and at the three people before the gate who had become so dear to me, who had quickly become entrenched in my life as never before. A great sigh escaped.

"Ready," I said.

I stared out the windows of the plane, the mountains and fields of Banff disappearing further in the distance with every passing minute. For a moment, I thought I caught a glimpse of Lake Louise, blinking in radiant sparkles of light from afar.

I turned to Peter, who sat next to me on the aisle seat. He had allowed me the window view without question—but in a way different from our trip to Canada.

He knew I needed it.

"Peter?"

"Yes?" Peter looked up from the book he was reading, his eyes alert. "What is it, Rebecca?"

A busy plane with dozens of other passengers hardly felt like the place to reveal my innermost secret. Besides, I reasoned, Peter would be staying in California for a time, and I would therefore have plenty of *time* to tell him. Which reminded me . . .

"So, how long will you be staying in California?" I asked, brushing back a lock of hair that had gleefully sprung in front of my eyes to impair my vision.

"I'm not certain. At least until the end of this month. But I did not make a return reservation yet."

Until the end of this month. Today was August 1, the birthday, I realized, with a pang in my chest, of my grandmother.

Peter would be staying for another month.

Excitement and confusion competed within me, allowing no rest. In the end, the confusion brought by curiosity won.

"Do you have any . . . specific plans for your trip?"

Peter's eyes relaxed, a casual gesture. "I plan to get a job for the summer," he said lightly. "School is out, and I would like the opportunity to earn more money."

"But why—"

Why not get a summer job in Banff? In Alberta? Even somewhere else in Canada? Especially since this wasn't a career change and just a temporary position.

Peter's eyes were fixed upon mine, and he smiled. "Well, I suppose I am also coming to 'hang out,' as you Californians love to say."

I looked at Peter, and knew, in a wave of impatience, that it was no use to attempt to break through the mystery that he so often employed. If Peter didn't want to say anything, I thought to myself in resignation, he would not say anything.

Much like myself, I admitted reluctantly.

Not that I am as mysterious as him and his vexing ways, I reasoned back.

"Ah, I see," I ventured, gazing back at the window view.

But.

"What kind of job?" I blurted out, turning from the window.

A wry smile formed at the corner of his lips, as if Peter expected my incessant chatter and questioning. "Well, that is to be determined, but I did apply for a position as a bank teller, having fulfilled that job description a few summers ago in Alberta. I have an interview on Thursday."

A bank teller. Peter was a bank teller a few summers back. And he had an interview on Thursday. *And* he was coming back with me to California.

I finally couldn't take it anymore, and the words came bursting from my mouth before I had a chance to stop them.

"Why are you coming to California, Peter?" I asked, my voice soft despite its urgency.

"It seemed," Peter said, looking back at me, "that there was more left to be done."

Chapter 36: Ametrine

I stepped off the plane, the chatter of conversation from a scattering of reunions in the vicinity quickly filling in the spaces, but I ignored it, scanning my surroundings for those whom I sought.

"Rebecca!" My mother rushed forward from where she stood waiting at the baggage check terminal, and pulled me into an embrace. "Welcome home."

I squeezed her once, and then withdrew, kissing her on the cheek. "It's good to be home," I said wistfully. "Though," my voice grew softer as Peter emerged from behind me, "it was an unforgettable trip."

"You'll have to tell us all about it once you get settled in." Dad gave me a bear hug, and then noticed the figure behind me.

He stretched out one hand. "Peter. Nice to see you."

"A pleasure, Mr. Veritas," Peter said formally, shaking my father's hand.

"Thanks for keeping my little girl safe."

"I would never have any other consideration in mind," Peter said fervently, his voice suddenly serious.

"Given what we have heard on the news and the recent texts from Rebecca, it's a miracle that you two are here safe and in one piece." Mom shook her head. "I'm so glad that you are both okay. We'll have to hear the whole story soon."

"Let's give credit where credit is due. She was just following my orders to stay safe." I felt someone's arms wrap around me from behind, and I turned.

"Hey, big brother," I said, hugging Alexander fiercely.

"Adriana couldn't make it," Alexander elaborated on her absence, his red hair striking as it glimmered in the sunlight like a beacon (I thought briefly of how his hair could serve as one of those airport signs notifying passengers of their ride). "She should be back from her vacation tomorrow."

"Thanks, Alex. I know . . . she emailed me," I said, briefly surprised that he had also been made aware of that fact.

Teresa and Amelia had dance class together, but they planned to visit with me sometime that week.

I yawned involuntarily, the exhaustion of the past several days suddenly catching up with me.

Alexander held up his hands. "No offense taken."

"I wasn't yawning at you, crazy head."

"Yeah, yeah."

"I think," Mom said, eyeing me, "that we had better take her home before she falls asleep standing up."

I laughed and heard a chuckle from behind me where Peter stood. "Probably."

I gazed around me, taking in the scene, the California summer—the sky, the ground, and even the sign reading LAX in bold white letters.

Home.

I breathed it in.

I sat on my bed, a red and white blanket beneath me, taking in every inch and corner of my childhood bedroom—my current bedroom, actually, since I had moved out of my apartment a year ago in order to be closer to my family.

Pale mint green walls surrounded me, fading almost into white like a secret that only those who looked closely would uncover. I smiled, recalling how I had once considered how mint green would make a lovely color for a bridesmaid dress, though, ultimately, my default of pink would naturally take precedence. At the thought, something within me sobered, and I continued surveying the room. A large desk made of maple and wood stood near the window, a work of art built for me by my grandfather. In it existed history and love, a testament to family and purpose.

I strode over to the desk, and a splash of floral pink design blinked into view.

I took the pen that Peter had given to me many years before, at age twenty, and considered it quietly.

And then I moved to what had once been my "toy shelves"—now simply shelves—a single purpose filling me.

My hand reached it, and then lifted the item closer.

The fairy prince and princess holographic painting sparkled in the light entering the window, flowers and small fairies of pinks, blues, and purples surrounding the taller fairy royalty. After seventeen years of it lying idly on the top layer of my shelves, examined only from time to time—and less so over the past year and a half—there were tiny tears in the border of black surrounding the picture, and the golden frame was, if only minimally considering the time passed, slightly rusted. Yet the images it presented could not have been more clear. The girl, pointed ears peeking out from beneath her curly brown hair, looked up at the prince, and he at her, and they clasped hands. It was as if the background existed only to fulfill their expression, caught in wonder and love, a reflection of all that they were, but almost forgotten as they could only see each other.

If that was a cliché, it was the truest cliché that ever was.

I took the foil painting in my hand, and, in one, steady movement, pressed it against the wall.

It looked back at me, shimmering in a vibrancy of color beyond any painting that had ever been created.

Beyond this room itself.

It was time.

Seventeen years I had waited to put up the painting. But then I had not known who the fairy prince was.

I placed the painting on my desk, then swiftly moved from the room. In a moment, I returned with a yellow-red hammer and silver nails.

When, some minutes later, the painting was affixed firmly to the wall, I stood back to examine it.

I gazed at the painting, and, in it, I found a truth, an array of color and form that filled that small room all at once with resounding depth.

It was home.

Chapter 37: Silver Pearl

"Hi, Grandpa." I sat down on the sofa lightly shaded in earth tones, and looked at him.

He was watching the garden through the lens of the sliding glass door, gazing out in silence, yet the gaze was less focused. He was not wholly present—not truly here.

"I remember, a few months before she got sick, this image, this picture in my mind," he finally spoke, but his voice was labored. "She was picking lemons, and the light was on her hair, and she turned back to me with a smile, this *beautiful* smile, and she was that eighteen-year-old again that I fell in love with the instant she stepped into that psychology class after the war."

I bit my lip, trying to stem the tears from coming. One tear, and I would lose it all.

"That beautiful, beautiful image of her in the garden. I told Fr. D'Angelo yesterday during his weekly visit, and he said it was a gift to me."

He turned his great eyes toward me.

"It was," I said softly.

"I never expected . . . her to go. I never expected to lose her. She was my life. She *is*, she is my life." Tears pooled deep within his large, Italian eyes, and within him was a truth conveyed to me, the knowledge that his heart would always be broken, always mourn the loss of the love of his life, as certain as the fact that I would miss Grandma until the day I died.

No, this loss was not one that would ever leave him, forever returning with the breaking dawn, even with the healing balm of time.

He could not forget. Nor should he.

But today, today I could try to take away—no, *alleviate*—some of the pain. For just a moment.

Sometimes, sometimes a moment was enough.

Or all we could have.

I touched Grandpa lightly on the shoulder. "Would you like me to read some of your poetry to you?"

Grandpa, aside from all his internal sufferings, was also slowly going blind.

The poet, the reader, the great intellect, *my grandpa*, struggled to read.

And it broke my already-shattered heart.

"That would be nice," he said.

"Any requests?"

"No, you can pick."

I stood up, leafing through the many volumes of his poetry on one of the shelves he had built years before in his library, before finally selecting his fifth published volume.

The cover. A scenic view.

A lemon tree.

And I began to read.

As I finished one poem, Grandpa requested another and another, and tranquility slowly settled over the room. When I finished the eleventh poem, selected out of order, I looked up, and the glimmer of a near-smile—not quite, but *something* focused, beyond the glazed expression cast in the distance of a man lost in time to one name as he yearned for his beloved—now, almost, found in it.

If only for a moment.

"You have a lovely reading voice, sweetheart. You mean the words." His voice was calmer, more thoughtful and measured.

"Thank you, Grandpa," I said quietly, and then more fervently, "And I do. I do mean them."

I squeezed his hand.

"Poetry is a special thing, isn't it?"

"The very best," I said. "But especially yours."

For a moment, he smiled.

"But we have one poem left to read before dinner," I said, turning to the next page.

It was a favorite poem—different from his war episodic and philosophical—yet somehow meaningful all the same.

It was about the time Grandpa uncharacteristically put on a pair of jeans, prompting a remark from Grandma that he looked like "an old Italian wrangler." He wore those jeans again when my family visited, completing the look with a cowboy hat, and I had insisted on a photo. Alex, Grandpa, and me, the muffled laughter of Grandma and Mom visualized mid-action in the background. Three wide, carefree grins lighting up the five-year-old photo.

I still had that photo on my desk.

I read the poem, using my "cowboy" voice throughout.

I was on the second verse when I heard it, and looked up.

My eyes burned as my heart was caught in my throat.

Laughter. Grandpa was laughing.

It had been so long since I had witnessed it. *So very long.*

I smiled through the tears that suddenly sprang to my eyes.

And then I joined in with him, meeting his deep chuckle with my own signature mark, peals of laughter echoing throughout the room, soaring far beyond.

One moment.

In the midst of our laughter, I saw, out of the corner of my eye, Mom peeking curiously around the edge of the library room. A peace and deep emotion settled in her eyes before she retreated, leaving the two of us alone.

"Grandma would have loved that," he said suddenly. "She'd be . . . is proud."

I took his hand.

"She was the best the world had."

"Yes," I managed to choke out. "As are you."

I squeezed his hand with a small smile.

And just, just for a moment, that moment was enough.

Chapter 38: Variscite

"So, how was your trip?" I twisted the phone cord absentmindedly.

"Pretty sweet. But clearly not as eventful as yours," Adriana's voice came from the other end of the phone.

"It was . . . something. And I haven't even told you the whole of it."

Such as Cedric, for one.

And your realization about Peter, for another, an inner voice chastised me.

That would be harder to tell somehow, even to my best friend.

"Dude. You didn't get kidnapped a *third* time, did you?"

"No, no, nothing like that. It just will . . . take a long time to explain," I said evasively.

"Gotcha. Any hints as to the subject?"

"Remember that old usher from church, Cedric?"

"Oh, yeah, I heard he just retired."

"In a manner of speaking . . . we actually ran into him in Banff."

"DUDE. Small world. Was he part of the adventure?"

"You could say that. It'll be . . . easier to explain in person, I think. Speaking of which, when are you free?" I asked. "We can even meet up tomorrow evening, if you want. I'll be free after 5."

"*Oh.* Gosh, I have plans tomorrow, actually. So sorry, dude."

"No worries," I reassured her. "Anything fun planned?"

"Yeah, it should be! I'm going to be spending some time with Peter at the new café on 5th."

Oh.

I froze, my hand suddenly no longer interested in twisting the phone cord, as it slowly unraveled itself.

In all the years I had known Peter, Adriana and Peter had never gotten together without me. And it was obvious that I was not invited to this get-together.

It wasn't that they couldn't.

But they weren't as close friends. They had always been more a part of The Trio element.

Until now.

"That . . . should be fun," I said, trying to still the quaver in my voice.

"Yeah, for sure! I visited their website, and the dinner menu looks really good."

And for dinner.

An image of Adriana and Peter at Dr. Yin's office, acting out a scene for the benefit of the bewildered secretary, emerged in my mind. Peter tipping his hat, as

Adriana feigned a blush. I had considered myself adept at the dramatics, but Adriana, and Peter—despite his quiet nature—showed *more*.

They had, in that moment, what you could call chemistry.
Why had I never seen it before?
"Rebecca?"
"Yeah, I'm still here." I forced myself to sound upbeat. After all, they were my two closest friends. "I . . . hope you two have a good time."
And maybe I was misinterpreting it all. Maybe . . .
"Thanks, dude. I'm really looking forward to it. I think there's a lot of potential for that evening."
The last bit of hope sank inside me, plunging beyond my heart to every dimension of reality I had ever known.
"I hope it's a beautiful day," I said.

Wisps of clouds scattered across the heavens, as if brought to their place by a great sigh. The imagery for a moment made me wonder what could cause such a sigh.
Perhaps it was one wrought with agony or joy.
Yet it was not enough to keep the bright rays of the sun at bay. One traveler might see golden brilliance splitting through the clouds like the crown of a princess on her coronation day.
Another day I might have been that traveler.
But today I could only feel oppressive heat smothering me, pushing against my old college T-shirt

with excessive warmth that tortured rather than comforted or enlightened.

It was only 80 degrees (by my last check on weather.com—which I had checked five times before leaving and approximately twelve since I had left my house). But, to me, it was at least twenty degrees hotter.

It's your fault, I told myself, as I neared Café Azalea on 5th Avenue. *You should never have come here. You cannot blame the weather. You are torturing yourself.*

And stalking.

Stalking your two best friends.

I glanced at my cell phone before crossing the street.

6:15 PM. Fifteen minutes after their meeting started.

Their date, I forced myself to say in my mind.

6:15. Maybe it *was* hot for 6:15. I could write a poem about various sci-fi scenarios that could lead to that effect . . .

I shook my head, glaring at myself within.

Always the poet freak. The words of another man circled through my head.

Or maybe just a freak in general. Not a freak-dork-nerd-geek. Just a plain freak.

Just weird. Not odd.

Did Peter think that?

I took a deep breath. *I had to see.*

And so, ignoring the thoughts that surfaced to distract me from the stabbing feeling in my chest, I crossed the street.

Café Azalea was a small, quaint edifice, the signature flower painted in three depictions of red and pink across the lavender sign. The building itself was ordinary fare, a brown and white structure with large glass windows inlaid around its center for customers to look out at the small park nearby with its grassy inclines, towering trees, and a smattering of its namesake throughout.

Or look in from the outside.

I stood by the window, my eyes scanning what lay within, as my heart pounded erratically in my chest.

Then, in an instant, I saw them.

They were sitting on the far side of the same long window from which I gazed, seemingly deep in conversation.

And then I saw Adriana laugh, as if at something Peter said . . . and then Peter smiled.

Peter's Grin.

My insides twisted into a tangle of mismatched parts, metallic and cold, not really here, not really alive.

I knew at that moment that I should have turned away. I should have averted my gaze, walked away, and gone home.

I should have.

But instead my face was glued to the screen, as if watching the climax of a movie—but this was a movie that I had never wished to see.

Adriana tossed her hair over one shoulder— playful, almost, for Adriana, coquettish, and threw another smile back at Peter as she rose to her feet. Her long, black hair fell in ripples down her back, and I was reminded of how beautiful my best friend was. How alluring she might be to any man, despite what she joked was an impediment in height.

Leave, Rebecca. Go. Just go.

Be happy for them and go.

Peter stood up and smiled again, his eyes resting on her. He moved closer until they were only inches apart, and began to speak.

I was only the girl behind the glass wall.

I could not hear what he said.

But, when his mouth stilled, Adriana smiled a smile I had never seen on her before, and offered her hand to him.

He took it and raised it to his lips.

I turned away, my cheeks burning, my feet moving of their own accord.

I approached the sidewalk, my eyes suddenly filling with moisture that did not allow me to see the cars approaching as clearly as I might have hoped.

I waited, waited for the blinding liquid to flee, to leave me alone, but a fresh batch arrived with each vehicle, as if connected to it.

They will see you. The voice inside of me pleaded desperately. *It's a miracle they didn't when you were looking through the window, spying on their intimate affairs.*

I shivered, wrapping my jacket around me tightly, no longer hung around my waist as the rays of the sun finally returned home, clouds moving to cover them with a lullaby of sleep. *How long had I stood here? Had it grown cold in a single instant?*

I finally wiped my eyes, staring at an empty street, my chin quaking as I bit my lip to stop its progress.

And then I crossed, a solitary figure leaving the reds and pinks behind, silent café laughter an echo severed, the grays and whites of the city streets solid and welcoming as I stared ahead and saw only shapes without faces.

From the Sidewalk

When you pick up
The scattered pieces of yesterday
I wonder what you will find
Oh, Magic Mirror.
It seemed it could have gone either way
Yet the path was farther along
Than I could have foreseen.
I seek my reflection
In echoes of shattered glass
Cast far in the distance.
Yet somehow
The half-conceived memories
Never realized yet believed
Remain with me . . .

CHORUS
When I close my eyes
You're holding my hand
I turn my head
And you're carrying me there
Your eyes look into mine
And for a moment,
Just a moment, you're mine.

I was a crazy anomaly
Certifiably weird
But you said
I was simply odd
To me, you were everything
Sunshine to every day
A guardian of the light
A beautiful kaleidoscope.
You showed me so much.

If only I had known
But I know now you're not mine
So, I'll have to settle for
The most important person in my life . . .

CHORUS
When I close my eyes
You're holding my hand
I turn my head
And you're carrying me there
Your eyes look into mine
And for a moment,
Just a moment, you're mine.

We were somewhere in between
The sea and the clouds
Partners in everything
From each race to the dawn
Somewhere in between
Snow White and her dwarves
A place
Where happiness overflowed
You captured my heart.
I do not know
How you remember it now.
But I hope you know
How real it was to me
How real it always shall be.

I've memorized that look
In your eyes
Expression so sweet
That crosses your face
Your voice
A song to my ears

For so long
It cannot be erased
Not later or now
But somehow, I'll remember
One day I shall remember . . .

CHORUS
When I close my eyes
You're holding my hand
I turn my head
And you're carrying me there
Your eyes look into mine
And for a moment,
Just a moment, you're mine.

I miss being allowed to love you.
Gazing at your words
Looking, and finding hope.
Enclosed in this embrace
Still yearning for your touch.
I miss being allowed to love you.
My sweet, beautiful
Guardian Angel.
I know you will
Never abandon
The keeper of
This Broken Heart.
[*Echo*]
Yet the world I've known is you
And today it's a globe of shattered glass. [*hold last note*]

If I could go back in time
I wouldn't be crying
As I write this line
Memories of you flooding my mind . . .

CHORUS
When I close my eyes
You're holding my hand
I turn my head
And you're carrying me there
Your eyes look into mine
And for a moment,
Just a moment, you're mine.

I know this may
Sound crazy
And that nothing can be done
Echo: Nothing can be done.
But I want you to know
This madness
Is the only truth I know. [*hold last note*]

CHORUS [*slower REPRISE*]
When I close my eyes
You're holding my hand
I turn my head
And you're carrying me there
Your eyes look into mine
And for a moment,
Just a moment, you're mine.

But what I want doesn't matter
The dream is over
Yet never forgotten.
I'll be content
To see you happy
I can even smile
And cheer you on
From the sidelines

Of a tapestry
Woven in my mind.

You never woke me
With a kiss
It was never meant to be
But I hope you know
I will never regret
Meeting you
Oh, it was no accident.
And when I think of it
With pain or sorrow
Bittersweet melancholy
It will still be beautiful
It will always be beautiful . . .

And then you will find
That your friend
I'll always be.
Perhaps one day
I'll remember
How to breathe.
So, smile, my love, smile,
I'll carry on
When I see you
On a mountain top
When everything you dreamed of
Has shone through your life . . .

CHORUS
When I close my eyes
You're holding my hand
I turn my head
And you're carrying me there
Your eyes look into mine

And for a moment,
Just a moment, you're mine.

It was so real
I know it's all gone
Some daydreams
Can't be won
So, I'll carry on . . .
I'll carry on
If I see your eyes smile.
Oh, smile . . .

When I can breathe without crying
The tears will still come
Echo: Still come
And I can't help saying
What lies in my heart
The saddest thing of all is
This truth will remain
I can't help saying
I still love you
Even as you walk away
You can't be more than this
But I'll still love you
From the sidewalk, I'll still love you
Forever I love you.
I love you.
I love you.
I love you.
I love you, my love.

I woke up, and the song I had written the night before could no longer rule my heart.

Maybe I was just too selfish.

I threw on my clothes and ran, my laptop lying open and forgotten on my bed from the night before, a new email blinking into view unseen.

> Rebecca,
>
> Dude, I don't know what to say. I am really, really stupid. About last evening . . .
>
> Okay, so, I had this idea. To get you and Peter together. I think you're in love with him, but I KNOW YOU, DUDE. It'll come out eventually, but it'll take you another five years or so. And, by then, Peter might find some nice Albertan girl to go out for a rip with to a shinny or a ride on a toboggan while eating timbits (or peameal and drinking pop), or offer his pencil crayons to—okay, so, I was looking up Canadian expressions on the Internet, don't shoot me! Anyway, dude, after you came back from Canada and your relationship status on Facebook didn't undergo a serious alteration or appear to be getting there, I thought I should take matters into my own hands. And, in true Adriana fashion, it was an epic fail.
>
> You see, I met with Peter last night to practice the script to this play I wrote. I'm thinking of submitting it to—well, never mind, that's not important now. But I needed a male lead, and I was going to rope Alex into it because, dude, what good are best friends' brothers

but to be forced to do stuff—but then I had this, again, idea. If I invited Peter out to practice as the male lead and told you about it without telling you *why* we were meeting up, that would make something CLICK in your brain and basically . . . make you go crazy and realize your undying love for him, and, once I explained to you later it wasn't a date, make you need to tell him ASAP??

So, I went ahead with my dumb idea. I invited Peter, explained that I needed help, and he graciously accepted. We practiced our parts.

And, yeah, I saw you staring at the street, dude. I know because I bought that purple sweatshirt with the butterflies for you our senior year of high school, so don't try to deny it was you. Besides, stalking is epic, so I totally get that and won't judge.

And, because I know you were there, you probably also saw Peter about to "kiss" my hand?

Well, you should know that he *didn't*. I wasn't going to make him anyway because he's your man, not that hand kissing is the same as other types. I mean, dude, even subjects kiss the hand of their queen, and it doesn't mean romance or anything.

But I lifted my hand, and he couldn't do it. He wasn't nervous, he wasn't shy, he just *couldn't*.

HE CAN'T EVEN KISS MY HAND IN PRETEND.

Dude, the guy clearly adores you.

Just marry Usher Dude already. Or at least go out on a date.

Again, I am *so*, so sorry. I would completely understand if you want to feed me to a dozen of those Sith birds you found at the library park. I would totally deserve it.

Love,

Your (still, I hope) best friend,

Adri

Chapter 39: Grandidierite

"Peter, are you in love with Adriana?"

I had marched into the bank, walked up to the counter where Peter awaited clients in his usual calm manner, and overrode traditional greetings by asking the question that had been pressing on my mind for the past sixteen hours.

Desperate times call for desperate measures.

When I saw the bewildered expression on his face, I almost felt remorse for my crazed outburst.

Rebecca doesn't act like this except in the farthest reaches of her over-active imagination.

"Rebecca, what are you—"

"It's fine, really, it is," I went on, absentmindedly ignoring his half-spoken query. "You can do whatever you want with . . . your life. Maybe you two will go on the stage together. Performances from two promising cross-national stars—"

"Rebecca—"

"... which really is ... pretty brilliant. You should do that. If you want." My voice cracked at those last words in spite of myself.

"Rebecca, I really—"

"And it's completely fine. And . . . this is a bank." I took out my wallet, my hands shaking. "I shouldn't leave without depositing some money."

I grabbed half a dozen bills and tossed them into the air, one by one. "It really doesn't matter, okay?"

Peter turned into a multi-skilled athlete/stealth man, half defense and half surveillance, simultaneously pulling back my arm in an attempt to halt the remaining flurry of paper bills and turning just as rapidly in an effort to distract curious eyes that wandered in the direction of the bills.

"Rebecca, what is going on—"

"Everything is perfectly fine!" My voice began to tremble again as I fought unwanted tears. "I'm . . . going to leave now."

I straightened my purse strap with any remaining dignity that I had, and walked calmly in the direction of the door.

It took about two steps before I started running, ignoring in my flight a familiar voice calling me back.

The tears had come fully now, streaming down my face. I gave up trying to stop them.

Why did I have to cry?

Why did it have to be him?

And why did I just turn my cash into a life-size, interactive green waterfall?

"Rebecca." I felt a familiar hand on my shoulder, and turned.

Peter Joseph Asturian stood before me, a mixture of concern and puzzlement filling his countenance.

"Oh." I looked away. "I'm sorry about the scene." Another tear, little and timid, escaped my eye.

"Rebecca, I don't care about that."

I looked down, not hearing his words. "You know that I don't . . . normally do things . . . like that. I . . . you can marry Adriana . . . you should really tell her. I wouldn't . . . I would be happy for you both. I—"

Peter's lips were upon mine, soft as the gentle sea breeze of a sun-set shore.

"Oh." I blinked. "I guess you're not in love with Adriana."

His eyes looked deeply into mine, and then he slowly shook his head. "Rebecca . . . I've been in love with you for the past four and a half years. Not always knowing . . . but it was there. And you . . ." Those great eyes returned to me. "What a puzzle you are. One moment, you're bashfully covering a poem that you just wrote, and, in another, you are throwing money at people. You are completely insane and random—and beautiful and genuine and true—and I love you for it."

"You do?"

"Yes."

Once again, I was having difficulty seeing.

"And," he continued, "I'm not sure where in the world you got it in your head that I was in love with your best friend." Peter shook his head again, finally smiling. "Rebecca, you really are . . . odd."

Another time, another place. Two young kids.

Silence surrounded us, the wind moving lightly with invisible hands. I could barely make out a blue jay's song.

I looked down shyly at my feet. "I never pictured you as the type to interrupt someone with a kiss."

"Nor I," Peter said quietly.

"Peter?"

"Yes?"

"I love you."

I had seen Peter's smile before, in all of its brilliance, but never like this, the pure radiance lighting up his face like a moonbeam.

"Do you?"

"Yes. Very much."

"Very?"

I looked at him. His eyes, too, were now filled.

"A thousand Intermissions and buckets of Duku jam over—"

"Farther than Antonio's lighthouse?"

"Like Antonio—"

"—and Patria."

"Farther than the sea itself."

"I love you."

"I love you."

I closed my eyes, and the world around me disappeared as a new one came to light.

There's no room for a thorn
In a heart meant to be whole
And so, I'll leave it behind.

When I drove down that road
In the afternoon light
I knew, in that moment,
That, at last,
I was ready to love again.
One week later, he appeared
In a glance from Heaven above.
I took the thorn from my heart
And he closed the wound.
He is my home and my rock.

CHORUS 3
This is a love song
But it isn't just for me
It's for the love I found
Beyond the thorns
With a gift from the One
Who was nailed to the Cross
With a crown of Thorns
I found the one that I sought.

[*quietly, more slowly*]
The Prince of princes
Brought a knight

Worth every moment of the thorn
With him, I found more.

BRIDGE
[*more loudly*]
Let the rain pour . . .

[*tempo increases; violin/guitar riff*]

This is a love song
[Let the rain pour]
Let your heart learn to heal
[Let it flow]
No cross or barricade
Is too much
[Flow over you]
Let the thorn in your heart
Fall away
[Over you]
As the pieces
Of its refuge
Form anew
You are worth so much more.

[*slower, more quietly*]
Let the thorn in your heart fall away
Your mosaic is enough.

Epilogue: Chrysocolla

"Oh, Peter," I breathed.

We were standing before a great lighthouse, which rose alabaster and tall on a rocky cliff against the august sea, foamy waves dipped in azure tumbling in serene ecstasy as a sea breeze caught their joy, blowing lightly across the scene. I lifted my head higher, gazing up to the very top, a red frame where a light would beam across the night to travelers at sea, beckoning them, bringing them safely home. In that moment, I heard a melody, strong and sure, yet as soft as the dancing waves, bringing within their folds a legend passed through bygone years to the present—once haunting, but now free—a story that a bard might once have told.

I was wearing The Green Dress, filmy puffed sleeves spilling across as light and dainty as the wings of a faerie, emerald sea green roses of form swirling across the top to cascade downward to my knees in billows of the same nimble effervescence.

Peter had told me, in that way of his, that he had a surprise for me, and, despite my protests and with that wry grin of his, refused to reveal the destination. I made an inner note to issue an official protest during our next incident of verbal sparring about his tendency to challenge my natural love for surprise—and torture my naturally curious mind. Yet all was forgotten as we stepped out of the car into the sunlight of a new summer day, and the lighthouse stood before me, words of welcome bidding me toward it like the sea.

"It has been so long since I have visited a lighthouse," I said breathlessly. "Not since I was a young teen. It has always lived in my dreams. Is it not strange then that I should only have experienced it in person once in my life?"

"I know. I wanted you to see it again . . . for more reasons than one. But, no, Rebecca, it is not strange. It is in your stories, and therefore in your heart," he said simply. His hand brushed against mine, and he squeezed it, his eyes alight. "Now, shall we go in?"

I eagerly strode forth as if to leap forward into the great structure, and then drew back, laughing. "Is that even a question?" And then, "Can we?"

"I would hazard a guess that it is the best course of action."

My eyes danced, meeting those of Peter with a smile that I could not contain—could no longer contain with him—tiptoeing closer until our feet were only inches apart. "Is it?"

Peter cupped my chin and tilted my head up to gaze into my eyes for an instant, solemn and smiling all at once, and then he kissed me, stroking my cheek lightly with one hand as I caught my breath, his lips warm against mine. It did not matter how often this occurred; it was as if it were the first time, the same sense of wonder and ecstasy never leaving me.

He drew back, profound affection written across his eyes with a depth greater than I had ever seen before addressed toward me.

This was the Peter who had been an essential part of my life—no, not a *part*, but *my life*—almost from the first day we met. This was the Peter of all the thoughts and memories, a film reel of all those times he had been there for me, sometimes showing up unexpectedly and even saving my life, from the days and nights he watched over me when I was in the hospital to the perilous adventures in Canada. I recalled each moment of trust and confidence like a snapshot in my mind.

I had realized that, although I had not admitted my love for Peter until years later, I would have had to admit—ever since I was twenty years old—that a life without Peter would have been unthinkable. Without having even expressed it, we had been one heart, one mind, for so long.

And now, now we were here.

For the past two years, Peter and I had dated, completely and utterly besotted, perfectly smitten—and deeply in love. The first year had been the most difficult, a romance conducted across the distance after Peter returned to Alberta at the end of the summer when we had first confessed our love to resume his teaching position in Canmore, a neighboring town of Banff. We visited each other as often as we could, which usually amounted to three or four times a year for a week to a month at a time, especially during the holidays. This was a time of forlornness and yearning—the realization and expression of our love seeming somehow to make the distance that we had become accustomed to for years even more unbearable than before. We began to discuss how that might change. At the end of the first year during a summer visit, Peter told me that he had been offered a teaching position about an hour away from Cedar Heights. Excitement had bounded across my heart and very being (hyperbole now real), irresistible before my eyes grew wide, and a sort of sadness remained with the realization that he was leaving his world for mine—his family and that beautiful Banff that I had come to love. I felt resigned, obligated to tell him that he should not do this for me, but he had expected that. He had told me, with great tenderness in his eyes, that he would miss it, but had not wanted to take me away from Albert and all the other clients dear to my heart who relied upon me—that my position here was needed, whereas he could find a new class to teach now that the school year was out.

"And, for you, I gladly do so," he had said.

I sighed, more and more in love, as I leaned against his shoulder, and he smiled down at me.

The best two years of my life.

I took his hand, never leaving his eyes until it became necessary due to my clumsy tendencies, and remained then content to feel his warmth against mine as we linked hands, and then walked arm in arm toward the great lighthouse.

"Adri's play still running?" Peter said conversationally as we neared the door.

"Oh, yes. And Alexander has gone to every single performance." I shook my head with a smile. "I still can't believe that they have been dating for a year. That I didn't even see this coming at all. I don't know which is crazier—that, or the fact that Amelia is starting her first year of college next year—or that Teresa is dating that Tom from Family Day at St. Vitus' after meeting him at the supermarket when she dropped all her groceries in a completely Rebecca-esque move, I might add. Adriana and Alexander. *A squared*. My brother and my best friend, for crying out loud!"

Adriana had submitted The Play—a scene from which I had mistaken for an actual romance with Peter, crazy that I was—to a promising agency. It had been greatly praised, and accepted, now performed to sold-out audiences in one of the best theaters in Los Angeles. The night of the first performance, my big brother Alexander had run up to her backstage, and, before he had a chance to tell her his feelings that had apparently been lying dormant for quite some time, Adriana, The Notorious-Unromantic-Yet-Not-So-Unromantic-Romantic-After-All and Mighty-Short-Person-Not-To-Be-Reckoned-With, had told him, point blank, "Okay, dude, yes, this is weird, yes, your sister is my best friend and I knew you when I was nine and I threw a water balloon on your head and made you cry, yes, I am crazy, yes, I am crazy about *you*, and, yes, I'll be your girlfriend! Just kiss me already, Spaceship Boy!" Alexander had apparently stood there, his mouth hanging open, completely flabbergasted—and, as I heard tell, that defined much of their relationship. And yet I had great hopes for it materializing into something truly splendid—and real. *Yes, it already was real.*

Peter's eyes teased me as he smiled. "All the best love stories start that way, do they not? I seem to recall a delightful young woman who was completely clueless when it came to the desires of her heart and who held it—"

"Hey!" I tickled him. "You're not allowed to go there!"

He tickled me back, and I leaned back against the lighthouse, laughing.

Peter pulled me to him, his hand around my waist.

"Hi," I said, my eyes alight as they gazed into his, darting back and forth with the jig of a piccolo, giddiness overtaking me.

"Hi." Peter brushed his lips against my forehead, and then lowered them to kiss my nose.

And then he kissed my hand, raising it to his lips, and his eyes penetrated mine, soft and unobtrusive, yet seeing me—my full essence—in a single glance.

He took my hand in his once again. "Shall we, my princess?"

And then we entered, hand in hand, taking in the scene as the light dimmed, the glow of a small room's candlelight the only remaining illumination.

A long staircase spiraled upward, circling onward like a maze, the tunnels of a labyrinthic home, leading perhaps to the room of the Lighthouse Keeper—and then beyond to the Light itself. The floor was simple, barren and gray brown, understated, yet, in its simplicity, reminiscent of the glory of another time—and therefore never barren and never simple. Brown walls extended on either side, peeling slightly around the edges and leading to a wooden bookshelf, dust collecting across worn volumes, and farther still, to an ancient grandfather clock, ticking to a rhythm that many had long forgotten. There was a small table, the same color and shade as the bookshelf, and a few miscellaneous tools, long fallen into disarray and disuse, lying about.

There was a timelessness here, and yet a sense of time greater than any before, that could only be found in a lighthouse.

For a moment, I recalled Cedric, and, with bittersweet recollection, *missed* him. But there was still a tranquility, a peace in my heart.

"I have . . . something for you," Peter said softly from behind me.

"The annual pink floral pen?" I teased him, twirling a curl around my finger lightly as I turned around. "It *is* a new year, isn't it? Hiding it in a lighthouse was an unexpected turn-of-events, but—"

"Yes, it is a new year," Peter said. "But, no, not the pen."

And, at that moment, I knew.

Yet, like any other girl before me, I could never truly *know*—not until . . .

"Peter." My voice came out in a whisper, and a small smile fell across my face and then retreated, as I became unable to speak.

And then, I turned again, not to avoid his gaze—and he knew this—not to prolong the moment—though perhaps I was—not because I did not want to hear it—oh, I did with all my heart.

Yet all Peter did as he looked back at me, betraying no sense of change in his countenance—still measured and undisturbed—was say, "Would you care to take the stairs?"

"Of course. I'd love to." The excitement of seeing the top of the lighthouse, the actual beacon of light that had inspired my imagination and heart—inspired me in my writing and defined my inner self—almost overtook me. Perhaps I had been mistaken about all else.

Peter kissed me lightly on the lips as I took his hand, before leading me toward the spiraling maze above.

And so, we ascended the stairs, taking a step at a time, Peter reaching back every so often to ensure that my footing was secure, reminding me of a moment long ago when we climbed a series of hills to eventually find a swing that would change everything.

When I reached the top—beyond the lighthouse keeper's room—only a step behind Peter, moving into the room beyond, I gasped.

Ahead of us was a porthole, looking out at the sea, waves glistening in a sunset that had just broken across the heavens. A small sailboat lingered in the distance, white sails billowing lightly in the wind. And, beside it, was the Light.

"*Oh.* This is a lovely place, Peter. Thank you for bringing me here. Oh, thank you—"

I turned.

Peter knelt before me on one knee, gazing up into my eyes. His large hazel eyes caught the light from a lantern hanging on the wall and seemed at that moment to be aglow. And, in one hand, was a thin, silver ring, broken only by a tiny, glittering diamond, like a tiny *swan* star.

My hand flew to my mouth. *So, this, too, was not a cliché.* This, too, was what occurred when one of the greatest moments—the greatest surprise—of your life came upon you. When your life would never be the same again.

"*Oh.*" This was all I could say, all I could utter, as my eyes filled, as they remained affixed on the kneeling figure. I stared back at Peter, whose eyes remained on mine. And then, as my heart soared, he opened his mouth to speak, still gazing at me with the most emotion I had ever seen contained in their depths.

"My Rebecca, when I met you, I was broken, walking in a desert, neither here nor there—resolved in my purpose to make amends, but fragmented, lost, all the same. Yet, when I looked into your eyes the first time, that changed. The more I grew to know you, the more that changed." Peter's voice softened. "I saw your beauty, the beauty of your eyes and your laugh, the curl of your hair, the beauty of your mind and your heart, your idiosyncrasies and quirks, and, most of all, the beauty of your *soul*." Peter paused, and, when he looked up, there was something glistening in his eyes. "Long ago, you told me that I was your rock. But you, Rebecca, are also my rock."

"Oh, Peter," I said softly.

Peter's eyes met mine, soft, warm—a caress.

"I've kept each moment from the past several years like the gems of a music box, a seamless melody of so many thoughts playing again and again, holding on to each memory, each smile or word, each moment we've shared, like a treasure, something precious and unbreakable in a fragile world—not knowing as I stared across the lake or left on the plane if I would be allowed the honor of another such moment—and I would have given anything, *anything,* for just *one* of those moments to hold in my memory, and in my heart, to forever keep. But I've grown greedy . . ."

A kaleidoscope of memories fluttered through my mind, slowing down for each important moment, from the first day I saw Peter holding the Offertory basket at Mass as an usher to our first kiss on that bright summer day, and my heart was caught in my throat.

". . . and, if you would allow me, I would like to spend the rest of my life collecting each and every moment that there yet remains to be—with you. Rebecca Veritas, will you marry me?"

Tears—beautiful raindrops of tears glistening on a summer leaf—overflowed, spilling liberally across my cheeks, and, with them, two words emerged:

"Yes, Peter," I said.

Here ends the final volume of the trilogy known as *The Veritas Chronicles*.

But . . .

Mr. Francis and Mrs. Patricia Veritas
invite you to the Nuptial Mass uniting their daughter
Rebecca Elizabeth
to Peter Joseph Asturian
in the Sacrament of Holy Matrimony

Saturday, June 20, 2020
two o'clock in the afternoon

St. Vitus Catholic Church
251 Knight Crest Road
Cedar Heights, California 92501

It is the event that you have all been waiting for! Along with two other *Veritas Chronicles* short stories, revealed in *One Word, One Moment, One Dance*, an upcoming collection of ten new tales by Gina Marinello-Sweeney, this highly anticipated event following the third and final novel, *Peter*, will be available for your literary perusal.

Get ready to RSVP when the book appears on Amazon and other retailers. The release date is yet to be determined. Follow the latest updates on the author's social media pages and official website.

Facebook:
www.facebook.com/ginamarinellosweeneyauthorpage

Twitter and Instagram:
@novelist_gina

Website:
www.ginamarinellosweeney.com

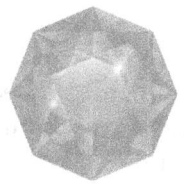

Acknowledgments

Thank you, God, for guiding me in yet another literary journey. I wouldn't have been able to do it without You. As this story comes to an end, I know that, in a way, it has only just begun.

For my wonderful fiancé, Vinnie, who has been there through so many joys and struggles in my life. You are the best man I could ever have by my side. Thank you for being the very first reader of *Peter*, and for all our conversations about the book—from your amusing sidenotes that kept me laughing to your sweet, thoughtful words, to your helpful suggestions. Thank you for being "you." I have in you not just the love of my life, but a best friend to whom I can tell anything, big or small. You accept me and my quirky nature, and are just as insane yourself. You make me feel like a princess and a partner-in-crime all at once. Most of all, you are my rock.

For my parents, who encouraged my dreams as a writer ever since I was a little girl. Thank you for your meticulous reading of *Peter* and subsequent suggestions. It seems that each beta reader has a special area of focus—unique aspects that stand out to them as individuals—and this process was no different. Your feedback has been immeasurably helpful. Thank you, as always, for your love and support. You are the best parents in the world.

For my grandma, who passed away a year and a half ago. I will miss you until the day that I die. I wish that you could read this final volume, you who perused the first two. Maybe God can let you read it from Heaven. And for Grandpa, who mourns her deeply, may you write many more poems with that great yard of yours as the backdrop. She remains with you always.

For Jansina, who continues to be the best publisher and most incredible friend, for her tireless effort, skill, and guidance. Your knowledge and attention to detail are, once again, astounding. Thank you for believing in this book and in me. Thank you for your support, patience, and encouragement throughout the journey of this series. Most of all, thank you for your friendship. I will always treasure it.

To my brother, the other Vinnie in my life, for being his epic, awesome self. Rock on, dude. Where's my spaceship?! By the way, thanks for being the best big brother ever.

And to the dear friends and devoted fans, here we are. *The Veritas Chronicles* may have reached its conclusion (other than a few side stories and perhaps an intermission I have up my sleeve ;)), but it will never really be over. All the same, I hope you enjoy the final chapter of sorts, whether you are #TeamPeterandRebecca (A special shout-out to my honorary sorella Kateri, the creator and ringleader of the team!) and have fought tirelessly for #Rebeter, or far removed from such notions. This story is for you, too. Thank you for all your love and support over the years. You continue to inspire and motivate me.

Readers, remember this, no matter what you are facing: When you feel too weak to stand, collapse on your bed, and look up at the ceiling . . . lean over and grab a flashlight like the song by Hunter Hayes. Point it at the ceiling and look at its small reflection of Light. As you stare at it, devoid of coherent thought, remember it. Remember it, even if now all you can do is hurt. Remember that, one day, you WILL be okay.

And, if the time comes when you feel that the bed is sinking to the ground, that you are lost there and content to remain that way forever, stand up. Hold on to goodness and beauty and Light, even if you cannot see them. Even if all you have is the memory of a shining torch.

Remember that a single pool of light still reaches the Greatest Eternity.

A broken heart will one day become a beautiful mosaic.

Thank you to the Whyte Museum of the Canadian Rockies for taking the time to answer my questions. Your help was greatly appreciated! As the museum is a focal point at the beginning of the adventure and inspires mystery, I can only hope that I did it justice. Best wishes.

And for the owners of the store Four Seasons, now closed but never forgotten, for once selling a foil painting of a fairie prince and princess. That little girl still has it.

Bonus Features

Fun Fact

Pietersite is the same gemstone as Tiger's Eye; that chapter is a turning point for Peter and also refers back to the poem Little Dan and Rebecca read. In addition to the overarching metaphor of the book itself, each rock chapter title was specifically chosen for a purpose. Can you figure out the significance of the other gems and their chapter correlation?

Bonus Songs

Alternate Song Ending to Ch. 38

Half Hope, Whole Heart

I've always been a dreamer
Kept my head and heart
Up in the clouds
I never let the pain tell me
That a future would not be true
But sometimes at night it was too hard.
And, of all the dreams and hopes,
I kept most dear and hoped the most
Unknown, he was in every one.
I knew, I know, I always had, I always will
There was only half a possibility
Not even sure if it was meant to be
But I dreamed of the half anyway.

I looked ahead at the play
But all I saw was far away
In some world I didn't know
Would ever come true
Yet in that moment
Everything was real
As real as anything could be
And then I believed it could
One day be true
You and I
Me and you
From the first steps
To the end
All in the flash
I saw it all . . .

CHORUS
I saw the day we first
Saw the light
I saw the day that we made a promise
To be kept until the Earth dies
I saw our children laughing
Walking with us, hand in hand
And I saw, I saw
You and I
Growing old together
One moment
One moment that had it all.

I knew there was half a chance that it would
Half a chance that it wouldn't
Because I'd been there before
Had my heart broken.
Left with no assumptions
But I still kept the hope alive
Half a hope, but never half a heart.

All in the flash
I saw it all . . .

CHORUS
I saw the day we first
Saw the light
I saw the day that we made a promise
To be kept until the Earth dies
I saw our children laughing
Walking with us, hand in hand
And I saw, I saw
You and I
Growing old together
One moment

One moment that had it all.

And even now, when it's gone
With a dream turned to dust
With one night
If I could go back
Would I change it now?
Noo, no, no
Never destroy your heart
By tearing apart
A dream made with love.

Half a hope, but never half a heart.

A Song Written by Rebecca Veritas for Peter Asturian Upon Their Engagement

Forest Firefly

[*Violin solo leads to simple piano melody*]

Deep in the forest
I wait for you
I'm not a damsel in distress
But I'm a lost princess far from home
Far from home.

[*Brief violin/piano interlude, which moves to solo piano. Violin returns intermittently in chorus, but piano remains consistent*]

Broken and twisted
My heart has been
Hopeful and filled with promise
'Til it was shattered to the floor.

But I never believed
That you were a Lost Boy
Never to leave
Neverland.
No, I've been tortured and cast aside
But the memory of a hope
Never died.

I knew you'd come.

[*Violin*]

And then I saw
Gleaming at the edge of the forest
Branches of silver and gold
Like the old tale
I have danced like the twelve
Waiting for your return
Though we've never met.

No, we've never met
Just in a dream.

[*Orchestral interlude*]

A figure tall, visage obscured
My hands outstretched, shaking
Is this it?
The cloak is drawn back
And I'd seen your face
Before.
But I had not known
It would be you.

I had not known it would be you.

Oh, I had not known it would be you
But now I'm home.

CHORUS
I dreamed of chandeliers
Strung from palace walls
But you're my firefly
Glimmering in the dark
Flying across the night sky
I'm standing by the shore
And I'm yours

Forever yours
Forest firefly
In my silver night.

Forest firefly,
It's been seven years
Six months less
If we're going to be precise.
Seven years of you
In my heart and in my life
Though not always knowing
Seven years
That I will never let go.

And I have waited
Dim echoes haunting
That fade away
With your touch
Like a record player
That would play again and again
Like the ones before
You would have left
But you stayed.
You stayed.

An enchanted mirror
Images fade away
Fade away
And turn to you.

CHORUS
I dreamed of chandeliers
Strung from palace walls
But you're my firefly
Glimmering in the dark

Flying across the night sky
I'm standing by the shore
And I'm yours
Forever yours
Forest firefly
In my silver night.

Chandeliers have beauty
But they cannot traverse the world
A world
You have become.
Chandeliers are a fairy tale
But you are more.
The greatest fairy tale
I have ever read
The greatest story
I have never penned
You look at me
And our eyes lock
Hearts beating faster still
It's as if we'd just
Fallen in love
Seven years more

Every day
I fall more in love.

Forest firefly
You have my heart.

CHORUS
I dreamed of chandeliers
Strung from palace walls
But you're my firefly
Glimmering in the dark

Flying across the night sky
I'm standing by the shore
And I'm yours
Forever yours
Forest firefly
In my silver night.

Will you spin gold
And ask my name?
I would give it
With all my life.
If a spell and an apple
Took me asleep
It would be your name
Of which I'd dream
East of the Sun, West of the Moon
I'd travel far to a kingdom of ice
Just to behold you
Once more.

Forevermore.

CHORUS
I dreamed of chandeliers
Strung from palace walls
But you're my firefly
Glimmering in the dark
Flying across the night sky
I'm standing by the shore
And I'm yours
Forever yours
Forest firefly
In my silver night.

Meet me at the ball
I'll wear a dress
Of midnight blue
Roses cascade above
Christmas lights echoing
Around and around
A glass tower.
I'd take your hand
Pied Piper
Held at bay
Your song is true
Aladdin's lamp
In my silver night.

Let us venture
To the sea
Merfolk
Forever free
But if I go near or far
Forest firefly
Be my prince
Aurora's refuge
Reflected in your eyes.

Palace of the forest
A chandelier no more
Dream spun to life
You're my chandelier
Lifted from the page
But you're real.

Forest firefly
In my silver night
I am yours.

An Interview with the Author:
Final Thoughts from Gina Marinello-Sweeney at the
Conclusion of a Series

1. How does it feel to have finished *The Veritas Chronicles* trilogy?

   Disbelief was one of the most dominant emotional reactions when I finished writing the last book. After so many years devoted to these characters and their stories, it was a near-unreality difficult to fathom that it had, more or less, come to an end. As much as I was elated to have finished writing the book after dedicating so much to its completion, there was also a strong sense of the bittersweet at saying goodbye. Perhaps that is why I still have a few tricks up my sleeve, even though the trilogy itself is complete.

   With that being said, writing a series is different from penning a standalone—particularly in terms of the time spent. As much as I loved getting to know the world of *The Veritas Chronicles,* I look forward to exploring other literary worlds and stories—both new and old.

2. What project(s) are up next?

   My next project is a short story collection. As of now, it is about halfway complete. I am excited at the prospect of sharing stories from a wide variety of genres and, in some cases, with stylistic differences from my first published series. However, there will also be three *Veritas Chronicles* stories included in the collection; there is one in particular that should be of especial interest to fans. ;)

   After the collection, I will either return to my much-neglected epic fantasy series (which I started writing and conceptualizing before *The Veritas Chronicles*!) or work on my Super Secret Project—a newer idea for another fantasy novel that, as a true FDNG, I'm pretty thrilled about. I also plan to eventually write a *Veritas Chronicles* Christmas novella or novelette that will take place approximately ten years after *Peter*. I'm curious as to what my characters will be up to at the time—and already have some preliminary ideas. I am especially excited to meet Little Dan as a twenty-year-old—incidentally and quite accidentally the same age as Rebecca at the beginning of the trilogy! Should be fun. Another project on the backburner is to return to the jam shop troupe and finally finish writing the complete *Intermission* play. Antonio and Monet deserve as much, don't you think?

One day, I also hope to delve into the genres of science fiction and historical fiction. I have a few ideas as to what that might entail. But the aforementioned list should cover the next ten years or so. ;)

3. What was the most memorable part of writing the novel *Peter*?

Too many to list! However, I will attempt to find a starting point . . .

There were portions of *Peter* that were very emotional for me to write—perhaps even moreso than previous volumes (though I do recall tearing up when writing a scene involving Albert in *The Rose and the Sword*, for example). In many ways, the characters are at their most vulnerable in this book. Other stand-out moments in the writing process were revealed in scenes involving and leading up to the answer to the #Rebeter question (shout-out to reader Jonathan F. for coining the term!)—I very much enjoyed writing them, especially since I had to hold back so much before and truly do love writing those kinds of scenes. For more comical considerations, the random insanity and joy of the first jam shop scene was a pure delight to pen.

Yet perhaps what stood out the most in the writing process—aside from the Peter and Rebecca moments and overarching emotional connection—was the experience of meeting and growing to know the elusive and somewhat enigmatic Asturian family. For the previous two books, Peter's family remained largely a mystery to readers—only referenced, not seen—and, while, as the author, I knew them to some degree earlier, previous conceptions were more clearly fleshed out as the series, and especially the final book, progressed. While I have found affection for all my characters through the writing process, Little Dan in particular earned a special place in my heart. I truly loved learning more about that wise and lively little boy—and, much like Rebecca, came to love him. Fictional or not, characters become "real" to the author.

4. What advice would you give to aspiring writers?

My answer may sound cliché, but I would advise that they find their writing voice. It must be authentic in order for a piece to work. At the same time, though, they shouldn't be afraid to explore new territory, whether it be a different writing style (that still speaks to them) or a crazy story idea. Most of all, never care about being popular. The only way that your work will truly find an audience is if it is genuine.

5. If *The Veritas Chronicles* were adapted for film, do you have any top choices to portray the characters?

    While it is highly unlikely that this would occur, I have to admit that I do have an imaginary movie cast in my head! It certainly is fun to consider, regardless.

    I think these two leads would especially be perfect for the roles, based on my observation of their performances and overall appearance:

    Rebecca Veritas –
    Rachel Hendrix (*October Baby*)

    Peter Joseph Asturian –
    Christopher Egan (*Letters to Juliet*)

    I also found an Italian actress named Jasmine Trinca who looked quite a lot like Rebecca (including some facial expressions) when she was a bit younger, but I haven't seen her in any roles and therefore cannot truly judge. Lily James is also a favorite actress of mine who could definitely pull off the role. But Rachel Hendrix really is the closest casting choice I have found thus far for Rebecca. It is also important to note that Mark Lester and Joel Blake, when they were young, looked a bit like I imagine Peter.

Additional Casting
- Alia Shawkat as Adriana Hanson**
- Amanda Seyfried as Chelsey Davis
- Licia Maglietta as Mrs. Veritas
- Pierce Brosnan as Mr. Veritas
- Anne Bancroft as Grandma Allegretti
- Michele Placido as Grandpa Allegretti
- Michael York as Cedric

- Laura Fraser or Paloma Baeza as Olivia Asturian
- John de Lancie as Dr. Everson
- Ralph Waite (RIP) as Albert
- Scarlett Pomers as Amelia?
- Lily James or Ellise Chappell as Teresa?
- Aidan Turner, Eduardo Verastegui, or Antonio Banderas as Tybalt

Intermission Cast
- Joseph di Mambro or Aidan Turner as Antonio Martinelli
- Stewart Finlay-McLennon as Monet
- Flor Nuñez as Morena
- Danielle Panabaker or Lily James as Elise (though Eleanor Tomlinson or Ellise Chappell could also pull it off)

**Based solely on appearance; I have not seen any of her work and therefore cannot really judge. So, I now submit an all-call for a young woman of the following specifications: black hair, short, feisty, quirky, *insane*.

The jury is still out in regards to casting for Jeffrey, Raphael Asturian, and Stacie, among others. ;) Little Dan (Daniel Asturian), too, although I have played with the idea of casting Harry Marcus, Jakob Salvati, or perhaps Jacob Tremblay in the role. Yet, while all three are wonderful actors, none of them seem *exactly* right for the vision in my mind.

Have any ideas? Feel free to tweet your casting choices for these characters, as well as ones previously listed for consideration, to @novelist_gina.

I would also love to cast the following actors in some role:

- Anthony Andrews (maybe Mr. Asturian?)
- Bruce Boxleitner (also a good option for Mr. Veritas, perhaps!)
- Robert Picardo
- Kyle Chandler
- Jim Caviezel (There's a bit of an Asturian in him, too . . .)

Author Bio

Gina Marinello-Sweeney is the author of *The Veritas Chronicles*, a YA trilogy. The first book in the series, *I Thirst*, received the 2013 YATR Literary Award for Best Prologue from Young Adult Teen Readers. Gina has been writing ever since she was a little girl and turned her bedroom into a "library," complete with due date slips and a check-out stamp. As her own stories were "checked out" by family and friends, she dreamed of a day in which her stories would be available in public libraries worldwide. Her dream of publication came true in 2013. Gina is also an avid poet in both the English and Spanish languages. In 2009, she was asked to present some original Spanish poems at an international literature conference in Costa Rica. Although unable to attend this event, a presentation of the poems was well-received at another scholarly event that same year. Graduating summa cum laude, Gina holds credentials in both elementary education and Spanish. In her spare time, she enjoys producing videos, going to the beach, reading, and dreaming of Prince Edward Island. Gina lives in southern California, where she is at work on a short story collection, as well as the first book in a fantasy series.

Visit www.ginamarinellosweeney.com for more information.

Rivershore Books

www.rivershorebooks.com
blog.rivershorebooks.com
forum.rivershorebooks.com
www.facebook.com/rivershorebooks
info@rivershorebooks.com